Praise for

the Novels of the Nine Kingdoms

The Mage's Daughter

"Engaging characters—family, friends, and enemies—keep the story hopping along with readers relishing every word and hungering for the next installment. [A] perfect ten." —*Romance Reviews Today*

"Lynn Kurland has become one of my favorite fantasy authors; I can hardly wait to see what happens next." —*Huntress Reviews*

"*The Mage's Daughter,* like its predecessor, *Star of the Morning,* is the best work Lynn Kurland has ever done. I can't recommend this book highly enough." —*Fresh Fiction*

"I couldn't put the book down . . . The fantasy world, drawn so beautifully, is too wonderful to miss any of it. I highly recommend this book, the series, and all of Ms. Kurland's other works. Brilliant!" —*Paranormal Romance Reviews*

"This is a terrific romantic fantasy. Lynn Kurland provides a fabulous . . . tale that sets the stage for an incredible finish." —*Midwest Book Review*

Star of the Morning

"Kurland launches a stunning, rich, and poetic new trilogy. The quest is on!" —*Romantic Times*

"Terrific . . . Lynn Kurland provides fantasy readers with a delightful quest tale starring likable heroes . . . A magical beginning to what looks like will be a superb romantic fantasy trilogy." —*Midwest Book Review*

"Entertaining fantasy." —*Romance Reviews Today*

"An enchanting writer." —*The Eternal Night*

"A superbly crafted, sweetly romantic tale of adventure and magic." —*Booklist*

continued . . .

"I dare you to read a Kurland story and not enjoy it!"
—Heartland Critiques

Dreams of Stardust

"Kurland weaves another fabulous read with just the right amounts of laughter, romance, and fantasy." *—Affaire de Coeur*

"Kurland crafts some of the most ingenious time-travel romances readers can find . . . Wonderfully clever and completely enchanting." *—Romantic Times*

"A masterful storyteller . . . [a] mesmerizing novel." *—Romance Junkies*

"One of our most beloved time-travel authors and deservedly so. Each new book is cause for celebration!" *—Fresh Fiction*

A Garden in the Rain

"Kurland laces her exquisitely romantic, utterly bewitching blend of contemporary romance and time travel with a delectable touch of tart wit, leaving readers savoring every word of this superbly written romance." *—Booklist*

"Kurland . . . consistently delivers the kind of stories readers dream about. Don't miss this one." *—The Oakland (MI) Press*

From This Moment On

"A disarming blend of romance, suspense, and heartwarming humor, this book is romantic comedy at its best." *—Publishers Weekly*

"A deftly plotted delight." *—Booklist*

My Heart Stood Still

"The essence of pure romance. Sweet, poignant, and truly magical, this is a rare treat." *—Booklist*

"Kurland out-writes romance fiction's top authors by a mile."
—Publishers Weekly

If I Had You

"Kurland brings history to life . . . in this tender medieval romance."
—Booklist

The More I See You

"Blends history with spellbinding passion and impressive characterization, not to mention a magnificent plot." *—Rendezvous*

Another Chance to Dream

"Kurland creates a special romance." *—Publishers Weekly*

The Very Thought of You

"[A] masterpiece . . . This fabulous tale will enchant anyone who reads it." *—Painted Rock Reviews*

This Is All I Ask

"An exceptional read." *—The Atlanta Journal-Constitution*

"Both powerful and sensitive . . . A wonderfully rich and rewarding book." —Susan Wiggs

"A medieval of stunning intensity. Sprinkled with adventure, fantasy, and heart." —Christina Dodd

A Dance Through Time

"An irresistibly fast and funny romp across time." —Stella Cameron

"Vastly entertaining time travel . . . a humorous novel of feisty fun and adventure." *—A Little Romance*

Titles by Lynn Kurland

STARDUST OF YESTERDAY
A DANCE THROUGH TIME
THIS IS ALL I ASK
THE VERY THOUGHT OF YOU
ANOTHER CHANCE TO DREAM
THE MORE I SEE YOU
IF I HAD YOU
MY HEART STOOD STILL
FROM THIS MOMENT ON
A GARDEN IN THE RAIN
DREAMS OF STARDUST
MUCH ADO IN THE MOONLIGHT
WHEN I FALL IN LOVE
WITH EVERY BREATH

The Novels of the Nine Kingdoms

STAR OF THE MORNING
THE MAGE'S DAUGHTER
PRINCESS OF THE SWORD

Anthologies

THE CHRISTMAS CAT
(with Julie Beard, Barbara Bretton, and Jo Beverley)

CHRISTMAS SPIRITS
(with Casey Claybourne, Elizabeth Bevarly, and Jenny Lykins)

VEILS OF TIME
(with Maggie Shayne, Angie Ray, and Ingrid Weaver)

OPPOSITES ATTRACT
(with Elizabeth Bevarly, Emily Carmichael, and Elda Minger)

LOVE CAME JUST IN TIME

A KNIGHT'S VOW
(with Patricia Potter, Deborah Simmons, and Glynnis Campbell)

TAPESTRY
(with Madeline Hunter, Sherrilyn Kenyon, and Karen Marie Moning)

TO WEAVE A WEB OF MAGIC
(with Patricia A. McKillip, Sharon Shinn, and Claire Delacroix)

THE QUEEN IN WINTER
(with Sharon Shinn, Claire Delacroix, and Sarah Monette)

Lynn Kurland

BERKLEY SENSATION, NEW YORK

THE BERKLEY PUBLISHING GROUP
Published by the Penguin Group
Penguin Group (USA) Inc.
375 Hudson Street, New York, New York 10014, USA
Penguin Group (Canada), 90 Eglinton Avenue East, Suite 700, Toronto, Ontario M4P 2Y3, Canada
(a division of Pearson Penguin Canada Inc.)
Penguin Books Ltd., 80 Strand, London WC2R 0RL, England
Penguin Group Ireland, 25 St. Stephen's Green, Dublin 2, Ireland (a division of Penguin Books Ltd.)
Penguin Group (Australia), 250 Camberwell Road, Camberwell, Victoria 3124, Australia
(a division of Pearson Australia Group Pty. Ltd.)
Penguin Books India Pvt. Ltd., 11 Community Centre, Panchsheel Park, New Delhi—110 017, India
Penguin Group (NZ), 67 Apollo Drive, Rosedale, North Shore 0632, New Zealand
(a division of Pearson New Zealand Ltd.)
Penguin Books (South Africa) (Pty.) Ltd., 24 Sturdee Avenue, Rosebank, Johannesburg 2196,
South Africa

Penguin Books Ltd., Registered Offices: 80 Strand, London WC2R 0RL, England

This book is an original publication of The Berkley Publishing Group.

Cover art by Dan Craig.
Cover design by George Long.
Cover hand lettering by Ron Zinn.

PRINTING HISTORY
Berkley Sensation trade paperback edition / January 2009

Library of Congress Cataloging-in-Publication Data

Kurland, Lynn.
Princess of the sword / Lynn Kurland.—Berkley Sensation trade pbk. ed.
p. cm.
ISBN 978-0-425-22568-4
1. Magic—Fiction. 2. Princesses—Fiction. I. Title.
PS3561.U645P75 2009
813'.54—dc22 2008041861

PRINTED IN THE UNITED STATES OF AMERICA

10 9 8 7 6 5 4 3 2 1

One

A dank chill filled the air, slipping down the weathered sides of crooked buildings to pool on glistening cobblestones. It hung in great tatters against the keep that sat perched atop a bluff like a great bird of prey. In the distance, a ship's bell tolled. The sound was muffled by the night air, as if the mist didn't particularly care to awaken anyone who might be sleeping inside that shadowy keep.

Morgan of Melksham understood that. She had no desire to wake anything in that keep either. In fact, she had no desire to get close enough to it for any unfortunate night-time interruptions to be a possibility. Only a madman would have approached those walls, shrouded as they were in spells and other unpleasant things of a wizardly nature.

Normally, she wouldn't have found herself anywhere near such a place. She was a very practical woman with a straightforward way of conducting her life, which generally included a fondness for sharp swords and a habit of avoiding whenever possible any associations with mages.

Or at least that had been true until the fall. It was then that her life had become something so far from what she'd expected it would be, she scarce recognized it as hers any longer.

It had all begun with a simple request from a man she loved like a father, a request to take a blade from the Island of Melksham all the way to the king's palace on the northern border of Neroche. She had agreed, reluctantly, but knowing that she couldn't in good conscience refuse. She'd expected the journey to be difficult, dangerous, and possibly fatal to her person.

She'd sorely underestimated the potential for all three.

The knife had revealed itself to be rather more magical than she'd been told, her travels had led her to discover things about her past she wouldn't have dreamt in her worst nightmares, and the companions she'd collected along the way—or one of them, rather—had turned out to be substantially more magical than she'd feared.

All of which had led, in a most roundabout fashion, to her standing uneasily under the eaves of an inn and feeling an unreasonable amount of trepidation at the thought of assaulting the fortress in front of her so she could steal something that was critical to another battle she intended to fight in a place she most certainly didn't want to go.

It wasn't the climbing over walls that bothered her. She had, during her long and illustrious career as a mercenary, ended more than one siege by slipping into a keep and convincing the recalcitrant lord there that it would be wise for him to just give up and give in rather than face what she could promise would be a very long and unpleasant war.

It wasn't even the theft that troubled her. Spoils were spoils and, when fairly won, really couldn't be considered plundered goods.

What bothered her was that the castle before her was so slathered in magic that even *she* could feel it from where she stood fifty paces away, and she was preparing to be about her nefarious business with a man who should have known better.

"This is a terrible idea," she said, not for the first time.

Mochriadhemiach of Neroche stood next to her with his arms folded over his chest, staring thoughtfully at the fortress in front of them. "We'll be in and out before anyone is the wiser," he said, also not for the first time.

"Have you ever done this before?" she asked unwillingly. "Here?"

"Aye," he said, but offered no further details.

She supposed she didn't want further details. She suspected he did this sort of thing on a regular basis to add to his already too-large collection of spells. At least he had the benefit of not being bothered by the magic. She wished she could say the same for herself.

But she wasn't one to shy away from the difficult, so she turned her thoughts back to the matter at hand. The keep had to be assaulted, and she needed to know the particulars of the defenses so she wouldn't make any mistakes in the taking of it.

"You said something about magic guarding the walls," she said, suppressing the urge to shiver from a cold that came from more than just evening mist. "You should tell me of it again." She looked up at Miach. "I wasn't listening when you tried before."

He smiled as he turned her to him and pulled her cloak up closer to her chin. "I imagine you weren't, so here is the tale. Several centuries ago, the headmaster, whose job it is to see to these sorts of things, determined that it would serve the wizards of Buidseachd to know who walked in and out of their gates."

"Or over their walls," she added.

"Aye, that too, I daresay," he agreed. "Master Ceannard crafted a spell that sets off an alarm in his chambers if any but he who has presented himself to the gatekeeper uses any sort of magic within the boundaries of the castle. Keeps the rabble out, I daresay."

"I daresay," she muttered.

He studied her for a moment or two before he reached out and tucked a strand of hair behind her ear. "You know, I wouldn't think any less of you if you stayed here."

"I can scale a wall as proficiently as you, my lord."

He smiled briefly. "You know that isn't what I'm talking about." He glanced at the keep, then looked back at her. "I fear, Morgan, that I will walk places tonight where you won't want to go."

She looked up at him, his face cast in deep shadows, and supposed she could have told him that what lay before them was the least of her worries, but she imagined he already knew that. She also could have reminded him that he was braving the place in front of them to fetch a spell for her use, not his, but she supposed he knew that already as well. This was merely another in a very long list of things he had done for her benefit alone. The least she could do was go with him and see that he didn't find himself with a sword thrust into his back.

No matter where his path led.

"I don't fear what's inside those walls," she said, wondering if saying it often enough would at some point lead her to believe the lie. "Just tell me how we're going to avoid that alarm."

He looked at her for another moment in silence, then sighed. "We're not going to use any magic as we're about our business."

"And just who you are won't set bells to ringing?"

"I'm going to hide who—and what—I am." He paused. "You'll need to do the same."

She knew she shouldn't have been surprised by how dry her mouth had suddenly become, but she was. She had faced countless men over blades and never once doubted her skill, yet there she was, terrified just the same.

Magic was, as her former swordmaster Scrymgeour Weger had said on more than one occasion, a very dodgy business indeed.

"I'm going to give you a Duriallian spell," Miach continued. "I think it will do for our purposes tonight."

"I didn't think the dwarves had any spells."

"They don't have very many, and they are, as you might imagine, exceptionally reluctant to share the ones they do have."

"Find yourself locked in some dwarvish solar without anything to do save poke about in books you shouldn't have been reading?" she asked pointedly.

He smiled. "I might have."

"Miach, someday you're going to get caught." *Just please don't let it be tonight.*

"I always have a good excuse for being where I'm not supposed to be," he assured her. "Now, the spell I'm going to give you is particularly useful when you want to hide something. A cache of gems, or perhaps piles of gold. Or yourself." He paused. "Or, rather, merely a *part* of yourself. As in, just your magic."

"But how can I use one of their spells?" she protested faintly. "I thought you could only use what magic you had in your blood." Well, unless you happened to be the archmage of some realm or other and then she supposed anything was possible.

"Magic is generally responsive only to what the mage has in his veins," he agreed, "but 'tis possible to use things you aren't entitled to by birth if you have enough power." He smiled faintly. "Are you truly curious, or merely stalling?"

"Stalling, if you can believe it." She purposely avoided looking to her right. "And I never stall."

He rubbed her arms briskly. "Then let's be about this before we think on it any longer," he said. "I'll give you the spell, then tell you two ways to undo it. One takes a handful of words; the other a single word only. I wouldn't use the second unless you've absolutely no other choice."

"Why not?"

"Because it will release all your power at once, much like a dam bursting. Everyone for miles will feel the echo of it."

She swallowed with difficulty. "And alarm bells will go off?"

"Probably in the throne room of Tor Neroche," he said dryly. "So please, be ginger. Now, the spell is laid thus—"

"Aren't you going to do it for me?" she asked in surprise.

He hesitated. "I could, but I don't think you'd care for it. You have power enough to use the spell successfully on your own."

"But if I make a mistake, we are lost."

He closed his eyes briefly. "All right, I'll see to it. But stop me if you find you can't breathe, aye?"

She nodded, but she couldn't help but think he was underestimating her ability to endure things that were difficult.

Or, at least she did until he started weaving his spell.

All her power, the power she'd spent weeks denying, then yet more time trying to accept—all that power didn't so much leave her as it was drawn into itself, then dropped down into some fathomless well. She looked over the edge of that well, fearing she had lost what she had never wanted but had so recently come to appreciate, but there it all lay, shining there in the dark like a treasure that was so lovely and so desirable, it almost brought tears to her eyes.

She had to pull away mentally from the sight. She was appalled to find how accustomed she'd become to that sparkle of magic cascading through her veins. It was the same sort of magic that whispered through the trees and sang as it fell down onto the ground like sunlight in her grandfather's garden at Seanagarra.

It was beautiful.

She looked up to find Miach watching her silently, his eyes full of what she'd seen.

"If your grandfather could see your face right now," he said quietly, "he would weep."

She took a deep breath. "I never intended . . . I didn't realize . . ."

"Not all magic is evil, Morgan, is it?"

She shook her head, because she couldn't speak. She could only go into his arms, hold him tightly for a moment or two, then step back before she gave into the urge to display some womanly emotion that wouldn't serve either of them. She waved him on to his business without further comment. She would think about magic, and mages, and other things that unbalanced her later. For now, 'twas best to do what had to be done.

Miach gave her both ways to undo his spell, and she memorized each faithfully. She didn't hear him say anything on his own behalf, but she felt his power disappear as surely as if he'd snuffed out a candle—or dropped all his magic into a well and then capped it.

She wasn't too fond of that last image, truth be told.

"Let's go," he said.

She nodded, then turned to slip through the shadows with him, giving no more thought to what she was doing than she would have any other offensive. They would be over the walls, find what they needed, then be back outside the keep before any of the mutterers inside were the wiser.

The outer walls of Buidseachd were relatively easy to scale, though very high. Heights didn't bother her, so she didn't trouble herself over them. She dropped onto the parapet with Miach, hid in the shadows as a sleepy sentry shuffled by, then followed him as he wound his way through towers and passages and up and down stairs. She didn't ask him where he was going, and he didn't volunteer any information.

Bells weren't ringing—save the one tolling the hour that almost sent her tripping into Miach's back—and students weren't pouring out of their bedchambers with spells of death on their lips. Perhaps they would manage their business after all.

They passed others, but those lads seemed to find nothing unusual about two cloaked and hooded figures wandering the halls in the middle of the night. Miach had told her that it was common to see both students and masters in the passageways at all hours, studying or thinking or working on some perplexing magical tangle of some sort or another. Morgan wondered how anyone bore the place. Despite her attempts to ignore it, the magic was almost stifling. She could feel it rising up from the ground like a foul mist. In time, she realized she was gasping.

Miach stopped suddenly and pulled her into an alcove with him. "We'll rest for a moment."

She leaned back against the wall instead of collapsing there, but doing so took almost more of her self-discipline than she had to spare. "Thank you."

"You're doing well."

She didn't think she was doing well at all. She never should have set foot inside the accursed place—never mind what she thought she owed Miach, never mind that she'd come over the walls fully expecting to not take a decent breath whilst she was there.

She had actually listened to Miach earlier when he'd said that Buidseachd was built on a spring of magic, and three thousand years of wizards puttering about inside it had added innumerable layers to what had already been there. She had stopped listening once Miach and her grandfather had begun discussing the wizardly mischief that had dredged up things under Buidseachd's foundations that perhaps had been better left alone, things that had left Sìle and Eulasaid of Camanaë and Proìseil of Ainneamh very nervous centuries ago. Perhaps she should have paid more attention to what those things had been. If she had, she might have been less likely to trust her ability to endure things far beyond what another might be able to.

She touched Weger's mark over her brow, the mark that had exacted an excruciating price in discipline to win, then forced herself to take a pair of deep, even breaths. She looked up at Miach. "None of this troubles you, does it?"

"I suppose that depends on where I find myself. There are places even here—" He took a deep breath, then shook his head. "Nay, it doesn't, for the most part, but I've been here before. We'll be swift."

She nodded, pushed away from the wall, then put her head down and merely watched his feet as he walked without haste in front of her. She was almost grateful when she felt a chill blow across her face.

Until she realized where the chill was coming from.

Miach continued to walk, though, and she continued to follow him because she could do nothing else. If he was affected by what was rapidly turning into bone-numbing cold, he didn't show it.

He finally stopped in front of a doorway that was so full of darkness, she could hardly make out where a doorknob might be located.

It was enough to know that this was the source of the coldness. Miach was still for quite some time, as if he listened. Morgan wished he would hurry. The longer she stood there, the more she dreaded going inside. At one point, as he picked the lock with skill even her most crafty mercenary companions would have been impressed by, she almost suggested that they return back the way they'd come.

But he opened the door before she could open her mouth and whatever else she might have been, she was no coward. If Miach could go inside, then so could she.

Though it took far more of her strength of will to cross that threshold than it should have.

The chamber was less dark than she'd feared it might be. A fire burned in the fireplace that faced the door and a servant slept on its hearth. Morgan jumped a bit when she felt Miach's hand on her arm, but he was only pointing toward a corner. She happily made her way there and stood in the absolute dark, grateful for its concealment. She could leap out at any moment and guard Miach's back. And given where they found themselves, she wasn't completely sure that wouldn't be necessary.

She didn't need anyone to tell her where she was, for she could feel the magic that lingered behind in the chamber like a vile odor.

Olc.

She could scarce believe this was where Miach intended to begin his search, but apparently he had a better idea of what sort of spell they needed than she did.

She forced herself to keep her focus part on Miach and part on the lad who lay snoring in front of the fire. The lad didn't rouse, but Miach gave him no reason to. He was absolutely silent as he walked around the chamber, investigating nooks and crannies, running his finger over books on shelves.

She watched him stop in front of a desk layered with manuscripts. She wondered how he could even touch things that made her ill just by being in the same chamber with them. Olc was an evil magic. She'd seen it worked—and worked it herself a time or two, unfortunately—and that had been enough to convince her that she wanted nothing to do with it.

Mochriadhemiach of Neroche had, she had decided in the past month, a depth to him that she suspected she would never plumb. It was reassuring somehow to have an idea of what he could endure.

And how quickly he could move.

She realized he'd leapt across the chamber only because he was shoving her back into a wardrobe—and he was doing that because there were voices that had stopped outside the chamber door and a key was being fitted into the lock. The doorknob squeaked as it turned. Morgan found herself backed into a coat hook and had to put her hand over her mouth to stifle her gasp of pain. She didn't dare move after that.

Actually, remaining still wasn't all that difficult. She was so terrified—she who had fought countless battles and never once puked in fear—that all she could do was stand there, hunched over and frozen, and pray she would live to see the other side of the next half hour without giving herself away by some untoward noise. At least Miach had managed to pull the door almost completely to so they wouldn't be easily seen. Unfortunately, she could still easily hear the voices on the other side of the heavy wood.

It would appear the master of the chamber had come back for the night. Morgan closed her eyes and wondered if she should have worked a bit harder to convince Miach this was a very bad idea indeed. She remembered vividly the conversation they'd had as they'd been leaving the safety of the inn.

And if they find you've slipped over the walls? she'd asked.

They won't.

And if they do, she'd insisted. *What then?*

He'd been long in answering. He had finally sighed heavily and looked at her. *Death.*

Even for you? she'd asked in surprise.

I can stand against many, Morgan, but not against all the masters of Buidseachd at once.

He hadn't offered any other details, but she hadn't needed him to. If he was caught, he would be thrown to the masters of Buidseachd and they would fall upon him mercilessly. She had no doubt she would defend him as best she could, but in the end, she supposed she would be overpowered as well, then they would both be subjected to whatever wizardly punishment the masters thought fit.

Death, she suspected, might be the more pleasant alternative.

The hook poking into her shoulder was terribly painful, but she ignored it. Harder to ignore was the stiffening of her back and the cramping of the muscles of her legs. She didn't move, though. She also didn't dare hope that the master of Olc would suddenly lose interest in retiring to his very comfortable solar for the night. She imagined he would soon be finished arguing with whomever he'd brought with him, then settle onto his sofa with a glass of wine and consider in a leisurely fashion all the ways he could make the final moments of intruders as miserable as possible.

She wasn't sure being trapped hunched over in a wardrobe shouldn't have had a prominent place on that list, but she wasn't about to suggest it to him. She closed her eyes and thought about Gobhann, about the bitter wind that blew there eleven months out of the year and the harsh summer sunshine that beat upon the rocks during the lone month of warmth. She thought about the strictures she'd learned from Weger and how he would have looked at her in disgust to learn she'd even given heed to any ache or pain she might have felt in her frail womanly frame. That helped, but not overmuch.

She and Miach were trapped.

And the only way out lay past a man who would never let them go willingly.

Two

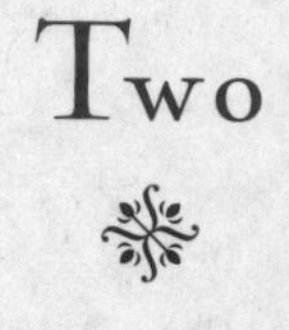

Miach suspected he might have indulged in a bit of plunder once too often.

He had slipped in and out of Buidseachd quite successfully before, but never with anyone else. It was also one thing to intend to have just a peek in the library downstairs. Assaulting the chamber of Droch of Saothair, the master of Olc, was another thing entirely. He should have insisted that Morgan remain behind.

Unfortunately, it was too late at present for regrets. All he could do now was decide what he might attempt if they were discovered. As he had told Morgan earlier, he could stand easily against one of the masters of Buidseachd, less easily against two or three, but not against all of them together.

At last count, there were ten wizards at the school, each the acknowledged master of his craft. Miach wasn't in the habit of doubting his own abilities, but there came a point where a man had to admit what his limitations were.

Even if he released his power, fought his way out of Droch's solar, and escaped the keep, he would be forced to slink back to Tor Neroche, shamed, ostracized, spoken of with disgust for centuries to come.

Which he would do without hesitation, if it came to a choice between that and Morgan's life. At least she might still care for him if he were disgraced. Better disgraced than dead.

But better undetected than disgraced. He would get them out without incident if he could manage it.

He fought to quiet his breath and his mind. He didn't dare reach behind him for Morgan's hand lest he brush something and give away their presence. Morgan was absolutely still, though her fingers were digging into his back, which told him she hadn't fainted from fright. He would have to tell her that the last thought had crossed his mind—later, when she could invite him outside and repay him for the slight with her sword.

"Give me tidings," Droch commanded, "and pray make them something useful."

"Aye, my lord," another voice said quickly. "Of course, my lord, there are the usual tales about those creatures that are wandering all over Neroche—"

"I know that already!"

Miach didn't doubt it. Droch wasn't one to leave his comfortable lodgings at Buidseachd very often, but he more than made up for it with the quantity and quality of his spies. Miach had encountered them on more than one occasion in places he wouldn't have thought to find them.

"But those monsters have been seen east of the Sgùrrachs," the man added gingerly. "There is no definite word on who sends them, but the rumor is that Lothar—"

"Lothar of Wychweald?" Droch said with a derisive snort. "He isn't capable of creating what roams through the Nine Kingdoms at present."

"But his art—"

"Art," Droch sneered. "I have art. He has a cobbled-together, inelegant patchwork of rubbish that works only because he's stumbled upon spells a child could master and puts a bit of flair behind them."

Miach might have smiled had the situation not been so dire. It was a well-known fact that there was no love lost between Droch and the black mage of Wychweald. He himself had perhaps a different opinion of the latter's power, though he certainly had to agree with Droch's assessment of Lothar's technique.

"What else do you have?" Droch demanded. "It had best be worth the gold I've given you, for what you've told me so far certainly isn't."

"There was a battle, Master," the man offered hastily, "less than a se'nnight ago, on the plains of Ailean. Many of those strange creatures were slain and 'tis said that the archmage of Neroche was slain with them. His runes were written in fire—"

"I saw his sign myself," Droch said coldly. "And if you think he allowed himself to be killed, you are a fool. He may be young, but he's neither stupid nor powerless. He hasn't skill to match mine, of course, but he shouldn't be underestimated." He made a noise of impatience. "These are not new tidings—"

"Then hear these," the man blurted out with the desperation of one truly terrified of whom he served. "There is a report that the king of Tòrr Dòrainn is staying at the Uneasy Dragon with his youngest son."

Miach closed his eyes briefly. Damn it. He'd known something like this would happen from the moment he'd taken the elven king to be fitted with discreet traveler's gear and Sìle had instructed the poor tailor to look a bit harder for silk instead of homespun. At the very least, he should have locked Sìle in the chamber at the inn, or insisted he conceal who he was beyond merely dressing plainly. Perhaps he should have demanded that Morgan's grandfather go back home to Seanagarra instead of coming with them to Beinn òrain.

But then Miach wouldn't have had the pleasure of Morgan's

company for the past se'nnight, and he wouldn't have found himself betrothed to the woman who was as still as death behind him.

He hoped they didn't pay a steep price for the concession.

"His younger son, you imbecile," Droch said. "He only has a pair of them. And what would Sìle of Seanagarra be doing here? We rid ourselves of his prying self centuries ago."

"He was trying to pass himself off as a mere traveler, but that isn't the interesting bit," the other man said, beginning to warm to his topic. "One of my local lads says he saw three others with them, one of whom he thought might have resembled the archmage of Neroche—"

The crack of a hand across a face echoed in the chamber. "Now you waste my time," Droch snarled. "The day the king of Tòrr Dòrainn endures the company of that brat from Neroche will be the day I sit down for tea with Eulasaid of Camanaë."

"I could continue to look—"

There was a bit of gurgling, then the unmistakable sound of a man being dragged across the room and thrown out the door. "Bring me proof of the elven king's presence here and I'll think about letting you live."

"Aye, my lo—"

The slamming of that door made the door of the wardrobe creak thanks to its breeze. Miach would have pushed himself back harder against Morgan, but he didn't dare do even that. He merely remained motionless and listened to Droch rage for a moment or two about gold wasted and the stupidity of local ne'er-do-wells. Miach closed his eyes and cursed. Even if Droch didn't believe the tidings at present, he would consider them when he'd calmed down a bit, and then he would begin to think things he shouldn't. Miach listened as Droch strode angrily around his chamber, then slowed to a halt in front of his desk.

He suddenly became very still.

Miach knew this because he could see a sliver of a reflection of the man in the enormous mirror hanging over the hearth. Droch ran his hand over his books, stopped, then turned and looked in the mirror.

Miach knew it wasn't possible that Droch could see him, not even through the slit left by the partially open wardrobe door, but even so his heart began to pound forcefully. He knew it was only in his own ears that it sounded so appallingly loud, but there was no comfort in that.

Droch walked over to the hearth and hauled his servant to his feet. The boy woke with a squeak.

"Aye, milord?"

"Has anyone been in here?" Droch demanded.

"Nay, milord," the lad gasped. "Nay, not a soul."

"Are you certain?"

"Aye, milord. My life upon it, milord. I just laid down but a moment ago."

Droch took the boy by the scruff of the neck and shoved him away. "Begone. I want privacy."

The serving lad scrambled with all due haste across the chamber. The door was wrenched open, then pulled shut behind him with a bang. Miach listened to Droch wander about the chamber, investigating corners and patches of dark that gave way to his werelight only reluctantly. He paused, then walked back over to his table and studied the books there. Miach had sensed no spell covering any of them—well, other than the usual bit of vileness that crawled over whatever tome contained Olc. Surely nothing that should have given his own presence away.

The master of the art came to a stop in front of his solar door. Miach could no longer see him, but he could hear him as he moved again, his boots very light against the stone of the floor. He walked to a spot directly in front of the wardrobe and stopped.

Miach was suddenly so overcome by the desire to fling open the door, he almost caught his breath. He wasn't sure if it was his own will faltering or if it were some sort of wretched spell that Droch was casting silently. That he couldn't tell spoke volumes, no doubt.

Droch stepped back suddenly, out of sight again. Miach didn't dare hope that would be the end of it. Morgan's fingers in his back didn't relax either, so perhaps she had the same thought. He closed his eyes and listened to Droch pace about the chamber several more times, pausing each time to linger in front of the wardrobe. Miach supposed they wouldn't be fortunate enough for Droch to wear himself out, then go have a little rest on that sofa long enough for them to escape.

Droch suddenly walked in the direction of the door. Miach didn't have to wonder for long what he intended, for he heard the words of a spell clearly enough. In time, he saw something begin to form itself in the middle of the chamber. Droch clapped his hands and the pile of what he'd created began to first shimmer, then take shape.

"That should take care of any vermin that might have slipped in unnoticed," Droch drawled. "And what an unpleasant way to die."

Miach closed his eyes and cursed silently as Droch left the chamber, slamming the door shut behind him and locking it. Unpleasant wasn't the word he would have used, but perhaps he would think of a better one when he had gotten Morgan safely away from what was now a mass of writhing, twisting snakes there in the middle of the chamber. He supposed it might have been prudent to wait a bit longer and see if Droch had merely pretended to leave, but he didn't think they would have that luxury. Consequences be damned. He and Morgan had to get out before those snakes warmed enough to slither about and find what they'd been instructed to seek.

Anything that moved.

Alarm bells began to ring in the distance. Miach swore, then flung open the armoire door and hurled the first thing he put his hand on across the chamber. The cloak he'd thrown landed on top of the nest of vipers, covering them temporarily.

He bolted for the window and worked on the latch with the knife Scrymgeour Weger had gifted him. Perhaps it possessed a magic he hadn't felt, for it cut through the spells there as if they'd been naught but tender flesh. He shoved open the window, boosted Morgan up, then jumped up himself.

"Miach!"

He looked down and flinched at the sight of fangs that were a fingerbreadth from his leg, stopped only by that same bit of steel he was holding in his hand.

Morgan said nothing else, but her knife flashed suddenly in the light from the fire. The viper's head and its body fell back to the floor separately.

Miach followed Morgan out onto the ledge, then jerked the window shut behind him. He wiped the venom off the knife and onto his boot, then carefully resheathed his knife. The venom of the Natharian viper was instantly fatal if it found home in flesh. He wasn't sure how long after the fact it remained potent, so keeping his hands away from his boots would probably be quite wise.

"We'll have to find somewhere inside the keep to hide," he said, feeling a little breathless.

"Are you mad?" Morgan exclaimed. "Surely they'll find us."

"We have no other choice. They'll be looking for us to go back over the outer walls. We'll climb up to the roof, join the hunt for a bit, then make our way somewhere safe."

She shot him a skeptical look, but followed him just the same. He wasn't any more eager to remain inside the keep than she was, but he saw no other alternative. Best to hide out for a bit and slip out when the masters had tired of the chase and gone to bed.

Within moments, they were running through the halls, mixing with hooded figures that were running about frantically as well. Miach considered where they might go, then settled for the library. Even in the middle of the night it wasn't unheard of for students to be laboring over texts. Given the evidence of untoward activities he and Morgan had left just inside Droch's window, he didn't think that simply hiding behind ale kegs in the kitchen would be any protection against discovery. Best that they appear to be about some sort of useful and ordinary labor.

Morgan made no comment as he led her swiftly through passageways, and down finally into the bowels of the keep. He walked into the library as if he had every right to, nodded deferentially to the librarian, then made his way back into the shelves. He hadn't but rounded the corner into a darkened row before he heard a voice behind him.

Droch's servant, unfortunately.

"Master Reudan, my master Droch said he feared an intruder was inside the keep!"

Miach took Morgan's hand and pulled her along with him deeper into the rows of shelves before he had to listen to the librarian's answer. He reached for a random volume and shoved it into her arms.

"Feign interest," he advised.

"Miach, behind you!" she whispered harshly.

Miach turned around—but too quickly for he caught the edge of his hood on a particularly large tome that protruded from the shelf. He yanked his hood back up but not before the man facing him had caught his breath.

"Excuse me," Miach said in a very low voice.

The other man's face was hidden in a deep cowl; determining his expression was impossible. He didn't seem particularly inclined to move out of their way. Instead, he reached out and put his hand on Miach's arm.

Miach looked down, then inhaled sharply. The hand that held on to his sleeve was horribly disfigured, as if it had been crushed under an unforgiving weight, then pulled free at great cost. Miach tried to see the man's face, but he pulled back farther into the shadows.

"Follow me," he rasped.

"But—" Miach protested.

The man kept his hand on Miach's arm, turned, and tugged.

Miach considered balking, but something stopped him. At least the man wasn't shouting for aid, or loudly announcing a neatly executed capture. Perhaps this was a gift from an unexpected source. If so, he would be a fool to spurn it. He wished he'd had a knife up his sleeve to loosen, but since he didn't, he would merely be wary.

Their guide led them through stacks of books to a chamber near the back of the library. Within moments, Miach found himself sitting on a stool with a needle and binding thread in his hand in a darkened corner of what was obviously a private workroom. Morgan was sitting on the floor next to him, hidden for the most part from anyone who might be looking inside from the doorway. He reached over and tugged her hood closer around her face, then put his hand briefly on her head before he moved his stool more fully in front of her. They were as inconspicuous as possible. There was nothing else to be done.

The man who had offered them sanctuary said nothing; he simply went about his work as if nothing were amiss. He was grappling with a set of shears when the door opened and guardsmen burst inside.

"Oh," said one of them, shivering and backing away immediately. "I thought the chamber was empty."

"Nay," said their rescuer in a voice that was as ruined as his hand. He pointed the shears toward the men. "'Tis my chamber, so be on your way."

Miach stole a glance at the lads who had backed out of the chamber itself but still hovered in the half-open doorway. He couldn't see their faces, but the shuffling of their feet bespoke serious discomfort.

"And those two there—" one of them ventured.

"My servants," the man rasped.

"I see," the guard said, shoving his companion behind him back out into the library itself. "We're looking for a lad who slipped over the walls tonight and we thought that perhaps . . ."

The man only made a sound that reminded Miach of the branches of a winter-hardened tree scraping against a glassed window. He supposed it had been a laugh.

"You thought he would dare come here?" the man asked.

The guards shook their heads as one, turned, then fled.

Their host shut the door, then put his ear against it and listened for some time in silence. Miach looked at Morgan. She was absolutely still, but he could see the dull gleam of steel in her hand. He nodded slightly, then turned back to watch their host.

The man remained where he was so long, Miach wondered if he'd fallen asleep. Before he dared say anything, the other pushed away from the door, turned, and walked across the chamber. He hooked a stool with his foot and dragged it over to the opposite side of the table. He sat stiffly, then set his shears down with a clatter. He tucked his hands inside the opposite sleeves of his robe.

"We'll seek the kitchens later. Lads will be coming in and out near dawn."

Miach nodded. He didn't dare ask him any of the questions that he so desperately wanted to, beginning and ending with *why did you help us?* He simply hoped the charity would last long enough to see them set outside the walls in the morning.

He didn't want to think about the alternative.

Several hours later, Miach found himself rather dirtier than he'd ever been before, trailed by an equally filthy Morgan of Melksham through a long passageway that led from the kitchens to the street outside the keep. He was carrying a basket of rotten flesh guaranteed to have everyone in Beinn òrain avoiding him willingly. He was fairly certain the basket of spoiled greens Morgan was carrying was even more pungent. Their host was leading the way with his arms full of much the same stuff. Miach promised himself a deep breath later, when he was sure it wouldn't fell him prematurely.

It had been a less-than-comfortable night, but he hadn't complained. Their host had said nothing, asked no questions, spared Morgan not so much as a look. He'd merely sat there with them save for the handful of times he'd risen and walked across the chamber to put his ear to the door. Miach had finally resorted to keeping himself awake by flipping through the randomly chosen book he'd given Morgan. It hadn't yielded any more answers than their silent host.

Their brief stop in the kitchens had been almost as risky as he'd suspected it might be, what with a cook who was far more inquisitive than he should have been and kitchen lads who were just as curious. Fortunately, their rescuer was not unknown—nor was he apparently very welcome—which had left them avoided by association. Miach had been profoundly grateful.

It was growing light outside when he followed their guide over to a row of compost heaps, happily deposited his burden in the appropriate place, then turned to look at the man who had saved their lives. He wasn't sure how to go about repaying the gift—or how to ask if the man might be willing to forget that he'd seen them.

"Thank you again," he said, settling for the simpler of the two.

The man brushed off his hands carefully, then nodded. "Be well," he said, his voice barely audible. "My lord Archmage."

Before Miach could respond, the man had melted back into the shadows of the keep and disappeared. Miach would have continued to gape after him, but Morgan elbowed him sharply in the ribs.

"You said your thanks," she said briskly. "Let's go."

"Think he'll keep it all to himself?" Miach asked, feeling a little winded—and not just from Morgan's elbow.

"Does it matter? Let's be off whilst we can."

He didn't protest when she pulled him after her down the hill, away from the keep but in a different direction from their lodgings. There was sense in that. The sooner they were able to blend in with the seedier elements near the docks, the better off they would be.

Half an hour later, he pulled her into a deserted alleyway and caught his first decent breath in hours. He almost wished he hadn't.

Morgan wrinkled her nose as well. "We stink."

"And thankfully we're alive to do so," he said, with feeling.

She smiled, apparently in spite of herself, then looked around her. "Do we dare have a dip in the river?"

"The Oan is filthier than we are," he said with a shudder. "Perhaps we should just wait until we're back at the inn. I imagine there's water in the garden."

"I don't think they'll let us in the garden."

"I'll bribe them. 'Tis a certainty your grandfather won't let us in that luxurious chamber I provided for him if we don't clean up first." He took a ginger breath, then looked at her. "How are you?"

"I'm not sure what was more unpleasant, hiding in that wardrobe and wondering when that horrible wizard would find us, or hiding in that horrible little chamber and wondering when guards would burst back in and leave us fighting our way out."

He couldn't have agreed more. It had been a thoroughly unpleasant night.

"What now?" she asked.

Back inside Droch's solar for another go was the first thing that came to mind, but he didn't suppose it would serve either of them for him to voice that thought given that he had no intention of taking Morgan with him. He merely picked a particularly rotten piece of spring salad off her shoulder and smiled. "Let's think about it later, when we can breathe again."

"I'm for that, at least. And quickly, if you don't mind."

He didn't mind at all. Half an hour and a substantial bag of gold in the cook's hand later, he was slightly cleaner and walking up the back stairs to the upper floor of the Uneasy Dragon. He ran into Morgan's uncle at the top of the stairs before he realized Sosar was waiting for them.

"You smell," Sosar said pleasantly.

"Thank you," Miach said with a grunt. "It was worse before, believe me." He steadied himself with a hand against the wall. "Any trouble?"

"Outside of my father raging half the night that he had changed his mind and planned to slay you?" Sosar asked with a smile. "Nay, it was very quiet. I heard a bell or two ringing inside the walls, though."

"I imagine you did," Miach agreed. "They're a busy lot, those wizards."

"No doubt." Sosar nodded down the passageway. "I've food waiting, which you can thank me for later. You'd best eat it. I imagine you won't have much appetite when you learn where we're lunching."

Miach blinked in surprise. "Where?"

"At Buidseachd. It would seem that Father was caught down at the stables very early this morning with your brother. Turah blurted out some ridiculous tale about having come to see a man about a sword, which my father says was completely unbelievable."

"Who saw them?" Miach asked, dragging his free hand through his hair. "One of Master Ceannard's lads?"

"Nay, the one who sent you this message a quarter hour ago." Sosar held out a note, pinched between as little of his thumb and forefinger as possible. "I couldn't bring myself to read it for you."

Miach opened the missive. Words of Olc slithered down the page to wind themselves around his fingers. *Next time alert me to your arrival, and I'll make certain to leave my door unlocked.*

The note burst into flames and Miach dropped it with a curse. He ground the smoking rubbish under his boot, then stared down at the ashes. Well, whatever else his faults might have been, Droch was no fool—and he had a knack for being able to tell who was behind him without looking over his shoulder. Perhaps there had been spells laid across the doorway or over the books that he hadn't seen. He looked at Sosar. "I suppose we'd best have a decent breakfast."

"As I advised," Sosar agreed. "I'll go now and see to clothes for this historic visit. You can find your own baths, though. I'm sure my father will aid you when he catches a whiff of your fragrant selves."

Miach cursed Sosar briefly as he slipped past them, then he took as deep a breath as he dared. "This is a boon," he said to Morgan with forced cheerfulness. "Perhaps I might even be invited into a few interesting chambers this time."

"Who was the missive from?"

He thought about attempting to dodge the question, but discarded the idea. If Morgan was going back inside Buidseachd with him, she had best know what they stood to face. "It was from Droch."

"He knows we were there, doesn't he?"

Miach managed a weary smile. "He believes that I was there, at least."

She put her hand on his arm. "Don't go back inside his solar, Miach."

"Morgan, this is but a bit of light work before the true labor begins," he said. "I cannot aid you when it comes time to use the spell we seek. At least allow me to aid you now by finding what you'll need to use."

"I don't like it."

He wouldn't have either, in her place, but there was nothing to be done about it. He held her close for a moment or two, then stepped back and reached for her hand. He ran his thumb over the back of that hand as they walked, feeling the scars there. Those were scars she had earned during years of swordplay in a place that was, in its own way, as terrifying as anything Master Droch could conjure up. Her hands had very recently learned to weave spells, something he knew she had come to accept at enormous cost to her soul. He also had a fair idea of the sort of spell she would have to weave to right the wrong her father's arrogance had caused. If there was something he could do to make that easier for her, he would.

Besides, who knew what sorts of things he might find whilst roaming about the keep on the pretext of stretching his legs?

He was willing to risk quite a bit to find out.

Three

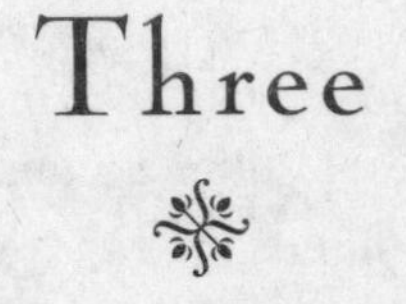

Morgan walked up the road that led to the castle, squinted briefly at the early afternoon sun, and wished desperately that she were walking anywhere else.

She had a decent selection of blades secreted on her person, but that was the only improvement over the night before. Her magic was hidden and her sword propped up in a corner at the inn, because apparently servants of archmages didn't have magic or carry swords. She had been selected to act as Miach's servant because their relatives had obviously had too much time on their hands whilst she and Miach had napped.

Or whilst she had napped, rather. Miach hadn't, but that wasn't anything new. There were times she suspected he never slept at all. She would have chided him for not resting—and for being a no-doubt willing party to the decision about her assumed identity—but he'd looked so weary, she hadn't had the heart to. She wasn't sure how he was still on his feet, but there he was, walking in front of her with his hands clasped behind his back and his head bowed.

She patted herself absently for weapons, just to lessen her unease. She had insisted that if she was going to go as Miach's servant, she should at least have first choice of all available gear lest she be called upon to protect him by more pedestrian means than a spell—and given the contents of Droch's missive to him, she wasn't sure she wouldn't find that to be necessary.

Her grandfather had drawn himself up and told her with a bit of a huff that he wasn't in the habit of stuffing blades up his sleeves, so he had nothing to offer her save a bit of advice on what might be considered appropriate *accoutrements* for elven princesses. She had a difficult time thinking of herself as such, so she had ignored his list and turned to her uncle. Sosar had justified his lack of steel by pleading an overwhelming desire to leave his flesh unnicked. Having seen him with a sword in his hands, she couldn't help but agree that was wise.

Turah, however, had surprised her with the number and quality of blades he'd pulled forth. She'd expressed her approval, then poached a pair of the best.

She'd then turned to see what Miach had to offer only to watch him hold out a pair of lovely, slim daggers, seemingly freshly forged, with hilts of bright gold.

"Did you buy these?" she'd asked in surprise.

He'd shaken his head with a small smile. "I made them for you, just now."

She had drawn each forth and blinked at the sight of what she'd already learned to recognize as runes of Tòrr Dòrainn and Neroche intertwined there. She *was* one to get a bit misty over the sight of a goodly blade, so she'd eyed the finely wrought steel with unabashed emotion, then embraced him and called him by a particularly heartfelt term of endearment.

Her fond feelings for him had departed abruptly when he'd

informed her that in addition to her being his servant, he thought she should be a mute one—which had led her to suspect he'd had much more of a hand in choosing her disguise than he'd admitted. He'd promised he wouldn't enjoy her silence. She'd promised him he would wish she were mute in truth when she had the chance to meet him in the lists and sharpen her tongue on him whilst she was about the happy labor of humiliating him with the sword. And damn him if he hadn't looked particularly intimidated by either threat.

It was impossible not to admire him a bit for that.

Of course, that had been whilst they'd been safely in front of their fire in the inn. Now they were walking up to a place she most certainly didn't want to visit again and she was having a hard time admiring much besides the way that led back down the hill.

She looked for a distraction. There were those aplenty, fortunately, and four of the most dazzling ones were walking in front of her.

Her grandfather had given up all pretense of being less than he was. Even if his terrible beauty and his kingly demeanor hadn't announced who he was, his clothing would have. His trousers were dark velvet, his tunic heavily embroidered and encrusted with gems. Over it all, he wore a cloak of ermine, trimmed in some other sort of fur that sparkled and shimmered in a way that demanded attention. He'd forgone the crown, but Morgan supposed that had been an oversight.

Sosar was dressed just as elegantly, in white trousers and a golden tunic, with a cloak that was slightly less showy than his father's, but no less luxurious. The sun shone down on his fair hair, turning it into pale, spun gold. She watched mere mortals stop to gape at him as he passed and understood why. He was nothing short of stunning.

Even Turah had been garbed in princely attire and wore a circlet of silver on his head. Perhaps the men he passed didn't stare at him, but the women certainly did. Morgan caught sight of a handful of winks he threw to an equal number of handsome wenches and had to smile. He might have looked like Miach, but they were completely unalike in temperament—which was probably fortunate indeed for the state of her heart.

Miach walked along with his brother, dressed very simply in unremarkable black, his crownless head still bowed and his hands still clasped behind his back. Only a fool, though, would have mistaken him for a common man. Even she could sense his power.

"Something wrong?" he asked, dropping back suddenly to walk next to her.

She had assumed that there would come a time where she would look at him and no longer be surprised by the flawless perfection of his face, but perhaps that was a vain hope. It certainly wasn't going to be possible today. "I'm not sure where to begin in answering that," she managed.

"Were you thinking kind thoughts about me?" he asked politely.

"I might be, but since I'm to be a bit short on conversation today, you'll never know."

He smiled, then reached out and tugged her hood up closer around her face. " 'Tis best you not tell me, I imagine, lest I blush. I will tell you, though, that you're far too lovely for anyone to believe you're a mere serving lad. You should keep your face covered, if you can."

"I'll try." She took a deep breath. "Aren't you anxious about this?"

He shrugged negligently. "For all they know, I've just come to town and am making a social call with my brother, my newly made allies the king of Tòrr Dòrainn and his son, and, of course, my obeisant servant."

She looked at him narrowly. "I wouldn't enjoy this overmuch, were I you."

"Oh, I fully intend to," he said, his eyes twinkling. "I imagine it may be the only time in our lives that you're this deferential."

What she imagined wasn't worth saying. She scowled at him and had a laugh for her trouble. "I think you shouldn't accustom yourself to my deference. I also think we're daft to go back inside these gates. Aren't you worried about Droch?"

"He might think he knows quite a few things, but he'll have a difficult time proving any of them. All will be well."

"Are you trying to reassure me, my lord Archmage, or yourself?"

He smiled. "You know, you're awfully cheeky for being the mute servant of a powerful mage."

"As if you would know how such a servant should behave," she said with a snort.

"I could learn, if you were that lass—"

"Oh, for pity's sake, Miach," Turah said with an exasperated laugh, "cease with that. You're being watched from the battlements, which I'm sure you know." He shot Morgan a brief look. "I apologize in advance, Morgan, for the way I'm going to treat you. And so does my brother. You can take him to task later. I'll keep him from escaping the field in fear as you do so." He dropped back and slung an arm around Miach's shoulders. "Come, brother, and leave the wench to her meditation on that happy confrontation."

Morgan slowed enough to allow them to walk on in front of her. Miach didn't look at her again, but he gave her a brief wave from behind his back. She sighed, bowed her head, and gave herself over to the contemplation of his freshly shined black boots. He might not have been nervous, but she most certainly was. It wouldn't have been the first time she'd gone back inside a keep she'd recently escaped from, but it was certainly the first time magic had been involved.

She slipped her hands into her sleeves and fingered the reassuring chill of steel.

Her second entry into Buidseachd was, unsurprisingly, no less unpleasant than her first. Though her magic was dulled and her senses should have been as well, she still felt suffocated the moment she walked under the barbican gate. She clasped her hands together and concentrated on breathing as she walked into the main courtyard.

From the look of things, this wasn't going to be a discreet, unobtrusive visit. There was an entire gaggle of wizards there to greet them, all dressed in their finest robes, all wearing very tall, pointed hats and attempting to look very important. A few of them were gaping at Sìle, but perhaps that couldn't be helped.

Her grandfather was in a courtyard with men who were by no means unimpressive, yet he somehow managed to look as if he was so far above and beyond anything the others might hope to achieve that they shouldn't bother. It was no wonder the wizards looked a bit small by comparison.

One of the masters stepped forward, made Sìle a flatteringly low bow, then began spouting titles, compliments, and other pleasantries that were apparently required for a visit of such unheralded magnitude and importance. Morgan listened for a few minutes, then fought the urge to look for somewhere to sit down. It was no wonder Miach preferred to tromp about in muddy boots and a patched cloak if this were the alternative. She wished heartily that she hadn't promised to remain silent. She might have managed to hurry them all along otherwise.

"And Prince Mochriadhemiach," said the wizard who was apparently the headmaster, making Miach a bow that wasn't quite as low as the one he'd made to Sìle. "An honor, as always. What brings you so far east in such august company?"

"A goodwill visit to Tòrr Dòrainn, Master Ceannard," Miach said easily. "When I indicated that it had been too long since I'd made a visit here, His Majesty was gracious enough to favor me with his company for a bit longer." He leaned in closer and lowered his voice. "The king of Tòrr Dòrainn is in an accommodating mood, I daresay. Fortuitous for relations between Buidseachd and Seanagarra, wouldn't you agree?"

"Indeed," Master Ceannard agreed, smoothing his hands nervously down the front of his velvet robes. "Perhaps we should discuss those relations in more detail inside. I believe luncheon has been prepared for your pleasure."

Sìle looked skeptical, but followed just the same. Morgan walked along behind the company, but not too far. The last thing she wanted was to become lost and be forced to cut her way through spells to find the front door.

The longer she walked, the less sure she became about whether she were dreaming or awake. She had become relatively accustomed to the magic that shimmered in the air in Tòrr Dòrainn and the fact that she was related to the souls living there, but now she was again in deep waters, drowning in a tangle of spells and magic and things that swirled around her, unseen but powerful.

She continued to watch Miach's boots and hope she wouldn't draw attention to herself by suddenly blurting out a plea for someone to carry her outside the walls so she could breathe.

She forced herself to walk into a dining hall paneled in dark wood and full of candles and torches that cast the shadows back into the corners. She looked for somewhere unobtrusive to sequester herself and saw a spot between sideboards already laden with bottles, glasses, and platters. Morgan found a stool there and sat, trying to blend into the woodwork. The hall was large enough to accommodate Sìle's entourage and no doubt all ten masters without the least trouble. Morgan filched a piece of bread when she thought no one was looking, but realized immediately that she wasn't going to be able to eat it. Obviously, she shouldn't have slept through breakfast. She set her bread on her lap, then pressed herself back against the wall and looked at the wizards in front of her, trying to guess who each was and what they did.

Miach had told her on their journey from Tòrr Dòrainn who the masters were and what they taught. Each of the seven levels of mastery were watched over by a particular wizard, leaving the headmaster, a wizard of no small amount of power himself, to see to the business of bringing students in and out of the gates.

Well, and dealing with miscreants who hopped over the walls.

The last two masters were ones that had no responsibility for doling out any of the rings aspirants came to try to win. Master Droch was one. The other was Soilléir of Cothromaiche, the man who had taught Miach the spells of essence changing. Miach had only said complimentary things about him, so Morgan supposed she would survive a meeting with him, though she suspected the fewer mages she encountered inside Buidseachd, the happier she would be.

Unfortunately, there she was in a chamber with a mob of them and she suspected lunch was going to drag on for most of the afternoon.

She leaned her head back against the wall and looked at the wizards sitting around the long, elegantly laid table. Some of them looked ancient, others surprisingly young, but all had that strange, otherworldly sort of radiance about them, as if they were definitely not just ordinary men. The glamour wasn't close to what radiated from her uncle and grandfather, but it wasn't insignificant either.

She would have been very happy to have been free of it, and the sooner the better, to her mind.

She wondered when they would begin to eat, then she realized what the delay was. There were two empty chairs, both across from where Miach had taken his seat. It occurred to her, with a sickening feeling, that she just might know who should have been filling at least one of those chairs. She looked at Miach, but unfortunately he had his back to her so she couldn't tell what his expression was. He was tapping his foot occasionally in a manner that didn't seem particularly frantic, so perhaps he was less troubled by the empty seats than she was.

The sound of a light footfall startled her. She looked up as a blond man walked into the chamber. At first glance, she thought him no more than a student. Then she realized that the magic surrounding him was too significant to have been tamed by a man who had no mastery of his art. His wasn't so much a tidal wave of power as it was a crystal shaft of sunlight that seemed to fall down over him and radiate out from him.

It was beautiful.

Miach stood immediately and walked over to embrace the other man briefly.

"Master Soilléir," Miach said deferentially.

Soilléir laughed and more perfect sunlight seemed to filter down into the chamber. "Prince Mochriadhemiach. What a pleasure." He stepped away and turned to make Sìle a very low bow. "And Your Majesty. An unprecedented and most undeserved honor."

Sìle acknowledged the compliment with a regal sort of nod, though he did deign to reach out and shake Master Soilléir's hand.

Morgan stared at the man in astonishment. It didn't seem possible that he could be the one who held spells of such import, but she supposed he could have been no one else. She looked around at the other wizards and found them watching Soilléir with expressions that ranged from disinterest to outright antagonism—along with a very substantial bit of envy.

Somehow that was rather reassuring. Power ofttimes begat a lust for more and Soilléir was certainly in a place where power was prized. That the masters should be so open about their feelings was something that made them seem slightly more like the lads she usually encountered. At least chewing on that thought for a bit would provide a pleasant respite from reality.

Unfortunately, her reprieve was interrupted sooner than she would have liked by a silent thunderclap. She looked to her left and saw a man standing just inside the door, a cold smile on his face.

It was Droch. It could be no one else. Master Soilléir might have been clear, beautiful light; Master Droch was darkness embodied.

Miach remained in his chair this time.

Morgan had to viciously suppress the urge to flee.

Droch sauntered into the chamber. "You waited for me," he drawled as he made his way around the far side of the table. "How pleasant." He stopped behind the last empty chair and nodded at Sìle. "Your Majesty. A pleasure—again. And your son. And a prince of Neroche." He paused and looked at Miach. "And the young archmage of that same rustic realm."

Morgan had to force herself not to stiffen at the tone of his voice, which wasn't so much contemptuous as it was dismissive—as if

Miach wasn't worth his notice. Morgan couldn't see Miach's face, but she imagined his expression would give nothing away. She also imagined this wasn't the first time Droch had insulted him.

"Master Droch," was all Miach said.

Droch sat down and snapped his fingers at his servant. Wine was immediately provided. That seemed to be some sort of signal, for the rest of the wizards set to their meals with the sort of swiftness men use when they fear their supper might be interrupted and they'd best get it down whilst they can.

"I haven't seen anyone from Seanagarra since . . . well, since I saw your youngest daughter, Sarait, Your Majesty," Droch said with a cold smile thrown Sìle's way. "She was here, climbing over the walls during the middle of the night to ransack my solar."

Morgan credited all her years in Gobhann for allowing her to keep her gasp inside her where it should have been and not out in the air for all to mark. No wonder the wizards had made quick work of starting their meals. Morgan supposed they would be fortunate indeed to finish their soup.

"I didn't catch her in the act, unfortunately," Droch continued. "I saw her the next day, visiting with one who indulges in a less serious form of magic."

Morgan watched Droch glance disdainfully at Soilléir. Master Soilléir only smiled blandly in return.

"I can't imagine what Princess Sarait wanted with me," Droch continued, turning back to Sìle. "Then again, considering she was wed to Gair of Ceangail, perhaps she was looking for some sort of spell to protect herself against him. Think you?"

Morgan caught the look her grandfather sent Droch. It should have had him shutting his mouth, but apparently Droch was impervious to intimidation—or the dictates of good taste. Morgan didn't consider her manners to be particularly fine, but even she knew when to keep her thoughts to herself.

"Perhaps she was looking for something else," Droch continued, stroking his chin thoughtfully. "I seem to remember that Gair had planned to open a well of evil, then contain it straightway, just to prove his power. And beautiful Sarait went along with him—presumably so she could be impressed by Gair's skill. She took all her children with her to enjoy the spectacle as well, didn't she? Seven sons, wasn't it?"

"Six," Sìle said flatly. "Six sons and a daughter."

"Ah, of course," Droch said, nodding expansively. "Six sons and a wee gel. I seem to remember that all the children were killed when Gair found his magic wasn't quite up to the task of containing what he'd loosed. Taking them along was certainly poorly done on Sarait's part, wasn't it?"

Morgan watched Sìle's hand shoot out and clamp down on Sosar's arm. Sìle only looked at Droch, his face completely devoid of all expression.

"I think, Master Droch," he said in a low voice, "that you speak of what you do not understand."

Droch smiled pleasantly, as if he knew he'd scored a particularly difficult point on a worthy opponent. "I'm perfectly happy to be corrected on the finer points of your late daughter's nature. Perhaps she had her reasons for putting the lives of her children at risk, though I can't imagine what they might be—"

"Let's move on to more pleasant memories," Master Ceannard said brightly, leaping to his feet. "A toast, all, to our esteemed guests. Let this be a day long remembered as the start of renewed correspondence between Buidseachd and Seanagarra, something we have longed for with particular fervor!"

Morgan couldn't help but feel for the man. He was doing his best to distract the others, but it didn't ease the tension. Master Ceannard continued with his efforts, the other wizards continued to squirm, and Sìle continued to look at Droch as if he was imagining up a score of different ways to put him to death, each more painful than the last.

Droch threw back an entire glass of wine, then tapped his glass impatiently for more. Once that was poured and drunk, he rose and began to wander around the chamber.

Morgan bowed her head and tried to be invisible. Footsteps came her way, but she didn't dare look up and see whom they belonged to.

Unfortunately, she didn't need to. She could tell by the sheer darkness of his presence that Droch was standing right in front of her, no doubt willing her to look up at him so he could see the guilt in her eyes.

She realized, with a start, that he was casting some sort of spell over her, something that tried to suffocate her. It was all she could do to keep her hands down in her lap and not claw at the catch on her cloak so she might draw in the breath she so desperately needed.

"Lovely pheasant," Miach said suddenly. "Don't you agree, Master Droch?"

Droch's foot moved, then both his boots turned away and carried him off with them. Morgan forced herself to merely draw in unremarkable breaths until the stars stopped swirling in front of her.

When she could see again, she realized that Droch had once again taken his place across the table from Miach. She wished she could have listened to whatever Master Ceannard was babbling about, but all she could do was watch the man who seemed to be drawing all the light in the chamber to him so he could extinguish it. He fingered his glass and ignored everyone else in favor of staring at Miach.

Morgan wished quite desperately that she'd brought her sword.

But as she hadn't, she settled for loosening the blades in the sheaths strapped to her forearms. She had heard Droch's voice before, which had been bad enough, but watching him was a thousand times worse. He was dark-haired, like Miach, and handsome, also like Miach, but that was where any similarities ended. The master of Olc's eyes were dark and soulless, lacking even the smallest amount of humanity. She shivered even though he wasn't looking at her. She supposed Miach was accustomed to it, for he didn't pause in the consumption of his meal. Then again, she'd never seen him be put off his food by anything. He had a strong stomach, for many things.

She, however, slipped her piece of bread under her stool and gave up thoughts of food anytime soon.

"Someone broke into my solar last night," Droch said.

Morgan held her breath. Not a soul moved. Well, perhaps that wasn't true. Her elven relations had apparently given up on any plans to continue their meal. Turah, very wisely to her mind, swallowed what he was chewing and didn't reach for anything else, presumably so he wouldn't spew it across the table when the battle began. Master Soilléir, whom Morgan could see thanks to the space between Miach and Turah, was watching Droch as if he studied a new species of vermin that might cause him irritation if he got too close. Miach only reached for his wine and sipped.

"It sounds like a popular activity," he remarked.

Morgan eyed the only exit from the chamber. If worst came to worst, she could fight her way—and Miach's—out the door.

"I know who it was," Droch said, looking at Miach pointedly.

"Do you, indeed?" Miach asked. "Interesting."

"You would find it so, I daresay."

"I doubt it," Miach said. "And given that such is the case, I'd appreciate it if you would keep your speculations to yourself and let me finish my meal in peace."

There were gasps from the other wizards at the table. Morgan cursed silently and wondered if it would be a misstep to point out to Miach that he was an idiot for provoking the other man. She could only hope she would be pointing that out later from outside the gates and not sooner whilst hanging from some uncomfortable gibbet, or whatever else it was that the masters of Buidseachd did with whatever miscreants they managed to find inside their gates. Given the expression on Droch's face, she had the feeling anything the masters could do to them would pale in comparison to whatever tortures Droch would devise.

Worse still, she suspected she would discover just what those might be sooner rather than later.

Four

Miach had had more enjoyable lunches.

It wasn't that the fare wasn't edible. It was certainly far superior to the dreck that was served in the buttery downstairs. He supposed the students didn't care what they ate, being too wrung out from their labors to speculate on what they might be missing. He had only vague memories of his first taste of the fare below. He'd come to Buidseachd during his tenth summer and his misery had been so complete, he hadn't noticed anything besides that. Adhémar had mocked him relentlessly for having used the excuse of homesickness to leave Beinn òrain, but he hadn't cared. What point had there been in staying when his mother had been able to teach him everything the masters could—and then some? He had hardly needed to be at Buidseachd to learn his craft.

Well, he'd been homesick as well, but perhaps that was an admission better left unmade.

He had presented himself a second time to the masters when

he'd been ten-and-six, once he'd become comfortable with the mantle of archmage. He'd done so only because there had been things that he'd wanted, things he couldn't have unless he possessed the seven rings of mastery. And so he'd endured a month of vile offerings in the buttery below in order to demonstrate mastery of both lore and craft to the six masters who doled out the usual rings, then spent another exhausting fortnight convincing the seventh wizard to hand over the rarely given, ferociously coveted seventh ring. Then, rings in hand, he'd turned his mind to what he'd actually come to Buidseachd for.

The spells of Caochladh.

They were spells of essence changing, taught only to those who possessed the seven rings of mastery, and only then if Soilléir of Cothromaiche found the candidate particularly worthy.

Miach had spent another month as Soilléir's apprentice, learning not a single spell but finding himself and his honor tested in scores of ways, relentlessly, unforgivingly, until he'd wondered if it was worth it. He had looked inside himself so long and so hard, he'd almost lost his sense of who he was. At the moment when he was certain he would never find his way back out of himself, Soilléir had announced it was enough.

Miach was fairly certain he'd wept.

A month later, he'd been grateful for the depths of himself he'd plumbed. The things that had been entrusted to him were so immense and overwhelming, he'd suspected that if he hadn't already been to the bottom of his soul and seen what lay there, he couldn't have borne what he'd been given.

He'd returned to Tor Neroche a much humbler young man than he'd left.

And he still preferred Master Soilléir's unrelentingly demanding spells to anything else, still preferred to spend time in the solar of a man who was clear and bright as noonday sun. He would have given quite a bit to be facing him across the table at present instead of the absolute darkness that was Master Droch.

"Are you telling me you know nothing about it?"

Miach looked up from his dessert. "About what?"

"About the trespasser in my solar last night!" Droch shouted.

Miach shrugged and helped himself to a bit more of a lovely mousse. "I can't imagine why anyone would bother with your chamber," he said, between bites. "Your spells aren't to everyone's taste, are they?"

There was more gasping by the others at the table, but Miach paid them no heed. He was far too busy wondering if Droch would leap over the table and throttle him before he could blurt out a spell of protection.

"Oh, I don't know," Droch said in a deceptively soft tone. "Some seem to manage them well enough. Especially those with a bloodright to them."

Miach smiled blandly, ignoring the barb. Droch was certainly one to talk there. At least he knew which parts of his blood to choose and which to leave alone. He suspected Droch had long ago passed the point of even having a choice.

"I want to know where you were last night, Prince Mochriadhemiach," Droch pressed.

"I can't imagine my whereabouts could possibly interest you," Miach returned, "so I think I'll keep them to myself."

Droch slapped his hands on the table. "I'll have my answers one way or another."

"Will you, indeed?" Miach said with a smile. "And just how do you think you'll manage that?"

Droch leaned forward. "By challenging you to a duel."

Miach suppressed the urge to roll his eyes, though he supposed no one would have noticed if he had. Half the masters were on their feet, shouting, and the other half were gaping at him as if he'd actually done something completely untoward.

Such as climb over the walls and slip into Droch's solar.

He glanced at Soilléir to find his former mentor sitting back in his chair, rubbing his finger over his mouth as if he strove not to smile. Miach scowled at him, then looked back at Droch.

"I'm busy today," Miach said, loudly enough to be heard over the others. "You'll have to find someone else to humor you."

"Damn you, I demand it!"

Miach considered, then shook his head. "Nay."

Droch's face was becoming a rather unattractive shade of red. Miach would have enjoyed that, but he didn't dare. A man could only poke a viper so many times before he found himself bitten as a result. He'd come perilously close to that the night before. He had no desire to tempt fate again.

"You cannot refuse a challenge!" Droch thundered.

"I think I just did."

Soilléir laughed, then rose and walked away from the table, shaking his head. He was still laughing as he pushed past the guards and left the chamber. Miach wished he could have done the same thing, but he couldn't. Challenges inside the walls of Buidseachd weren't issued lightly and when they were, they were, as Droch had said, never refused. To do so was incredibly poor form.

Not that Miach had any intentions of truly begging off. He simply wanted to make certain that Droch was to the point where he was willing to agree to what Miach truly wanted.

"I might accept," Miach said when Droch paused in his shouting long enough to take a breath, "if the prize was worth the risk."

Droch looked at him furiously. "And what would you consider to be such a prize, boy?"

"An hour of free rein in your solar."

"And I'll have a recounting of where you were last night," Droch shot back without hesitation. "Signed with your blood."

Miach ignored the new round of shouting from down the table that threatened to deafen him. An hour of rifling through Droch's private books or his death.

It seemed reasonable to him.

"Agreed, then," he said.

Droch shoved his chair back and stood. "Now."

"When I've finished my wine."

Even Sìle choked at that. Droch stood there with his arms folded across his chest, simply radiating hatred. Miach wasn't sure if that was an improvement over his threats or not; it was probably something better left undecided.

He did decide, however, that a year spent in Lothar of Wychweald's lowest dungeon, learning to ignore even the most vile of things pressing down on his mind, had been of more use to him than he had ever thought it would be. Ignoring the very powerful wizard glaring at him was relatively easy. Droch had a poor opinion of Lothar's skill with a spell, but he might have thought differently if he'd had a decent taste of Lothar's cruelty.

Miach finished his wine in his own good time, thanked the masters for a delicious lunch, then pushed his chair back without haste and looked at Droch.

"Where to, my lord?"

"Just shut up and follow me," Droch threw over his shoulder as he strode from the chamber.

Miach raised his eyebrows briefly at the other's rudeness, then shrugged and started along after him. He didn't make it five paces before he ran bodily into the king of Tòrr Dòrainn.

"You're mad," Sìle said in a low voice. "Do not have anything to do with him. No good will come of it."

Miach put his hand on the elven king's shoulder. "Your Majesty, I want what he's willing to give. I won't lose."

"Damn these wizards and all their foul doings," Sìle muttered. He looked at Miach from under bushy eyebrows. "You needn't capitulate to their rules, you know, nor to their ridiculous challenges. You're beyond that."

Miach smiled in appreciation of the compliment. "Thank you, Your Grace. But if it eases you any, I don't imagine Droch will use much imagination in his choice. He'll likely settle for a simple game of cards. I'll fare well enough considering that your son taught me almost everything I know about cheating."

Sosar laughed uneasily and pushed back from the table. "I did not," he said, standing. "You were proficient enough in that without my aid. We'll come along, of course, though I'm not sure what assistance we can offer."

"You'll think of something," Miach said with a slight nod over his shoulder. If something happened to him, they would have to look after Morgan, which Sosar surely realized. Miach glanced at Morgan. "Come along, Buck, and wait for me whilst I'm about this fine entertainment."

Morgan's hands were hidden under her cloak, no doubt holding on to those lovely knives he'd made for her. He supposed it wouldn't be inappropriate to hope she wouldn't use them on him before Droch could have at him.

She fell into step behind him as he left the chamber. He wasn't sure who was cursing in a less successful whisper, Morgan or her grandfather. Sosar and Turah were, blessedly, refraining from the same.

"Buck, my arse," Morgan hissed from immediately behind him. "You idiot, what are you doing?"

"Just a little sport," he said easily, loudly enough that Droch could hear from where he walked twenty paces ahead of them. "We'll be on our way come sunset, I imagine."

Morgan said nothing else, but he imagined she was silently calling him all kinds of fool. Perhaps she had it aright, but there was nothing to be done about it now. He had to have the spell Gair of Ceangail had used to open that well of evil and Droch's solar was as good a place as any to look for it. Especially if he actually had the freedom to look without worrying that he might be caught whilst doing so.

He followed Droch with Morgan walking behind him and the rest of their kin trailing along behind her. The chill increased as they continued down a particular passageway not far from where Droch's solar lay.

Without warning, he walked out suddenly into a garden that reminded him so much of a particular glade near Ceangail that he came to an abrupt halt. Morgan plowed into his back so hard, he stumbled. He reached behind him to steady her, then steeled himself for another look.

The garden was open to the sky, for what that was worth. The sunlight that fell down through the bare trees wasn't what shone on other parts of the world, of that Miach was certain. It was viewed through a filter of Droch's magic, a filter that rendered it unpleasant, garish, and somehow completely without warmth.

"Vile," Sosar breathed.

Miach agreed, but he didn't say as much. He squeezed Morgan's arm briefly, then stepped out into the garden. There was a life-sized chessboard there to one side, built from alternating slabs of black and gray marble. Miach looked at Droch.

"Chess?"

"If you dare," Droch snarled.

Miach shrugged with a casualness he didn't feel. "Whatever suits you. Are there pieces, or are we to man the board ourselves?"

"You could use your servant as one," Droch suggested. "Or your brother."

"No, thank you," Miach said without hesitation. "I value the first's ability to shine my boots and the latter's to sharpen my sword."

"Then I'll provide the players," Droch said. He gestured and his servant ran across the chessboard and over to doors set into a rock wall. The lad opened those heavy wooden doors, then stepped back.

Miach could scarce believe his eyes.

Chess pieces, pieces that were not only life-sized but terribly life-*like,* shuffled out of the closet. He watched, openmouthed, as creatures who seemed human enough continued their slow, weary march onto the board. First came pieces dressed in black, then another contingent of players dressed in what might have been white at one time but was now a dingy gray that seemed a too-accurate reflection of the absolute bleakness of their souls.

Miach waited until they'd taken their places, then he walked out onto the chessboard, feeling slightly dazed.

He looked at the black players, but he could see instantly that if they had been alive before, they were that no longer. Their eyes were empty, their souls long since drained of anything that might have made them mortal.

It was so shockingly reminiscent of what Lothar did with his captives that Miach thought he might be ill.

He turned away and looked at his own warriors. He saw, to his horror, that they were most certainly not dead. They were encased in some sort of resin. They looked at him with a desperate hope that was difficult to behold. He rubbed his hands over his face, then went to examine each of the pieces in turn.

The pawns, he realized immediately, were faeries from Siabh-reach, trapped helplessly like butterflies inside a gray, granitelike prison. He took a deep breath, then approached each of them, looking into their eyes and willing them to trust him, hoping to gain their loyalty.

When he had finished, he went in turn to each of the rooks, stewards of mighty keeps: the knights with their long, sharp swords: then the mages with their tall, pointed hats frozen along with them. Last, he paused before the king and queen and searched back through his own memory of tales and lore for who they might be.

Uallach and Murdina of Faoin.

The names came to him as if they'd been spoken aloud. A power-hungry and foolish pair who had traded what magic they had for spells that had seemed more . . . but hadn't been.

Olc was a seductive magic indeed.

The king struggled to put his hand on his sword, but failed. He looked at Miach, his expression one of utter defeat.

Miach reached up and put his hand on the king's ice-cold shoulder. "Your Grace," he began helplessly. He cast about for something to say, but found nothing of substance. He finally merely inclined his head, then turned and looked for Droch.

Droch was standing next to his own king, smiling coldly. "Have you sufficient courage gathered, young one?"

"Almost." Miach gestured to his pieces. "What happens to them if I lose?"

"I take more of their souls and they continue on their relentless journey toward black," Droch said. "And I'll see that you join their ranks—after I've had your confession." He smiled. "I think an archmage would make a particularly fine acquisition, don't you? Instead of your death for trespassing, I'll have you forever tucked away in my closet, where I might pull you forth now and again and admire you."

Miach suppressed the urge to close his eyes. He had no doubt Droch would do just that. He wasn't afraid of death—indeed, he'd come within a breath of it not a fortnight before—but he was very afraid of leaving Morgan alone. She was skilled and courageous, but there were things that hunted her, things that might catch her unawares and carry her where she didn't want to go. Given that he knew where that place was and what she would face, he was particularly interested in making sure she didn't find herself there.

And he had to admit that he wanted to believe that in some small way she might miss him.

He was so tempted to turn, reach for her hand, and pull her up into the sky with him, he could hardly stop himself from doing just that. But if he looked at her, Droch might suspect she meant something to him and then who knew what mischief he would combine against her. As much as Miach wanted to tell her once more that he loved her, he knew he couldn't. He simply took a deep breath and looked at Droch.

"What now?"

"Your move."

Miach nodded, walked over to one of those beautiful faeries from Siabhreach, and asked her politely to step forward. He could almost see the imperceptible flutter of her wings as she attempted it.

In the end, he had to help her step across the boundary from gray to black and back to gray again.

The moment she did, all hell broke loose.

It was as if someone had taken an ordinary game of chess, tossed it into a whirlwind, and bombarded it with spells of all varieties coming from all sides at once. It was pieces and spells and strategy; it was war, only compressed, bloody, unrelenting, exhausting.

And Droch was very good at it.

Miach lost half his pieces before he understood the threat he faced and managed to get his feet underneath him. He almost cost himself the game at first by his reticence. He realized all too quickly that it was either fight to win, fight to the death and disregard the pieces of Droch's he'd captured that were now lying lifeless on the side of the board, or lose the game and find himself as one of them.

He sought to out-finesse Droch, but the man was like a sledgehammer, ruthlessly smashing through defenses, obliterating pieces in his way as if he had no interest in how or where they were won or lost. Miach dug deep for every strategy his father had taught him over countless games of chess in the family's private gathering chamber at Tor Neroche, considered the things he'd learned in his own life, even searched through his memories of that year spent in Lothar's dungeon for something underhanded and foul to use as an honorless gambit.

All it won him was finding himself with two bloodied, exhausted mages defending his king. He watched in desperation as the trap Droch had laid for him began to close.

And then he realized that it wasn't the attack from Droch's knight that he had to worry about.

It was from Droch himself.

Miach found himself being bound, just as the pieces had been. He stood there, already half frozen next to his king, and searched frantically for a spell of Olc to counter it. He knew more of that magic than he cared to think about, had walked in many very unpleasant places to learn it, had paid his own share of peace for the spells he knew.

He shouldn't have been surprised that none of it served him now.

He wondered with a growing feeling of fury just what Droch was using on him. It wasn't Olc, or Wexham, or half a dozen other things he could have easily identified. It was something he'd never encountered before, a slow but relentless piece of magic that surrounded him, leaving him more unable to draw breath each time he exhaled. Fighting it, even knowing *how* to fight it was almost impossible. In desperation, he continued to try spell after spell, all with the same result. He turned his head to look at his king.

There was pity in the old man's eyes. Pity and fear.

Miach heard himself crackle as he turned back to look at Droch. He could hear Sosar shouting at Droch and Droch bellowing for Sosar to mind his own bloody business. Miach saw, out of the corner of his eye, spells go flying over his head from both sides of the board. Olc and Fadaire mingled in the putrid air, becoming something ugly and rancid. For himself, Miach found that he couldn't shout at all. He could scarcely breathe.

And still the spell hardened around him.

He realized that time was indeed running out for him. And all for a bloody ridiculous game of chess where he'd been too stupid to recognize where the true danger lay. He would have shaken his head, but that was now quite impossible, so instead, he did what he'd done countless times in places where he'd been out of his depth: he took the best breath he could and stilled his mind. He calmly and very deliberately gave thought to the tangle and how he might best unravel it.

Almost without thinking, he put his hand on the simplest spell of binding he could, something a village sorcerer would have taught an apprentice on the first day.

And then he reversed it.

Nothing happened. He started to repeat the words, then he noticed a tiny crack appearing in Droch's spell. It took rather longer than he would have liked for that crack to deepen, but once it had, there was no stopping the damage. Fractures in Droch's spell raced from Miach's initial break outward so quickly, Miach couldn't follow them. He caught sight of Droch's expression of shock as his spell shattered right there in front of him—in spite of his efforts to stop it.

And whilst Droch was otherwise occupied, Miach leapt forward and shoved one of his mages, sending him skidding to a halt just out of reach of the black king. The black king crackled loudly as he turned his head to look back over his shoulder along the same gray diagonal the white mage now threatened. His steward stood behind him, frozen in place, wearing a look of horror on his face. There was now no escape for either of them.

Miach leaned over with his hands on his thighs, gasping for breath. He lifted his head and saw Droch gaping in surprise at his king who was now in check. The game was now over except for final formalities.

Droch reached out suddenly and tore the sword from his knight's scabbard. He thrust it through his own king's heart with a vicious curse.

The black king fell to his knees, clutching his chest. Then he looked up at Miach.

His soulless eyes were full of tears.

Miach suspected those were tears of relief. He watched as Droch's king fell over onto the board. Droch jerked the sword free, then glared at Miach. Miach straightened.

"An hour," he said, drawing in a great lungful of air and not feeling the least bit inclined to complain about the sour taste of it.

Droch crossed the board, kicking one of his dead pawns out of the way, and stopped just in front of Miach.

"Someday," he said in a low, dangerous voice. "Someday, Mochriadhemiach, you will find yourself alone, perhaps unwell, perhaps careless. You will find things do not go so well for you then."

Miach inclined his head just the slightest bit. "I'm certain you would be grieved at such a day."

Droch looked around Miach and glared at a lad standing nervously nearby. "One hour. You mark the time and mark it well, else you'll answer to me." He turned back to Miach. "I won't forget this."

Miach imagined he wouldn't. He watched Droch spin on his heel and stalk off, then looked at the carnage around him. He walked over to the black king. He was no longer frozen, but he was most certainly dead. The rest of the black pieces lay on the ground, lifeless. Perhaps there had never been any hope for them. Miach turned to look at his own king. The man looked about himself, as if he'd just woken from a terrible nightmare. He flexed his fingers, then swung his arms a bit. His gaze came to rest on Miach and he frowned.

"Who are you, lad?"

Miach walked over to him and made him a low bow. "Mochriadhemiach of Neroche, Your Majesty."

"I have you to thank for my life, apparently."

Miach managed a weary smile. "Nay, King Uallach, you fought well, as did your men. And your queen."

Uallach looked at him. "You know me?"

"Of course, Your Grace. Your fame extends far beyond the bounds of your own land."

The king harrumphed a bit in pleasure, clapped a hand on Miach's shoulder, then went to gather his queen back up to her feet from where she lay sprawled on the grass. Queen Murdina looked as dazed as her husband did. Once she had gotten her bearings, she went into her husband's arms and wept. Miach left them to it because he understood. He was damned tempted to weep himself.

He would have searched for Morgan but his way was blocked by the mages who had glided over to stand in front of him. Miach didn't know either of them, but he was the first to admit he didn't spend enough time in Buidseachd to know who was who.

"You look like Gilraehen of Neroche," the mage on the left said.

The mage on the right shook his head. "Nay, Anghmar of Neroche," he insisted. He frowned at Miach. "You a relation?"

Miach smiled. "I might be."

The man frowned. "I heard a rumor he was slain, rescuing one of his witless sons from the dungeon at Riamh."

"The son was indeed witless," Miach agreed, unoffended, "and he was indeed rescued. And aye, his father the king died as a result. His mother too, unfortunately."

The man on the right clapped a hand on Miach's shoulder. "You're not a bad chessman, lad. Fine command of magic for being a simple village brat."

"He didn't say he was a simple village brat," the other mage said, drawing the first aside. "He said he might be kin to the king of Neroche—the late king, rather." He shot Miach a look. "Perhaps a cousin. Let's go nose about in the library and see if we can find his name."

"They won't let us in the library any longer. Not after the last time."

"That was decades ago. Surely they've forgotten by now. And if not, we'll feign hunger and sit on the bench by the door. You make a great production of calling for food, whilst I sneak off to look for books of Nerochian genealogy to filch."

Miach watched them go, then turned to see if Morgan was standing, sitting, or waiting for him to come closer so she could stab him. He'd barely caught sight of her when his line of sight was obscured by a flurry of wings. Eight giggling, fluttering, very silly faeries were crowding around him, touching his hands, his hair, his face, and, heaven help him, fighting over who would be the one to kiss him first.

He wondered if it would be impolite to bolt.

He managed to catch sight of Sosar, who was only standing there laughing at him.

"Help!" Miach called.

Sosar put his arm around Morgan's shoulders. "I believe I have my hands full here."

Miach looked desperately about for Turah, but his brother was only smirking as well. Even Sìle was smiling just the slightest bit.

He would have shot the king a pleading look, but he was borne to the ground and overcome before he could.

And he thought he'd survived the most dangerous part of the afternoon.

Five

Morgan wished, not for the first time that day, that she'd had her sword. She wasn't sure on whom she would have used it first: Sosar or Miach. Well, perhaps not on Miach. He couldn't help the fact that he was currently under assault. Her uncle, however, could most certainly have helped his unnecessary mirth. It was levity sorely misplaced after what they'd just watched. She glared at him, then turned to see how Turah was taking the events of the day.

He looked as gray as she felt, though he seemingly managed a smile in spite of it. "Well," he said, "that's done."

"Your brother takes terrible risks," she managed.

"He always has. Perhaps you should talk to him about it."

"I've tried, but he ignores me." She took a deep breath. "I need a chair."

"So do I. And since you're Miach's servant, why don't you be a love and run fetch us one?"

She looked up at him in surprise only to have him wink at her. She wasn't sure she knew him well enough to do damage to him, but thought an elbow to his ribs wasn't anything more than he deserved. He laughed weakly.

"I can see you're not inclined to do any fetching," he said, "so perhaps we'll just soldier on as best we can until Miach is finished with his, er, business there. I don't suppose you'd want to hurry him along, would you?"

"Aye," Sosar agreed. "I should think you would want to rush over and defend your lord's abused honor. Those lassies are notoriously . . . well, they're notorious."

Morgan gave them both looks of warning that they should have taken more seriously, then turned back to the spectacle in front of her. Was it not enough that she'd spent the past half hour wondering how she could possibly save Miach before he was killed; now she had to watch him be fawned over by half a dozen truly lovely women?

"Faeries," Sosar corrected. "And there are eight of them."

"Are you reading my thoughts now, my lord?" she asked shortly.

"You're muttering."

She didn't want to think about where she'd learned that bad habit, but she suspected it might have been from Miach, who had learned it from Adhémar. Reason enough not to investigate any further.

She took a deep breath and clasped her hands together under her cloak where no one would be able to watch them tremble. It had nothing to do with the faeries; it had everything to do with the battle she'd just witnessed. She wasn't terribly fond of chess. She'd played it with Weger to humor him, and bested him a respectable number of times, but she far preferred to be out on the battlefield instead of merely playing at it.

The speed of the game had been swift, the battle ruthless, and the outcome far from certain. Indeed, the entire thing had come about too swiftly for her to decide what, if anything, she could do to be helpful. She wouldn't soon forget the sight of Miach becoming increasingly bound by Droch's spell.

She tried to distract herself with the sight in front of her, but that was no better. The faeries had now formed a very ladylike, sedate line in front of Miach, who had managed to get back to his feet without help.

Well, the faeries were sedate until the first of them took what was apparently more time than she was allowed. All-out war ensued with pauses only for one faery to shove another of their ranks aside and take her place immediately in front of the hapless archmage of Neroche.

Morgan wondered, absently, just what they were. Some species of elf, perhaps, though they were not so unrelentingly beautiful as her relatives were. These creatures were alluring in an entirely different way, as if they'd been flowers that were so sweetly luscious that any bee with sense wouldn't have passed them by.

And damn them all if they weren't *still* fighting each other to be the one closest to Miach. They hovered behind him, in front of him, on either side of him, their gossamer wings fluttering coquettishly.

Morgan gritted her teeth and wondered if this was indeed what jealousy felt like.

The only thing that eased her any was how profoundly uncomfortable Miach looked. He was very red in the face and looked pathetically grateful when the knights who had fought for him demanded their own turn. After those goodly lads had discussed the battle to their satisfaction, the stewards took a turn. The faeries began to murmur unhappily. Apparently discussions of strategy that didn't involve how to get themselves as close to the exceptionally handsome prince of Neroche as possible didn't interest the ladies much. They fluttered off, disappointed and disgruntled. In time, the rest of the players wandered off as well.

Miach rubbed his hands over his face, then heaved a sigh and walked over to where they stood near the wall. He stopped in front of her.

"How are you?" he ventured.

"Unkissed," she said tartly. "Not that you find yourself in a similar situation."

He laughed uneasily. "I would see to remedying that for you if I could, but perhaps later, when we've a bit of privacy." His smile faded. "That was unpleasant."

"I will be happy to see the last of this place," she whispered. "I'm sorry we came."

"Reserve judgment for another hour," he said. "We might just find what we need, then we'll count the journey worth it." He looked at their companions. "Thank you all for staying."

Sìle grunted. "What a disgusting display from that reprehensible mage." He paused. "I will allow that you did well."

Miach made Sìle a bow. "Thank you, Your Majesty. Now, if you wouldn't mind taking—"

"I'm not leaving you," Morgan interrupted shortly, certain that was what he intended. "No discussion."

"I'll come keep watch over her," Sosar offered. "Father, perhaps you and Turah might distract a few souls and provide Miach with an extra measure of privacy."

Morgan watched her grandfather consider, then nod briskly.

"Very well," he conceded. "We'll be off and see to a few things of a more clandestine nature, if Prince Turah manages to keep his mouth shut for a change." He took Turah by the scruff of the neck and pulled him away. "Come with me, young one, and let me teach you a bit about not answering questions you don't care to. Your mother was a master at it. Did you learn nothing at her knee?"

Morgan would have smiled at the look of panic Turah threw them over his shoulder before he was dragged off, but she was still standing in a garden full of vile spells and all she had the strength for was to hope she could stumble out of them.

The servant Droch had spoken to made Miach a bow, then turned and walked off as if he expected to be followed. She was quite happy to do so, simply because it meant she could leave Droch's garden behind her. She would be long in forgetting the sight of the chess pieces still lying motionless on the board behind them.

"Who were those people?" she asked Miach quietly as they walked through passageways that were only slightly less unpleasant than the garden had been.

"Kings ensnared by a lust for power, queens ensnared by the desire for riches, knights wishing for something extra in battle to impress those who might want to hire them. They went looking for those things in places they shouldn't have." He shrugged. "Olc can be a very seductive magic. Once a mage who had no bloodright to it realizes how much of his soul the learning of it costs, the price has been paid and he is too enamored of the power it gives him to try to pull away."

"Like Gair?" she whispered.

"Aye," he said, just as softly. "Like Gair. Droch has a right to it, so it hasn't killed so much of his soul. Then again, I daresay he didn't have much of a soul to start with."

She frowned. "Then why did the faeries find themselves trapped? Surely they weren't interested in power."

He smiled. "They're lovely, but not very smart. They were most likely just caught with a net."

She bumped him companionably with her shoulder. "You are a dreadful man."

"I'm still blushing."

"I don't know that I've seen you blush before when kissed."

"Given that you have your eyes closed most of the time when we're about that pleasant activity, I daresay you don't know what I do, do you?"

She wanted to smile, but they were walking along passageways that were suddenly all too familiar, and she couldn't. She swallowed, hard. "I'm so sorry you're going in there."

"I've been in worse places," he said easily. He shot her a quick look. "Thank you for waiting for me, though. I daresay it will help."

"You can thank me later."

"I will, when I can burst into tears safely away from prying eyes." He took a deep breath, then stopped. "Here we are."

Morgan realized he was right. Her uncle shuddered visibly as they stopped in front of Droch's door. She watched their guide pull an hourglass from his pocket, look at Miach, then set the glass on the floor.

"One hour, Archmage of Neroche."

Miach nodded, looked at Morgan again, then walked into the chamber and shut the door behind him. Morgan leaned back against the wall and wished for the comforting chill of her swordhilt beneath her hand, not the horrible, bone-numbing bitterness that seemed to freeze more than just her body. She hadn't noticed it the night before—perhaps she'd been too terrified to—but Olc's darkness seemed to not only chill her form, it began to work on her mind as well. Unreasonable fears assaulted her, fears of things that lurked in shadows in the depth of night when there was no light to drive them away.

She took a deep breath, then looked around Sosar at the glass on the floor. Unfortunately, only a barely discernable amount of time had passed.

She looked up at her uncle, but his eyes were closed and he was breathing very carefully. Perhaps he was walking in the garden at Seanagarra where songs of Fadaire whispered through the leaves and his father's spells kept the worst of winter away.

She closed her eyes to attempt the same thing, but once she did, she was immediately assaulted by visions of the serpents she'd seen inside Droch's chamber the night before. No aid from that quarter. She opened her eyes and looked about her for some other, less evil distraction.

She found it in the person of the tall man who was walking down the passageway toward them, looking for all the world as if he too strolled peacefully in Seanagarra's pleasant gardens. She elbowed Sosar, and he opened his eyes reluctantly. He looked, then smiled at the ageless man who stopped in front of him.

"Master Soilléir," Sosar said, inclining his head, "I didn't have the chance to greet you properly at luncheon today."

Master Soilléir made him a very low bow. "Not to worry, Prince Sosar. The circumstances there were less than ideal. Tell me, how long has it been since last we met?"

"Three," Sosar began, squinting up at the ceiling, "perhaps four hundred years?"

"Too long," Soilléir said without a hint of irony. He turned to her and held out his hand. "I'm Léir," he said simply. "And you are . . . ?"

She took his hand in a firm grip and answered before she thought better of it. "The archmage's servant." She made what she hoped was a gruff, manly noise as she pulled her hand back and tucked it into her sleeve. "Buck."

Soilléir only looked at her with one eyebrow raised. "Indeed, Buck. I thought you were mute."

"It comes and goes."

He laughed. "I imagine it does—to your lord's edification, no doubt. Would you mind if I kept vigil here with you and Prince Sosar?"

Morgan shook her head. "I'm sure Miach—I mean, my lord Mochriadhemiach—would appreciate it."

Soilléir gave no indication of having marked her slip. He merely leaned against the wall next to her and folded his arms over his chest. He looked around her now and again, as if he checked the hourglass as well, but said nothing more. Morgan didn't want to credit him with more sterling qualities than he deserved, but she had the feeling he was just as interested in keeping Miach safe as she and Sosar were.

The hour passed with excruciating slowness. Morgan tried not to think about what Miach might be finding, or—worse still—not finding. She had no choice but to believe he had been in more terrible places than Droch's solar, but that was of little comfort.

And still the sand dropped one grain at a time.

Droch appeared precisely as the last grain fell. He pushed the servant out of the way, then threw open his door as if he expected Miach to be plundering his coffers. Morgan saw Miach standing just inside the door, as if he'd been preparing to come out. She knew this because in the scuffle, she'd moved to stand where she might most advantageously fling her knives into Droch's back if he tried anything untoward.

Droch shoved Miach aside roughly, then strode inside his chamber. Miach said nothing. He simply came out into the passageway and pulled the door shut behind him. He leaned back against the wall, his face ashen.

Soilléir walked over to speak to the servant, who had picked up the hourglass. "I'll be the archmage's escort from here, my friend. Thank you for your service to him."

The lad nodded, shot Miach an uneasy look, then hurried away. Soilléir turned to Sosar. "I'll take him to my solar for a bit of peace. You're welcome to come as well, if it pleases you."

Sosar smiled. "I imagine I should go make certain my father isn't trying to discover ways to undermine the foundations of the keep."

Morgan might have laughed, but she supposed such a thing wasn't beneath her grandfather. Soilléir seemed to find it humorous enough, though, for he laughed and clapped a companionable hand on Sosar's shoulder.

"I'm sure Master Ceannard would appreciate that. Perhaps your father will have finished with his explorations by supper. I'll have it prepared in my chambers and send for you then, shall I?"

"That would be lovely," Sosar agreed. He looked at Miach. "Be well, Miach. And you, Buck, be a good lad and do just as your master tells you."

Morgan cursed her uncle under her breath, then resheathed her knives and jumped forward just in time to catch Miach as he swayed. She drew his arm over her shoulders and put her arm around his waist.

"Let me aid you."

"Nay," Miach protested, "I am well."

"You're a fool. Lean on me."

Master Soilléir sighed, then put himself on Miach's other side, taking much of Miach's weight on him. Miach didn't protest, though Morgan supposed she should hold off on congratulating him on his show of sense given that he was having difficulty even standing. If they hadn't been holding him up, he likely would have fallen on his face.

"Let's be off then, shall we?" Soilléir said easily, as if they were merely heading out for tea in the garden. "Down the passageway, Buck, and up the stairs. Miach, lad, one foot in front of the other."

Morgan was more grateful for the aid than she wanted to admit. Miach was much taller than she was and while he was lean, he was also quite heavy when not sailing fully under his own power, as it were. She took what of his weight Soilléir would accord her and was happy to listen to Soilléir speak of naught but meaningless gossip and useless political tidings as they made their way slowly down the passageway. The longer Miach walked, the less he trembled. Perhaps just being away from Droch's lair was enough to restore him to himself.

They wound their way through hallways and up flights of stairs until Soilléir stopped before a heavy wooden door. He opened it, then stood back to allow them to go inside first. Morgan only made it a handful of paces before she had to stop and stare.

She was struck first by the sight of floor-to-ceiling windows along one side of the room. There was so much glorious light pouring into the chamber, it was difficult to take in.

"Beautiful, isn't it?" Miach whispered.

She nodded, because she couldn't speak. She turned in all directions, looking at the windows, then walls covered with bookshelves, then at an enormous hearth set into the wall at the far end of the chamber. The chamber reminded her greatly of the gathering hall in Weger's tower, but here there were the true luxuries of carpets on the floor and tapestries lining what walls weren't already lined with books.

And there was the light.

It was exactly the sort of place she knew Miach would be comfortable in, somewhere where he could put his feet up on the furniture and talk about his turnip crop whilst being bathed in glorious daylight. She imagined, based on his surroundings, that Soilléir was that sort of man as well.

A pair of very large dogs scrambled to their feet and raced across the chamber toward them, jumping first on their master, then turning to see about more interesting victims.

Miach submitted to a thorough investigation of his person, but Morgan wasn't so sure she wanted to. She patted the enormous dogs, then tried to shoo them surreptitiously away. It was an instruction they ignored entirely. She found, to her consternation, that the beasts were as determined to shadow her as she was Miach. Soilléir invited Miach to come sit in front of the fire. Morgan trailed along behind them because Soilléir nodded at her as well.

Miach fell back to walk alongside her. "Will you be well here?" he murmured.

"If the dogs fail in their plan to make a meal of me," she said, "aye, I will be well enough."

He smiled. "Perhaps a rest would serve you. We'll leave after supper, I promise."

"You are the one who could do with a rest," she said, "though I'll concede that you look better than you did a quarter hour ago." She wanted to ask him what he'd found—if anything at all—but she couldn't bring herself to. He looked a bit like a man who'd woken from a horrific nightmare only to find he hadn't been dreaming.

She walked with him to the hearth, then settled for a small stool near the fire where she could watch the door yet still hear whatever conversation might go on. She looked up as a hooded servant stepped forward and poured wine into cups for both his master and Miach. The bottle trembled as he did so, but it was obvious it wasn't from any nervousness on his part. His hands, Morgan could see, were horribly scarred.

She realized with a start that it was the man who had helped them the night before.

She looked quickly at his face, but it was hidden too deeply in shadow for her to see his expression. He hadn't lingered near Miach, nor had he leaned down to whisper in his master's ear about Miach's traitorous activities of the night before, so Morgan supposed all she could do was wait and see if he attempted anything foul.

Miach didn't seem concerned even though she had seen him mark the man's hands as well. Perhaps he was also willing to wait and see what the rest of the afternoon would bring. He sat back in his chair and sighed in contentment.

"Thank you," he said to Soilléir.

"First good breath of the day, eh, lad?" Soilléir said with an amused smile.

"Actually, it is," Miach said. "I appreciate the peace to enjoy it."

"You've been busy," Soilléir said. "And not just today, I suspect."

Morgan fingered the hilt of one of her daggers, because it made her feel more comfortable. She would have liked to have believed that they were safe, but they were still in a nest of mages and mages were unpredictable. There was no sense in not being prepared for the worst.

"It was a taxing journey here," Miach said, lifting his shoulder in a half shrug. "There is always a bit of weariness that follows such a journey, isn't there?"

Soilléir slid Miach a skeptical look. "You're hedging, Mochriad-hemiach, but I won't press you until you look a bit less like you'll sick up your lunch on my rug. Give me tidings instead. I've heard rumors about powerless swords, foul creatures roaming in places one wouldn't expect, and archmages escaping death."

"Is that all?" Miach asked, smiling.

"Of course not. I've heard all sorts of things about all sorts of other things. I'm just giving you an easy place to start."

Morgan imagined Miach appreciated that more than he cared to show. He humored Soilléir by giving a rather vague recounting of his activities in the fall, starting with his sending his brother the king on a quest to find a certain thing and finishing with his and Adhémar's return to Tor Neroche. He made no mention of anyone who might or might not have been the wielder of the Sword of Angesand—or who might or might not have taken the Sword of Angesand and smashed it to bits against the king's high table—and for that she was most grateful.

"You were looking for a wielder for the Sword of Angesand?" Soilléir asked when Miach finished.

Morgan pursed her lips. She had apparently begun to breathe easily a moment too soon.

"I thought I might need the sword's power," Miach conceded, "since Lothar took Adhémar's. I've come to the conclusion, though, that I can do without it at present."

"Has Adhémar regained his power, then?"

"Nay," Miach said slowly. "And worse still, he's now captive in Lothar's dungeon. He was fool enough to take his bride too near the border without a large enough guard. Not that any sized guard would have served him, I suppose."

"Why haven't you gone to rescue him?" Soilléir asked mildly.

"I have business to see to first."

Soilléir studied him in silence for a moment or two before he spoke again. "I thought it was interesting table conversation earlier."

"I tried to ignore it."

"I don't know how you could have, especially when Droch brought up Gair's well."

"Droch has no manners," Miach said.

"Was it only bad manners, or something else? He couldn't have been merely provoking Sìle, surely."

Miach shrugged. "I wouldn't presume to guess."

Soilléir scowled at him for a moment, then laughed. "Damn you, Miach, you're going to make me work at this, aren't you?"

Miach smiled. "I'm just assuring myself you haven't entered fully into your dotage and lost all your powers of sight. No doubt you can divine Droch's motives without my aid."

"Dotage, my arse," Soilléir grunted. He sat back and propped his ankle up on his knee. "Well, since you're not going to be of any help, perhaps I'll humor you and tell you what I saw."

"Do," Miach said.

"Don't," Morgan said, realizing only after the word was out of her mouth that she and Miach had spoken at the same time.

Soilléir shot her a look of amusement, then turned back to Miach. "I'll temper my remarks, then, for your servant, who has suddenly become quite vocal. We'll also leave Droch for a bit later, though I'm hazarding a guess that his topics of conversation have more to do with your business than you want to admit. I'll start with your elvish companions. I didn't see much change in Sile or Prince Sosar, but their lives are long and the passing of seasons does not affect them as it does others. You, however, have changed quite a bit since last we spoke."

"Have I?" Miach asked. "How so?"

"You bear Scrymgeour Weger's mark, for one thing."

Morgan looked at Miach pointedly, but he only smiled and lifted one of his shoulders in a half shrug. Fortunately, perhaps, Soilléir didn't seem to mark any of the exchange. He was suddenly watching his servant struggle to open another bottle of wine. Morgan wondered why he didn't offer any aid, then decided he was perhaps seeking to save the man's pride. She found herself surprisingly relieved when the cork came free and the man no longer had to wrestle with it.

"What possessed you to go inside Weger's gates?" Soilléir continued, turning to look at Miach. "Temporary madness?"

"Nay, I went in to fetch something."

"Something?"

"Someone," Miach amended.

"Curious."

"Isn't it, though."

Morgan found that Soilléir was looking over his shoulder at her. She shifted uncomfortably before she could stop herself. She knew him to be the keeper of the spells of Caochladh, but somehow he didn't look old enough to have mastered anything past the turning of a good row or two for spring planting. Then again, Miach had become archmage of Neroche at ten-and-four, so perhaps looks were deceiving. All she knew was that when Master Soilléir looked at her, she wanted to run lest he see too much.

He turned away, though, and began to speak with Miach of more inconsequential things. It seemed a very normal bit of business, sitting in front of a roaring fire and listening to the talk of men. She'd done it in Nicholas of Lismòr's solar as a girl; she'd done it in Scrymgeour Weger's gathering hall as a young woman and an adult. That she should find the same bit of normalcy in the midst of spells and wizardry should have alerted her to the fact that she was becoming far too comfortable in her untoward surroundings.

"Your servant bears Weger's mark as well," Soilléir said at one point.

Morgan clapped her hand over her forehead before she could stop herself and cursed silently. It was nothing more than she deserved for letting down her guard. Obviously he'd marked it earlier and chosen, for his own nefarious purposes, to discuss it only now.

She wondered, though, how he knew. Her face was too far in shadows for him to have seen anything that might or might not have resided over her left eyebrow.

"An interesting thing for a woman to have won," Soilléir continued.

Morgan looked quickly at Miach, but he was quite obviously fighting a smile. She turned to Soilléir and frowned.

"What is it you think you know, good sir?" she demanded. "If I'm allowed to ask."

"Likely more than you'd be comfortable with, lass," Soilléir said. "If you'd like to join us, you might have an easier time using one of your blades on me if I vexed you overmuch by telling the rest of what I know."

"Does the university frown on bloodshed?"

"It frowns on many things, but bloodshed is quite a bit farther down the list than sneaking over the walls with a man who definitely should have known better. Come join us, lady. Miach, why don't you go fetch a chair for Princess Mhorghain."

The sound of glass shattering startled Morgan so badly, she had both of the knives Miach had given her in her hands before she realized she'd reached for them.

But it was only Soilléir's servant who had dropped his bottle of wine.

Soilléir looked up quickly. "I'm sorry, my friend," he said, rising. "That was poorly done on my part. I also should have poured for you. Let me see to the shards."

Morgan looked at Soilléir's servant and saw that he had cut himself badly. She would have offered aid, but Soilléir was already wrapping a cloth about his hand. She thought about being surprised that Soilléir had apparently known her without her having shown her face, but decided there was little point. Miach had, after all, warned her of his particular skills. Perhaps she should have taken them more seriously.

She set aside her cloak, then went to stand next to Miach after he'd fetched her a chair. "You, serving me," she said pointedly. "What a pleasure."

He pulled her into his arms and smiled down at her. "You know I prefer it that way."

She did know that, actually, which would save him a mighty thrashing in the lists later, which she supposed he knew as well. She glanced at Soilléir, then back at Miach. "Is he the only one who knows, do you think? About me, I mean."

"Aye. I can guarantee the other masters didn't look past their plates this afternoon. You're anonymous enough for our purposes."

Morgan watched Soilléir talking quietly with his servant. She was sure that was the same man from the night before, who had been in no doubt of Miach's identity then and was in no doubt of hers now. She wondered how that boded for their safety.

"And Soilléir's servant?" she asked with a nod in his direction.

"Time will tell, won't it?"

She didn't find that particularly comforting, but there wasn't really any other answer to offer.

"I think an afternoon here would do us good," he continued. "If you can bear it."

"I will allow that this is the least objectionable chamber I've been in so far."

"I'm sure Master Soilléir would be greatly relieved to know that."

She scowled at him, but he only tugged on her braid, smiled at her, then walked unsteadily away presumably to find more wine.

Morgan sat, but she didn't relax. Miach obviously needed a bit more time to recover from the events of the day, but she would watch him and suggest they leave the moment he looked equal to it. They might have been in a chamber where the company was pleasant, but that said nothing for what lurked outside the door.

The sooner they were away from the fury Droch was no doubt nursing, the better off they would be.

Six

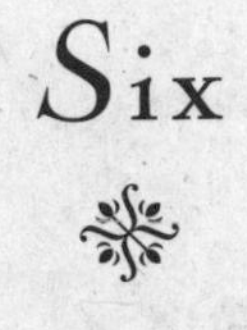

Miach fetched a new bottle of wine, then poured glasses all around. He looked up as Léir's servant walked unsteadily back to stand in the shadows, his hands tucked into the folds of his robe. He wondered who he was and how he had come to find himself in Léir's company. Or if he'd come upstairs earlier that morning and told Léir everything he'd seen.

Perhaps that was something better reserved for later contemplation, after he'd stopped shaking and could think clearly again. And perhaps later he would also think on the spells he'd memorized in Droch's solar, the books he'd thumbed through, the personal diaries he'd managed to free from their locked box in the darkest corner of the chamber. He would consider Droch's fury with Gair over his stinginess with his knowledge, speculate on the other magics Droch was certain Gair had unearthed from unpleasant places, and give himself time to wonder why Droch seemed to be so concerned that Gair might have passed on to others spells he shouldn't have had.

He hadn't found what they needed in Droch's solar, true, but he'd found an entirely new set of things to chew on.

But not now. For the moment, he was quite happy to be where he was: safe, warm, and in a chamber where the books on the shelves didn't make his skin crawl. He drained his cup, then set it aside and turned so he could watch Morgan. What he wanted to do was pull her into his arms again and hold her close until his heart was no longer so cold, but he was nothing if not discreet. He settled for pressing his booted foot against hers and enjoying the simple pleasure of watching her.

She looked at him in surprise, then rolled her eyes and reached for his hand. She laced her fingers with his, then turned back to Léir. Miach looked at Léir as well, smiled sheepishly, then sat back and let the conversation wash over him.

It took a while, but Morgan finally decided that Léir was deserving of at least a few tales of her time in Weger's tower. It was with obvious relish that she related to him the strictures she'd learned on the first day alone, ones that seemed to relate in a particular way to ridding the world of the plague of finger-wagglers.

Miach shook his head in silent wonder. Morgan was sitting across from a man who, half a year ago, she would have spotted for what he was at a hundred paces, then either killed him or avoided him—yet now she was chatting almost as easily as if she'd been in Nicholas of Lismòr's solar. Perhaps it was Soilléir himself. He was a man without guile, skilled enough that he no longer worried about his place in the world, and old enough that he likely no longer cared. Miach knew he terrified most of the other masters and baffled the remainder. He also tended to have mud on his boots during most of the year thanks to the time he spent tramping about in his garden.

The conversation deteriorated rather quickly into a polite argument about what was more useful, a sword or a spell. Miach supposed Léir would never convince Morgan it was the latter, though she did concede after a bit that spells were not quite as abhorrent as she had once thought and Léir agreed that a knife up the sleeve could indeed come in handy in the right circumstance, such as when a lad might be slipping over a wall in the middle of the night and didn't particularly care to use any magic.

"What do you think, Miach?" Leir asked.

"I think Morgan is lovely, your wine is lovely as well, and I might need a nap soon," Miach said lazily.

Léir pursed his lips. "Stay awake long enough to discuss this. Why is it, do you suppose, that the lad who made a clandestine foray into the keep last night didn't just use the front gates?"

"Not challenging enough?" Miach suggested.

"What did you want from Droch, my friend?"

Miach sighed and waved a fond farewell to any hope of a rest anytime soon. Léir was relentless when he was in the pursuit of answers.

"I needed a particular spell," Miach admitted, "and I thought I might find it in Droch's chambers. I was, as you might imagine, less than eager to have him know I was looking for it."

"Indeed," Léir said with interest. "And what is this particular spell meant to do?"

"Close a well of evil."

"Ah," Léir said slowly. "Gair's well?"

"Aye," Miach said. He sat up and rested his elbows on his knees, holding Morgan's hand in both his own. He considered for a moment or two, then looked at Morgan. "May I be frank with him about what we've seen?"

"You said he was trustworthy," she said.

"And so he is," Miach agreed. He took a deep breath and looked back at Léir. "What I left out earlier was that it was Morgan I was traveling with in the fall. I began to suspect at one point that the dreams she was having of Gair of Ceangail were actually memories, and that she might be Gair's long-lost daughter. Nicholas of Diarmailt confirmed this to both of us at different times. I thought that perhaps Morgan should meet her mother's family—giving me a chance to ask her grandfather permission to wed her—so we traveled to Seanagarra." He paused. "I also thought I might have a little peep at the books in Sìle's library whilst we were there."

"Miach, you are going to nick one too many spells someday," Léir said, sighing lightly.

"So I tell him," Morgan agreed without hesitation, "constantly. He's incorrigible."

"Well, in this case it turned out to be useful," Miach said seriously. "I found directions to the well Gair opened, then traveled there myself. Not only is the evil still trickling forth, that evil is being shaped by a spell into the creatures that are roaming unchecked."

"And whose is the latter spell?" Léir asked. "Lothar's?"

Miach pursed his lips. "That isn't much of a surprise, is it?" He started to say more, then looked at Morgan. "I didn't tell you everything I learned there, but I likely should now. Care to hand me all your blades before I do?"

She blanched. "I think you've been traumatized enough for the day. Carry on."

He smiled at her, then turned back to Léir. "These creatures fashioned from the well's evil have instructions to hunt two things: those with Camanaë magic and those with Gair's blood. The heirs of Camanaë are to be slain." He couldn't look at Morgan, but he supposed he didn't need to. She was holding his hand so tightly it pained him. "Those of Gair's legacy are to be captured and carried back to Riamh."

Morgan was absolutely silent. Léir only continued to watch him without surprise.

"Avoiding the monsters is, perhaps, the least of our worries," Miach continued. "We must shut the well once and for all. I tried to shut it myself, but failed, of course. I thought to have a look inside Droch's solar and see if there might be something there that would lead me to the spell we need."

"Why did you think Gair's spells would be Olc?" Léir asked.

"Because of a letter Sarait left for Sosar," Miach said. "It contained as much of Gair's spell of closing as she could piece together.

I'm not certain if it was one he'd used before, or one he intended to use, though I suspect the latter. It was mostly Olc with a bit of Camanaë thrown in for good measure, if you can fathom that."

Léir pursed his lips in distaste. "I'm not surprised. Gair was famous for taking pieces of whatever suited him and forcing those pieces into things new and revolting." He stopped abruptly and looked at Morgan. "I'm sorry, Mhorghain, to speak of your sire thus."

She shook her head sharply. "Until the end of fall, I didn't know who he was, much less suspect he might be my father. I'm under no illusions about his character." She paused. "Did you know him?"

"Aye, quite well," Léir said with a faint smile. "He was younger than I am, of course, so I was able to watch him grow into his power—which was formidable. He was a restless man, never content with his situation or his heritage. He roamed the Nine Kingdoms for decades until he settled upon Ceangail as home. How he came to be lord there is something better left in the shadows, as are the years he spent there, stretching his power. I encountered him in various locales and grieved for what he could have been but chose not to be. When he wed Sarait, I hoped he had turned his back on the darkness."

"But he hadn't," Morgan said quietly, "had he?"

Soilléir reached for the bottle of wine and poured himself a glass. "Nay, though I can't say I was surprised. He had sought out and taken for his own spells that he never should have had. As for his using spells of Olc, nay, that doesn't surprise me either. The only assumption you're making that you shouldn't, Miach, is that Gair would ever beg anything from Droch, or use anything that Droch had laid claim to. To say they were enemies is understating the truth badly. Droch loathed Gair with a fury that bordered on madness and Gair reciprocated in equal measure. Gair was the far superior mage, of course, and used whatever magic suited him, which galled Droch no end—especially when he saw that Gair could bend Olc to his will when he had no bloodright to it."

"But I can use it," Morgan said very quietly.

Léir slid her a sideways look. "How do you know?"

She took a deep breath. "I have nightmares, and that seems to be the language of magic that comes out of my mouth during them. I keep dreaming that Miach is Gair and trying to kill him before I realize he's not." She paused. "I haven't had those dreams in a while, though."

Léir smiled at her kindly. "Your dreams will fade as you settle into yourself and then Miach won't have to sleep with one eye open any longer. And you can perhaps sleep more easily knowing that even if you use a spell on our good archmage there, he will always be capable of countering it—unless you catch him completely by surprise. Even then, you likely won't manage to best him."

"Why not?" Morgan asked.

Miach watched Léir turn to him expectantly and knew there was no point in even attempting a dodge. He turned to Morgan. "Because Olc is a blood magic, like Fadaire or Camanaë. Only those with it in their veins can truly harness its full power, though others who do not claim it as their heritage can use it—with enough power." He sighed deeply. "If you care for the history, I'll give it to you."

"Perhaps you should," she managed. "I might feel better about it the next time I try to do you in."

He squeezed her hand briefly. "You might. As for the magic, there are, as it happens, only a handful of well-known practitioners of Olc in the world because they were the only ones to manage to survive into adulthood. The first master of Olc was Duaichnidh. His descendants were in the habit of having children, waiting until they were grown, then killing off all but the strongest lad."

"What of their girls?" Morgan asked, looking horrified.

"I suppose there are a few of them still roaming the wastes past Aonaranach," he conceded, "but I wouldn't want to seek them out. Outside of those few lassies who escaped, the blood has remained concentrated in only a few over the centuries until Dorchadas of Saothair. He had eight sons and killed all but two because he couldn't choose between them. He set them to fighting each other, but neither prevailed, so in at least that generation, the line was split into two. Droch is one of those lads. I believe he has a pair of sons as well, but you'll notice they aren't standing at their father's elbow, waiting to pour him his wine."

"Who was Dorchadas's other son?" Morgan asked.

Miach took a deep breath. "Wehr of Wrekin."

"Your mother's grandfather?"

"Aye."

"You use Olc very reluctantly," she said softly.

"Very. I make a point of concentrating on those parts of myself that come from more noble ancestors. My mother taught me that much."

She looked at him for quite some time in silence. "There's a lesson in there for me as well, I daresay."

"Aye, I daresay," he agreed. "Of course, none of it matters when I'm facing Master Soilléir. He sees both the good and the bad regardless of what I might like to hide." He looked at Léir. "Isn't that so, my lord?"

Léir nodded, watching them both thoughtfully for a moment. Then he reached out suddenly and pushed their sleeves up over their wrists. He looked at the runes of gold and silver that sparkled there in the light from the fire, then met Miach's eyes.

"Runes of betrothal and ascension to the throne of Tòrr Dòrainn," he said. "Unprecedented. How in the world did you convince Sìle to give them to you?"

"He's resigned to the fact that I love his granddaughter," Miach said with a small smile. "The bit about the crown is, I suspect, simply to annoy my eldest brother."

"No doubt," Léir agreed with a brief laugh. "Does Làidir know? Or Sosar?"

Miach shook his head. "Làidir doesn't know about the runes yet, but I imagine he'll have quite a bit to say when he finds out."

"What did Sosar say about finding himself yet another step away from his father's throne?"

"He said, and I quote, 'Good, now I can wed some ill-mannered tavern wench and live out my life with my feet up.' "

"I daresay," Léir said with a smile. "It is Sìle's choice, of course, until he dies. Then I suppose you'll be fighting Làidir's heirs for the crown, despite what else you might want for yourselves."

"Thank you just the same, but nay," Morgan said with a shiver. "We'll quite happily keep ourselves far from it, if possible. But if I might ask, how did you know about the runes?"

"Well, I wasn't sure about you at first, Princess," Léir said, "but there was something different about your betrothed lord there. Another layer of power added to his, a vast stretching of what lengthy life he had already, a shimmer of glamour that he didn't have the last time he was here."

Miach watched Morgan look at Léir in surprise.

"You can see all that?" she asked.

"I can," he said. "That makes it challenging to wade through the layers of useless and unwise things mortals and mages heap upon themselves by their choices. It was particularly difficult to watch your father, who could have done much good, choose to do evil with the gifts he'd been given." He sighed, then looked back at Miach. "I understand why you came to search here, but I can tell you that I would be very surprised to find that Gair had limited himself to either Olc or Camanaë—or to a combination of the two—unless he was using them in a way I cannot see. It would have laid his trail open and easily imitated. If you've learned anything about him, either of you, you've surely seen that he was not one to make the trail plain. He guarded his spells jealously, never writing them down in their entirety, never using a single source of magic in their fashioning. Add that to his habit of twisting magic to his own ends and I daresay determining what he intended to use as a spell of closing will be extremely difficult, if not impossible—never mind what Sarait supposed."

"In truth?" Morgan asked faintly.

"Her guesses would be close," Léir conceded, "for she was a canny weaver of spells herself, but nay, Princess, I don't think even she knew what was in Gair's mind." He paused, looked off into the distance blindly for a moment, then turned back to Miach. "I saw your game with Droch this afternoon, though I didn't pay heed to the particular spells being bandied about. Sosar was making far too much noise for me to be able to concentrate. I'm curious, though, as to what spell you used to break out of Droch's trap."

" 'Twas a simple spell of binding," Miach said. "I reversed it."

Léir looked at him for so long, Miach began to grow uncomfortable under the scrutiny. His former mentor seemed not to notice, for he didn't look away.

"I wonder," he said thoughtfully, "if Gair might have considered the same thing at the well when he realized he couldn't control what he'd unleashed."

"A simple spell of binding?" Miach asked in surprise.

"Nay," Léir said, "reversing his spell of opening."

Miach felt his mouth fall open, then he shut it and shook his head. "Too easy."

"Is it?" Léir asked. "What if in that precise moment when he knew he would die if he didn't close that well, Gair reached for the simplest thing to hand, as you did today?"

"But where in the world would I find his spell of opening?" Miach asked crossly. "It isn't as if . . ."

He felt time grind to an unsteady and ungainly halt. He'd intended to say *it isn't as if I know anyone who was there*, but that wasn't exactly true.

He was quite certain he would remember that moment for years to come. The precise way the shadows had lengthened on Léir's floor. The way the fire crackled and popped in the hearth, as if it would rather have been celebrating a merry gathering of friends. The look on Léir's face, as if he knew he wanted knowledge that was beyond dreadful, but knew he had no choice but to seek it.

And the exact moment when Morgan realized just exactly what Léir was asking of her.

She caught her breath, but so softly, he would have thought he was imagining it if he hadn't felt her hand tighten just the slightest bit against his at the same time.

Miach shook his head sharply. "There is absolutely no guarantee that reversing the spell will shut the well. Indeed, all signs point to that not being the case."

"But," Léir said slowly, meeting Miach's eyes, "what if it were the case?"

Miach heard no change in Morgan's breathing, felt no trembles in her hand. She was now so calm, it worried him, for he knew what her stillness was costing her.

He had seen what her nightmares had done to her in the fall. He'd watched her in waking dreams casting spells against her sire who had killed her family with his arrogance. He wasn't going to ask her to revisit those memories. He might as well ask her to walk into hell.

He shot Léir a dark look. "You can rip my soul into shreds as fully as you like—"

"Which I've done," Léir said mildly.

Miach swore at him. "In this case, my lord, you do not know what you're asking. I do. And I will *not* ask this of her."

"I'm merely suggesting—"

Miach heaved himself to his feet and pulled Morgan up with him. "My thanks for a lovely afternoon, my lord. We'll be off now."

"Miach," Morgan began quietly.

He ignored her and pulled her away. She dug in her heels, but he merely took both her hands and continued on toward the door.

She was, he found, stronger than she looked.

He stopped halfway to the door in the end because she gave him no choice.

"Miach."

He took a deep breath, then turned and drew her into his arms. He bent his head and buried his face against her neck, partly so he wouldn't have to look at her expression and partly because he didn't want her to see his. He had to admit, it had been a very long day so far and it was lengthening still. He wasn't one to concede the battle prematurely, but he thought he just might be on the verge of it. Had it not been enough to spend an hour in Droch's solar that afternoon and time before that in the midst of a whirlwind of Droch's spells? If he had to watch Morgan delve into her memories to dredge up more of the same . . .

He took a deep breath, then lifted his head and looked across the chamber at Léir. "Why are you doing this?" he said harshly. It occurred to him that he'd said that more than once during his own month of hell in Léir's solar, but that had been just his soul being shattered, not Morgan's. "She should *not* be forced to think on that."

"If she cannot face the memory of the spell," Léir said, and there was pity in his eyes, "how will she face the glade again? And I understand very well what you haven't told me: Mhorghain will have to close that well herself because only one with her father's blood and power can do so."

Miach felt Morgan's hands on his cheek. He looked down at her.

"Morgan—"

She only shook her head, then pulled out of his arms. She led him back over to his chair, then put her hand in the middle of his chest and pushed him until he had no choice but to sit. She drew her chair up close to his, then sat and looked at Léir.

"If you'll fetch me what I need, Master Soilléir, I'll write down for you what I can remember."

Léir smiled at her. Miach recognized that smile. It was one he'd had himself numerous times when Léir had asked him to go deep inside himself and look for things he hadn't particularly wanted to see, and he'd been foolish enough to agree to do so. Miach closed his eyes briefly, then took Morgan's hand in his left and put his right arm around her shoulders.

Morgan shot him a look. "I am not a weak-kneed maid," she managed, though there was no venom behind her words. Miach squeezed her shoulders briefly.

"I'm holding on to you for my own sake, not yours," he said quietly.

Léir clapped him on the shoulder as he passed, then went to rummage about in his desk. He drew up a small table in front of Morgan and laid out a sheaf of parchment, ink, and a quill. Then he pulled up the chair across from her and sat. He looked at Miach.

"Keep her grounded here."

"I'll repay you for this," Miach growled.

Léir smiled gravely. "I don't doubt it."

"Could he?" Morgan asked quietly.

"Oh, aye," Léir said with a rueful smile. "Miach is very powerful, though he is very self-deprecating about it all. I wouldn't have taught him anything otherwise."

Miach knew Léir was humoring him; Léir was powerful in ways he was too modest to admit. He was also cruel in ways that didn't bear admitting either.

Never mind that that cruelty was usually for the best.

Miach watched Morgan as she bent over the sheaf of paper. She considered for a moment or two, then quickly wrote out in a very fine hand a very complicated spell of opening. The words of Olc slithered in and out of spells of Camanaë, twisting them, uprooting them, turning them into something ugly and repulsive. There were other things there as well, glimpses of magics that were equally as vile. But Miach wasn't a weak-kneed maid either, so he read along as Morgan wrote, pitying her that such things were inside her head, casting a shadow over her soul.

She finished suddenly, shoved the quill at Léir, then pushed her chair back. She leapt to her feet and pulled Miach up to his.

"Let's fly."

"We cannot," he said, seeing by the haunted look in her eye just how much what she'd done had cost her. "You cannot use your magic here lest everyone know who you are." He paused. "We could run, though, if you like."

She nodded and pulled him toward the door. Miach spared Léir a look before he shut the door.

His servant was sidling over to him, hugging the shadows as if he couldn't bear to be in the light. He stopped behind Léir and looked down at the paper still lying on the table.

Miach would have given that more thought, but Morgan's fingers tangled with his were starting to cause him pain. He supposed there would be time enough to unravel other mysteries later, when she'd agreed to come back inside.

He wouldn't have blamed her if she wouldn't.

Seven

Morgan paced about Master Soilléir's chamber restlessly, unable to sit and enjoy the after-supper conversation. Her legs ached from an hour spent running around the inside of Buidseachd's bailey, but that discomfort wasn't distraction enough from the darkness she now found creeping toward her again.

She wandered around the room, touching books, looking at tapestries, searching for something else to think about besides where she was and what she'd done that afternoon. Finally, she came to a stop at the window. Soilléir's windows faced north, which she supposed was pleasant enough during high summer. Now, though, the sun had set and the gloom outside was very disquieting. Not even the reflections of the candles on the table behind her and the men she was quite fond of helped her overmuch.

The words of her father's spell swam before her eyes and the darkness of them was complete.

She turned away and started to make another circle of the chamber.

The occupants of the table didn't pay her any heed. Her grandfather was too busy being flattered by Master Ceannard, who had somehow slipped into Soilléir's chamber along with supper. Sosar and Turah were busy discussing things she imagined had to do with ill-mannered tavern wenches. Miach was sitting there with his eyes closed, working on his spells of ward. He'd been willing to pace with her, but she'd declined his offer. He was exhausted and Neroche's defenses had to be attended to before he could sleep. Perhaps Master Ceannard could be persuaded to leave soon, so he could be about the latter.

She stopped in front of the fire and stared into it for several minutes before she realized she wasn't alone. She looked up to find Master Soilléir standing next to her.

"Am I forgiven yet?" he asked politely.

She shot him a weak glare. "I'm thinking on it."

He only smiled, a small, charming smile that made her suspect he had his own share of faeries fawning over him whenever possible. "I'm sorry, Morgan," he said, his smile fading. "If I might call you that. I'm sorry for what you've faced in your childhood, for what I forced you to face earlier today . . . and for what you'll face next."

"I'm not afraid of difficult things," she said, lifting her chin.

"I imagine you aren't," he said. "And I suppose I shouldn't wish away the pain of the road you'll walk along. A blade is only strong because of the fire it passes through, isn't it?" He studied her for a moment or two. "Have you ever forged a blade, Your Highness?"

Morgan shifted uncomfortably. "I haven't." She had certainly destroyed one, but perhaps his sight wasn't clear enough to see that.

"Perhaps you'll have the chance someday," he said. "If you do, you might like to incorporate a few more magical elements into the fashioning of it, as many have done before you."

"You mean like Catrìona of Croxteth?" she asked, happy to turn the conversation to someone besides herself and something besides the ruined Sword of Angesand. "Miach told me her tale one night when I couldn't bear to sleep."

"I was thinking of her, actually." He looked at her casually. "You know, I gave Catrìona the spell to make her sword sing."

"Did you?" Morgan asked in surprise.

"Aye. I also taught it to Mehar of Neroche, but only after she'd already forged her very famous sword. She used it on the knife you carry in your boot and the ring you wear on your hand. Her sword always seemed to sing on its own, though, for some reason." He looked at her with a faint smile. "Or at least it did when it was in one piece."

Morgan shut her mouth with a snap when she realized it was hanging open. "I have no secrets, I see."

"Not many," he agreed. "I see echoes of the shards of the Sword of Angesand floating in the air around you, shimmering with power, much like the runes your grandfather placed about your wrist."

"And here I thought I was keeping my unsavory deeds to myself."

He only smiled. "I wouldn't presume to pry into why you did what you did, though I imagine you had cause. I will, however, give you Catrìona's spell before you go, if you like."

"Would you?" she asked, doing her best to mask her surprise. She knew the tortures Miach had gone through simply to apply to the man for a few spells. "Why?"

"Penance," he said, his eyes twinkling.

She smiled in spite of herself. "Then I accept."

"I thought you might."

She nodded, then felt her smile fade. Thinking about spells for swords reminded her that she needed spells for other things. She cast about for something else to talk about so she could avoid the unpleasant a bit longer.

"Do you see things about everyone?" she asked Soilléir, latching onto the first distraction she could think of.

He nodded solemnly.

She wasn't one to delve too deeply into any species of magic, but she found herself more curious about his particular sort of it than she should have been. Perhaps it was that she had seen so much of Olc that day that anything else would have been a relief to face. And given that Weger wasn't there to needle her if she asked questions he wouldn't have approved of, she thought she might venture one or two more.

"Does it work on everyone? For instance, do you see things about my grandfather?"

"Aye," he said with a small smile. He turned to look at Sìle. "I see the echoes of his runes first and foremost. Then gossamer layer after layer of the centuries he has lived. Every spell, every flaw in the cloth that overextension of his power has left, every marring of his soul that grief has left behind; 'tis all there for the viewing. But mostly I see a riot of colors, glittering and beautiful, as if out of a dream."

She found, to her profound surprise, that she wished she could see as Soilléir did.

But that would require the seven rings of mastery, then whatever other tortures Soilléir would put her through until he deigned to give her a spell or two. Miach might have managed it, but she was quite certain she wouldn't.

That she had even considered the price was truly appalling.

"Prince Sosar carries that same beauty about him," Soilléir went on, "though it has not run so deeply in him yet. He is still but a sturdy sapling, of course, compared to the mighty oak that is his sire, but age and experience will no doubt color him as well at some point."

"And Miach?"

Soilléir clasped his hands behind his back and studied Miach for a moment or two. "Miach is Neroche," he began slowly, "with its ancient mountains sending their roots deep in the earth, its terrible winds sweeping across the plains, its highland meadows full of endless flowers. He is Chagailt with its painful beauty, its bubbling brooks laughing as they cascade over rocks and tumble along banks, its endless rain. His foundations stretch so far down into the earth that there's no separating him from the land, or the realm, or its magic.

And now, laid over it all, is the glamour of Tòrr Dòrainn, something he's entitled to by birth and is now heir to because of his love for you." He turned slightly toward her and smiled. "Do you think?"

She had to take a deep breath. "Aye, I daresay it describes him very well."

"Shall I tell you what I see in you?"

"Can I stop you?"

He looked at her with the same gentle pity Miach had often in his eyes. "Morgan, no one is completely full of light. Not your grandfather, nor your father, nor your love over there pouring the bulk of his strength into spells meant to keep the darkness at bay." He studied her thoughtfully for a moment or two. "I think you have the courage to know what I see."

She swallowed, painfully, then nodded.

He lifted the hood back away from her face and studied her. "I see the fire that burns along a freshly forged sword, the beauty of the light of first sun on the peaks of the Sgùrrachs, the shadows of Ceangail where no spring ever comes. You are those dreams that tangle men's feet as they walk through Seanagarra, under the boughs of trees that whisper Fadairian songs, through the air full of the sweet smell of spring and the sharp taste of rain. And underneath all that," he continued, "is a well of power that springs from sources that are pure and beautiful. Ainneamh, Camanaë, Tòrr Dòrainn . . . the heritage you claim from those sources will color you just as it has your grandfather." He smiled. "You have drunk deeply from a very bitter well, my dear, but there will come a day when you'll have the chance to drink just as deeply from a well of joy."

She had to take several deep, steadying breaths before she trusted herself to speak. "I think you flatter me."

"Never," he said seriously. "I will say, though, that you won't see those things yourself until you dispel the darkness—a darkness that you did not choose, by the way. But often we cannot choose what surrounds us. All we can do is choose to change ourselves to master it."

She nodded, then found herself unable to move. A thought occurred to her, a thought that filled her with such dreadful hope, she hardly dared voice it. She was standing next to the man who had given Miach all the spells of essence changing he knew.

What if he could change more than just fire to air?

She gathered her courage and looked at him. "Miach says you can change the nature of things with your magic."

"Judiciously."

She plunged ahead before she thought better of it. "Could you change what spews from my father's well?"

He winced. "That is a terrible question."

She only waited. She couldn't unask it.

He sighed. "Perhaps I could, but I dare not. To change either good or evil would unbalance the world in a way that would destroy it." He smiled at her. "Besides, if there were no evil, what would there be for good men to do?"

"Put their feet up in front of the fire and enjoy?"

He smiled. "Dull."

"Safe."

"But at what cost?" He shook his head. "Nay, Morgan, there are things in this world that shouldn't be made to be other than what they are. To change them is to the change the fates of men and mages both."

She nodded, because she knew he was right. There were no easy answers for what she faced, no matter how much she wished otherwise.

"And you don't know, lass, that you weren't given this place in the history of the Nine Kingdoms because you were the only one who could see what needed to be done—and had the courage to do it. To take away what will refine you in a fire you didn't create would be to rob you of the light you were meant to have."

"I wish it were a battle with swords."

He laughed and put his hand briefly on her shoulder. "I daresay you do, gel. I daresay you do."

Morgan sighed, thanked him kindly for the pleasant conversation, excused herself and began her circle of the chamber again before she had to think any longer on what they'd discussed. Aye, it would have been easier indeed had the battle been with swords.

She touched Miach's head in passing before she thought better of it, then realized she'd also neglected to pull her hood back up over her face.

Master Ceannard dropped his fork onto his plate so loudly, she jumped. He stared at her for a moment or two, then leapt to his feet and looked at Sìle in astonishment. "My eyes deceive me."

Sìle sighed gustily. "My long-lost granddaughter, as you can plainly see." He shot Ceannard a pointed look. "I wish that her identity remain secret, for reasons that are known only to myself. Those who help me in this endeavor might find themselves invited to her wedding at Seanagarra."

"Wedding?" Ceannard squeaked.

"To the archmage of Neroche," Sìle said heavily.

Ceannard's eyes couldn't have been wider. "Of course," he said, nodding enthusiastically. "A fine choice. We've always thought very highly of him."

Morgan watched Miach pull himself away from wherever he'd been, turn, and look at Ceannard in disbelief. The headmaster drew himself up.

"Well, we have."

Miach grunted, then heaved himself to his feet with a groan. Morgan found herself thereafter with his arm happily around her shoulders as he pulled her away from the table and started on another circle about the chamber.

"Finished?" she asked.

"I have a bit more to do, but I'll see to it later."

"Miach, you need to sleep."

"I'll do that later, as well. For now, allow me the pleasure of you as much in my arms as I dare with all these chaperons." He looked at her closely. "How do you fare?"

"Better, now. Time away from this afternoon has helped." She continued on with him for some time before she could bring herself to voice her thoughts. "What do you think of that spell?" she asked. "My father's spell?"

"Apart from its very vileness," he said with a weary smile, "it was brilliantly wrought. Whatever else your sire's faults might have been, he was certainly a talented mage. I'll have to look at it a bit longer to see what usefulness can be taken away."

She shivered. "I don't know how you can bear to read any of it."

"Desperation is inducement for quite a few things."

"But surely this all can't be as simple as reading the bloody thing backward," she said doubtfully. "Surely."

"Much as I would like to believe it is, I dare not—and I think we shouldn't go to the glade until we've at least a fair certainty of what will work." He tightened his arm around her shoulders. "We'll find the answer, Morgan. Somewhere."

She stopped him, then turned toward him and put her arms around his waist. There were a dozen things she wanted to tell him, mostly having to do with the things she loved about him, but all she could do was stand there, hold on to him, and be grateful for what he was sacrificing to help her. She laid her head on his shoulder.

"I'm ready to go," she said. "Unfortunately, I don't think the road ahead is any less unpleasant than this place."

"I don't think so either, but I think we'll have an easier time of facing difficult things in the sunlight."

She had her doubts about that, but she didn't bother to say as much. She merely stood there for a moment or two longer, then pulled away and started again about the chamber with him.

In time, she found herself with Soilléir's servant in her sights. Soilléir had taken a place with her family and Turah at the table, so she supposed he wouldn't notice if they made free with his man. The servant was standing against a wall with his hands down at his sides. The one with the rag tied about it was obviously still bleeding from where he'd cut it on the bottle of wine. Morgan hesitated, then cast caution to the wind.

"Can Master Soilléir not heal that for you?" she asked.

The man shifted. "I do not heal . . . well," he said, his voice very faint. "Your Highness."

Morgan couldn't see his face, so she couldn't decide if he was uncomfortable because of her scrutiny or uncomfortable around strangers. She could understand both, so she let it pass. She chewed on her words a bit before she dared utter them.

"I have a spell of my grandfather's that might work just the same," she offered. She paused. "It might hurt, though. I'm not good at it."

The man was motionless for an excruciatingly long period of time, then he slowly held out his ruined hand.

Morgan took it in hers, felt a shiver run through him, then she looked up at Miach. "I forgot that my magic is hidden. Can you . . . ?"

"Of course." He wove an elvish spell of concealment that sprang up and over them, then cascaded down to enclose the three of them within the walls of a translucent tent.

"That's mine!" Sosar protested with a laugh.

"And you're surprised?" Sìle demanded. "Damned boy, always pinching spells he shouldn't."

Morgan smiled at Miach, carefully undid the Duriallian spell that hid her magic, then sighed in spite of herself at its return. She decided immediately that it was likely better not to examine that feeling too closely.

She unwrapped the rag from around the man's hand. The wound was bleeding freely, still.

She put her hands over it, then repeated the spell her grandfather had given her to use on Miach in that dreadful battle when Miach had found himself with a very large hole in his chest. That wound had been so severe, it had taken her grandfather's power as well as hers to heal him. This wound was a paltry echo of that one, but even so, her spell was still inadequate.

She considered as she kept the man's hand in hers, then looked at Miach. "Shall we try together?"

Miach looked a little winded. "Aye, if you like."

Morgan nodded and waited for him to put his hands over hers. She wove the spell again, then heard Miach take a quiet breath before he spoke the last word with her.

She heard someone squeak.

She supposed that someone might have been her. The magic that streaked through her was not that white-hot business she'd felt when her grandfather had joined his power to hers. This was a hundred times more powerful, a mighty rushing wind, a wall of water unleashed from a bitterly cold mountain pass, so clear and cold and unexpected that she couldn't catch her breath.

She felt as if the palace of Tor Neroche had just been dropped on her.

She happily pitched forward into blackness.

She woke at some point during the night. She lay still for a moment, trying to catch her breath. She ached abominably from head to toe and her magic was again hidden, only this time it was not only at the bottom of a well, the well was capped, and the entire thing buried under layers of illusion so thick, she had a brief moment of panic during which she was quite sure she'd lost it all forever.

She was going to have something to say to Miach about that.

She sat up silently and looked around to get her bearings so she could do just that. The fire still burned brightly in the hearth, and pallets had been set up in front of that pleasant warmth. Her grandfather, uncle, and Turah were sound asleep. Soilléir's servant was stretched out by the fire and even Soilléir himself was asleep there on the other side of the hearth.

The cot next to her, however, was empty.

Morgan had no doubts that Miach had gone to the library. Why he thought it was a good idea to go alone when he was in the same keep with Droch was something she would discuss with him—loudly—as soon as she found him.

She rose silently, pulled her cloak up from the foot of her bed and wrapped it around her, then crossed Soilléir's chamber soundlessly. Hoping that just opening his door wouldn't set off alarm bells, she left the chamber, then pulled the door closed behind her. She considered, then turned to her right. The library was in the bowels of the university, so surely if she continued downward, she would find it eventually.

She hadn't gone fifty paces before she realized she was being followed. She didn't dare turn and see who it might be—not that it would have done her any good considering the gloom in the passageway. She tucked her hands in her sleeves and took hold of the blades there. Comforted by the feel of cold steel in her hands, she stopped the first student coming her way and leaned in close.

"Library," she said in her huskiest voice.

"Left after the apothecary's chamber, down the stairs, then continue on ever downward," the lad said absently.

Morgan pursed her lips. That much she had supposed without aid. She thanked the lad just the same, then brushed past him, hastening down the passageway as if she truly had some urgent bit of business to be about.

Unfortunately whoever was behind her had the same sort of haste.

She ducked into a stairwell and bolted down the circular stairs, wondering as she did so which she dared do first: stab the lad following her, or rip the covering off her magic and send the entire school into a panic.

A heavy hand clapped onto her shoulder as she exited the stairwell. Before she could protest, she was dragged under a torchlight and the hood was shoved back away from her face. She had her blades up in front of her before the man she faced had gasped in surprise.

She understood the feeling, though she supposed her surprise was more of an unpleasant sort.

Master Droch stood there, looking at her in absolute astonishment. "Sarait? But nay, that is impossible."

Morgan would have stabbed him, but he caught her by the wrists before she could. She was so repulsed by the combination of his handsomeness and his absolutely vile magic that she could hardly think clearly. She grasped for Weger's strictures only to find them slipping away from her as if she'd only glanced at them, not burned them into her soul.

Droch released her hands and stepped backward. Morgan realized with a start that her knives were no longer in her possession. She heard them clattering down the hallway to her right. She pulled one of Turah's knives from her belt, flipped it so she was holding onto the blade, and flung it.

He raised a hand and the blade bounced harmlessly off the wall behind him.

"Mhorghain," he said and even the sound of her name from his lips was abhorrent. "I thought you were dead."

"Apparently not." She looked at him for a moment, feinted left, then turned and fled right. She didn't make it five paces before he'd caught her and slammed her back against the wall. She looked around frantically for aid, but saw only someone scuttle into the safety of the circular stairway she'd just exited.

She tried to wrench herself away from Droch, but with no success. "Let me go," she spat.

"When I have Gair's daughter here, with all her power within my grasp?" he asked with a smile. "You must be mad."

Morgan reached for the word that Miach had given her to undo the dwarvish spell, then realized that Droch was looking for the same thing. And in that moment, she realized with startling clarity what he would do if either of them managed to release her magic.

He was going to take it from her.

"Well, aye," he said pleasantly, "I will. And if you think that brat from Neroche could possibly have given you anything to stand against me, Your Highness, you are sorely mistaken. The easiest thing for you to do is simply hand your power over to me."

"You underestimate me," she managed. Never mind that what he underestimated was her ability to do anything with her magic besides try to ignore it most of the time. It was probably better that he not know that.

"I think you'll find it's in your best interest to surrender voluntarily," he continued as if he hadn't heard her. "I can take your power from you, of course, but you wouldn't care for that. At least I'm offering you a choice. Your father didn't even do that."

"You'll have nothing from me," she said with as much coldness in her tone as she could muster.

"I think you're wrong."

Morgan saw darkness spring up around him, darkness that was full of things from the worst of her nightmares. She fumbled for the pendant around her neck, the amulet that her grandfather had made as a protection for her mother, only to remember that she'd left it in her saddlebag at the inn lest it reveal her presence inside Buidseachd.

She cursed Droch, but found she was fast losing the ability to do anything but struggle to breathe and stop herself from screaming. Damnation, she should have at least brought her sword. It might have been some protection from the man who simply stood a handful of paces from her, smiling, waiting for her to give in.

She kicked him full in the belly before she allowed even the thought to take shape in her mind. He cursed her and stretched out his hands—no doubt to throttle her. Morgan held up the knife she'd jerked from her boot, the knife Mehar of Angesand had made to go with her sword.

It burst into a song of Camanaë.

Droch drew back in disgust, but only for a moment. He didn't take the knife from her; he simply smothered the knife's song in a song of his own, a melody that wove itself around her blade and began to crawl up her right arm, a melody so discordant that she almost clapped her hands over her ears in an effort to block it out.

And still the darkness increased.

"You know why Gair killed your aunt, don't you?" Droch remarked pleasantly.

"I don't care," Morgan said through gritted teeth. The spell had slithered up her arm, around her neck, and now was crawling down her other arm toward her wrist. She frantically tried to wipe it off, but it was impossible to dislodge.

"You might find it interesting. Lismòrian's eldest son, Reil, found one of Gair's complete spells, a spell for draining a mage of his power. Gair called it Diminishing, but I always thought that to be too tame a term for it."

"What would you call it, then?" Morgan managed.

"Gifting," Droch said in a deceptively pleasant voice. "It's what mages do when I ask it of them. It's what you will do, Mhorghain, and you'll thank me for the pleasure afterward. I think Lothar calls it Taking, but that seems a pedestrian sort of term for it, doesn't it? Anyway, your sire was particularly loath for anyone to know about this business of appropriating another mage's power. It made him particularly angry to learn that Reil had the complete spell. The lad of course immediately told his brothers what he'd learned and the lot of them decided to confront Gair."

Morgan started to see stars. Better that than the darkness full of shapes and claws and endless, bitter cold. She realized Droch was suffocating her as well. She understood how desperate Miach must have felt whilst battling on that chessboard with him. The temptation to do as Droch wanted so the darkness would abate was so overwhelming, she almost gave in. She clung to both her will and sanity with all her strength, trying to block out his words.

She focused on the blade she held with both hands, then realized with a start that Droch's magic had stopped just short of her left wrist. It writhed there like a live thing, but it wouldn't cross the runes that encircled her wrist.

Damnation, but she wished she knew more Fadaire. Even a simple spell of defense to counter what Droch had assaulted her with would have been useful.

"Of course, the lads didn't realize that their mother had followed them in a panic," Droch continued relentlessly. "Lismòrian overheard Gair taking the lads' power away, which left Gair with no choice but to kill her as well, given that she had heard his spell. I would have used her as some sort of bargaining piece in a game of chess with King Nicholas, but I have more imagination than your father had."

"But less power," Morgan managed.

The change in his mien was swift and terrible. She closed her eyes, but it didn't matter. The darkness was complete. Not even Mehar's knife was any comfort any longer.

"Stupid girl," Droch snarled. "I'm finished negotiating with you."

He ripped Mehar's knife out of her hand and threw it down the passageway, then threw her after it so hard and so far, she was certain her feet didn't touch the ground. She was caught by other arms and fought them furiously until she realized they belonged to Miach. She scarce had the time to thank him before he had shoved her behind him. She found herself behind yet another body with a scarred, ruined hand holding her there.

She looked around Soilléir's servant to watch what was happening. Alarm bells were ringing wildly, but she couldn't imagine that would do anything to stop the battle of spells raging in the passageway in front of her. Miach was in a fury, but then again so was Droch, so perhaps there was little hope for either to gain the upper hand. Morgan had once watched Miach fight another battle with spells of Olc and supposed she wouldn't see anything worse here.

She was wrong.

She reminded herself of what Master Soilléir had said about her own sorry self, that she was full of both darkness and light. It surely applied to Miach as well, though she suspected she was being treated to a full view of his darkness at present. He was every bit Droch's equal. Perhaps it was because he was angry, perhaps it was that he had things to repay Droch for, things she wasn't privy to.

Before she could decide what it might be, she found her view again blocked first by Sosar, then Turah, then her grandfather. Soilléir's servant had taken up a place behind her and put his heavy hands on her shoulders, as if he feared she might rush ahead and try to defend Miach. She was no coward, but she was also no fool. She had no means of standing against Droch.

She didn't want to think about what that boded for her trip to her father's well.

"Enough."

Morgan escaped the servant's hands, ducked past Turah, and elbowed Sosar out of the way. She stood next to her grandfather and watched the collection of masters standing in the passageway. They were, to a wizard, gaping at Miach and Droch. Soilléir was there, standing in front of them all, the only voice of reason in a gaggle of men who should have had the good sense to stop what was going on.

"Enough," he repeated.

Droch whirled on him. "Who are you—"

"Capable of turning you into a rock, that's who I am," Soilléir shot back. "Care to test it?"

"One day," Droch spat, "one day you won't dare. I vow it."

Soilléir stepped in front of Miach. "I look forward to that day as I'm sure you do."

"Gair's get had best watch herself—"

Soilléir thrust his arm out to keep Miach behind him, then simply stood there until Droch cursed viciously and walked away. Miach leaned over with his hands on his thighs, gasping for breath. Morgan pushed past her grandfather and ran up the passageway. Miach straightened as she reached him and yanked her into his arms.

"How did you know?" she said, her teeth chattering.

"I laid a spell over Soilléir's door," he wheezed. "I knew the moment you left his chamber. It took me far longer to get here than I wanted it to. I think I plowed over Soilléir's servant on his way to fetch me."

"I thought you shouldn't be alone in the library," she said weakly. "I feared Droch might come for you."

He laughed a little, then tightened his embrace so quickly, her back popped in protest. "I should have left you a note."

"You should have woken me."

"I tried. You wouldn't wake."

She pursed her lips. "I daresay that's your fault. You almost killed me with the end of my grandfather's spell."

"Your friend's hand is healed, though."

"The price was high."

"But he was grateful. And don't look now, but I think you have other admirers."

Morgan turned to find that there was a rather long line of wizards behind her who were perfectly happy to greet her in the middle of the night. Most were in their nightclothes with their nightcaps askew. She supposed she didn't look any less rumpled and undone, so perhaps it didn't matter.

It was a very long reception line.

An hour later, she found herself back in front of the fire with her weapons at her feet, her love sitting next to her on the floor, and her pride hanging in shreds around her. She looked at Miach.

"I don't know why he didn't take my power," she said bleakly. "I suspect he was simply toying with me."

"And I suspect you're stronger than you realize," Miach said with a faint smile.

"It might have been your spell that held."

"I didn't want to say as much, but aye," he agreed with a small smile, "it might have been."

"Cheeky, aren't you?"

"Terrified," he said frankly. "I've never run so fast in my life. I'm not sure I ran. I think I might have arrived as a bitter wind. I'm a little hazy on the details, truth be told."

Morgan smiled, but she didn't think it had been a particularly good smile. She glanced at Soilléir, who was sitting apart, lost in some sort of wizardly stupor.

"Who is he?" she murmured. "In truth?"

"Among other things, he is the one who keeps Droch in check," Miach said quietly.

"He'd better have someone taste his wine for him."

"I imagine he does."

She took a deep breath, then reached for Miach's hand. "What were you looking for in the library?"

"I'm not sure," he said with a shrug. "I couldn't sleep and I hoped I might stumble across something useful."

Morgan looked down at his fingers intertwined with hers. She trailed her fingers over the back of his hand, studying the scars there, then turned his hand over and did the same with the calluses. Those she was fairly sure he'd earned from swordplay. She wasn't sure if magecraft left any outward sign of what it cost to learn. Then again, with some magics perhaps it did. The coldness in Droch's eyes was indication enough of what he'd traded for his power. She looked at Miach and found him watching her gravely.

"What is it, love?" he asked.

She had to force herself to spew out the realization that had plagued her for the past hour. "My skill lies with the blade, not with spells. I think I could spend a year learning every spell of Olc and still not be able to do what I must."

"Morgan, all it takes is the right spell and the daring to use it."

"But I couldn't even face Droch." She swallowed, hard. "It was as if everything I'd ever learned, all those hours in Weger's tower learning to master my fear, every battle I'd ever fought—all of it vanished." She paused. "I was petrified."

He studied her thoughtfully. "You know, even here at Buidseachd, an apprentice is not required to know advanced spells at the start. And there isn't an apprentice alive who would think to face Droch and come away unscathed."

"Not even you?" she asked quietly. "Not then?"

He shook his head slowly. "Not during my youth. He did catch me in the passageway after I'd earned the rings of mastery and was trying to pry the spells of Caochladh from Master Soilléir." He smiled faintly. "Léir rescued me then just as he did tonight."

"You didn't need rescuing tonight."

He shrugged uncomfortably. "Who's to say? Perhaps I didn't, but I have walked in places where Droch's sort of magic reigns, no light is possible, and he is not the master. I am able to fight his spells because I know them myself—and because they are my bloodright. I don't expect you to know those spells, nor to want to use them."

"But he doesn't frighten you—"

"Morgan, he scares the hell out of me, but if I showed it, Léir would never let me forget it." He squeezed her hand. "And before I think on that possible humiliation overlong, let me put you to bed."

"Nay, I'll keep watch," she said. "You need the sleep worse than I do. I'll tell you a tale to help you along. Some elvish rot."

He smiled and leaned over to kiss her softly. "Perhaps it will put us both to sleep. You'll have to whisper it over your grandfather, though, since he seems to have placed himself between our beds." He paused. "Well, perhaps not whisper. He's a bit of a snorer, isn't he?"

"That's your brother."

He laughed softly and rose, pulling her to her feet. "So it is. The noise will cover all the slanderous things you're about to tell me. Come lie next to me, Morgan. We have chaperons enough, I warrant, to satisfy even your grandfather."

Morgan made herself at home on his bed with her head on his shoulder. She suspected her grandfather would wake and boot Miach onto the floor for sleeping within ten paces of her, but that would come later. For the moment, she was content to have Miach's arms around her and several layers of his recently laid, impenetrable spells cascading down around her.

"My tale?" he prompted.

Morgan wasn't sure she managed a single sentence before he fell asleep.

It was quite a bit longer before she managed the same thing.

He'd said it would merely take the right spell and a goodly amount of courage to close her father's well. She had the second, to be sure.

But despite all their efforts and all the unpleasantness they'd both faced at Beinn òrain, they were no closer to finding the first than they had been two days ago.

Where they were going to look now was anyone's guess.

Eight

Miach walked across Buidseachd's outer bailey, following an escort truly worthy of the leave-taking of the king of the elves. Sìle led the procession with Master Ceannard trotting alongside him, heaping compliments and pleasantries upon his head as if the very future of the university depended on it. It didn't, of course, but Miach couldn't blame Ceannard for being a little dazzled by Sìle's sheer splendidness. Miach managed to avoid the same, but then again, he had much on his mind and none of it was pleasant.

He'd spent breakfast reading over the spell that Morgan had written down for Léir. As if having it almost put him off his food hadn't been enough, he'd also come to the conclusion that simply reversing it would not do what they needed. The spell was far too different from what Sarait had written down, and Miach had to believe that Sarait had managed to piece together most of what Gair had intended to use. She had been a deft mage herself, and she'd had seven compelling reasons to want to free herself from her husband's arrogance. Her spell was accurate.

It was also unfortunately quite incomplete.

"See anything interesting?" Soilléir asked.

Miach realized that Léir was talking to Morgan. He looked to his left to find Morgan studying the company in front of them with a frown, as if she tried to discover things about them they might not particularly care to reveal. He supposed she was doing the like in an effort to distract herself. She had put on a good face at breakfast, but she hadn't been able to hide her unease. The encounter with Droch the night before had unsettled her greatly and Miach knew why. It was one thing to fight with steel and courage; it was another thing entirely to fight with spells.

He'd thought about it earlier, then decided that perhaps if she had even a handful of things to reach for without thinking, she might be better prepared to fight the battle that lay before her. He'd asked her that morning to think on Weger's five most useful strictures, then trade him those for his five best spells. It wasn't a question of courage; it was one of habit.

Though he supposed she would probably never lay a hand on a spell first before she laid her hand on her sword.

"Princess, you're going to give yourself a headache."

Miach smiled at Morgan's scowl.

"I'm trying to see," she grumbled. "It is, if you can believe it, the first magic I think I've truly wanted. I'm trying not to think about *that* overmuch."

"I daresay," Léir said dryly, shooting Miach a look over Morgan's head. "And lest you ruin yourself for all useful labor today, why don't you leave off for now. Come back with your love after your task is finished, and I'll teach you what you want to know."

Miach blinked in surprise. The art of seeing was one that required serious study and a great amount of power. Miach felt Morgan's hand tighten around his, though she gave no sign of being affected by such a historic offer. Léir was even more stingy with those lessons than he was with the spells of Caochladh.

"Miach will be jealous," Morgan managed.

"Miach may eavesdrop," Léir said. "If he likes."

"Feeling guilty about past torments, my lord?" Miach asked politely.

"Or he can wait outside in the passageway," Léir said pointedly. "It will, as usual, depend on my mood."

Miach smiled to himself and continued on, listening to Léir and Morgan discuss whether or not she would need to present seven rings of mastery to get inside the gates—and whether or not Miach's own rings would serve if she could find them where they no doubt languished under his most uncomfortable set of court clothes—or if simply repeating a few of Weger's more terrifying thoughts on mages would do.

They had still come to no useful conclusion by the time the gates were reached. Miach stood with Morgan and watched the masters taking advantage of one last opportunity to flatter Sìle. He wasn't surprised to find they were all there save Droch. Miach snorted to himself. The sunlight likely pained him. He was heartily glad he wasn't the mage keeping that one in check.

Miach stood aside as Sìle was sent off with even more compliments and praise than he'd been welcomed with. Sosar and Turah were also farewelled in a manner befitting their station. He went through his own rounds of good-byes, though he had to admit he had little patience for them. They might have passed a relatively pleasant pair of days in Beinn òrain, but in the world outside, creatures were still roaming about and Gair's well was still spewing evil. The sooner they saw to both, the better.

Léir put his hand on Miach's shoulder as they stood just under the barbican gate. "I wish you good fortune in your journey, my friend."

"Thank you for the refuge," Miach said. "We needed it perhaps more than you might guess."

" 'Tis always here for you when you need it." He hesitated, then looked at Miach seriously. "You should keep your lady close, lad. I daresay Droch isn't the only mage she needs to avoid."

"Aye, I daresay you're right."

"Keep your eyes open," Léir suggested. "You never know what you'll see where you didn't think to look."

Miach didn't dare speculate. He thought he might have seen enough to last him quite a while, but he didn't say as much. He merely thanked Léir again for his hospitality, bid him good-bye, then caught up with his company, which was already ahead of him.

"Well, that's behind us," Sìle said once they had all cleared the outer gate. "I'm reminded of all the reasons I haven't missed talking to those pretenders for the past millennia."

"You must admit, Father, that they treated you with a proper amount of deference," Sosar said, fighting a smile. "Perhaps you might even allow the occasional bit of correspondence."

"Aye, when that correspondence contains reports of how Droch looked with his head on a pike outside their gates," Sìle grumbled. "I'm not sure why they keep him here, but perhaps they think he's more easily watched inside their keep than out. Miach, lad, how do you fare?"

Miach was surprised enough at the question to look up from his contemplation of the cobblestones at his feet. "Your Majesty?"

"Last night was unpleasant," Sìle said gruffly. "In fact, I imagine the whole visit has been unpleasant for you. I hoped you hadn't suffered any permanent damage. Only for my granddaughter's sake, of course."

Miach smiled. "I am well, Your Grace. Thank you."

Sìle grunted and dropped back to draw Morgan's arm through his. "I don't suppose you found what you needed." He nodded knowingly. "For the business we're about."

Miach wouldn't have told Sìle about the spell Morgan had written down under pain of death, and what he'd found in Droch's solar wasn't fit for casual conversation, so he merely shrugged. "I eliminated a few possibilities, which was useful. I'm thinking on other things."

"Where to now?" Sìle asked.

Miach started to speak, then noticed out of the corner of his eye a shadow near one of Buidseachd's bulwark foundations. Normally he wouldn't have paid it any heed past deciding to avoid it, but Léir's words came back to him suddenly.

You never know what you'll see where you didn't think to look.

He turned away from the sight, but he didn't dare ignore it. He had the feeling he knew just who was standing there. More importantly, he suspected he might know why that soul was taking his life in his hands to leave the protection of Buidseachd to take up such a post.

"Miach?"

Miach felt Morgan squeeze his hand and he put on a smile. "Sorry. Not enough sleep. Where to now, Your Majesty? I think the stables, don't you? It would likely serve us to make a great production of leaving the city. We'll decide on a destination once we're beyond the range of prying eyes."

Sìle nodded, then gathered the company up and started down the hill. Miach waited until they were ten paces from the Uneasy Dragon, then he stopped suddenly.

"I'm sorry," he said, trying to put just enough regret in his tone to sound believable, but not so much that Morgan looked at him askance, "but I think I've forgotten the notes I was making. In the, er, in the library."

"Did you, indeed?" Morgan asked, one eyebrow raised.

Damnation, he was going to have to learn to lie more skillfully. He gave her the best look of innocent bafflement he could muster. "In the confusion of the night's events, of course."

"Well, then let's return for them."

"Nay, love, you go on with your grandfather. I'll run back and fetch them, then meet you at the stables."

"If you do not return," she said slowly, "you will regret it."

He imagined he would, for more reasons than just what she would put him through. "I give you my word." He embraced her briefly, then stepped back. "A quarter hour at the most."

Morgan caught him by the arm before he could walk away. "Miach . . ."

"To the keep and back," he said seriously. "I vow it upon my life, Morgan. The one you've already saved for me once. I don't count that gift cheaply."

She released him reluctantly. "Don't force me to do it again."

"I won't." He made her grandfather a brief bow, smiled at Morgan once more, then turned and strode back up toward the keep. He didn't dare look back until the road had bent to the left and he knew he wouldn't be marked by any in his company. He looked over his shoulder, but saw nothing but ordinary townsfolk going about their business.

He slipped into the shadows, drawing a spell of un-noticing over himself, then walked swiftly up the street and to the servants' entrance of the keep.

He leaned back against the wall and concentrated on simply staying out of everyone's way. He waited for quite some time with no sight of anyone he might or might not have wanted to see. He had almost given up hope when a shadow detached itself from the row of houses adjacent to the keep and eased its way with a hitching step along the wall. Miach removed his spell of concealment, then waited.

The man who came to a stop next to him didn't offer any details. There was no determining his expression either, thanks to the cowl that cast all his face in complete shadow. Or it did until the man turned Miach's way and a shaft of sunlight revealed more than the man apparently cared to. He pulled back and rearranged the material to cover his visage.

Miach wasn't surprised by what he'd seen, but he made no note of it. The ruin wasn't limited to the other's hands, unfortunately. Miach wondered how he'd come by the injuries, but he wasn't going to ask.

Soilléir's servant slid a roll of papers out from his sleeve and handed it over. Miach unrolled what he'd been given and glanced through the sheaves. He closed his eyes and suppressed the urge to fall to his knees in gratitude.

In his hands were page after page of fragments of Gair's twisted spells along with their original sources.

It took him a handful of moments before he thought he could speak with any success. He opened his eyes and looked at the man standing next to him. "*Thank you* seems inadequate," he managed.

The other only let out a long, slow breath, as if he'd been holding it for years. "You're welcome just the same."

Miach rolled up the parchment sheaves and shoved them down the side of his boot. "Where did you find these?"

"In the library," the man answered in his ruined voice. "They were hidden in the margins of books."

"But there must be thousands of books in that library," Miach said, stunned.

"I've been looking for years."

Miach imagined he had been and he imagined he knew just how many years the man beside him had been looking. He had wondered that first night when he'd been sitting at the man's table in his workchamber, watching him try to accomplish simple tasks with his ruined hands, if he might have an idea who had rescued them. He'd dismissed it as fanciful imaginings—until he'd watched their unforeseen rescuer's reaction to Morgan's true name.

And then he and Morgan had healed the man's hand and he had known beyond all doubt.

"I hoped someone would come wanting these," the other man continued slowly. "I'm somehow not at all surprised to find it is you. Use them well, my lord Archmage."

"I will, Prince Rùnach."

The other man froze, then bowed his head and let out his breath slowly. "How did you know?"

"Last night, when we healed your hand. Your essence is very powerful."

"But my power is nonexistent."

Miach blinked in surprise. "Why—"

Rùnach looked over his shoulder, then shook his head. "I must go. Be well, Your Highness."

Miach watched him go and fought the urge to dash after him and ask a score of questions beginning with how long he had been at Buidseachd, why his body was destroyed, and why he hadn't gone to Seanagarra?

And what had he meant about his power being nonexistent?

Miach watched Rùnach of Ceangail slip back into the kitchens and thought back to the night before. It was true enough that he hadn't felt anything but Rùnach's essence, but that had been all he'd managed before he realized he'd sent Morgan tumbling into oblivion. If Rùnach didn't have any magic, perhaps it made sense to masquerade as Léir's servant. Léir had the power and stomach to protect him from Droch—though Miach was certain Droch didn't know who was lurking in Soilléir's chambers. He would have tried to kill him, else.

He wondered, too, if Rùnach had come for the same reason Sarait had spent so much time in libraries: to find Gair's spell.

Miach now had more questions than answers, but that seemed to be the way of things, so he wasn't particularly surprised. He was, however, desperately curious about what was now stuffed down his boot. The sooner they were away from the city, the sooner he could have a look and see just how great a gift Rùnach had given them all.

He waited in the shadows for several minutes more, then pushed away from the wall and made his way quickly back to the inn. He saw no one save Turah, who was waiting for him under the sign of the Uneasy Dragon.

"What took you so long?" Turah asked crossly.

"I was having a rest," Miach said with a sigh. "Where are the others?"

"At the stable," Turah said, nodding down the way. "Let's be off. And whilst we're walking, tell me how it is you managed to pry not two, but four horses now from Hearn of Angesand's stablish vault."

"He likes Morgan."

"I can see why," Turah said. "What she sees in you, I don't know."

Miach smiled in spite of himself. "Thank you."

"I think after we're through with all this," Turah said, smoothing his hands down the front of his tunic, "I will make a journey to Melksham and see what King Nicholas can do for me. Or perhaps I'll venture inside Gobhann and see if there might be another shield-maiden of Morgan's ilk available. It can't be that difficult to get in and out of Weger's gates."

"You've no idea."

"Oh, come now, Miach," Turah said with mock surprise. "Are you telling me that isn't a pity mark over your brow?"

Miach glared at his older brother. "Pick up a sword in the next day or two, Turah, and see for yourself."

Turah slung his arm around Miach's shoulders and laughed. "I'm provoking you. Haven't you been sleeping well? You're terribly cross."

"And you're a dolt," Miach muttered. "You wouldn't like Gobhann, brother. It's a magic sink."

Turah blinked in surprise and pulled away. "Is it?"

"Aye."

"Well, I haven't much magic anyway, so it wouldn't matter."

"Oh, I wouldn't be so sure of that," Miach said, because he knew it would gall his brother. "Mother once told me that you were next in line after me for the lovely office of archmage."

Turah gave Miach a hearty shove. "That isn't amusing."

"She told me as much after you'd blundered into a pair of her favorite rosebushes and cut your way out of them with your sword, so perhaps she was merely vexed." He shrugged. "Who knows?"

"I wouldn't wish that curse on anyone," Turah said with a shiver. "Look what a sourpuss it's turned you into. Ah, there are the stables—"

Miach found himself suddenly jerked back into a deep doorway. He had his knife out of his belt before he realized who was holding him captive by the back of his cloak.

A long, slender-fingered hand pointed over his shoulder toward the street. Miach turned around and saw none other than Droch of Saothair, who had apparently braved the overcast skies to see what mischief he could stir up in town. It was his companion, though, who left Miach gaping.

"Who's that with Droch?" Turah asked, pushing himself back farther into the shadows.

"Cruadal," Miach murmured. "A prince of Duibhreas whom Sìle thought to see Morgan betrothed to. And before Morgan tells you as much, you may as well know that he shoved a sword through my chest less than a fortnight ago. I daresay Cruadal wants me dead almost as much as he wants to make Morgan his wife."

"Understandable." Turah turned to look at Morgan. "Are you still looking for a current spouse and might I—*oof*—very well, never mind answering that. Goodness, Morgan, you're testy. I think, though, that you're beginning to feel quite comfortable with me, if these displays of affection are any indication."

"Turah," she said with a sigh, "be quiet."

Turah only rubbed his side where Morgan's elbow had recently resided and turned back to the street.

Miach smiled to himself, then took Morgan's hand, more relieved than he wanted to admit to find it free of any blades. He watched for several minutes as Cruadal tried to carry on some species of conversation with Droch. The master of Olc merely stood there with his arms folded over his chest and watched as Cruadal became increasingly agitated. Finally he simply looked at Cruadal with the same distaste he might have a steaming pile of dung and walked back up the street.

Cruadal cursed loudly for a moment or two, then threw up his hands in frustration. A heartbeat later and in full view of everyone on the street, he turned himself into a black dragon and leapt into the sky with a harsh cry of anger.

But it was Beinn òrain, after all, so none of the villagers did much past looking up, yawning, then returning to their tasks.

Miach let out an unsteady breath, then turned to look at Morgan. It was too dark to take full measure of her expression, but he didn't suppose she was smiling.

"How long had they been there?" he asked.

"I don't know," she said. "I'd forgotten a knife and run back to the inn to fetch it. I saw them as I was coming back down the street."

He started to ask her if she'd gone farther than just the inn, then thought better of it. Even if she had shadowed him, she couldn't possibly have heard any of his very brief conversation with Rùnach.

Though he wondered if it might have been better if she had.

"Let's go find the others," he suggested. He leaned out of the doorway and looked up and down the street. Droch was nowhere in sight and no dragons hovered overhead, so perhaps they were safe enough for the moment.

They walked quickly down to the stables to find the rest of their company waiting for them.

"Took you long enough," Sìle said impatiently. "Now, how are we to escape this accursed place?"

"What say you to flying?" Miach asked.

"Elves do not shapechange," Sìle said, though he didn't sound as convinced about it as he usually did.

"I wasn't suggesting *we* shapechange," Miach said. "I was thinking perhaps that we might convince the horses to take wing. Turah can take my horse and I'll fly with Morgan. If the beasts are willing."

"Hearn won't like it," Sosar said in a singsong voice. "And you *know* the horses will tell tales when they return to Angesand."

"Go convince them for me," Miach said pointedly. "Your elvish beasts, too. It is either that or leave them behind—which would probably be safer for them but less comfortable for us. Speed is, I daresay, of the essence."

Sosar nodded readily and went into the stables, followed by his father, less readily. Miach turned Morgan to him and put his arms around her, resting his cheek against her hair. He looked at his brother, but Turah was only watching him with the gravest expression Miach had ever seen him wear.

"Be careful with yourself," Turah said. "And I say that for the most selfish of reasons. I don't want to be taking over any positions of . . . well, any positions in the kingdom, if you know what I mean."

Miach nodded. He had his own reasons for wanting to be alive and well, and they were certainly no less selfish than Turah's.

Turah put his hand briefly on Miach's shoulder, then went inside the stables. Miach continued to hold Morgan, watching the street as he did so. She was very quiet, far quieter than she should have been. That she had no questions for him about his supposed return inside Buidseachd's gates led him to a conclusion he didn't think he could avoid any longer.

"You followed me back to the keep, didn't you?" he asked.

"I thought it wise."

He smiled. "A spell or just skill?"

She pulled back far enough to scowl at him. "The latter, assuredly."

"Did you hear any of my conversation with our erstwhile rescuer?"

"Nay, but I saw you shove something down your boot, which makes me very curious about what it was your friend found in the library during all those years he spent looking."

"Morgan, where *were* you?" he asked with a half laugh.

"Twenty paces behind you."

"I didn't see you."

"Of course you didn't."

He smiled down at her. What a marvel she was. "Weger would be impressed."

"Nay, he would have chastised me for not having rid you of both your papers and your purse whilst having left you feeling as if but a gentle breeze had stirred your cloak. I've grown horribly soft." She looked at him in silence for a moment or two. "It was Soilléir's servant, wasn't it?"

Miach nodded.

She was silent for quite a bit longer. "Was it Rùnach?"

"Aye, but surely you couldn't have heard me call him by name."

She smiled briefly. "My powers of eavesdropping are not so formidable." She shook her head. "Nay, it was what happened last night. I healed his hand, then I dreamed about him. I never dream of my brothers." She shrugged, though she didn't look very blasé about it. "I wondered."

"I think it made him happy to know you were alive," Miach offered.

She nodded slowly. "I should like to see him again. If we're successful."

He tucked stray strands of hair behind her ear. "We'll do our best. In the meantime, we can rest easy knowing that Léir will keep him safe. Now, do you have anything else to tell me?" he asked politely. "Any more nuggets gleaned from eavesdropping? Spells stolen from under the very noses of powerful mages? Purses pinched and papers pilfered?"

She looked at him with one eyebrow raised. "Nothing so exciting, though Master Soilléir did tell me something about your mother this morning whilst you had your nose buried in a book. I think he relished the tale, truth be told."

"I imagine I will as well."

She leaned up and pressed her lips against his cheek briefly. "What a wonderful woman she was and what a wonderful son she raised," she whispered, then she sank back to her heels and smiled. "Apparently, there had been a time when she too scaled the walls of Buidseachd and broke into his solar for a particular spell she wanted."

"Did he catch her?" Miach asked, smiling.

"Nay. He slept right through the, um, borrowing."

"How did he know she'd been there?"

"She left him a thank-you. He said you could stand to learn a few things from her yet."

"I daresay," he agreed with a half laugh.

"My mother did the same sort of thing," she said, sobering. "Only she didn't assault his chamber."

Miach didn't bother asking where Sarait had gone, for Droch had said as much earlier. And the thought of her having to resort to breaking into Droch's chamber in order to protect her children against their father made him rather ill.

"I know you don't need me to," he began very quietly, "but I will keep you safe, as often as you'll let me. 'Tis what your father should have done for your mother. I'm sorry that he didn't."

She took a deep breath. "I am, too. And I thank you for the offer. I'll return the favor."

He nodded, then gathered her close again. He hoped she never had to, but he would be the first to admit their road was not likely to be a pleasant one. He certainly couldn't guarantee safety for either of them.

He waited silently until the rest of the company appeared, leading the horses. He kept his arm around Morgan's shoulders as he took Fleòd's and Luath's reins from Sosar. "Did you ask them what they thought?"

Sosar smiled. "They were of the opinion that they could already fly, but were willing to consider other shapes to see if more speed might be achieved. Cheeky lads, those."

"Did they express an interest in merely adding wings, or would they prefer to try dragonshape?"

"The latter, definitely. Bragging rights, apparently, are worth any potential discomfort."

Miach smiled. "I daresay. And your beasts?"

"I think there may be a bruising of dignity when it comes to inhabitants of Seanagarra's stables, but they weren't completely opposed to the idea, especially after Hearn's beasts looked down their very aristocratic noses at them for not readily embracing the idea. I'd turn your horses first, though, then see how ours react."

Miach looked around to see if anyone might be marking their progress, but saw no one out of the ordinary. There were a few locals who gaped at Sìle, but that wasn't unexpected. Wizards from up the way and their accompanying antics were one thing; the view of an elven king in all his haughty glory was something else entirely.

Miach followed Morgan's grandfather down the road and along the way to the garden of Gearrannan. Sìle opened the gate and led them along the path that wound up to the top of the hill. Miach looked at Morgan to find her watching their surroundings with a grave expression.

He understood. He had knelt with her in that beautiful grove of trees on the top of that hill and plighted his troth with her . . . was it two days ago? Three? It felt like months.

He was actually rather relieved to find that he was needed to change the horses into something less equine, for it gave him reason enough to think on something that wouldn't make him weep. He went into the mind of each beast in turn, showing them what he planned to do to them, then made the change when he thought they could bear it.

Hearn's horses took to dragonshape with roars of approval; Sìle's beasts with little sighs of resignation.

Within moments, they were wheeling up into the morning sunshine. Miach put his arms around Morgan and concentrated on keeping his seat.

"Thank you for the reins this time," she shouted over her shoulder.

He smiled and squeezed her hands. If only the rest of their troubles could be addressed so easily.

He hoped Rùnach had found something that might make that possible.

Nine

Morgan paced around the edge of their hastily pitched camp, too restless to sit, too unsettled to take a watch. It wasn't the journey so far that had bothered her. Riding Hearn's horses-turned-dragons hadn't been any more troubling than turning herself into a dragon. Leaving Beinn òrain behind had actually been a pleasure. She was once again out in the open with air that wasn't full of spells and streets that weren't full of mages. Unfortunately, being back out in the open reminded her of what hunted them, where those creatures had been created, and what they were fashioned of.

She wasn't a coward, but she couldn't say she was anticipating with pleasure encountering either the trolls Lothar had created or her father's well. She was also not a fool, which was why, the moment she'd had the chance, she'd put on the amulet her grandfather had fashioned for her mother. Its power had enveloped her like a cloak that had been warmed by the fire. She had sighed in spite of herself.

That she should have been reduced to relying on a piece of jewelry instead of her blade . . . well, it was galling.

She'd actually taken the thing off at one point and forced Miach to try it around his neck. He'd paused for a moment as if judging its efficacy, then draped it back over her head. He'd assured her that he would manage quite well without it. She supposed he would, but that didn't lessen her feeling that she was walking into a battle where she would be the only one who wouldn't have that battle touch her.

She stopped at the edge of the firelight and looked at the souls gathered around it. Turah was sharpening his sword, pausing between each handful of strokes to gauge how the firelight slid along the blade. A handful of blades lay on the ground next to him, waiting their turn. She nodded her approval of the activity when he looked up. He winked at her, then went back to his work.

Her grandfather was sitting on a tree stump, clad in simple traveler's garb, looking about him every now and again as if he measured the strength of the glamour he'd woven about their camp. When not about that noble labor, he was watching the other two souls there who were currently arguing in less-than-dulcet tones.

"I cannot believe you're not going to let me look," Sosar was saying, incredulously.

Miach dragged his hand through his hair. "The spells are very unpleasant."

"You idiot," Sosar said, throwing up his hands, "don't you think I know that already? I might actually be of some *help* to you."

"Sosar—"

"I sat with you for *three* days in the library at home, Miach, filching things from father's private books."

Sìle rolled his eyes and sighed.

"I think you can trust me with what you have there," Sosar added pointedly. "Don't you?"

Miach looked at Sosar for several long moments in silence. "I'm trying to warn you."

"You succeeded. Now, don't be a fool. Hand over a bit of that and let us be about this business so we might be finished with it."

Miach sighed deeply, then handed Sosar half the stack sitting in front of him.

Or almost half.

Morgan supposed if she hadn't been watching Miach so closely, she never would have seen the sleight of hand he used to slip the bottommost sheaf of paper back under what he was reading. The question was why, but it was one she suspected she could readily answer. Miach was again trying to save those around him by keeping the most terrible things of all to himself. It hadn't worked out very well for him a fortnight ago. She didn't suppose it would work out very well this time either.

All the more reason to have a peek at that sheaf at her earliest opportunity.

She walked about the edge of the camp for another hour, long enough for Miach and Sosar to stop arguing and start discussing quietly what the spells they'd found might mean. She paused, leaned against a tree, and watched them for a bit, grateful that both of them had become a part of her life when she hadn't expected it.

Sosar's hair was as fair as Miach's was dark, as golden as his father's crown. He was light and laughter and, as Master Soilléir would have said, full of all the shimmering dreams that made up his father's realm. He didn't seem to mind getting his hands dirty, though, for he didn't hesitate to discuss with Miach spells that made Sìle turn up his kingly nose in disgust.

Miach presently sat with one knee bent, his other on the ground, alternately dragging his hands through his hair and rubbing them over his face. He cursed a great deal as well, but he didn't seem any more inclined than Sosar to give up the discussion.

It was actually one of the more polite exchanges she'd listened to over the past se'nnight. There had been a marked lack of pleasantries when they'd been just inside the border of Tòrr Dòrainn and Miach and her grandfather had been discussing their destination.

Morgan had stood with Làidir and listened to her grandfather and her betrothed argue very loudly about whether or not Sìle should just go back home. Miach had been quite serious about leaving her grandfather behind, and her grandfather had been equally adamant that he continue on with them to Durial.

The impasse had lasted a full half hour before Làidir had finally simply started to fill his father's saddlebags with fresh supplies for their journey.

The discussions since then about destinations and dangers hadn't been as antagonistic, but the topics for discussion had made up for it with their sheer unpleasantness.

Morgan sighed and took another turn about the camp. She paused and admired Turah's blades, then paused behind her grandfather and took his hand when he reached up for hers.

"You should sleep, Mhorghain," he said quietly. "Whilst you can."

"I don't think I can, my liege."

He released her hand, then rose and began to make her a bed by the fire. He put his hands on her shoulders, kissed her forehead, then turned her toward the blankets. "Try."

Morgan relented and lay down partly because she was exhausted and partly because she thought it might pass a bit of time to at least pretend to sleep.

She wasn't sure why she wanted time to pass, however, given that every minute that marched by brought her closer to somewhere she didn't want to go, without what she needed to have.

She surprised herself by waking as the sky grew light overhead. She sat up and found her uncle and grandfather asleep, Turah gone, and Miach sitting in the same place she'd left him. He was still staring down at the pages laid out in front of him, as if he expected them to suddenly leap up and tell him what he wanted to know.

He looked up and smiled at her. "Good morning, love."

"You haven't slept."

"I couldn't." He held out his hand for her, then pulled her over to sit in front of him. He began to carefully work the tangles from her hair with his fingers. "I worked on my spells for a bit, then spent the rest of the night watching you sleep."

"You didn't."

"Oh, I did," he said, sounding as if he were smiling, "and not simply because I had stopped seeing what was written here before me. You looked very peaceful."

She felt him begin to braid her hair. "Then when you're finished with that, you take a turn."

"We need to leave—"

"Miach, an hour or two of sleep won't make any difference to our journey. It likely won't make any difference to you either, but it won't hurt you."

"As you will," he said, finishing her hair. "Have any interesting tales to tell me to send me off to blissful slumber?"

"Aye, one about an archmage who fell off his horse, dashed his head against a rock, and angered his betrothed so much because of it that she healed him just so she could kill him for the trouble he'd caused her."

He laughed and put his arms around her. "Indeed."

She leaned her head back and kissed his cheek. "Indeed. Go to sleep. I'll watch over you this time."

He sighed deeply, then reached out to gather the sheaves of parchment into a pile.

She stopped him with a hand on his arm. "I'll see to it."

"Almost finished anyway," he said, shuffling things together. He tucked away the papers in his pack, then plumped that pack to use as a pillow. He stretched out and smiled up at her. "My tale?"

She pursed her lips and reached out to brush her hand over his eyes. "You wouldn't want that one I threatened you with. It would just give you a headache." She dragged her fingers through his hair slowly. "Sleep. I'll keep watch."

He reached for her hand, closed his eyes, and was asleep within moments.

Morgan waited another quarter hour, just to be certain, then looked about her. Her grandfather and uncle were still sleeping soundly and she couldn't see Turah in the forest. She supposed it was safe enough for what she intended to do. She disentangled her fingers from Miach's, then rose silently to her knees and inched her way alongside him. She didn't hesitate before she slipped her hand into his boot and carefully removed what she'd watched him unobtrusively slide into it earlier.

She rose quietly and walked away to find a bit of privacy. She stopped under a tree and made herself a discreet bit of werelight. She held the sheaf up to it and looked at the spells written there. She couldn't say that they made any sense to her. They were merely bits of things—Olc, Camanaë, and perhaps even Fadaire—though she was the first to admit she could only guess at that and not be certain. The wobbly writing reeled drunkenly across the page. It was obviously the product of her brother's hand.

She had to pause for a moment to come to terms with that. It was one thing to realize that she had grandparents and aunts and uncles still living. To have a brother . . . well, that was something else entirely.

All the more reason to be successful at the current business, that she might return to Beinn òrain and convince him to come to Tor Neroche with her.

She flipped the sheaf over to read through the unsteady lines there as well. Nothing made any more sense there than did the business on the other side. She half wondered why Miach had thought it so important to keep it to himself. Or at least she did until she reached the very last handful of lines, things that surely hadn't been added as an afterthought—

"Aid! To me!"

Morgan shoved the paper down her boot and drew her sword almost before the echo of that shout registered. She reached Turah just as Miach did to find him fighting off a handful of trolls. She slew two without hesitation, watched Miach do the same and Turah finish the one in front of him. There was only one left, one shrieking, misshapen creature, drooling in his fury. Morgan found her mother's amulet in her hand without remembering having reached for it. She held it in one hand and her sword in the other and approached the beast.

He threw his hand over his eyes and fell back, crying out in fear.

Morgan only hesitated slightly before she drove her sword through his heart. There was nothing else to be done, of course, for it wasn't as if he had once been a man and subsequently turned into something abominable. He had been created, so Miach had said, out of her father's evil.

Still, she couldn't help but stand there and look at him, felled at her feet, and feel a small bit of regret that such an existence had been his.

"That was interesting," Turah said, breathing rapidly.

"Didn't you see them coming?" Miach asked pointedly.

"Of course I saw them coming," Turah said with a snort. "But they didn't see me until I stepped outside the king's glamour. Well, that isn't accurate. I think they *thought* they could see me, for they stared my way rather intently. But when they started to move off and test the strength of the king's spell in other areas, I thought it best to engage them. Bloody disgusting characters, aren't they?"

"Very," Miach agreed.

Morgan allowed him to take her sword out of her hand and clean it on the grass. She looked at him when he handed it back to her and found her thoughts reflected in his eyes.

"We must stop the evil," he said quietly. "For many reasons."

She nodded and resheathed her sword. She tucked the pendant back down inside her tunic, then looked at him. "Your rest was short-lived."

He smiled. "I'll survive. I think, though, that we should break camp and move before we have any more uninvited guests."

Morgan nodded and followed him back to camp, wondering how she was going to get the paper she'd shoved into her boot back into his. She finally decided that perhaps a bald-faced lie was her best choice. Miach was so bad at them himself, he likely wouldn't recognize one if it announced itself to him as such.

She waited until they'd reached the fire before she leaned down and pretended to pick something up off the ground.

"You dropped this," she said, handing him the sheaf.

He was obviously sleepier than he wanted to let on because he only nodded, took it back, and put it with the others in his pack. Morgan supposed he might realize later that he'd been duped, but by then she would have decided what she was going to do with what she'd learned. The last words written in that untidy scrawl came back to her unbidden:

I didn't have the strength to attempt a search myself. Not after what happened at the well.

Aye, she had quite a bit to think about.

It took her until the following afternoon to decide on a course of action.

She was going on a little explore—and she was going alone. Much as she might have wanted to believe differently, when everything was weighed and measured, she was the only one who could manage what she planned.

Miach was the far superior mage, which put him ahead of her in matters of magic. There was no difference between the two of them when it came to sneaking into a keep, which evened the score a bit. But what tipped the scales firmly in her direction were, oddly enough, the trolls that hunted them. Despite Miach's skill with both spell and sword, she was the one for whom her mother's amulet worked. A spell didn't do Miach any good if he were overcome by creatures fashioned from absolute evil.

And if her path led into a particular keep shrouded in darkness and heaven only knew what else, it followed that she, having the amulet, was the best one to slip past that evil without harm coming to her. She knew Miach wasn't going to want her to go, which was reason enough to leave when he might find himself otherwise occupied.

She came back to herself to find that Miach was leaning against a tree some ten paces away from her with his arms folded across his chest. He was watching her silently.

"How long have you been there?" she said, her voice cracking unexpectedly. She cleared her throat. "How long?"

"Long enough," he said quietly.

She wondered how many of her thoughts had shown on her face. She was going to need a fortnight in some uninhabited chamber in Tor Neroche where she might review several of Weger's more strenuous rules of comportment before she felt her disciplined self again.

Miach slowly held open his arms.

Morgan hesitated only slightly before she crossed the distance separating them and walked into his embrace. She rested her head on his shoulder and simply breathed in and out, content to be silent and still.

"Have I told you," he said, at length, "how much I love you?"

She smiled in spite of herself. "Nay, not today."

"Then I apologize. I daresay I've thought it a score of times."

Morgan closed her eyes and allowed herself to enjoy the feeling of his hand smoothing over her hair. "I daresay I have as well."

He fell silent and Morgan didn't protest. She heard the crunch of twigs under a boot, heard Turah apologize quickly for the interruption and walk away, heard the steady beat of Miach's heart beneath her ear.

"I'm wondering, love," he began slowly, "where you found—"

Morgan leaned up on her toes and kissed him. It was for less-than-romantic reasons, but once she began, she decided that it didn't matter what her initial motivation had been. Now that she was about it, there was no point in not doing a proper job of it.

By the time she pulled away, he was breathing raggedly.

"You're distracting me."

"Trying," she agreed.

"Succeeding."

She smiled and hugged him tightly for a moment, then pulled out of his arms. "Let's go back to camp."

He shifted uncomfortably. "I've no doubt I look quite ravished. Your grandfather will shout at me."

"I'll protect you," she said, reaching for his hand. "You can keep yourself out of his sights by drawing me a map of our route. I'm curious as to where we're going."

"If it means he won't stab me for taking liberties where he thinks I shouldn't, then gladly. If you like."

She did like, and for a more pressing reason than she was willing to let on. She walked back to camp with him, then sat down near the fire. Sosar and Turah were playing cards. Her grandfather was standing in the shadows of the trees, watching the countryside that lay outside his spells.

She sat with Miach in front of the fire and watched as he smoothed over the dirt in front of him.

"I'm no cartographer, but I'll do what I can."

"I'm no map reader," she said, "so I won't judge you too harshly."

He smiled. "I was going to tease you about that, but I don't think I have the heart to. We'll just soldier on together as best we can."

She nodded, though it cost her quite a bit to do it casually. "Aye. Draw the whole area for me, if you will. Just so I'll know." She paused. "For the future."

He didn't look at her askance, so she assumed he thought nothing of her request. He pulled Weger's knife out of his boot and backed away from the fire a bit so he could draw in the dirt.

"The Sgùrrach mountains run south from Durial," he began, "with a branch that forks to the west along the eastern border of Wychweald. Ceangail lies to the east of Neroche and Penrhyn, through the mountains here." He paused. "The well is here. The keep, Dìobhail, lies to the east of the well, perhaps a day's enthusiastic march. The village is farther east still, east and a bit north, up in the mountains." He looked at the map for a moment or two, then shook his head. "I'm not sure why anyone lives there. The climate is not hospitable. Whether that has created the temperament of the people, or those of Ceangail's ilk settled there because of the climate, is difficult to say. I know there have always been rumors there of darkness. There are places within its borders where . . ." He took a deep breath. "Where no magic is possible. Well, no magic save a particular sort."

"Olc?"

"Nay," he said, "Lugham. 'Tis the magic of Ceangail."

"Ceangail has its own magic?" she asked, surprised.

"It hasn't always." He shrugged. "Ceangail used to be part of Wychweald, though my cousins have become increasingly loath over the centuries to claim it as part of their realm. King Renauld, my cousin Stefan's grandfather's grandfather, ceded it to . . . well, to your father, as it happened, some five hundred years ago. Ceangail's magic is actually a bastardization of Wexham, if you want to trace the history of it."

"Do you know any of it?"

He smiled briefly. "More than I'd like. I have in the past, and definitely without Stefan's permission, set spells of ward just inside Wychweald's borders. They would have been useless spells indeed if I hadn't known how to counter Ceangail's magic."

She looked at his map and considered for a moment or two. "Do you think my father would have used that magic?"

"Never," Miach said without hesitation. "His detractors can say what they like about his character, but when it came to magic, your sire was a connoisseur of splendidly wrought spells. He never would have lowered himself to use the vulgar magic of Ceangail."

She looked down at his map for a moment or two. "If you were to try to counter those spells," she asked in as offhanded a manner as possible, "what would you use?"

"It depends on how you wanted to do so," he said, shooting her a faintly quizzical look. "If you wanted to smash the spells ruthlessly but cleanly, you would use Wexham. If you wanted to accomplish the same thing yet terrify your foe in the bargain, you could use Olc. I suppose you could cast a Fadairian glamour over yourself and confuse whoever was coming at you. That seems to have worked well enough for us so far, but I don't think it will keep Lothar's creatures from us forever. Of course, you could use Lugham. 'Tis a very ugly magic, though not ineffective." He paused. "I don't know if you'd want to learn it any more than I would want to teach it to you."

Morgan thought back to the spells Miach had given her the day before in return for three of Weger's strictures. They had been spells of Wexham, Olc, and Fadaire—but those had been spells of defense. Useful, but not if she wanted to attack.

She trailed her finger through the borders of Ceangail that Miach had drawn in the dirt, then looked up at him. "You owe me two more spells, you know."

"You owe me two strictures for them."

She smiled, considered, then gave him two of Weger's most violent strictures of offense. He laughed uneasily, then gave her what she'd asked for.

"What were those?" she asked.

"Croxteth and Wexham."

"Does Camanaë have no spells of offense?"

He shook his head. "None that would serve you in our present business. Camanaë's purpose has never been to fight wars, though certainly those who possess it have done so. The intent of those who first fashioned their bloodright into spells was that Camanaë be primarily a magic of healing. There are spells of offense, aye, but their design is to strike out as a last resort whilst the mage was protecting those who could not protect themselves."

"Very matriarchal," Morgan said quietly.

He shrugged, smiling faintly. "It is what it is, and there have been mothers aplenty over the years who have protected the vulnerable quite well with spells of Camanaë. I wouldn't exaggerate things to say that the ferocity with which those spells have been used has convinced more than one ambitious mage to take his fight elsewhere. But as useful as those spells of offense might be in the right circumstances, they won't serve you now. I think you should stay with Wexham and Croxteth. You have the power for it."

"But you'll teach me the others eventually?" she asked. "Those Camanaëian spells of offense?"

He was silent for a very long time before he looked at her from under his eyelashes. "I would, Morgan, but I imagine you'll find those spells coming to you unbidden. Your mother would have known them, because they would have been effective against your sire who was of Camanaë lineage. I can't imagine she didn't teach them to you the moment you could memorize them."

Morgan had to take a deep breath before she could manage even a nod. "Of course."

His hand covered hers. "Why don't you rest a bit, then let's be on our way. I think we should continue to make for Durial. I have the feeling we might find aid there that we might not be expecting."

Morgan nodded, because she suspected he might have it aright. She also suspected the reason he hadn't pushed harder to have her grandfather remain behind in Tòrr Dòrainn was that he wanted him to see her safely to Durial whilst he went off to Ceangail.

Rùnach had been very specific about what he thought might be found there.

Miach wiped away his map and resheathed his dagger. "Rest, Morgan. You need it."

"Later. I don't think I could stomach it now. Let's join Sosar and Turah for a game or two of cards instead."

He hesitated, then nodded. "What shall I have as my prize when I win?"

"What do you want?"

"You, in my arms, in some secluded spot in the forest without your grandfather threatening to skewer me for daring to kiss you."

"You have but one thing on your mind."

"I have many things on my mind," he countered, "but that, I will freely admit, is the most pleasant."

"Done, then," she said. "I'll have the same thing when I best you."

He laughed and rose to his feet before he held down his hands for her.

She happily collected her winnings an hour later, watched Miach work on his spells, then bested him in one last game of cards and took for her winnings his going to sleep first. Once she was certain he was truly senseless, she quickly wrote a note and left it under a rock near his head.

She looked at the company sleeping there, Miach, Turah, and Sìle, then turned and melted into the forest before she thought better of her plan. With any luck, she would do what she had to and catch up to them within a handful of days.

She ran bodily into her uncle within ten paces. She cursed as she looked up at him.

"Excuse me."

"And just where is it you're going?" he asked. "In the dark? Alone? In such haste?"

"Don't ask."

"Mhorghain," he said, putting his hands on her shoulders and looking at her seriously. "I know I can't stop you without finding a blade in my belly, but I'm begging you to reconsider whatever rash thing it is you've decided to do."

"I have a simple bit of business that's better carried out alone." She managed a smile. "I have the amulet, my sword, and a handful of daggers. That is far more protection than I'm accustomed to."

"I imagine you weren't dealing with mages before, though, were you?" he asked pointedly.

"Nay, but I'm very adept at spotting them so I might avoid them." She supposed it would have been imprudent to mention that she'd been under the care of Nicholas of Lismòr for a good part of her life without realizing that he was—or had been—the wizard king of Diarmailt, and that she hadn't recognized Miach for what he was until she'd been standing in the throne room of Tor Neroche with the Sword of Angesand blazing in her hand and both Mehar's knife and her ring deafening her with their song. She leaned up on her toes and kissed her uncle on the cheek. "Be a good lad and keep your mouth shut."

"Miach will torture me for the tidings."

"Be a man, Sosar, and refuse to tattle."

He didn't smile. "I don't like this. Where are you going?"

"To see a man about a spell." She pulled away from him. "I'll see you in Durial." She hesitated, then looked at him seriously. "Don't say anything. Upon your life."

He considered her for a moment, then shrugged. "I'll think about it."

"Swear it."

He only folded his arms and said nothing. Morgan supposed she would have nothing else from him, and there was little point in forcing bloodshed.

She turned away and walked quickly into the forest until she thought she dared run. With any luck, Miach would read her note and leave her to do what she needed to. If not, she would outrun him and be over the walls of where she intended to go before he could reach her—and she had the feeling that the only way to breach the defenses of her intended keep was to slip over the wall, alone.

She started to run.

Ten

Miach woke to a weight on his chest. He usually woke quite well, with his head clear, fully aware of his surroundings. That he didn't at present likely spoke volumes about his weariness. He needed a long succession of days where he had a full night's sleep whilst someone else saw to the defense of the realm.

But since that wasn't going to happen in his lifetime, he would just make do. He shook his head to clear it, then opened his eyes, expecting to see Morgan sitting next to him with her hand resting on him.

Instead, what he saw was the furious king of Tòrr Dòrainn standing over him, with Turah and Sosar on either side of him looking unsettled and faintly amused, respectively. The weight on his chest was the point of Sìle's sword. The only reason it hadn't impaled him was because it was occupied by impaling a sheaf of paper instead. He looked up at Sìle in surprise.

"I didn't know you had a sword."

Sìle growled at him. "I made a very sharp one, just for you."

Miach rolled out from under the king's blade and was on his feet with Turah's sword in his hands before Sìle could begin to curse him.

"Impressive," Turah said, his eyes wide.

Miach shot him a glare, then turned back to Morgan's grandfather. "What did I do this time?"

Sìle held up the missive gored onto the end of his sword. "You slept through the writing of that, apparently. I did, too," he admitted stiffly, "but I woke quickly enough when Sosar prodded me and said what he'd found."

Miach blinked. "Is Morgan on watch?"

"Nay, she most certainly is not!" Sìle roared.

Miach had to rub his hand over his face and yawn before he felt even slightly more awake. He gingerly plucked the sheaf off the end of Sìle's sword before the king could stab him. He read, his heart sinking more with every word.

Miach,

I'll meet you in Durial. I have protection none of the rest of you do, which is why I must go on my errand alone. Keep my grandfather from following me, please.

I love you,
Morgan

"Well?" Sìle demanded. "What are you going to do about that?"

"Determine where she's gone, first off," Miach said wearily. He looked at the three men facing him. "I don't suppose any of you has any idea. Sosar?"

Sosar held up his hands. "I almost gave my word I wouldn't say anything. I made sure Father woke you, which didn't seem unreasonable. I imagine you'll come up with the rest on your own."

Miach looked at his other two companions. Turah was merely watching Sìle continue to curse loudly. No aid from either of them.

He considered for a few minutes in silence, then realized what had been so odd about that morning.

Morgan had handed him something of Rùnach's that he hadn't lost.

He reached down into his pack and slowly pulled Rùnach's papers out of it. He glanced at the top sheaf, the one he had shoved back inside when Morgan had given it to him that morning, then noticed that it had been creased differently from the rest. Obviously, he'd either slept too much or too little.

He turned the sheaf over and looked at the final words scrawled there, words he'd not wanted Morgan to read, words about what might or might not find itself in Ceangail.

There is a book in the library at Ceangail, hidden, a book containing all my father's spells in their entirety. I looked for it during my youth, as boys do, but never found it. All the books are covered by a powerful magic that causes the titles to change even whilst you're staring at them. It might take a while to find the right book. That and more magic than I have.

I didn't have the strength to attempt a search myself. Not after what happened at the well.

Miach looked off into the distance and gave that a bit of thought. Rùnach had seen the book himself, which meant that it had at one point definitely existed. It was entirely possible that the book was still there, hiding amongst other things in that library. And if it did exist, and if they could find it, it might quite possibly solve all their problems.

All of Gair's spells in their entirety. The very thought of that was almost enough to make him want to sit down.

Morgan had obviously gone off to look for it herself. Perhaps she thought Sarait's amulet would give her protection that even he couldn't match. How she thought that would help her strip spells of illusion off books, he couldn't have said. It certainly wouldn't be because she wouldn't try.

His first instinct was to immediately go after her, but he forced himself to stop and think. It was another two days' march to Dìobhail, and he doubted she would be making that journey on wing. He had time for a little investigation of his own.

His spells of defense were still far more intact than he was used to finding them. The only possible reason he could divine for that was that Lothar was concentrating his efforts elsewhere.

Perhaps closer than any of them would have liked.

He also wanted to see if he couldn't find some trace of Cruadal. Morgan could best the fool with a butter knife whilst half asleep, but that didn't mean that he couldn't still stir up mischief of some untoward sort. Even but a few hours spent nosing about might tell him where their enemies were.

And thereby save them grief later.

He realized belatedly that Sìle was shouting at him. He looked at the king of Tòrr Dòrainn and frowned.

"What?"

"I want to know when you're going after her!" Sìle bellowed. "And why you didn't see this coming!"

Miach leapt back and narrowly avoided finding himself impaled on the end of Sìle's sword. It was then that he realized Morgan's grandfather fully intended to try to kill him. And the king of Tòrr Dòrainn was not a poor swordsman, when it came right down to it. Miach clutched the sheaves of paper in one hand and fended off Sìle's attack with the other.

"Well?" Sìle demanded, his chest heaving.

"I'm thinking on it," Miach said, sending Sìle's sword suddenly flying up into the air. He caught it, crunching the sheaves of paper as a result, then stabbed it point down in the dirt with Turah's. "I feel sure she's gone to Dìobhail to see what might be found there."

Sìle gaped, standing there with his hands hanging down by his sides. "Then go follow her, you fool!"

"She told me not to."

He wasn't surprised by the volume or the violence of Sìle's reaction to that. And once the king of Tòrr Dòrainn stopped swearing at him, he looked at him, coldly furious.

"You'll send her to her death, just as Sarait went to her death," he spat. "I cannot believe I trusted you with her."

"Your granddaughter, Your Majesty, is perfectly capable of taking care of herself," Miach said patiently. "She has sword skill, and spells, and Sarait's amulet—"

"I *knew* 'twas a mistake to gift her that!" Sìle glared at him. "You must follow her and make her listen to you. She does not know what's best for her." He cursed again. "What would have possessed her to go to such an accursed place?"

Miach wished he'd had a better time or place to give Sìle the tidings, but unfortunately he had neither. He bought himself a bit of time by replacing Rùnach's work in his pack. Then he straightened and looked at Morgan's grandfather gravely. "I didn't tell you who gave me those sheets of spells."

"I didn't ask," Sìle said shortly.

"Nay, Your Majesty," Miach said quietly, "you didn't, and I don't blame you for that. But I think you should know who it was. You'll recognize the name." He paused. "There is no easy way to tell you this—"

Sìle blanched suddenly. "Not this again, you dratted boy."

Miach smiled briefly. "It was Rùnach, Your Grace. He has been hiding at Buidseachd all these years, searching for a way to undo Gair's evil. And until we're finished with this task before us, he asked that we keep his secret for him. He has lost his power, though I can't imagine how. Soilléir is keeping him safe—"

"From Droch," Sìle said, fumbling for Sosar's shoulder and leaning heavily on his son. "I should have killed that piece of filth long ago."

"It isn't worth the cost to your soul, Your Grace."

Sìle's mouth tightened briefly. "There is where you're wrong, lad, but we'll leave it there. We'll see what happens when I go back to Beinn òrain for my grandson." He straightened and put his shoulders back. "I see the wisdom in it. So, Rùnach, that clever lad, found you things you needed. It was obviously something that sent Mhorghain off on an ill-advised adventure."

"He thought something useful might be found in the keep at Ceangail," Miach agreed. "I think he would have a fairly good idea of what was there, wouldn't you?"

Sìle took a deep, unsteady breath. "That hardly seems worth the risk to Mhorghain, no matter what Rùnach might think he knows."

"She'll be safe enough," Miach said. "She's very adept at sneaking in and out of keeps."

"And you'll leave her unprotected whilst she does," Sìle said flatly.

"I never said that. Please, Your Majesty, do as Mhorghain asks and go to Durial. We'll be along in a few days."

"I most certainly will not!"

"Your Grace," Miach said patiently, "if you come with me, then those who might be following us will continue to follow us. If you go—loudly—to Durial, they might assume your granddaughter and I are still traveling with you. I will be discreetly about a bit of my own business, find Mhorghain, then join you hopefully before you reach Uachdaran's kingdom."

Sìle started to speak again, then shut his mouth. He stared at Miach in silence for several very long moments. "I'll think on it," he said finally.

Miach nodded. He supposed he couldn't expect anything else. "Perhaps it would be wise to go in different directions entirely," he said. "To throw our enemies off our scent."

Turah blinked. "Think you we're being followed?"

"I don't think so," Miach said slowly, "I know so. We have been since we left Beinn òrain." He didn't say by whom, but he had his suspicions. He turned to his brother. "Turah, I think you should go home. You might see how Adhémar fares."

"In Lothar's dungeon?" Turah asked, blinking in surprise.

"Nay, not there," Miach said impatiently. "Go home and ask Cathar what he's learned. Tell him what we're doing and that I'll be along when I'm able. It will ease his mind."

"I think seeing your lovely face will be the only thing to do that," Turah said with a smile, "but I'll do as you ask. Do you want me seen, or not?"

"Aye, be very visible," Miach said. "And fly hard." He turned to Sìle and Sosar. "If you two could take up your journey north in the same very visible manner, I think it would be of great use. Your glamour would hide the number of your company, yet lead whoever might be following on a merry chase."

Sìle sighed heavily, then looked at Sosar. "Well? Do we march, or do we fly? Perhaps leaving our horses behind was a mistake."

"Fewer mouths to feed," Sosar said with a shrug. "I say we walk for a day or two, Father, to give Miach and Mhorghain time, then fly the rest of the way. Durial is perhaps, what, five days' hard march from here?"

Miach nodded. "And the countryside is inhospitable, to say the least."

Sìle pursed his lips, then spelled his sword into oblivion and went to fetch his pack. Sosar put out the fire and went to find his own gear. Miach handed his brother back his sword.

"Be careful."

"I'm not the one with the well in front of me, brother." He paused. "Are you certain you don't want me to stay? I haven't been of any aid to you, I don't think. Well, besides vexing you whenever the opportunity presented itself."

"Which made all seem right with the world," Miach said with a faint smile. "Thank you for that. Your company was greatly appreciated. Now, go hold Cathar's hand and tell him we'll be there as soon as possible. Reassure him that I'm still minding the spells of defense."

"I will." Turah embraced him roughly, then took several steps backward and turned himself into an enormous eagle. He leapt up into the sky, cried out in a harsh voice, then turned and wheeled toward the west.

Miach looked to find Sìle watching the sky with resignation.

"He isn't an elf," Sìle said to no one in particular. "Not a full-blooded one, at least. He doesn't know any better."

Miach smiled and made Sìle a low bow. "We'll meet you in Durial, Your Grace. A safe journey to you and Sosar both."

"Take care of Mhorghain."

"I will." He exchanged a look with Sosar, then turned himself into a bitter wind.

"Disgusting," Sìle said loudly.

Miach suppressed the urge to ruffle the king of Tòrr Dòrainn's hair in response, then rose swiftly into the air. He paused and searched briefly for Morgan's essence. He wasn't looking in Neroche or any of her territories, so he wasn't terribly surprised that he couldn't sense her.

Well, that and all of Ceangail was covered with spells of confusion and aversion.

He would be about his business quickly, then search by more pedestrian means.

Dawn was just breaking when he reached the glade containing Gair's well. It wasn't a place he returned to gladly, for he'd been there a fortnight ago and had unpleasant dreams about it ever since.

It was no wonder Morgan had had nightmares in the fall.

He allowed himself to seep through the spells of illusion that still covered the forest, but he didn't dare resume his proper shape when he reached the ground. He simply kept himself intermingled with the dank air there.

He merely watched for several minutes, waiting to see if anything had changed from his last visit. The well was still slightly open, still oozing evil. Miach watched as the evil dropped bit by bit into a depression made in the earth directly in front of the opening. In time, when enough evil was gathered there, a creature began to form itself from a spell that had been laid there for that exact purpose.

It was a spell he had destroyed a fortnight earlier. That it had been repaired since then said that Lothar had been busy whilst Miach'd been off doing other things.

Miach had no sense of him there at present, but that wasn't a guarantee of anything. Lothar was not an apprentice and he had spent centuries perfecting the art of lurking in darkened corners where he might work his foul arts in peace. Miach could understand Sìle's loathing of Droch, but his own hatred of Lothar of Wychweald made Sìle's pale by comparison. It wasn't something he thought on often, which was probably for the best. He wouldn't be unhappy, however, to thwart Lothar in the piece of iniquity before him.

He very slowly and with great care floated across the glade. The creature who was now fully formed paid him no heed, which boded well. Miach allowed it to go its way unmolested, then he hung over the well and looked down to see if there might be anything useful there. It took him a moment to realize that the well's cap was not as he'd left it.

Admittedly, the last time he'd been there trying to shut the thing, he'd been chased off by trolls. It was conceivable that he was remembering things amiss—but he would have bet gold that the cap had been tampered with. As if someone were trying to open it.

He cursed. There was surely nothing Lothar would have wanted more than to have opened that bloody thing fully and taken all its power to himself. It was, after all, what he did best.

And he might have managed to harness the power of the well now that most of that power had been lost a score of years ago when Gair had opened it. At least it wouldn't erupt so violently that Lothar would find himself crushed beneath its contents as Gair had. Miach had no way of knowing what was left, but the fact that it was even trickling twenty years later said there was at least enough to make the effort of having it worth the price to be paid.

He started to float away, then something caught his eye. He looked more closely and saw that someone had indeed been trying to pry the cap off.

With a sword.

The marks were there, scratches in the rock that hadn't been there before. Miach would have gaped if he'd been able. He looked a bit longer, saw not only the marks from a sword, but little bits of ash as if someone had tried to burn the rock itself. *Two* people trying to remove the cap? Those attempts were nothing Lothar would have stooped to. Those were the marks of someone without any useful magic and a decided lack of patience and good sense. He considered, then decided to call the effort what it was.

Completely daft.

He supposed Cruadal might have been frustrated enough to try to set the cap on fire, but he couldn't imagine him trying to use a sword to open Gair's well. He looked around carefully, but saw nothing in the glade save the troll who was now walking into the trees. No sign of either black mage or irritating elven prince. Indeed, there was no sound at all, as if nothing living could bear to remain nearby. He could understand that very well.

He looked about the glade, made certain it was as empty as he'd found it, then forced himself to float up and through the spell above without any haste whatsoever. He'd proved to himself that Lothar was indeed still obsessed with what the well could do for him, found something that was too ridiculous to even be taken seriously, and come to the conclusion that leaving Morgan alone was a very bad idea indeed. There was no guarantee that Lothar was in the area . . . but there wasn't any reason to believe that he might not be either.

Miach turned and bolted east.

Eleven

Morgan sat next to a very small fire she'd built in an equally small clearing and permitted herself a brief moment of reflection on the undeniable truths she was currently faced with.

First, she was not and never would be very good with a map—especially a map that had been drawn in the dirt and erased before she could truly commit it to memory. She was fairly certain she had been going in the right direction for the past two days. She could, after all, still tell east from west and she felt fairly safe in betting that as long as she went up into the mountains, she was going north. Then again, she didn't remember Ceangail's keep being due north from where they'd been, so for all she knew, she was headed off toward paths she wouldn't particularly care for.

Second was a puzzle of a slightly more unsettling nature. She was being followed. She'd realized it within hours of leaving her companions behind. She would have credited it to Miach simply being perverse by following her in a guise other than his own form, but the shape—or lack thereof, as was the case—was covered in Olc. And if that hadn't been unsettling enough, she'd been almost positive that the first shape had been joined by another sometime during the previous night, but she was the first to admit that she wasn't at her best at present and it had much to do with the fact that she hadn't slept very much in the past two days.

And that lack of sleep had everything to do with the companions she'd acquired.

She lifted her head and looked around her at the lads who sat in a circle just outside the light of her fire. Monstrous trolls, the lot of them. The first ones who'd stumbled upon her had tried to capture her, then howled when they realized that for some reason, they dared not. She had put several of that batch out of their misery without hesitation. The remainder had stopped shouting, apparently preferring to merely snarl at her. Morgan had stared at them for several minutes, Mehar's knife in one hand and her sword in the other, until she realized what had probably been saving her. She had slipped Mehar's knife back into her boot, then reached under the neck of her tunic and pulled out her mother's amulet.

The trolls had shrieked in fear and fallen back.

That might have been a boon if they'd actually scampered off to bother someone else. Unfortunately, they seemed to find her to their liking. They had followed her as she had taken up her journey again, collecting fellow brutes on the way, until she found herself with quite an escort as she made her way into the mountains. It must have been a terrifying sight, but she supposed it had likely saved her from more unsavory hands.

Well, save that lad covered in Olc who seemed to be following her just for the sport of it.

She hadn't dared sleep except in very brief fits. Every time she'd woken, the creatures had been sitting just as they were now, in a circle around her, just out of the light of her fire, just out of the reach of the magic contained in her mother's pendant.

Damnation, what was she going to do now?

Well, she was going to do what she'd done in the past. She was going to sneak inside the keep, catch the lord unawares, then put a knife to his neck and threaten him with acute harm until he gave her what she wanted. If Ceangail was full of darkness, the lord should be full of spells, and he should have a good idea of where the worst spells his library had to offer were kept. And perhaps he was as susceptible to a blade in his back as the next evil lord.

She had to believe it. She had no other choice.

She got up, stomped out the flames of her small fire, then considered her options. She supposed she could continue on with her companions, but it wouldn't help her any to arrive at the keep with a score of terrors at her heels announcing her presence. She looked at the creatures that were now on their feet as well, their gazes locked on her. There was, she supposed, no point in trying to reason with them or tell them what she planned.

She took a deep breath, then leapt up suddenly into the air as a hawk. She chose that because she only knew how to change her shape into two things and she supposed dragonshape might not be all that inconspicuous. As an afterthought, she drew a spell of un-noticing over herself, then flapped off away from the sunlight that was now beginning to spread from the east.

The trolls were not pleased. She supposed any hope of secrecy had been ruined by their howls of dismay. She couldn't say that she was going to miss them particularly—they were spectacularly frightening-looking—but she had become accustomed to them. Weger would have been appalled.

Then again, knowing what she knew about him now, perhaps he wouldn't have been.

She decided, an hour later, that taking wing had been a wise choice. The only reason she found the keep was because she saw it in the distance—well to her left, not in front of her.

She landed carefully atop a bit of parapet that was still intact. Perhaps flying had been the wisest choice for more than one reason. It was a miracle that any of the stones still remained standing atop each other. Trying to scale that wall would have been nigh onto impossible.

She hopped down onto the walkway, then resumed her proper shape, flattening herself against the stones until a guardsman walked past her, yawning. She had hoped for a keep full of drunkards so she might be about her business whilst they slept off their stupor, but the lad who walked past her was unfortunately quite sober. Perhaps she would have better luck inside.

She followed the guardsman in front of her as he made for the tower door. She slipped in behind him as he opened it, then leapt out of his way before he could shut it on her.

He did, apparently, try to shut it on someone else.

The only reason she knew this was that she could hear that someone else cursing. She certainly wasn't going to look behind her to see who might or might not have been there.

She never allowed herself to panic, but she also wasn't one to linger where moving suited her better—especially when moving might prevent her from having to see what was in the guardsman's way.

Obviously now that she didn't have her gruesome companions, that soul who had been following her—Cruadal, she decided without hesitation—had decided she was unprotected enough to be taken. Why he'd thought doing so inside Dìobhail was wise, she couldn't fathom, but it was yet another reason to believe it was Cruadal. He was a fool—and a dangerous one.

She ran lightly down the circular stairs, leaping aside to avoid someone coming up them. She stepped out of the stairwell—

And felt her spell of un-noticing be stripped from her instantly.

Spells tangled about her and held her in place. She tried to pull her feet free of them, but with no success. She groped for Mehar's knife and used it liberally. She was almost surprised to find that it severed the spells as if they'd been naught but worn threads. The only thing that ruined that happy bit of good fortune was the fact that once she cut one spell, another sprang up to take its place.

She cursed viciously as she continued to cut through spells. The sooner she found the vile lord of Ceangail, the better off she would be. At least she could force him to call off the magic that tormented her.

She drew her sword and carried on as best she could. She continually fought both the spells that caught at her and the men who confronted her. The man behind her seemed to be doing the same thing. It was either take the time to dispatch him or press on. She chose the latter. And once she had the lord of the keep at her mercy, she would demand that he toss Cruadal into a dungeon that would hopefully be full of very unpleasant spells.

She bested the guards standing in front of what she hoped were the great hall doors, then commanded the doors to open. They obeyed her without hesitation, which surprised her, but she didn't pause to examine it. She strode inside and was vastly relieved to find that the floor was no longer swimming with things she was going to have to wade through. That was made up for, though, by the number and viciousness of the men who attacked her from all sides.

That, at least, was something she was accustomed to.

She fought Dìobhail's guardsmen coldly and with a detachment that might have earned her a nod of approval even from Weger himself. That might have eased her if it hadn't been for the darkness that had followed her inside.

She couldn't see who it was, but she could feel him in her wake, ten paces behind her, without a sword drawn or a knife flashing in the torchlight, sending men sprawling with spells alone. She didn't recognize the magic that rendered him unseen, and she didn't understand the spells that he used to fling his enemies away from him.

Damnation, she was *not* going to find herself in over her head again. Once she had Ceangail's lord well in hand, she would turn and use the spells of offense Miach had given her. She refused to be intimidated by a lad who didn't have the spine to even put his hand to steel.

She calculated furiously, but she couldn't manage a full count of the men in the hall. Lads were strewn along the floor behind her in various stages of being overcome, but still more came at her. It would have been very useful if the bloody place had possessed even the smallest of windows. Apparently light wasn't a sought-after commodity in Dìobhail.

She saw, in the gloom, a raised dais at the end of the hall. There was a chair there, not quite a throne, but more than a simple seat for supper. A man sat there, swathed in darkness, unmoving. Morgan supposed it might take her all morning to reach him, but she had no other choice. She needed free rein in the keep and 'twas obvious secrecy wasn't going to win her that. She would have to capture him openly.

She continued her slow progress to the end of the hall. She was tiring more quickly than she should have been and that made her angry. She dredged up another measure of fury and continued, sending men scattering in front of her.

She realized, suddenly, that the man behind her was now fighting with swords as well.

It occurred to her, just as suddenly, that he was fighting *for* her, not against her.

She looked over her shoulder, then felt something rush through her. She wasn't sure if that something was surprise, anger, or relief.

Miach stood there.

"What spell of un-noticing was that?" she demanded.

"Lugham," he said, shivering. "Very unpleasant."

Had it been him following her the entire time instead of Cruadal? She wasn't sure if she should be furious that he'd felt the need to do so, or grateful that he had bothered. Perhaps she would determine that later, after she'd decided whether or not she should kill him.

She turned back to her own fight and continued inching her way forward.

After there were no more lads for her to fight, she turned on Miach. Fury it would be and he deserved every bit of it, the lout, for not having listened to her.

She realized that she'd forgotten, oddly enough, that he also bore Weger's mark and his swordplay said that he had earned it, no matter how brief his stay. It took her quite a bit just to stand against him, and she supposed it would take more strength than she had to best him. She finally caught his blades between hers, then gave him a mighty shove backward.

"Damn you," she said fiercely, "I thought you were going on without me."

"I did," he said, his chest heaving.

She blinked in surprise and lowered her swords. "Then you haven't been following me?"

He rested his blades against his shoulders and simply caught his breath for a moment or two. "It wasn't for a lack of trying," he said with a dry smile. "I went on a little errand of my own, then turned back to look for you. I've been hunting for two days." He paused. "You were going in the wrong direction."

"I know that," she muttered.

He smiled briefly, then sobered. "Cruadal was following you, which I imagine you knew. I caught him before dawn and clunked him over the head with my sword as he resumed his proper shape to fight me. I did him the favor of sparing his nose this time."

"Good of you."

"Aye, I thought so."

She dragged her sleeve across her forehead, grateful for a brief moment to rest and enjoy the chill of the hall. Her cloak had been the first thing to go near the hall door, flung into some poor man's face so she could have his sword. She looked at Miach and attempted a frown. "You didn't need to come after me at all, you know. I would have met you in Durial."

He looked at her gravely. "I know you don't need my protection, Morgan, but I thought it best to offer it just the same."

She pointed toward the dais with her sword. "I think I could have captured *him* more easily on my own. You might not like to watch what I have to do."

Miach chewed on that for a moment. "I wonder if he has an opinion?"

Morgan looked to her left to find that the lord of the hall had risen to his feet and was standing there stiffly. It was difficult to judge his expression, for he was swathed in a darkness she couldn't see through. Obviously more of that Ceangail magic that even Miach found unpleasant.

She put herself in front of Miach only to have him pull her behind him.

"Damn you, move," she said, stepping around him.

"Nay—"

"Aye!"

"Absolutely not—"

Morgan decided, as she caught sight of the lord stumbling off his step, that arguing with Miach could wait. Miach backed into her, hard, when the man took a step closer. The lord looked at them in silence for several protracted moments, then lifted his hand.

Morgan watched as scores of men poured into the great hall. She turned to put her back against Miach's but saw immediately that there was no point in it. They were sorely outnumbered.

She was appalled to find herself willing to let go of her blades because she knew she had magic at her disposal, but she had done several appalling things over the past few fortnights so perhaps this was just another to add to the list.

She listened to Miach toss his swords onto the stone floor, then did the same herself—almost without hesitation. She did, however, protest when Ceangail's lord came to face her and held out his hand for her knives. Miach elbowed her in the back, so she acquiesced grudgingly. The knife Weger had made him was already there, so perhaps he had a plan for getting them all back.

The lord of Ceangail handed off their gear, then nodded to his guards, a handful of whom drew their swords and looked prepared to do business with them. Morgan walked with Miach out of the hall, through more passageways laden with spells, and up stairs into a chamber that at least had light from windows set into one of the walls. Even though winter was fading, the light streaming into the chamber was cold. Perhaps the sun didn't shine very well in Ceangail.

Morgan found herself turning around again and again, unable to find a comfortable place to rest her gaze. There were window seats set into the wall to her left, tapestries of battle lining the far wall in front of her, a hearth set into the wall to her right, stone floor beneath her feet that was uneven in spots . . .

She felt her mouth fall open. The stone floor beneath her feet was uneven in spots that she recognized.

Miach's arm was suddenly around her shoulders. "Are you going to faint?" he whispered urgently.

She shook her head sharply, but willingly allowed him to keep her on her feet as she continued to gape at the chamber she was in and let unbidden and unwanted memories of it wash over her.

She had lived in the keep she was standing in.

She was surprised the possibility of it hadn't occurred to her before, but she'd never stopped to consider it. She'd been thinking about spells and magic and righting wrongs. She hadn't been thinking that she might be walking back into a place where she had lived as a child with her family.

"Leave us," the lord of Ceangail demanded of his men.

"But, my lord," one of the guardsmen protested, "surely not. There are two of them, and only one—"

The lord laughed. Well, it might have passed for a laugh if a great amount of imagination was used. Just the sound made Morgan shiver.

The man walked his guardsmen to the door, telling them all along the way quite bluntly how he would reward their disobedience. Morgan took a deep breath, then looked up at Miach.

"Tell me again how this is better?"

"We're being underestimated."

She wished suddenly that she'd had her cloak. She was far colder than she should have been, given the circumstances. "I'm not happy with you," she muttered.

He took off his cloak and wrapped it around her. "Would you dance with me just the same if our good lord of darkness here could produce any minstrels?"

She shot him a glare, though it was a weak one. "Are you trying to distract me from my unpleasant thoughts about this chamber, or my unreasonable fears about this chamber's lord?"

"A bit of both," he said with a grave smile.

Morgan smiled in spite of herself and was cheered, also in spite of herself. There was something about Miach that was very grounding, as if he were a keep whose foundations reached deep into the earth, with soaring battlements, scores of chambers full of unexpected delights, and several pairs of boots near the door encrusted with mud from the garden.

Well, that and he had a very lovely smile.

"I suppose we could fight our way out with magic," she said with a sigh.

"Difficult."

She looked up at him in surprise. "Even for you?"

"I'm not particularly eager to have anyone know I've been here," he said. "A battle would require quite a substantial bit of magic considering what's here, magic that would leave my presence very plain to anyone who cared to look for it." He shivered. "This place is so slathered with Olc, it's making *me* queasy. Can't you feel it?"

She shook her head. "I just thought I was hungry. I haven't eaten in two days."

He smiled at her, an affectionate smile that was almost sweet enough to make her forget where she was. He started to speak, then looked up and sobered abruptly. Morgan found herself pulled behind him. She would have argued, but he had taken her hand and put it against his back.

There was a dagger shoved through his belt, hidden by the back of his tunic.

"I think I just might dance with you as a reward for this," she murmured.

He tightened his hand around her wrist briefly, then put his hands down at his sides.

Morgan supposed the lord of Ceangail wouldn't find them as cooperative as he'd hoped.

Or perhaps he wouldn't even find them worth his notice. Morgan looked over Miach's shoulder and watched in surprise as the man took their weapons from his final guardsman, shoved him out the door, then barred it. He then turned and walked across the solar to the hearth, tossing their weapons onto a long bench set against the wall as he did so. Without comment, he squatted down and kindled a fire by eminently pedestrian means.

Morgan wondered at that. Perhaps he was so full of magic that he didn't fear what they might do to him. Apparently that was the case, for he merely fetched a bottle of wine and three silver goblets from a table near one of the windows, then came back to the fire where he set his burdens down on a low table surrounded by not-uncomfortable-looking chairs.

"What's he doing?" Morgan whispered to Miach.

"I have no idea."

"Food, then torture?"

"I don't know. Maybe he heard your stomach complaining and thought to appease it."

She pursed her lips. "Are you ever serious?"

"About food and dancing? Always."

"Well, the first I believe," she muttered. She pulled the dagger out of Miach's belt and hid it behind her back. If things went south, at least she would have some means of protecting them. She hadn't bothered to hide her magic and she was actually surprised to find that Miach hadn't either. Surely this lord of Ceangail could sense what they were, if not who.

Perhaps he could, but he certainly didn't seem to care. He merely stood in front of his fire with his back to them. Darkness surrounded him, a darkness so complete that he almost wasn't discernable. The firelight flickered quite merrily over the wine bottle and the goblets, but it made no mark on him. He was mad if he thought she and Miach would simply sit down and have a pleasant afternoon drink with him.

She leaned closer to Miach. "What now?"

"I have no idea," he said with a shrug. "We could rush him, I suppose, or try to dazzle him with a spell or two. I'm inclined to merely wait and allow him to make the first move."

She wasn't surprised by that tactic, and she would have told Miach so, but the lord was slowly turning around to face them. Morgan took a step forward and stood shoulder to shoulder with Miach. If nothing else, they would fight together. She took a firmer hold on her blade and prepared herself for the worst.

The lord of Ceangail took a handful of steps closer to them.

And then he pulled his hood back from his face.

Twelve

Miach gasped, but his was covered quite handily by Morgan's. He wasn't unaccustomed to finding things where he hadn't been looking for them, but this was something else entirely. If he hadn't known better, he would have thought he was looking at a ghost. But the man standing in front of them with hands that trembled slightly wasn't a ghost.

He was Keir.

Keir was watching Morgan with the same expression of dreadful hope that Sìle had worn when he'd first seen her. Miach would have offered Sarait's eldest son a shoulder to lean on, but Morgan needed it more. She was leaning against him so hard, he had to brace himself to keep from being pushed over. He put his arm around her shoulders and felt her hand come up to hold his, almost painfully.

And all the while Keir looked at her, as if he simply couldn't believe what was before his eyes.

"Mhorghain?" Keir said hesitantly.

Morgan cleared her throat, then nodded very slightly.

Keir of Ceangail threw his cloak onto one of the chairs, then strode across the distance that separated them. He hesitated a pace or two away, then reached out and pulled his sister into his arms. He bowed his head and made several rough noises, as if he sought not to weep.

Miach stepped away and let them have a bit of room. Actually, releasing Morgan's hand let him drag his sleeve across his eyes, but he supposed that might escape anyone's notice but his, which was as it should have been.

Morgan stood in her brother's embrace, then turned her head and looked back at him. Her eyes were dry, but they were full of absolute anguish. Miach smiled, pained, knowing what she was thinking. All the years she'd thought she was alone in the world and now to find out she needn't have been. Miach imagined Keir was thinking something akin to that. He watched Morgan's brother hold her as if he simply couldn't bring himself to let her go. Miach understood that as well.

Keir finally pulled back and looked down at his sister.

"You look so much like Mother," he said faintly. "In truth, I thought for a moment that you *were* Mother. But that isn't possible." He shook his head. "Little Mhorghain. But you're no longer a child." He let out a shuddering breath. "I thought you were dead."

"I thought you were too," she managed.

Actually, Miach knew it was worse than that. She hadn't even remembered that she'd had brothers until the fall.

Keir continued to stare at his sister in silence, as if he feared his eyes were deceiving him, then he looked up and frowned.

"Prince Mochriadhemiach—or am I mistaken?"

"Nay, Your Highness," Miach said gravely, "you aren't mistaken."

"You look like Gilraehen the Fey."

"So I'm told," Miach agreed. "Often."

Keir didn't smile. "You also look a great deal like yourself, though you too have grown since last we met. Why are you following my sister?" He looked at Morgan. "Why are you here? Where did you learn to fight as you do? Where have you been?" He frowned at Miach again. "Why are you with her? Does my grandfather know she's alive? If he does, he certainly wouldn't approve of a wee mage prince keeping company with her."

Miach opened his mouth, but found there wasn't a good answer to any of Keir's questions. Damnation. Yet more relatives to appease.

"Don't you know?" Morgan asked. "Don't you know anything about Miach?"

Keir's expression darkened considerably and he pulled Morgan to stand under the protection of his wing, as it were. "The tidings that reach my ears are few and far between indeed, but one thing I can tell you, sister, is that we don't associate with mages. They aren't our sort of people."

Miach would have laughed, but he didn't dare. Keir couldn't have sounded any more like Sìle if he'd been reading from a script Sìle had prepared for him. Miach also refrained from pointing out to Keir that he was something of a mage himself and had no room to criticize. Then again, perhaps Keir chose to ignore parts of his heritage in favor of the more savory ones.

Miach understood that very well.

He dragged his hand through his hair, searching for a decent way to begin to answer Keir's questions. The next thing he knew, Keir had hold of his right hand in a grip of iron. He shoved Miach's sleeve up his forearm and looked down at the runes surrounding his wrist in astonishment.

"What," he began in a garbled tone, "are these?"

"Ah—"

"Did you steal them?" Keir demanded.

Miach shot him a look. "That'd be a bit difficult, wouldn't it?"

"You insolent boy, how dare you speak to me that way," Keir said haughtily. "I am a prince of the house of Tòrr Dòrainn. You, however, are—"

"A prince of the house of Neroche," Miach said wearily. "And the youngest of that house, aye, I know. I also happen to be one who loves your sister."

"Love?" Keir echoed incredulously. "Who in the *hell* do you think you are presuming—"

"I—"

Miach found himself suddenly with Morgan standing in front of him, as if she were protecting him, which he wasn't altogether certain he didn't need at the moment. Keir's expression was thunderous.

"Mhorghain, come away from him."

"I will not." She held up her left hand. "Here are my runes, runes which are echoes of Miach's. Grandfather gave them to us freely when he gave me the gift I wanted most, which is the man standing behind me. If you intend to do damage to him, you'll go through me first. Otherwise, cease. I'm tired, hungry, and I would very much like to simply sit down."

Keir opened his mouth, apparently to protest a bit more, then he scowled. "I'll give this more thought later." He turned a much lighter expression on his sister. "I'll have food brought. It won't be particularly edible, but it might be hot if I'm very cross with my servant. Perhaps if we feed the mage there, he'll release you."

"I'm the one holding on to him," Morgan pointed out, pulling Miach's arms around her.

Keir grunted, then turned a glare on Miach. "You would be better served to keep your hands to yourself, little lad."

Miach only nodded to Gair's eldest with what he hoped was the appropriate amount of gravity as Keir walked away. Then he took a deep breath and turned Morgan around.

"Well?"

She looked almost as devastated as she had when she'd first realized who she was. "This was not what I expected to find here," she said, her voice barely audible. "Do you think Rùnach knows?"

Miach brushed her hair back from her face. "If he did, he didn't say aught to me. You know, I've heard various rumors over the years about how Keir met his end. I always thought it curious that no one seemed to know exactly what happened. I don't think anyone believed anyone had survived the morning at the well, but the makers of tales are often wrong. We should ask him what happened—if you can bear it," he added.

She shivered as she put her arms around his waist. "It can't be any worse than my dreams. Aye, I'd like to know. I'm also curious why he remained here when he's but a handful of days from Seanagarra."

"He must have his reasons, just as Rùnach does."

She nodded, then fell silent. Miach turned them both so he could watch the door. He couldn't have said why, but he didn't think Keir had all that much control over his servants. In time, the door opened and Keir came back inside the solar with a tray laden with food. He stopped halfway across the chamber and almost dropped their supper. He righted the tray and scowled.

"Sorry," he said gruffly. " 'Tis a bit startling to see my sister as a grown woman. 'Tis more startling still to see her touching the youngest prince of Neroche." He continued on his way over to them, then deposited the tray on a small table. "I never would have considered such a match, though I'll allow that your mother and mine did discuss such a calamity more than once. My father was not at all pleased with the idea."

"I can't imagine he would have been," Miach said ruefully, "though I daresay I'm flattered to have been discussed."

Keir threw him another glare, then dragged up a chair to the table. "Sit. I cannot guarantee the quality, but at least 'tis hot."

Miach found chairs for himself and Morgan, then sat down next to her. Keir didn't seem particularly pleased with that arrangement, but he didn't draw any weapons or cast any spells, which was progress. Things could have been worse.

What was worse was the food. Miach ate it anyway, gratefully, and so did Morgan. He watched Keir watch his sister and couldn't help but smile at the continued look of disbelief the man wore. Miach supposed the kindest thing he could do was leave them both a bit of privacy to digest the morning's events. He finished a glass of terribly bitter ale, then turned to Morgan.

"I should see to my spells," he said quietly. "If you wouldn't mind?"

"I'm perfectly capable of seeing to my sister," Keir put in pointedly.

Miach nodded deferentially. "I never doubted it. I was just trying to be polite."

Morgan leaned over and kissed his cheek. "I'll save you a spot for a nap."

Miach rose and walked away before he had to listen to Keir's response—which he was sure, based on the tone of his voice, had not been polite. He pulled up a chair in front of what small windows there were in the solar, then sat down and let out a long, slow breath. He was slightly ill from the Olc he'd covered himself with even briefly to follow Morgan, and the Lugham he'd used downstairs, and yet again by the Olc that drenched the castle they were in. Truly, Sarait had borne much to even set foot in it, though perhaps Gair hadn't been so open about his preferences in the early years of their marriage. In this chamber, though, it was not so oppressive. He looked up at the ceiling and examined what else it was that he felt.

It was the slightest hint of Fadaire.

He knew he shouldn't have been surprised. For whatever reason, this had been Keir's home for the past twenty years and he was, as he had said earlier, a prince of the house of Tòrr Dòrainn. He never would have subjected himself to the brunt of Olc, or Lugham, or whatever else the mages of Ceangail favored.

Miach looked over his shoulder at Morgan and Keir sitting in front of the fire. Keir was holding on to her hands and wearing again that expression of incredulity.

Miach understood. He smiled to himself, then turned back to his own business.

It was late afternoon before he came back to himself. The spells of defense he'd set along the borders of Neroche—and Wychweald too—were unsettlingly intact. Lothar was obviously concentrating his efforts elsewhere—no doubt trying to find someone to open Gair's well for him.

Miach rubbed his hands over his face and grimaced. They had to find the proper spell and use it, sooner rather than later. And once the well was shut, Miach had a slew of things he was going to pile atop it, things that would take even Droch several months to undo.

There is a book in the library at Ceangail, hidden, a book containing all my father's spells in their entirety.

Rùnach's words came back to him as clearly as if he'd been standing there speaking them, and Miach felt the urgency of them. If the book was as difficult to find as Rùnach had suggested, the sooner he got to looking for it, the better.

He turned to find Morgan asleep on a hard, high-backed bench near the fire. Keir was simply sitting there, watching her. Miach looked at Gair's eldest son and marveled that in all the years he himself had lived, he'd never considered that one of Gair's children might have survived that horrible business at the well.

Keir didn't look to have borne the ravages of time very well. Being heir to Sìle's wellspring of youth, he should have looked no more than a score and a bit. Instead, his dark hair was heavily sprinkled with white, and his face was lined with care and sorrow. His had certainly not been an easy life and the past twenty years had obviously taken their toll.

Miach rose, stretched, then walked over to the hearth. He took a blanket from off the back of the bench and covered Morgan with it, then sat down opposite Keir. "Your Highness," he said, inclining his head deferentially.

Keir studied him for quite a while in silence, then cleared his throat. "She says you're the archmage now. And that Adhémar is king."

Miach nodded.

"I'm surprised there's anything left of Neroche with him looking after it," Keir said with a snort. "Your brother is an ass."

Miach suppressed a smile. He might have felt sorry for Adhémar and his reputation, but his brother had certainly gone out of his way to earn it. Miach suspected there wasn't an elf living that Adhémar hadn't insulted to some degree. He certainly never had an easy time of any of his blessedly infrequent visits to either Ainneamh or Tòrr Dòrainn.

"How did your parents die?" Kier asked.

Miach managed not to flinch, especially since he had equally prying questions to ask of Morgan's brother. He took a deep breath. "My mother died rescuing me from the dungeons at Riamh, where I had been held captive for a year. My father died a fortnight later from wounds received in that battle."

Keir's mouth had fallen open. He shut it with a snap. "You poor fool."

"Aye."

He considered for another moment or two. "Mhorghain says she loves you and that Grandfather gave you permission to wed her."

"I think she does love me," Miach said slowly. "And 'tis certain that I love her. And aye, your grandfather did give me permission to wed her." He paused. "I would have asked you for her hand, Prince Keir, if I'd known you were alive. I will ask you now, if it isn't too late."

"I imagine it is very much too late," Keir grumbled, "since Mhorghain seems to consider the matter closed. I don't suppose I can credit you with enchanting her."

"I don't enchant," Miach said. "Actually, I haven't even wooed her very well yet. Ask her as much when she wakes."

"I already did. I understand you made her a pair of blades, which she approved of, and that you braved the gates of Gobhann to bring her to her senses. She mentioned something about hay, but wouldn't elaborate. Do you care to?"

Miach smiled in spite of himself. "I don't think I dare. Nothing untoward happened, if that eases your mind any."

"I'm not sure anything would ease me at present." He sighed deeply. "Perhaps you might be so good as to distract me with tales of the outside world. If I think on my sister, I will weep. Again."

"I wouldn't blame you if you did, and I imagine your sister is just as overwhelmed. But I'll happily give you whatever tidings you want. Where shall I begin?"

"I've been here twenty years, lad," Keir said grimly, "with scant contact with the outside world. Anything would be new to me."

Miach waited, hoping Keir would elaborate, but he seemed disinclined to do so. Once Miach realized that no details would be forthcoming, he helped himself to a glass of wine, sat back, then worked his way from one end of the Nine Kingdoms to the other. Keir merely listened greedily, like a man who had been perishing from thirst without realizing it. He smiled at some things, cursed at others, and shook his head at most everything else.

"Well told," he said after Miach had finished, "and I thank you for it. It has been many years since I had such accurate reports." He studied the liquid in his cup for a moment or two in silence, then looked up. "I must now admit to being slightly confused as to why you're here, you and Mhorghain both. It cannot be mere chance."

"Nay, Your Highness," Miach agreed, "it isn't chance. We're here for a particular spell."

"And what is this spell to do?"

Miach knew there was no point in not being honest. "We're trying to shut your father's well. I understand there is a book here, a private book that contains all your father's spells. I hadn't expected to have you here to help me in finding it, but I'm grateful—"

"It's gone."

Miach was fairly certain he'd heard that awrong. "I beg your pardon?"

Keir smiled without humor. "I watched the library downstairs be reduced to ashes soon after I arrived. If the book had been there, it is there no longer. I can personally guarantee it isn't anywhere else in the keep. I would have found it by now if it had been."

Miach looked up into the blackness of the vault above him. It had been a brief hope, but perhaps 'twas one better left unfulfilled. If Gair's lifework had fallen into the wrong hands . . . well, that didn't bear thinking on. It was better to believe it had been burned.

"I don't know why you'd want it anyway," Keir continued, "for it wouldn't serve you. Only someone with my father's . . . blood . . ." He looked at Miach in astonishment. "You can't mean . . ." His mouth fell open. "You can't mean for Mhorghain to close that bloody well."

Miach looked at him in consternation. He realized at that moment what that feeling was that he'd had when he first realized Keir was alive.

Relief.

Morgan was no longer the only one with the power to shut the well. Rùnach could not aid them, but Keir was whole and sound.

He wondered, absently, why Keir didn't look equally relieved.

"That was our plan," Miach admitted, "but that was before. Now that I know you're alive—"

Keir threw himself to his feet and walked away with a curse before Miach could finish. He paced about the room in a frantic fashion, much like a man who had just learned a truth so dreadful, he couldn't take it in. Miach could offer him no comfort. The reality was the well had to be closed and Morgan had been the only one to do it.

She wasn't now.

Keir finally came to a halt in front of him. "You cannot be serious."

Miach looked up at him, confused. "But I am. That well is still spewing evil even after a score of years. Lothar has found it and is using what evil still seeps forth to create monsters to hunt those with Camanaë magic, as well as those with Gair's blood in their veins. I have reason to believe that Lothar is actively looking for a way to open it. Worse still, I fear there are others with the same idea. I must shut it before Lothar—or anyone else—is successful. Can you imagine the devastation that would cause otherwise?"

"Actually," Keir said curtly, "I can."

Miach closed his eyes briefly. "Forgive me, Your Highness. I spoke without thinking." He paused. "I know you've been away from the world, but surely you've heard tell of those creatures roaming through Neroche—through all the Nine Kingdoms now. Have you seen none of these monsters of Lothar's make here at the keep?"

Keir cast himself back down in his chair. "No one comes here," he said flatly. "There is a very substantial, if not a bit tatty, spell of aversion laid over the keep. I'm surprised you didn't feel it."

"Oh, I did," Miach admitted. "I just ignored it."

Keir looked at him. "Who told you to come here?"

"Your brother, Rùnach. He's hiding at Buidseachd."

Keir shook his head, wearing again a faint look of wonder. "I didn't dare hope anyone else had survived, but I suppose I shouldn't be surprised. I'm also not surprised he made his way there. I take it he's lurking in the library?"

"Aye, whilst also posing as Soilléir's servant."

"That surprises me even less," Keir said with a sigh. "Soilléir is likely the only one who has the power to protect him from Droch. Not that he has any power left for Droch to take."

Miach watched Morgan's brother again study his cup, as if it contained answers he couldn't bring himself to look for elsewhere. Miach looked up and watched the shadows dance from the light of the fire and wished for a few answers himself. Why hadn't Keir been able to stop book-destroying mages who had surely been inferior to him in both power and skill? Why was he hiding in Dìobhail, and why had he had no tidings of the outside world?

He also wanted to know why Keir hadn't gone back to the well and tried to close it himself before now.

"Do you know anything about that day?"

Miach pulled his attention back to Keir. "At the well?" He waited for Keir's nod, then shook his head. "I've heard your sister's memories and read your uncle Làidir's diary. I have a letter your mother sent to Sosar detailing her plan. But as to the actual events, nay, I don't know enough." He paused and wished for a better way to ask the question that burned in his mouth. "My lord, perhaps this is an impertinent question, but I can't help but wonder why you couldn't simply shut the well your—"

"I have no power."

Miach blinked. "What?" he asked, astonished.

"I have no power," Keir repeated. "My father stripped it from me—or most of it, rather—just before he opened the well."

Miach rubbed his hands over his face, then blew out his breath. He wasn't sure what was more devastating: entertaining even briefly that someone besides Morgan might be able to see to the task before them, or imagining how Keir must have felt to have lost something so integral to who he was. Having seen Lothar do the like countless times over that very unpleasant year passed in his dungeon, Miach had more familiarity than he wanted to have with what that snatching of power did to a mage. He could hardly imagine having it happen to himself.

"I'm very sorry," he said quietly. He paused, then looked at Keir. "Would it grieve you overmuch to give me the entire tale?"

Keir shook his head. "Nay, not now." He bowed his head briefly, then looked back up at Miach. "My mother goaded him into the whole thing, of course. He had become so . . . agitated. Nothing pleased him. Worse still, he became convinced that we were plotting against him.

My mother felt she had no choice but to push him into doing something foolish and hope that he would destroy himself. I suppose we could have brought ourselves to kill him eventually—since he threatened the same against us so often—though it wouldn't have been easily done. My father's power was formidable, and he wasn't one to be caught unawares."

He fell silent. Miach waited for him to continue, but he seemed to be lost in some unpleasant memory and only stared into the distance as if he witnessed events only he could see.

"Your Highness?" Miach prompted when he dared.

Keir focused on him. "Rùnach and I stood with my dam in that accursed glade to protect her," he continued, as if he'd never stopped talking. "Brogach, Gille, and Eglach distracted my father whilst Ruithneadh and Mhorghain went into hiding. I had assumed my father would try to harm my mother first, but instead he attacked Rùnach, taking all his power with a single word. Brogach's as well. Gille and Eglach he simply slew. He then attacked me just as he began to open the well. My mother deflected his spell that it didn't kill me as well, but it cost her, which was a disaster for us all. She had counted on me for added strength to fight him."

Miach could only imagine Sarait's panic. She had been powerful in her own right, but facing a mage of Gair's strength who had just increased that power—not only by the stealing of his son's but by the evil contained in the well itself . . . it was a miracle she had managed to shut the well as far as she had.

"The evil sprang up," Keir went on, "then fell upon my father. My mother deflected it from me and Rùnach, though because of that it caught her fully. She managed to pull the cap back down most of the way—on Rùnach's hands unfortunately. I pulled him free with the last of my strength." He paused for quite some time. "I am ashamed to say I then fainted. I'm not certain how long I lay there, but it must have been at least most of that day, for the sun was sinking when I woke. My mother was dead, as were my brothers who had apparently been washed away in that first wave of evil. I tried to look for Mhorghain and Ruithneadh—Rùnach, as well—but I couldn't find any of the three and I was too weak to manage a decent search."

"Are you certain your father was killed?"

"Of course," Keir said without hesitation, then he paused. "He couldn't possibly have survived the initial spewing of the well. He is dead and rotting in some place where I hope he will suffer forever."

Miach couldn't help but agree with that sentiment. "What then?"

"I crawled off to find aid, then I made my way here. And so you don't have to ask any particulars, I'll tell you freely that I can still conjure up werelight, light a fire, and use a spell of un-noticing. Things any witch gel can do once she can speak. I can still weave a bit of elven glamour, but nothing else."

Miach wasn't quite sure what, if anything, he could say, or should say. He closed his eyes briefly. "I'm sorry."

Keir shrugged. "I won't say it doesn't gall me, because it does, but there's nothing to be done about it."

"Indeed?" Miach asked in spite of himself. "Why not? Could I not undo the spell?"

Keir smiled without humor. "Know you nothing of this vile art?"

"I've watched Lothar do it a time or two." That was an understatement, but there was no point in dredging up his own past at present.

"Lothar's spell for the like is but a shadow of what my father could do," Keir said frankly. "Lothar claims to drain his victims of their power, but at best he might capture half of what they have. My father could strip a mage of every drop of his strength, completely, wholly, mercilessly." He shot Miach a look. "That's why Droch hated my sire so intensely. Because he could steal power and Droch cannot. Droch tried many times to have the spell, by bribery, by threat, by merely asking politely, but my father never humored him."

"Your father was notoriously stingy with his spells."

"Thankfully, I daresay, or we would all be nothing but shells of ourselves." He sighed. "Unfortunately, that leaves me of no use to you."

Miach frowned. "I don't mean to be obtuse, but I don't understand why I or your grandfather—or both of us, for that matter—couldn't restore what you lost."

"Because only the mage who took the power can give it back," Keir said, "and that because he alone holds what is yours. That is the nature of the spell and the reason it is so powerful. And believe me when I tell you that by the time the mage has used the spell even once, he does not have any interest in giving back what he's taken. He would no doubt prefer death first. Not that any of it matters. I don't have the spell of closing you're looking for and I have no power to aid you. And," he said, shooting Miach a look of warning, "I will not allow my sister to do that work in my stead."

"Then what will you have me do?" Miach asked seriously. "I am no more eager than you to see her anywhere near that glade again, but if not Mhorghain, then who? The well must be shut and she is now the only one left with the right to use your father's spells."

"And if she fails?"

Miach took a deep breath. "She cannot. And she will not. She has more courage than anyone I've ever known. She came along with me when I slipped over the walls of Buidseachd and into Droch's solar—"

Keir gaped at him. "You bastard."

Miach smiled faintly. "We argued for a full three hours about it beforehand. Your sister the grown woman is, I imagine, much like your mother. You will not find her easily dissuaded when she decides on a plan. I've found the best course of action is to agree with her, then follow along behind and offer her protection she certainly doesn't need. She spent six years in Gobhann and though she's never elaborated, I would imagine she earned Weger's mark quite quickly. She was a master there for quite some time, honing her skill past where you or I could have borne the discipline."

"She'll listen to reason from me," Keir said confidently.

Miach couldn't stop a brief smile. "You're certainly welcome to try."

Keir glared at him briefly, then buried a curse or two in his cup.

"If I might ask something else," Miach began gingerly.

"Can I dissuade you from it?" Keir asked sourly.

Miach smiled. "I'm curious about why you haven't gone to Seanagarra. Or to Cladach to see Sgath and Eulasaid. Either pair of grandparents would have been overjoyed to welcome you."

Keir studied him for a moment or two in silence, then leaned forward stiffly and rested his elbows on his knees. "I cannot leave—and that through no fault of my own. There are others who keep me here."

"Others?"

"The rumor that my father had no bastards—or that he killed them all—is false. I honestly couldn't say how many there are out in the world, but there are at least two here in the keep with me. They've woven spells over the keep that I can't best. A third left last summer and I've had no word of him since. I shudder to think of the mischief he's been stirring up. The eldest of the witchwoman of Fàs is also out roaming the world. He thinks his brothers are ruling me here, his brothers here think I'm in league with the eldest, and I'm keeping myself alive by promising them both a spell they know will die with me."

"And that spell would be?" Miach asked, because he couldn't help himself.

"The spell of Diminishing," Keir said. "What else?"

"Do you know it?"

"Of course I know it." He smiled briefly. "I memorized as much of my father's private book as possible whilst he wasn't looking."

"Very interesting."

Keir pursed his lips. "Next I suppose you'll ask if I'll give you all the spells."

"I had considered it."

"Along with the spell of Diminishing, no doubt."

"Would you?" Miach asked with a smile.

"How many rings of mastery do you have?"

"Seven."

Keir lifted one eyebrow. "Droch has those as well."

"But he doesn't have the spells of Caochladh."

Keir's mouth fell open. "Soilléir gave those to you?"

"I earned them, believe me," Miach said, with feeling. "What of my soul the mantle of archmage didn't shatter, he did."

Keir looked at him as if he were seeing him for the first time. "What would you do with my father's spells if I gave them to you?"

"Catalog them along with a score of other things I'll never use," Miach said.

Keir considered, then looked at Miach again. "I'll think on it." He paused. "I would advise you to never use that spell of Diminishing. It would destroy you."

"I'll remember that."

"You may call me Keir."

"Thank you, Your Highness," Miach said with a smile. "And I'd be pleased if you would call me Miach."

"'Tis better than that other mouthful," Keir said with a snort. "Besides, I've heard 'tis bad luck to use your full name."

Miach laughed in spite of himself. "So they say."

Keir managed a faint smile. "I knew you when you were a wee thing, you know. Your mother brought you often to Seanagarra. You could at four read everything you saw, and work most all of what you read. I daresay you—how shall we say it?—appropriated the first of my grandsire's spells at that tender age."

"I don't remember it," Miach admitted.

"You might not, but your mother certainly did. She teased my grandfather unmercifully about it every time she visited thereafter. He didn't dare chastise her, of course, for he was terribly fond of her, even if he pretended otherwise."

"He's never been terribly fond of me."

"You haven't your mother's charm, I daresay," Keir said dryly. "And trust me, if my grandfather hadn't already engraved his approval upon your wrist, I would have quite a bit to put you through before I agreed to give my sister to you. I cannot believe you intend to send her to that well."

Miach sighed. "You know I have no choice. I have tried everything in my power to see she came nowhere near it. Unfortunately, we are ofttimes not offered the choice of our adversities, which I hardly need to tell you. I cannot take Mhorghain's path away from her. All I can do is walk it with her."

Keir studied him for several minutes in silence, then he cleared his throat roughly. "Perhaps my grandsire didn't bestow his blessing amiss."

"Thank you."

Keir sighed deeply. "I can see there is nothing else to be done. I'll help you as I can. Do you have the letter my mother wrote Sosar with you? I'd like to see it again."

"Aye, I have it." Miach paused. "I also have a dozen pages full of spells that might have been your father's, or your father's sources for them."

"Rùnach's been busy."

"Aye," Miach said with a smile.

"He had a knack for ferreting out things from unlikely sources. What else do you have?"

"Your father's spell of opening, which Mhorghain wrote down for us in Soilléir's solar. I don't imagine merely trying to reverse it will be enough."

Keir shook his head. "My father was too cagey for that. It wouldn't have done for anyone to have duplicated one of his spells. Let me see what you have. I might see something to jog a memory or two." He looked at Miach briefly. "A brother and a sister, when I thought I had none. 'Tis truly a miracle."

"Aye, Your Highness, it is."

Keir sat up and rubbed his hands together. "I'll fetch a pair of candles, you pull the table back over, and we'll see what you have there."

Miach nodded and did as Keir bid, then he walked over to stand next to Morgan. She was still sleeping peacefully, for which he was most grateful. Perhaps Keir would give her other details of that fateful day, but surely she didn't need them at present. He wouldn't be unhappy if she slept through the rest of his conversations with Keir. The fewer of her father's spells she was forced to listen to, the better off she would be.

He reached down and settled her blanket, then turned back to wait for Keir. Perhaps Morgan's brother would be able to make something of what they had.

Miach honestly had no idea where to look if not.

Thirteen

Morgan lay on the hard bench in front of the fire and continued to feign sleep. She wasn't above that sort of subterfuge when it stood to provide her with details she might not have had in a more straightforward fashion. She had to admit, though, that she'd heard things she likely could have gone on quite happily without knowing.

She had hoped, at one point during her eavesdropping, that Keir might have had all the answers they needed. She had also hoped, even more briefly and with a distinct feeling of shame, that he might be able to take on the task of closing the well and save her having to face it. She'd been even less proud of the dismay she'd felt when she'd heard that he had no power.

Weger would have been appalled at her craven lack of courage.

She had continued to listen as Keir and Miach had discussed spells and potential locations for other spells that might help them. The sound of her brother's voice had been terribly familiar and that mixed with the sound of Miach's voice, which she had come to love . . . well, it made her feel as if she were dreaming, encountering at every turn things she hadn't expected to, and finding bits of her past becoming enmeshed with the whole of her present. She was as bemused as if she'd been walking in her grandfather's garden under the full strength of his glamour. She couldn't say she wasn't looking forward to having her life settle back to normal, truth be told.

If normal could possibly have anything to do with palaces and spells and court functions. At least at Tor Neroche she suspected she could count on Miach to meet her in the lists once a day.

She made a production of waking up. She sat up and shivered at the feeling of spells pressing down on her. She could sense, now that she had the time to do so, that the air was not so oppressive in the solar where she sat, but she supposed Keir had woven some sort of glamour about it—either he or Miach. Even so, it was appalling to think she was in a place she'd been as a child. She wished she could have denied it, but she couldn't. The truth was all around her.

She pushed herself to her feet and crossed the handful of paces to stand next to Miach's chair. He and Keir were looking over the pages Miach had gotten from Rùnach. He put his hand on the small of her back and smiled up at her.

"How do you fare?"

"Very well," she lied. "Did you find anything interesting?"

"A few things."

Morgan nodded and smiled at her brother as if what he and Miach were discussing was limited to them perhaps starting a shop together, or building a new barn that straddled their properties. It was better than acknowledging what it was they discussed. Of course, it wasn't that she was afraid of the spells, or the magic, or the terrible reality of what she now knew only she could do at the well. Nay, she wasn't afraid.

She was terrified.

She put her hand on Miach's head briefly, nodded again to her brother, then turned and looked for the best route to use for running away from that fear. She found a route all too quickly, which unsettled her even more. The echo of familiarity that grasped at her at every turn was startling. It was so unpleasant a sensation that she found it difficult to breathe. She felt an inescapable sense of inevitability, as if she were walking toward a darkness so complete that there was no light possible and in that darkness was her death . . .

She realized her breath was coming in gasps, but she couldn't help herself. It was the same feeling of doom she'd had in the passageway at Buidseachd when Droch had surrounded her with his spells and was slowly cutting off any hope of escape—only this was worse. She was in the heart of her father's darkness.

If that doom had instead been a tangible foe, aye, that she could have conquered. She could have drawn her sword and finished it with a bare minimum of fuss. But this was magic—and unpleasant magic at that. If her mother, with all her centuries of spells and all her power drawn from the springs of Tòrr Dòrainn and An Cèin, Camanaë and Ainneamh, hadn't been able to fight Gair's evil, who did she think she was to even try?

For the first time in her life, she was tempted to sit down and give up. Not even during her first few months at Gobhann when weariness had gnawed at her and Weger's students had used every slur and barb possible against her had she entertained such a thought. Not even during her first few months at Lismòr when she had been suffocated by university rules and what had seemed a complete loss of her freedom had she ever given in to the temptation to take a step backward.

Not even during those profoundly miserable years as a young girl when she'd traveled with mercenaries and been favored with only occasional moments of kindness from them had she done anything besides stick her chin out and soldier on.

But now?

Mhorghain, love, come and sit with me.

Morgan turned around, all the way around herself in surprise until she stood facing the fire. And there, wrapped in a faint glow of elven glamour, with her arms open and beckoning, sat her mother.

Morgan caught her breath at the sight. She'd seen her in dreams and in a portrait that hung in her grandfather's palace, but now there she sat, as if she truly lived and breathed.

Morgan would have moved, but she couldn't. All she could do was look at her mother and feel herself be wrapped in a sensation she hadn't expected. She was too startled to have the wit to identify it, but it wasn't unpleasant. On the contrary, it was a feeling that sank into her heart and eased the fear there. Sarait of Tòrr Dòrainn was beautiful, serene, and wore such an expression of love that Morgan found her own eyes beginning to burn. If she could have even a part of what her mother radiated so effortlessly, she might have the courage to press on.

She took a step forward, rubbing her eyes to ease them, only to realize with a start that her mother was gone.

Now, in her place in front of the fire, sat two men who pored over spells and spoke in quiet tones. Miach lifted his head and looked for her suddenly. He smiled, a smile full of love that was very reminiscent of her mother's, then turned back to his business.

Morgan stepped backward and leaned against chilled stone, trying to regain her balance. She fully expected to be assaulted by a feeling of bereavement, but instead, what she had seen in her mother's smile washed over her again. It wasn't at all diminished by the sight of her brother and her love searching desperately for a way to save their lives and their land.

She stood there in the shadows and wondered, absently, if her mother had actually done what she'd just seen and heard, if she'd drawn her into her arms, held her close, kept her safe.

She let out a shuddering breath. Perhaps it didn't matter if it was dream or memory. Perhaps it was enough to know there were others, seen and unseen, who loved her and believed she could do things that seemed impossibly difficult.

And perhaps she didn't need her mother's power or her father's skill. Perhaps Miach had it aright. All she needed was her own courage and the right spell.

She took that thought and held on to it as she started to pace again. This time, the familiarity of the chamber didn't trouble her as much. She made the circuit a handful of times more, then came to a stop near the fire. Miach rose, fetched a chair, and set it next to his. He sat down with her and ran his hand over her braid.

"How are you?"

"Better now."

He smiled, then took her hand and held it in both his own as he turned back to the spells laid in front of him. Morgan leaned forward and looked, but not for long. The spell of opening she'd written for Soilléir was laying there atop the rest.

Keir looked up. "You remembered all this?"

"Aye," she said, "but I'm not sure if the order is right."

"I think this is almost exactly what he used," Keir said, sitting back. "You have a good memory, sister. Much better than father's was. I don't know that he could have written this again without aid."

"Are you telling me your father wrote things down on his arm and pulled his sleeve up as needed?" Miach asked with a smile.

"Nothing so clever, I assure you," Keir said with a sigh. "He was, though, wont to jot things down in various places to jog his memory. The notes Rùnach found in the margins of books at Buidseachd are a good example of it."

"But I've heard he never wrote things down in their entirety," Miach said slowly. "Except for the book that no longer exists."

"That is true," Keir agreed. "He wouldn't have wanted any other mage to have copied what he'd done. But 'tis also true that his spells were generally so complicated that he couldn't remember them perfectly. Hence the jotting down of notes in margins."

Morgan was surprised by that, though she was certainly not one to judge. She couldn't remember her father casting any sort of spell, but perhaps her mother had protected her from it. She watched Miach think about something for a moment, then frown.

"So, if he were to make a substantial piece of magic, would he have taken notes with him?" Miach asked. "Or would he have gone to the spot ahead of the moment and left something there?"

"If it was a single spell he stood to cast, he wouldn't have needed anything," Keir said. "More than one spell and he might have taken something with him, but he would have incinerated it the moment the spell was begun. Of course, that doesn't cover the things he would have left behind."

Miach lifted an eyebrow. "And what would those have been?"

"Some visible mark that he'd been there," Keir said with a shrug. "His name, a word, a piece of the spell. A very small piece, mind you. Just enough to let the world know he had been there with his fearsome self and his wonderful magic. Why do you ask?"

"I was just curious."

"I imagine, lad, that curiosity lands you in spots of trouble now and again."

"Ah, but that trouble always yields interesting things."

Keir laughed. "I imagine it does."

Morgan sat back and listened to them veer off into topics that had nothing at all to do with the spells in front of them but a great deal to do with the different sorts of trouble they'd gotten themselves into over the course of their lives. She listened for a bit and smiled at the tales, grateful for the distraction from more serious things.

She realized at some point during that discussion that the peace she'd felt before was still surrounding her, as if it had been a quiet spell of elven glamour cast by someone who loved her. The contrast between that and the spells of evil that sat on the table was startling, but she found that she could tolerate it more easily now. She looked at Miach as he laughed at something her brother said and wondered if he had that same sort of tranquility somewhere deep inside him, a peace that not even the horrors of Lothar's dungeon could touch.

She suspected so.

The conversation soon turned to things less magical, settling finally on famous battles in the past. Keir, despite his having been trapped in Ceangail for years, was apparently a serious student of the history of the Nine Kingdoms. She suspected that he knew many of the players he mentioned, just as Miach did. She listened for a bit, then looked at the spell in front of her, wishing quite desperately that it would simply up and reveal its secrets.

The longer she stared at it, the more the words began to move on the page. She pulled Mehar's knife out of her boot and fingered the hilt, just to keep herself where she was and not lost in some horrible forest of Olc where what sun that shone down was cold and flat. It was a pity that there was no way to fight magic with a blade. It would have made it so much more tolerable.

She watched her hand as it reached for the quill and ink that was sitting on the edge of the table. She slowly turned the top sheaf over, then sat down on the floor and began to rearrange the words she could still see swimming in front of her eyes in a less magical pattern.

She tried first to put them in precise, disciplined columns, but they didn't seem to care for that. She arranged them then in rows that marched across the page with precision and order. That made the words slightly less disgusting, but no less eager to be managed.

She considered all the battle plans she had studied during her time at Gobhann, plans for sieges successfully mounted and wars successfully won. Her preferred route was to simply slip over the wall in disguise and threaten the lord with death until he opened the front gate to her fellows, at which point she would slip back into the background lest the lord recognize her and be wary of her the next time. She'd done it more than once, with great success. It wasn't, however, a very showy, grandiose way to go about it. If she were going to lay siege to a keep and make certain everyone for miles knew she'd done it, she would have gone about it far differently.

She thought back to a book she'd read in Weger's gathering hall more than once, a tome written by Gleac of Gairn, the general who had stopped the Eastern Ravages hundreds of years ago. She'd liked his writings partly because he'd had a very wry sense of humor and partly because he'd been a brilliant tactician.

She thought back to a particular chapter in that same book where Gleac had presented a score of battle plans suited to the ego of the commander in charge. She'd found it to be ridiculous at the time, but over her years as a mercenary, she'd begun to see the truth—and the humor—of it. Not that she'd allowed her ego to become involved in what she was about, but she'd seen scores of other lads do so.

She now chose one of the more flamboyant plans of assault that came to her and began to arrange the words of her father's spell in the order that Gleac would have moved his men. She flipped the sheaf over a time or two to study the words of the spell to make sure she wasn't missing anything. When she was finished, she blew on the ink to dry it, then set the sheaf on the ground.

And her writing, words that had come from her hand, began to glow with a red light that had nothing to do with the fire in front of her.

She leapt to her feet, overturning her chair as a result, and stared down at the sheaf on the floor in horror. She heard other chairs scrape as they were pushed back, then felt Miach's hand on her arm. She looked at him, then at Keir. Both of them were staring down at what she'd done with openmouthed astonishment.

"What," Keir asked in a garbled tone, "have you done?"

"I don't know," she said, wrapping her arms around herself and pricking herself with the quill. She threw it down on the floor next to her arranged spell, then hugged herself again. "I don't know."

Miach stared at the spell for a moment or two, stroking his chin thoughtfully. Then he looked at Keir.

"Fetch a bottle of wine, my lord."

"But—"

"A bottle," Miach said, shooting Keir a look. "Unopened."

Keir looked positively green, but he nodded just the same and walked away. Morgan watched him go, then shivered.

"What have I done?"

He turned her to him and put his arms around her, pulling her close. "I'll tell you when I'm certain of it. First, tell me how you knew to arrange those words that way."

"I didn't know anything," she said, fighting the urge to shiver. "I was just trying to distract myself. Magic bothers me, as you know."

His laugh was nothing but the slightest of huffs. "An understatement, but I'll let it stand. Go on."

"Do you remember Gleac of Gairn?" she asked.

"Aye. He was the captain of Nicholas of Diarmailt's armies at one time."

She felt as if someone had just kicked her in the stomach. It took her a moment or two before she could catch her breath. "Is that so?"

"I thought you'd find that interesting," he said, sounding as if he smiled. "He was a brilliant soldier, General Gleac. Still is, I daresay. But I'm pulling you away from what you wanted to say. What about him?"

"I was considering his schemes for mounting sieges. I thought that it might ease my mind to take a spell from a pompous mage and try to wrestle it into a pattern created by a very showy soldier." She paused. "It was just for sport."

"Interesting sport."

She pulled back far enough to look at him. "The words are glowing, Miach."

"So they are, love." He tucked a lock of hair behind her ear. "Some spells do that, given the right circumstances. Their perfect order. A powerful mage. A powerful mage writing a spell down in its perfect order."

She took a deep breath. It had to have been simple coincidence. She was not a powerful mage and that spell had been arranged thus simply as an amusement.

"I was just curious, you know."

"Dangerous," he said with a smile.

"You've corrupted me."

He smiled. "I imagine I have. At least now we have each other to add a bit of protection whilst curiosity is satisfied."

She looked into his very pale eyes. "Aye, so we do."

"Would you do me a favor?" he asked seriously. "I vow I'll return it."

She looked at him for a moment in silence, then sighed. "I know what you want. I won't go again without telling you."

"I won't either."

"Vow it."

He took her left wrist, put his fingers over the crown of Neroche engraved on the inside there, then met her eyes. "I vow it. Now, 'tis your turn."

She made the same vow to him, had another quick embrace for her trouble, then stepped away as Keir came back to the fire with a bottle in his hand. He handed it to Miach.

"Well?"

Miach took the bottle and set it on the floor. He reached down for the spell, then set it aside on the table. He considered for another moment or two, then looked at Morgan.

"Want to try?"

She nodded, though she had no desire at all to attempt it. But a coward, she wasn't. "Won't everyone here feel my magic?"

"Not after I weave Sosar's spell of concealment over us."

Morgan watched him do so, smiled at Keir's cursing, then realized there was nothing else to use to delay the unpleasant. She looked up at Miach. "The spell has its final pattern, but how is it woven, do you suppose?"

"If you were a soldierish sort, how would you use those words if they were your men?"

She blew out her breath. She supposed a spell of opening was the same no matter if one wanted to open a keep or a bottle of wine. She thought about it for a moment or two, then began to use the words of the spell as she might have soldiers on the field of battle. She paused, then spoke the last word.

The cork flew out of the bottle so hard, the bottle shattered and wine gushed everywhere.

"Bloody hell," Keir said, leaping out of the way.

Morgan managed to get her boots out of the way of the flood, but she managed nothing else besides finding her chair and sitting down on it. It was Keir who mopped and Miach who retrieved broken glass and put it into a bucket for rubbish.

Once the floor was clean, Miach drew up a chair next to hers and collapsed into it.

"Well," he said.

"Well, indeed," she said weakly.

"Is there a stricture for that?"

"I don't think so, but I read the book in Weger's library. Does that count?"

"Cheeky wench," he said as he reached out to tug gently on her braid. He rubbed his hand over her back for a moment or two, then took her hand. "Are you game to give something else a go?"

"Always," she said weakly.

Miach fished Sarait's letter out of the pile and handed it to her. "I wonder what would happen if you did your same bit of rearranging with this?"

Keir leaned forward intently. "But that spell isn't complete."

"Let's see what Morgan—Mhorghain, I should say—can do with it. We might see what's missing if we have the proper pattern for the rest."

Morgan felt time begin to march on very oddly. She was Morgan; she was Mhorghain. She was taking magic and trying to bend it into strictures and structures she'd found in a place where no magic was possible. She was who she had been and who she had become.

She felt quite ill, actually.

Miach took her hand and squeezed it. "We can rest a bit, if you like."

She looked at him. It took her a moment before she could see him. "Nay, I am well," she croaked. "I'm not afraid."

"Of course you aren't."

But he didn't release her hand and she didn't pull away. She took several deep, steadying breaths, then waited until Keir had pushed the table in front of her and put a clean sheaf of paper out. He set their mother's letter to the side where she could see it, put the quill in her hand, then sat back down and waited, silently.

Morgan looked at the words there, then considered for quite a while. She called to mind Gleac's most brazen strategy and considered its implementation. Men stationed themselves at the four corners of a keep, distracting as others slithered over the walls and took over those same four guard towers from the inside, and they waited whilst yet another team of more skilled mercenaries took up the same positions just inside the great hall, each group pressing inward until the lord of the hall was ringed about in his own keep by lads who were not his. The final blow came from the commander who merely walked through the front gate and into the hall without resistance, either taking the lord prisoner, or slaying him on the spot. Not quick, but exceptionally showy, leaving the lord in question no doubt as to who had been behind the attack.

Morgan looked at the words written in her mother's hand, then arranged them in the same way, from the edge inward, layer upon layer, gathering the spell's power as it closed about the center spot. She wrote the last word she found in her mother's hand as she stood in front of that imaginary lord—but there was no killing blow.

But the final word was not there on the missive.

She looked at Miach and Keir. "I think all we lack is the last word."

Keir nodded. "Mother had thought so even at the time. I think she hoped Father would close his own spell, or give away the last piece of the puzzle. For all I know he did, but I certainly didn't hear it." He paused. "I don't even think he would have written it in his book, though I could be wrong. I think he had been planning to open the well for quite some time, so perhaps he did write down what he intended to use. It doesn't matter, though, does it, since we don't have the book."

Morgan watched Miach stare thoughtfully at the spell. He ran his fingers over words that, thankfully, didn't glow, then sat back and looked at Keir.

"Tell me again about how your father would leave his mark."

"As I said, it would be his name, or a bit . . ." Keir's face was suddenly ashen. "A bit of the spell."

"In the place where the spell had been wrought."

Keir nodded, mute.

Morgan was heartily glad to be sitting down. She put her hands over her face and felt Miach's arm go around her shoulders. She reached up and took hold of his hand, hoping belatedly that she didn't bruise his fingers. She sat there until she thought she could speak without making some unwelcome noise of distress, then she looked at him.

"We'll find it at the well," she said quietly. "Won't we?"

"If it is to be found at all, aye, I imagine we will find it there." He looked at Keir. "What do you think, Your Highness?"

Keir rubbed his hands over his face, then put his shoulders back. " 'Tis possible. Perhaps written on some stone in the glade—perhaps the well itself. Did you notice anything whilst you were there?"

"Nay," Miach said, "but I didn't think to look."

Morgan started to speak, but a sudden banging on the door almost sent her tumbling forward onto the table instead. Keir cursed, then rose and walked to the door. Morgan didn't say anything to Miach; she simply turned and put her arms around his neck. He held her close and trailed his fingers up and down her back as if he sought to comfort her. She was happy to let him try. It was one thing to think to enter that accursed glade with spell in hand; it was another thing to attempt an assault when she wasn't fully prepared.

As her mother had done.

She held Miach for a moment or two longer, then pulled back when she heard Keir slam his door shut. She attempted a smile, but failed. Miach managed it better than she had, but he had a very strong stomach indeed. He looked up as Keir walked swiftly across the chamber, cursing fluently.

"What was that about?" he asked.

"Prince Cruadal of Duibhreas is downstairs," Keir said with another curse, "demanding an audience."

"I wonder what he wants?" Miach murmured.

"Something to ease his headache, no doubt," Morgan said with a snort.

Miach smiled at her, then turned to Keir. "Do you know him?"

"I knew his family," Keir conceded. "He was perfectly horrible as a child, so I can't imagine he's improved with age. I take it he's not unknown to you two?"

"Grandfather presented him to me as a suitor," Morgan said. "I left it to Miach to express my aversion to the idea."

Keir lifted an eyebrow briefly. "I would be interested in the tale, but I fear we've no time for it." He hesitated, then looked at them with a very grave expression on his face. "It has been very joyous to me to have you here. Both of you. But I fear that the time has come for you to make your escape." He took a deep breath. "I'll entertain young master Cruadal and keep the guards busy whilst you do so. I suggest flight from the roof, if you don't mind shapechanging."

Morgan exchanged a look with Miach, but she supposed that had been unnecessary. He smiled slightly at her, then rose and made Keir a small bow.

"Whilst we appreciate your generosity, we can't accept it. We can't leave you here."

Keir shook his head. "Impossible, lad, as I told you before."

"Keir, you must come," Morgan insisted. "I'm not going to lose you after I just found you again."

He dragged his hand through his hair with a sigh. "The thought of leaving is, I'll admit, appealing."

Morgan walked over to him and put her arms around his waist. "Come with us," she urged. "Think on the freedom you'll enjoy."

"I agree," Miach said. "You cannot remain here, Your Highness. Not now. Not after today. Mhorghain and I can counter whatever magic holds you here. I'll hide your essence for you."

"He did it for me at Buidseachd," Morgan said, looking up at her brother. "Very well, actually."

Keir shot Miach a glare. "I should come with you simply to repay you for that—and to see you never do anything so foolish again." He shifted uncomfortably. "I'm surprised to find I'm nervous at the thought of leaving."

Miach put his hand on Keir's shoulder. "The world outside is not such a terrible place, my lord. And your grandparents would be very happy to see you."

Keir swallowed, apparently with quite a bit of difficulty. "I'll think on it."

"Don't," Morgan said firmly. "Don't think about it. Just come."

She watched her brother exchange a look with Miach, a look full of dreadful hope and not a small bit of panic. Miach only smiled at him.

"If you want to think on something," he said, "think on the sunlight."

Keir shuddered. He took a deep breath, hugged Morgan tightly, then stepped away. "Very well, let us see to the fool downstairs, then we'll make our escape. There are other ways out besides the front gate."

Morgan went to gather her blades with a lighter heart than she might have expected otherwise. She didn't protest when Miach hid her magic as thoroughly as he had the second time in Soilléir's chamber. She didn't even flinch as she walked across the solar for the last time, though she felt as if she were walking over her own grave.

She shivered, once, then put it behind her and followed her

brother out the door, trying to look as much like a prisoner as possible. It was difficult, because in spite of it all, she was happy.

Keir was planning to come away with them, and Miach was behind her humming a battle dirge she was quite certain he'd learned in Gobhann.

It was surprisingly cheering.

Fourteen

Miach stood in the shadows of the great hall, wearing a spell of un-noticing under a spell of aversion under yet another spell of Olc. It was unpleasant and stifling. He could safely say he would be relieved to never need set foot inside Ceangail again, though he wasn't unhappy that he had at present. Seeing Morgan's reunion with her brother had been worth any unpleasantness.

Now, if they could just rid themselves of the unpleasantness in front of them, he would have been content.

Cruadal of Duibhreas swayed a bit as he stood a score of paces away from the lord's chair. Perhaps his head pained him more than he cared to let on. Miach almost wished he'd done him in, but he hadn't been able to shake the feeling that Cruadal had yet a part to play in the history of the Nine Kingdoms. He comforted himself thinking that Yngerame of Wychweald and Symon of Neroche had faced the same dilemma when they'd had Lothar in their power and considered slaying him. Though Miach wasn't so sure that *that* wouldn't have been a boon for them all.

But it might have upset the balance of good and evil in the world, as Master Soilléir was wont to say, so perhaps Yngerame and Symon had made the right choice. Miach could only hope he was doing the same thing.

Cruadal squinted as he peered into the darkness that surrounded Keir. "I am here for a spell."

"Oh, are you," Keir said, without a shred of inflection to his voice. "And you think I have one to give to you?"

"I know you do. And you'll surely want to once you realize what *I* know."

Miach couldn't see Keir's face thanks to both the spells that surrounded him and the hood he'd drawn over his head, but Miach could readily imagine his look of skepticism. Cruadal was bold, Miach would give him that. It took a particular sort of confidence to walk openly into a hall where one had no leverage and think to sway the lord by words alone.

Then again, perhaps Cruadal had a bargaining piece they didn't know about.

"And just what is it you think you know?" Keir asked. "And you'd best make it very interesting. I don't care to be called away from my private affairs without good reason."

"Oh, nay," Cruadal said, shaking his head gingerly. "Not that easily. There is a price to be paid for even a small bit of information."

Keir laughed a bit. "Well, you've cheek, I'll give you that. I'll allow you to draw breath long enough to amuse me a bit more. Go ahead and name your price."

"I want you to give me a spell. Actually, I want two of them, but I'm willing to wait for the second."

"Ah, well, you are a patient lad, aren't you?" Keir asked smoothly. "But so you have been for quite some time, haven't you? It takes quite a bit of that to slowly administer poison to the siblings in your way of your father's crown."

Cruadal gaped. "How did you—"

"You are not young, Cruadal," Keir interrupted, "and you are not careful. I think you would be surprised by how many know of your doings."

"Rumor only," Cruadal blustered.

Keir shrugged. "Perhaps, but that isn't our argument today, is it? Now, instead of wasting my time any longer, why don't you spew out what you truly want so I can tell you nay and go to supper?"

"Very well, then," Cruadal said angrily, "I want to destroy the archmage of Neroche and I want a particular spell to do so."

Miach was somehow not at all surprised.

"Just go slip a knife between his ribs whilst he's sleeping," Keir said with a yawn. "Surely you can manage that without any of my spells."

Miach rubbed his chest before he could stop himself, then felt Morgan's arm steal around his waist. He caught her hand and squeezed it gently, then put his arm around her shoulders and pulled her close.

"I don't want him dead," Cruadal said. "I want him to watch me for the rest of his unnaturally long life and realize that I have what he lost."

"And what, pray tell, would that be?"

"His power and his woman."

Miach tightened his arm around Morgan to stop her from moving, but realized it was unnecessary.

"I wasn't going to go stab him," she muttered, "though I'll admit the thought crossed my mind."

"I imagine it's crossing your brother's mind as well," Miach whispered. "At least we know what Cruadal wants—not that it was ever in question. After all, he's already tried to kill me and found the experience unsatisfactory enough to want to try again."

She looked up at him and smiled faintly. "You are never serious."

"I am now and again. And I'm taking that fool there seriously enough. I wonder what His Lordship will say?"

"I can hardly wait to hear."

Miach turned back to listen to Cruadal and found himself unnerved, but not at all surprised, by what he was hearing.

"I don't think you'll find the archmage of Neroche so easily trapped," Keir was saying negligently, "but I suppose you could try. So, if you don't want me to hold him down so you can fumble your knife into his gut, what is it exactly you want from me?"

"A spell of Diminishing."

Keir laughed out loud, a sound of genuine humor. He had been leaning back in his chair with one ankle propped up on the opposite knee, but now he dropped both feet onto the floor and sat forward. "And why is it, my wee elven prince, that you think I would *ever* give *you* such a thing?"

"Because I have a name, a name you'll be most interested in."

"So, let me understand this," Keir said, sitting back again. "You want to give me a name. And in return for that name, you want me to give you the most powerful spell in existence. Well, outside of the spells that a particular master in Buidseachd teaches, but I can't imagine you ever slithered through the doors of the schools of wizardry, much less stayed long enough to earn enough of the rings to even darken that mage's door."

Cruadal's hands were clenched down at his sides. "I wouldn't have bothered with anyone in Beinn òrain, and I couldn't care less about any ridiculous rings. And you *will* want this name. I can't imagine you want any of your father's rightful get running about, ruining your hold over Ceangail."

Keir tilted his hooded head to one side. "Who do you think I am, boy?"

"Not one of Gair's legitimate children, though I imagine you'd like to be," Cruadal said promptly. "Wouldn't you?"

"Why would I?" Keir asked, rubbing his hands together absently.

Cruadal took a step closer. "Give me what I want and I'll tell you who might come knocking on your door, wanting to sit in your chair."

"I'm not particularly eager to share my spells," Keir said, "especially that one. You might try Lothar."

"I don't have anything that Lothar want—" He shut his mouth with a snap. "Never mind."

Miach felt himself grow cold at the thought. He'd feared a fortnight ago that Cruadal would eventually decide to join forces with Lothar, or at least try to strike up some sort of alliance. He'd supposed that Cruadal would use Morgan's name and whose daughter she happened to be as his bargaining chip. At the time, Miach had feared that Lothar would come for Morgan because he would want to take her power.

But now he was certain that Lothar would do that only after he'd forced her to open the well.

Cruadal clasped his hands behind his back. "Perhaps, since you're not inclined to give me what I want, I might be willing to settle for the second spell I wanted from you."

"And what would that be?"

"A spell of opening."

"Well," Keir said very softly, "that's an interesting thing to want. What is it you intend to open?"

"Nothing in particular," he said. "Nothing of import. It would be a trivial thing to give when weighed against what I would give you in return. Trust me, this soul would truly be a threat to your comfortable life."

Keir looked at him for a moment, then called for parchment and ink. He penned something quickly, handed it to a servant, then looked at Cruadal. "You give me the name; I'll give you the spell."

"I want the spell first."

"I imagine you do," Keir said coolly. He waved his servant on, then stopped him just before he handed Cruadal the paper. "The name."

"Mhorghain of Ceangail."

"She's dead," Keir said.

"She's not," Cruadal returned. "I saw her with my own eyes. She is a legitimate heir to your father's throne, which might trouble you a bit, don't you agree?"

Keir lifted a shoulder in a negligent shrug. "I can't imagine why."

Cruadal took hold of the sheaf. "Which bastard are you?"

"I'm none."

Cruadal tugged until the servant finally released the paper with the spell written on it. Cruadal glared at the man, then at Keir. "Who are you then?"

Keir lifted his hood back off his face. Cruadal gasped.

"Who . . ."

"Keir," Keir said easily. "The eldest."

Cruadal cast a spell of binding. Miach stopped himself with a spell of protection half out of his mouth. Spells had already sprung up around Keir, strong ones, ones he could see from where he stood. A handful of mages stepped out of the shadows, their eyes fixed on Cruadal. He suddenly was quite still. Miach could see very unpleasant spells of Lugham wrapped around him. Keir only smiled.

"I am not without protection, as you see. I'm quite happy to remain here in my comfortable seat, no matter which of my siblings might be alive. Now, since you have your spell, why don't you be on your way?"

Cruadal apparently couldn't speak.

"Let me help you," Keir said politely. He beckoned and a dozen lads came forward to pick Cruadal up and carry him from the hall. Miach felt Morgan lean against him.

"He won't be happy with that."

"I would love to see his expression when he manages to free himself from that spell," Miach agreed. "I daresay we should be on our way long before that happens."

She looked up at him. "Can we manage it?"

"To be free of this keep? Of course. I don't particularly want to fight my way out of here with spells, but we will if we have no choice. We won't leave without your brother."

"And Cruadal?"

He tightened his arm around her. "We need to hurry, Morgan. I am very much afraid that when Lothar finds out you're alive, he won't merely want your power. He'll want you to do for him what he cannot do for himself."

She was very still. "Open the well?"

"Aye."

"Can't he do it himself?"

"Not now. Not after your mother shut it even partially using your father's spell." He paused. "I don't think he hasn't managed it, though, from a lack of trying. He simply doesn't have the power to overcome your father's spells and he doesn't have the bloodright to remove them. It will make you doubly attractive to him. Cruadal is stupid enough to believe he'll be able to be a part of any of it." He shook his head. "He won't like what happens to him once he's told Lothar what he knows."

She took a deep breath. "I'm ready for this to be over."

"We'll hurry."

She tightened her arm around his waist briefly, then pulled away. He heard the distinct sound of knives coming from sheaths.

He remained in the dark with Morgan and listened to Keir give instructions to his servants and thank his mages kindly for their aid. He rose only to run bodily into another man who had appeared suddenly next to him.

The menace was easily seen.

"Dìolain," Keir said pleasantly. "How lovely. Did you come to rescue me?"

The other man made a noise of disgust. "Rather I should have let him have you."

Keir shrugged. "You could have, my beloved bastard brother,

given that I am defenseless. There must be something you want very badly to leave me alive."

Dìolain leaned closer to him. "I could torture it from you."

Keir smiled without humor. "I think you've tried that before, and failed. I suppose you'll have to think of something else. Bribery, perhaps, or just a very polite request. You never know when I'll decide to accommodate you."

"Make it soon," the other said in a low, dangerous voice. "My patience has grown perilously thin."

Keir shook his head, as if the other's stupidity was simply beyond comprehension. He pushed past him, then paused and turned. "You might want to follow that slippery elven prince. I wouldn't trust him as far as I could heave him."

"I had planned to," Dìolain said sharply. "What spell did you give him?"

"A spell of opening," Keir said dismissively. "Unfortunately, the only thing it will open is his mouth—and that for an uncomfortable amount of time. He'll be quite furious by the time he determines how to undo what he did to himself. I guarantee it."

Dìolain snorted, then turned and walked away. Miach watched Keir come toward them. He didn't look at them, or make any sign he'd marked them. Perhaps he couldn't see them at all, which Miach supposed was likely the case.

Miach put Morgan in front of him and followed Gair's eldest along passageways and down tight, circular stairs until they reached a very dank cellar. They walked through the kitchens and back along another very claustrophobic passageway that led to an equally unpleasant set of cells.

A guard stood immediately. "Oy, and what would you be wantin'?"

"I came to torture the prisoner," Keir said firmly. "Open the cell."

"But, Lord Keir, there is no prisoner—"

"And how can you tell, Dudley? I didn't realize you'd been in my books, looking for spells of seeing."

The guardsman swallowed uncomfortably. "Beg pardon, Lord Keir. I'm just doing my job, aren't I, and avoiding . . . well, you know what I'm avoiding."

"Open the door, friend, and let me go in and have speech with the prisoner. He was brought down last night. I'm positive you were having a well-deserved meal at the time and missed his arrival. For all we know, there were others here during the night who rendered him senseless. I should think you would want to know as little about that as possible."

Dudley gulped, nodded, then opened the cell. Miach took a deep breath and hoped he wasn't making a monumental mistake. He slipped inside and tried not to protest when Morgan did the same thing. He didn't suppose Keir would lock them in and walk away—or find it a permanent solution for them—but Keir's hand was very unsteady as he held onto the door.

"Prisoner?" Keir called sharply. "Answer."

Miach let out his breath slowly, pushing away the unpleasant suspicions. It was Olc and Lugham and all their permutations that worked on him, nothing more. He dredged up the most feeble tone he could manage. "Aye, lord. I'm here and I plead again for mer—"

"Silence!" Keir thundered. He looked at Dudley. "I'm going to go in and torture him with a spell or two. He won't make any sounds, but that is of my choosing. Your task is to keep the door locked and pretend you haven't seen me. I have a particular grudge against this lad and don't want to be interrupted in my labors. If you do, or if you allow anyone else to do so, it won't go well for you."

Dudley nodded again, quickly shut the door behind Keir and locked it, then turned away and put his back to them. Keir walked swiftly to the back of the cell and began to feel along the wall. He finally murmured a handful of words. A spell of Fadairian glamour rent itself softly from top to bottom. Keir then fitted a key to a lock in the wall. A metal panel swung open soundlessly.

"Pray this works," he murmured.

Miach was ready to. He wasn't fond of dungeons, for obvious reasons, and the pitch blackness was more unsettling than he'd considered it might be. He felt Morgan grasp for his hand and squeeze, hard. He took a deep breath, nodded, then followed her into the yawning darkness.

He caught his breath as he ran into Morgan, who had run into what he could feel was a solid wall of spells.

"This is what I cannot best," Keir said quietly.

Miach removed the spells of concealment he'd placed over both himself and Morgan, then felt for Keir's arm. "Give me the key."

"What are you going to do?"

Miach forced himself to take deep, even breaths. "I'm going to lock the door behind us, then we'll see to these spells here. I don't think they're impenetrable. We may have to change ourselves into something less substantial to get through them, but we'll manage." He took the key, fitted it into the lock, then turned. He was tempted to lay a spell of aversion on the other side of the door, but it would have taken too much time and energy. He gave the key back to Keir, then felt for Morgan's hand. "Can you simply walk through those spells?"

"I'll try." She stepped forward, then suddenly made a noise of disgust. "I'm through," she said. She sounded as if she were trying to wipe the remains off her sleeves.

Miach put his hand on Keir's shoulder. "Let me hide your essence. I think the spell was, as you say, created specifically for you. Hiding who you are should be enough."

"You can try," Keir said, sighing deeply.

Miach supposed he could have been gentler, but he also supposed Keir would survive. He drew what little power—and it was a very little, indeed—Keir still had into the center of his being, then ruthlessly buried it along with any bits of himself that spoke too loudly of who he was. Keir gasped, then cursed Miach thoroughly.

"Try now," Miach suggested.

Keir walked through the spell. Miach followed along behind without hesitation. Keir stood next to Morgan, shivering.

"I wish I could repay you for that," he said grimly.

"You're welcome," Miach said with a smile.

Keir grunted. "I'll thank you when I think I won't be ill. For now, let's run. Straight ahead for a quarter league and hope to heaven no one's blocked the exit."

Miach shared that hope. He supposed he might be able to manufacture a trio of shovels, but that wasn't an appealing alternative to just finding the passageway open. He put his hands on Morgan's shoulders and put her in front of him.

He had no idea how long it took them to keep up a stumbling run along a floor clogged with things he didn't want to identify. Bones, rocks, filth: it could have been anything, or nothing at all. He didn't dare make any light. He merely ran behind Morgan, who was following Keir, and divided his time between trying not to trip over her when she stumbled and listening for things tripping over themselves behind him.

They burst out of the tunnel's end into a crisp, beautiful twilight. Miach placed a spell of un-noticing over their exit at Keir's request, then watched as Keir stood there, hunched over with his hands on his thighs, for far longer than was required to simply catch his breath. He straightened eventually, then dragged his sleeve across his eyes. Morgan embraced him before he could say anything, then continued to hold on to him for several minutes in silence. Miach met Keir's eyes over Morgan's head.

"Thank you, Miach," Keir said quietly.

"You would have done the same for me."

"Perhaps with a bit more finesse," Keir said with a faint snort. "I feel as if I've just had a sledgehammer dropped on my head."

Miach smiled. "I was in haste."

"Which we should be," Morgan said, pulling away from her brother. "I don't like the feeling here."

"We're near the house of the witchwoman of Fàs," Keir said.

"You have it aright, Mhorghain. 'Tis not a place to linger." He looked at Miach. "Where now?"

"Durial."

Keir took a deep breath, blew it out, then nodded. "We'll have to run."

Miach agreed. They weren't safe until they were behind King Uachdaran's very substantial walls and the journey was going to be longer than any of them would care for.

They had no other choice.

Two days later, Miach walked into a chamber full of souls he would have greeted pleasantly at another time. At the moment, he wished so desperately for a bed, he thought he might weep.

As awful as the passageway had been, the subsequent journey had been worse. They'd run for hours at a stretch and rested uneasily when they hadn't been able to run any longer. Finally, Miach had changed Keir's shape for him in a very businesslike and brisk manner to save his pride, and they'd flown the rest of the way under cover of spell. He'd helped Keir resume his proper form just outside palace walls and accepted his thanks and threat of retribution at some future date with a smile.

In truth, he wasn't sure he would have borne it so well himself if the roles had been reversed.

They'd been allowed in the gates of Léige, the palace of the king of Durial, thanks to some sort of miracle wrought by Sìle the day before. Miach supposed he would have the energy to listen to the tale at some point, but at the moment, it was all he could do to force himself to stay awake long enough to see Sìle's face when he caught sight of Keir walking into the chamber behind him.

It was worth the effort.

Sìle gaped for a moment or two, then strode forward and threw his arms around his grandson. He made many, many gruff noises that Miach was sure were substitutes for expressions of grief. Sosar clapped his nephew on the shoulder, then came to stand next to Miach.

"I sense a tale here," he said with a smile.

"I'll give it to you tomorrow," Miach said with a yawn, "or you can try your niece tonight. I don't think I could possibly do it justice right now."

"I'll tell you in a minute or two," Morgan said, taking Miach's hand. "Miach, look, there are the lads."

Miach looked blearily across the chamber to see Morgan's mercenary companions huddled there in a group, looking slightly overwhelmed. He allowed her to pull him across to the hearth where chairs had been set up along with, blessedly, a handful of cots.

He greeted Paien, the eldest of Morgan's companions, and Camid, a dwarf who looked particularly happy to be where he was, but he couldn't manage up any energy for the last two. Glines of Balfour would no doubt suggest a game of chance, which Miach would lose badly, and young Fletcher of Harding wouldn't do aught besides watch with wide eyes as Miach was robbed blind. He managed to acknowledge them both with a nod, but no more. Paien shoved a chair out of the way and pulled a cot over closer to the fire.

"Lay yourself down, Miach my lad, before you fall there."

Miach did, stretching out with a sigh of pure pleasure. He didn't protest when Morgan sat down with her back against his bed, though he was certain she would have been more comfortable in a chair. He kissed her cheek happily, then realized he didn't need to close his eyes because they were already closed.

He forced himself to at least check on his spells of defense. Tonight, again, things didn't seem as bad as they had been over the past several months.

He yawned hugely in spite of himself, then surrendered to weariness. His defenses were as secure as they had been the night before and he could do nothing else to strengthen them. A handful of hours spent sleeping wouldn't do any harm. He turned toward Morgan and put his arm around her shoulders.

He listened to her laugh at Paien and Camid's tales of foes vanquished along the way, marvel at the weight of Glines's purse and wonder at the percentage of it that might be credited to ill-gotten gains, and then quiz Fletcher about his improvement with the sword.

"My lady," Fletcher said in hushed tones, "I heard tell that yon archmage of Neroche entered Gobhann, but I can't believe 'tis true."

"Why not?" she asked. "Think you he is unequal to its horrors?"

Fletcher made a noise of distress. "He is powerful, surely, but, my lady Morgan, 'tis Weger's tower. No one gets out once they've gone in."

"You would be surprised," Morgan said dryly.

"I also heard," Fletcher continued, sounding awed, "that he went in to fetch something. It must have been something powerfully important to him to brave such a thing, don't you think?"

Miach felt Morgan squeeze his arm, then reach back to touch his face gently.

"I daresay, Fletcher, that it was," she said quietly.

Miach couldn't have agreed more. He caught Morgan's hand, kissed her palm, then remembered no more.

Fifteen

Morgan opened her eyes and looked up. Firelight flickered against an intricately carved ceiling high above her head, and the faint echo of song whispered across her mind. For a moment, panic assailed her. She'd woken in a strange place before with an unknown song ringing in her ears, but that chamber had been in the palace of Tor Neroche and the song had been one sung by the ring on her hand and the knife in her boot.

That day hadn't ended particularly well.

She wasn't at Tor Neroche now. She let out her breath slowly and peered into the darkness above her. She realized with a start that it wasn't wood that was so elaborately carved, it was stone. The song that marched through that stone was pleasing in a precise, stately sort of way, as if a clan of warriors from the north had bid their piper play something not quite a battle dirge, but surely not a love song.

She remembered then that she was in Léige, home of the dwarvish kings of Durial. She had watched her grandfather the night before as he'd fallen upon Keir's neck and wept. She had lost very badly in a quick game of cards with Glines as her other mercenary companions had told her of their journey there, bragging expansively about marvelously dangerous exploits that they would add to their already full tally of such accomplishments. She remembered taking Miach's boots off him as he lay where he'd fallen in front of the fire and doing him the favor of covering him with a blanket before she too had succumbed to slumber.

She sighed deeply, then turned to see who, if anyone, had been left behind to tend her whilst she slept.

Miach was sitting on the floor a handful of paces away from her, leaning back against a sturdy-looking sofa, resting his elbows on his bent knees, watching her.

He was, as she had often pointed out to herself, remarkably handsome with his dark hair falling across his forehead and his very pale blue eyes full of good humor. She wasn't sure if Master Soilléir had secretly gifted her a bit of his sight or she had just come to know Miach better, but she thought she could see something else around him, some layer of elvish glamour that he hadn't had before.

Or that could have been merely because he looked so clean. His hair was damp, as if he'd just come from a bath, and his boots were shined. All she knew was that she was quite thoroughly happy to see him first thing in the morning. On the floor next to him were all the blades she'd left behind in Tor Neroche. She suspected her companions had brought them for her, but she was quite certain Miach had laid them out in her preferred order.

She met his eyes. "I love you."

"I must have done something particularly pleasing to have earned that," he said with a smile.

She propped her head up on her hand. "Am I so stingy with my expressions of affection?"

"No indeed," he said, his eyes twinkling. "I was just teasing you and enjoying the fact that I'm at liberty to do so in a place that's safe."

She felt her smile fade and couldn't stop it. "Are we safe, then?"

"Aye," he said quietly. "King Uachdaran's walls wouldn't protect us indefinitely, but they are very strong and he is very powerful. We're safe enough for the moment."

"It was kind of him to offer us a refuge."

Miach smiled. "He has a long-standing affinity for lads and lasses from Neroche. My father made a point of sending him bolts of the finest Neroche's weavers can produce, a tradition my brother Cathar has kept up behind Adhémar's back. I daresay we're benefiting from that diligence."

"The dwarves aren't weavers, then?"

"Carvers of stone, miners of gems, and makers of very fine swords," Miach said. "But nay, they aren't much for weaving." He rubbed his hands together, then blew on them. "They aren't much for hot fires, either."

"You could come sit closer to me," she said casually. "Just to be closer to the fire, of course."

"Why, I think I just might."

She watched him walk over to her on his knees, then reached up and put her hand around the back of his head to pull it down where she could kiss him. She smiled up into his eyes.

"Is this one of those moments when the darkness recedes and we take a bit of peace for our own?"

He sat down next to her and smoothed her hair back from her face. "Please," he said with feeling. "Please let us have as many of those moments as possible today."

"Is that why you stayed with me?"

"Aye," he said quietly. "That, and I just wanted to watch you sleep. You're very beautiful, you know. And you looked very peaceful."

She felt neither beautiful nor peaceful; she felt ragged and drawn out, as if she'd been in a siege that had lasted far too long. But if Miach wanted to compliment her in ways she didn't deserve, she wasn't going to stop him. "Well, at least I don't dream anymore."

"A fact for which I am most grateful."

She smiled and reached out to brush his hair out of his eyes. "Did we miss breakfast?"

"Aye, but I imagine I can find the kitchens if you're hungry. You've been promised a bath as well, if you like. Servants await your pleasure outside in the passageway. I think we can hide out for another hour or two, then we'll most likely need to make an appearance. There are those in the palace who would like to see you."

"I hesitate to ask who."

"I'll tell you after you eat, when you've the stomach for it. They're mostly my relatives, which I'm sure eases your mind greatly. They have all pointed out to me that I'm very fortunate to have caught your eye at all, so perhaps your mind should be eased in truth."

She smiled. "I don't know if I deserve any ease, given what my grandfather put you through. Keir as well." She paused. "Sìle was happy to see him, wasn't he?"

"He was in tears, though I'm not sure if that had more to do with seeing your brother, or his intense headache."

She folded her hands together and rested her chin on them. "What happened to him?"

Miach settled himself more comfortably. "Well, there is a bit of a tale there, but since we're at our leisure, perhaps you won't mind my relating it."

She managed a smile, loving him all the more for knowing how desperately she wanted to hide for a bit longer. "Thank you."

"Surely you jest," he said, leaning forward to kiss her softly. "You, in front of a marginally useful fire, without a chaperon in sight? I should be thanking you for the excuse to linger. I'll tell you tales all day for the privilege, if you like."

She nodded happily. She had forgotten in the madness of elves and wizards and darkness pressing against her from all sides just how pleasant it was to sit with Miach and enjoy his company.

Would that she might do so long into her old age.

"Now, as you might imagine," he began with a thoughtful frown, as if he discussed something of particular import, "elves and dwarves have traditionally not gotten on very well. That problem is only exacerbated by an elvish belief in their race's inherent, um—"

"Superiority?" she offered.

He shot her a smile. "Aye, that. Fortunately for us, King Gilraehen and his lovely bride arrived a se'nnight ago and smoothed the way for us all."

"Did they?" Morgan asked, finding that her heart was suddenly beating uncomfortably fast. "Queen Mehar is here? I hesitate to ask why."

Miach brushed stray strands of hair back from her face. "To give you whatever aid you ask of her, I imagine. She convinced King Uachdaran to allow us to use his smithy—which wasn't hard, actually, considering this was where she forged the Sword of Angesand in the first place. She also made certain your lads were allowed in and that the gates weren't barred against your grandfather. I think your friend Camid also put in a good word for anyone of our particular company from last fall, even though he is a northern dwarf and is therefore under suspicion since he prefers roaming to mining. But you can thank your grandfather for the luxury we're enjoying and the niceties we'll enjoy later."

"What did he do?"

"It would seem that by the time he arrived, King Uachdaran was prepared to choke back his gall and humor your grandfather with all manner of concessions, beginning with grudgingly providing a very fine, delicate wine at supper to appease the dainty sensibilities of the elven king. What I heard from a very reliable source is that Sìle looked at the goblet in front of him, then at the heavy pewter mug in front of his host, then he turned to King Uachdaran's page and said firmly, 'I'll have what he's having.' Their Majesties then descended happily into their royal cups filled with very strong ale, only to later stumble together from the hall singing raunchy Duriallian pub songs. Relations between Durial and Tòrr Dòrainn were thus forever changed."

"You jest," Morgan said, fighting her smile.

"Sosar assures me 'tis the absolute truth. I suspect Làidir won't recognize his father when he sees him again."

"Is this a good thing?" she asked.

Miach smiled mischievously. "Sìle has terrorized and intimidated his neighbors for centuries. It wouldn't hurt him to make a few friends amongst them for a change. There are, after all, only nine kingdoms making up the council of kings. He might like to make an ally or two on that council for a change. I don't think the exclusivity of his kingdom would suffer for it."

"Eyewitness reports of his splendidness would only enhance his reputation, is that it?"

Miach laughed. "Precisely. The tremors that will run through your family will be felt for generations, no doubt."

She trailed her fingers over the back of his hand resting on the edge of the cot until she trusted herself to speak. "You know, it is difficult to think on. All that family," she added, meeting his eyes. "I was very fortunate to be cared for as a child and during my youth, truly, but I can't deny that it is a pleasure to know there is somewhere I belong only because of my blood."

He smiled and captured her hand, holding it tightly with his. "I think Keir is just as overwhelmed. Rùnach is as well, no doubt. I know it doesn't make up for all those years of being alone, Morgan, but I hope it will add happiness to your future."

She leaned over and kissed his hand before she thought better of it. "You were more than enough for my future," she said quietly, "but I'll be happy to have them as well."

He blinked rapidly, then frowned at her. "Damned smoky fire," he said gruffly.

She smiled and squeezed his hand. "You have a tender heart, my lord, and apparently very sensitive eyes." She sat up and dragged her hands through her grimy hair. "I would love a bath, I think, then something to eat before I'm presented to relatives and lose my appetite."

He crawled to his feet and pulled her up to hers. " 'Tis just Gilraehen and Mehar. Well, and Yngerame and Màire." He paused. "And Harold and Catrìona."

"So many of them?" she asked uneasily.

"And those are just mine. We haven't discussed yours." His smile faded. "Morgan, you are a wielder of the Sword of Angesand. Mehar and Gilraehen came to offer you strength in the reforging of that sword. Yngerame and Màire came to do for you what they can—and to give us their blessing. I daresay Catrìona merely wanted to meet the woman who has me so turned about." He paused. "I understand Harry only came because he wanted one last chance to tell you to run."

She laughed a bit. "I can't imagine that—" She stopped and looked at him in surprise. "You said Catrìona. That isn't the same one who taught her sword to sing, is it?"

"Aye."

"But you said she was dead."

He smiled. "I never said she was dead, I said she had lived a very long time ago. You were having nightmares; I didn't want to burden you with unnecessary details."

She considered. "Was she one of the wielders of the Sword of Angesand?"

"You can ask her yourself, but I don't know if she'll tell you. Her tale is shrouded in mystery."

"Are you again avoiding burdening me with unnecessary details?"

"I might be," he agreed with half a laugh. "I know you don't need the spell to make your sword sing, but I'm quite sure Catrìona will share many others with you, if you like. A very resourceful gel, that one."

"Isn't she your grandmother somewhere back in the mists of time?" Morgan asked, looking at him sideways. "Do you think it's entirely proper to call her *gel*?"

"Meet her and see," was all he said as he smiled and pulled her toward the door.

Three hours later, bathed, fed, and dressed properly in a black velvet gown with a discreet silver crown atop her head, Morgan was ready to find the nearest guard tower, climb to its height, and fling herself off in dragonshape.

It wasn't the food, which had been wonderful, or the sight of astoundingly beautiful dwarvish women alongside particularly unattractive dwarvish men, which had been startling, or being bowed and scraped to by almost everyone she'd seen, which had been just as uncomfortable as it had been in Seanagarra. It was the fact that even though she'd managed to miss a formal lunch by hiding with Miach in the library, she now had no more excuses and she was doomed to face her future.

Or her past, rather.

Future, past, present: she wasn't sure where she was in any of those, or what she was getting ready to walk into. All she knew was on the other side of those exquisitely carved doors were relatives she couldn't remember, friends she could, and discussions about the task that lay in front of her that she couldn't bear to listen to any longer.

"Your hand is cold."

Miach brought her hand to his mouth and blew on it, though it did little to aid her. She was happy to have him standing there next to her dressed in black, as usual, though he'd forgone the circlet of silver on top of his head. His sword was propped up with hers back in the enormous chamber they seemed to be sharing with most everyone they knew, but he had Weger's dagger tucked down the side of his boot. That, at least, was reassuring since she'd had to leave Mehar's knife behind, not having had a decent place to stash it. She'd left her other blades in the chamber as well, for the same reason. The knives Miach had made her, however, were strapped to her forearms and her long, dripping sleeves hid them well enough, though she supposed those sleeves wouldn't do much to hide the trembles she couldn't seem to stop.

"I'm nervous," she said, adding a curse that didn't do anything to aid her. She took off her crown and looked at him. " 'Tis ridiculous."

He turned and put his arms around her. "It isn't."

"You're not nervous."

"Oh, I am," he said with a half laugh. "You would be too if you knew how furious Sgath is going to be that I took you to Tòrr Dòrainn instead of Lake Cladach. I imagine my ears will be ringing for quite some time to come."

"No wonder you wanted to skip lunch," she managed. "You're more devious than I give you credit for being."

"Guilty," he agreed, then he pulled back far enough to smile at her. "A distraction?"

"Only if it's the kind where we dash for the nearest open space and change shape to fly off into the sunset."

"I've corrupted you."

"Thoroughly. And since you have, 'tis your duty to now distract me."

He smiled briefly, then bent his head and kissed her. Morgan put her arms around his neck and held on partly because her knees tended to buckle when he kissed her and partly because she was indeed very nervous and it seemed the best way to stay on her feet. Now, if she'd been facing a keep guarded by scores of well-armed and highly trained guardsmen, she wouldn't have given it another thought. Dozens of lads with her death on their minds and their swords gleaming dully in the moonlight? Not worth a yawn. But a chamber full of relatives and potential relatives-by-future-marriage she didn't know?

Terrifying.

"Morgan?"

She had left off kissing Miach and instead buried her face against his neck where he might not notice her trembling. "Aye?"

"They've opened the door. I think they've seen you."

Damnation. Too late to escape. She pulled away reluctantly. "Don't leave me."

"I won't." He took her crown from her and plopped it onto her head. "Let's go."

She took a deep breath, then turned to face the gaggle of souls she was sure she wouldn't recognize.

Only that wasn't the case. She knew Eulasaid and Sgath immediately. She had thought that perhaps Keir resembled Sìle, but now she could see he resembled their other grandfather to a greater degree. Eulasaid was simply stunning; not elvish, but so full of power and beauty of an entirely different sort that Morgan caught her breath in spite of herself.

But most startling of all was that she knew them. She remembered sitting on her grandfather's lap and listening to him tell of the wonders of Ainneamh where he had grown to manhood. She could now bring to mind several walks along the shores of a beautiful lake with her grandmother, listening to her memories that stretched back into the far reaches of time. They had loved her and protected her and kept her close whilst they could.

She walked over to them, feeling as if she were floating. She released Miach's hand to embrace her grandmother, felt her eyes burn at Eulasaid's tears, then turned to be embraced and wept over by her grandfather.

Sgath took her face in his hands, kissed her on both cheeks, then pulled her close again. He cleared his throat roughly. "Miach, lad, I have a few things to discuss with you."

Miach sighed lightly. "I thought you might, my lord."

"I can't scrape those runes of Sìle's off your wrist, you miserable little wretch, but I could cover them with many unpleasant things. Well, not Mhorghain's, of course, but yours? Aye, I could do that without much effort at all."

"I imagine you could, my lord."

Morgan looked up at her grandfather. "It isn't his fault," she said, attempting a smile. "I honestly didn't know who I was. I wasn't convinced until we reached Seanagarra, and not even then, at first. Once I knew, we had no choice but to keep pressing forward."

Sgath put his hands on her shoulders. "I know, love. Sosar told us all about your adventures. I'm just trying to instill the proper level of respect and terror in your betrothed. He thinks I'm nigh on to doddering about like an old fool, so I take every opportunity to remind him that that isn't the case."

He smiled at Miach as he said it, so Morgan supposed he wasn't all that serious about any of his words. Eulasaid was embracing Miach warmly, and smiling up at him, so obviously she wasn't overly opposed to him either.

Keir soon joined them, followed in time by Sìle and Sosar. Morgan listened to them talk about things that had happened long before she was born and was happy to stand beside Miach and discuss things that had nothing to do with her.

And then Miach took her hand.

"Ready for the others?"

She supposed there was no point in being honest, so she merely nodded as if she were indeed ready, then allowed Miach to lead her over to meet others she might want to know. She was happier than she likely should have been to have his hand to clutch as she found herself introduced to the relatives that seemed to have come not only for his benefit.

She had no trouble identifying Gilraehen of Neroche, mostly because he and Miach did look indeed very much alike and they definitely shared the same pale, spooky eyes, as Weger had once said. Unfortunately, meeting Gilraehen meant meeting his wife.

Morgan faced Mehar of Angesand and wondered if she was more uncomfortable meeting a woman who had long outlived many others of her vintage, or if she were uncomfortable because she'd taken the woman's sword and smashed it to bits.

Morgan made Mehar a curtsey, happy that she'd taken the trouble to learn how, then straightened and wondered how best to begin her confession.

Mehar took her hands and saved her the trouble. "So, you're Mhorghain," she said, smiling. "I'm happy to finally meet you. I understand you've had quite a few adventures during the past few months."

Morgan swallowed, hard. "I'm sorry about your sword, Your Majesty."

"Call me Mehar and don't fret about the sword," Mehar said dismissively. "It had seen more than its share of battle and likely needed a bit of refurbishment. We'll reforge it tomorrow and add to it things that will serve you for your turn as its keeper. I understand from your companions, particularly young Fletcher, who admires you greatly, that the sword sang for you."

"It did," Morgan agreed. "As did the knife. And the ring." She paused. "Do you want those back?"

"No, indeed," Mehar said. "I left them with Nicholas for you long before you were born, which I suppose you know by now. The ring won't serve you as a weapon, but it might offer you comfort. The song it sings is a love song." She smiled. "I imagine Miach knew that, didn't you, love?"

Morgan felt Miach's arm go around her shoulders. "Of course, Grandmother."

Gilraehen clapped a hand on Miach's shoulder. "Mhorghain, you can do what you like with the ring, but I suggest you keep that dagger close. You can use it on your lord here when he gets too cheeky, which he has a tendency to do."

Morgan agreed and tried to concentrate on listening to Mehar and Gilraehen both tease Miach about various things, but she was soon distracted by the other conversations going around her. She hadn't anticipated that it would be simply a reunion of relatives who hadn't seen each other in a bit, but she was surprised by how casually those relatives were discussing the conditions of the Nine Kingdoms and what had to be done at Gair's well.

She wished heartily that she and Miach were still hiding in the library.

She found herself introduced to others in time, most notably Catrìona of Croxteth, lately of Neroche, who ran into the chamber with a man who was apparently her husband, Harold. She was breathless and laughing and her husband was blushing. Morgan watched them after they'd both greeted her with hearty kisses on the cheek before hastening off to talk to others. She slipped her arm through Miach's and leaned up to whisper in his ear.

"I think there's a hayloft here."

He lifted one eyebrow. "Think you?"

"Aye. And I daresay King Harold and his bride have recently been in it."

Miach glanced at them, then laughed. "I told you that you would like her. A perfectly cheeky gel, that one. I think she missed more court functions during her time at Tor Neroche than she attended."

"I hesitate to ask what she was doing."

He winked at her. "Grinding her guardsmen into the dust, among other things. I'm sure she'll have a few suggestions for you about it all."

Morgan imagined she would as well.

Miach was soon pulled away by Keir to discuss spells with Gilraehen, leaving her wandering from group to group, looking for the least uncomfortable conversation to be a part of. It wasn't that she wasn't interested in what the others had to say about Gair and his well; she just wasn't particularly interested in talking about it herself.

Besides, it didn't matter how much anyone talked about it, the facts were the same: Lothar was actively trying to open the well, Cruadal was actively seeking to use her as a bargaining chip for what he really wanted, and she needed the time to get to the well, find the word she needed, and close the bloody thing before either of them could manage it. As far as she was concerned, there was only one thing to do and that was get to that business as quickly as possible and have it over with.

She came back to herself to find Miach watching her gravely from across the room. She looked at him, then tilted her head ever so slightly toward the door they'd come in earlier. He nodded, just as slightly. She looked about her casually, then backed up, preparing to flee.

"And just where do you think you're off to?"

Morgan whirled around to find Catrìona of Croxteth standing behind her. She took a deep breath. "I need air."

"Is that all?"

Morgan reached up and plucked a piece of straw from Catrìona's hair and handed it to her. "You missed that."

Catrìona blinked, then laughed softly. "Thank you, Mhorghain." She studied her for a moment, then smiled. "I like you. Come and stay with us for a bit after you and Miach wed. Do you ride?"

"Barely."

"But you bear Weger's mark, which means you're my sort of gel." She looked over Morgan's shoulder, then moved past her. "I'll distract your grandfather Sìle for you now, if you'd like to bolt. I think he's moving this way with the express intention of talking to you."

Morgan thanked her most kindly, ducked behind some former king of Neroche or another, then hurried toward the door. She hastened out into the passageway, then leaned back against the wall and sighed, grateful for the simple pleasure of quiet. She closed her eyes and enjoyed it for only a handful of moments before Miach came hurrying through that same door.

"Run," he said.

She did. She ran with him through passageways, past elaborately carved wooden doors, and out into the open. Miach pulled her back to a walk and laughed a bit as he caught his breath.

"Thank you," he said, with feeling. "I was ready not to talk any longer. You, too?"

"Very," she said, pulling her crown off her head and slipping it over her arm like a bracelet. "Where to now?"

"The hayloft is likely off-limits, but I would settle for a walk in Uachdaran's gardens. Interested?"

"Please. Anything to be out of that chamber."

It wasn't but a quarter hour later that she was walking with him under trees that were like none other she'd seen. They were gnarled and tangled, full of intricate twistings and turnings, looking a great deal like the ceiling she'd woken underneath that morning. Perhaps that had been intentional on the carver's part. The trees that made a canopy over her head now didn't leave her feeling stifled, though, they left her feeling embraced. The breath of air that found its way through the still-leafless branches carried with it a song, the same sort of song she'd heard in the stone that morning.

There were, she decided, many things she'd seen over the past half year that she never would have dreamed might exist.

"Well?" Miach asked finally. "What do you think?"

She sighed and looked up at him. "In truth? I think you and I should slip out during supper and be about this task. We could be back before they finished their wine."

He put his arm around her shoulders and continued on along the path they were taking. "I am tempted to agree," he said, "but we cannot. We need the power of the Sword of Angesand."

"Do we?" she asked, looking up at him in surprise. "Why?"

He looked at her thoughtfully. "Were you truly asleep whilst Keir and I talked in your father's solar, or were you eavesdropping?"

She sighed. "The latter, which I'm sure you already knew."

"Aye, I suspected as much." He took a deep breath. "Then you heard what he said about how your father took both his and Rùnach's power?"

She nodded.

"Unfortunately thanks to that additional power, your father's strength was far greater than it should have been when he wrenched open that well. That leads me to believe that it will take more than the usual measure of strength to close that well."

"But how will I have any of the sword's power?"

He smiled. "You'll put your hand on the hilt, it will blaze with magelight, and you'll feel as if a horse has just trampled you."

She pursed her lips. "I know that feeling. It was what I felt when you helped me heal Rùnach's hand."

"Only this time, you won't faint," he said. "I promise. The sword will know you, just as it did in the great hall of Tor Neroche. The power may startle you, but it won't crush you. It will give you strength when you've exhausted your own. We'll make certain of that tomorrow."

"If you say so."

He laced his fingers with hers and smiled at her. "Just walk with me now, Morgan, and leave the rest. We'll face it soon enough."

She nodded, then walked with him until they reached the outer wall and the path ended. It seemed a fitting reflection of their situation.

She looked up at Miach. "What now?"

He turned her to him and took her hands. "We'll reforge the sword in the morning, send out scouts to see what's afoot, then set off ourselves to do what we must. Then, after the well is closed, I think we just might go back to Seanagarra and sleep for a se'nnight."

She smiled and put her arms around his waist. "You could use it."

"So, my love, could you. But for now, let us see if we might find a quiet place to rest a bit whilst I see to my spells, then we'll hope for supper and a bit of dancing. King Uachdaran does set a remarkably fine table and he employs only the finest musicians."

She nodded, but she didn't release him, nor did he release her. He merely ran his hand over her hair again and again, breathing lightly, not speaking. Finally, she pulled back far enough to look at him.

"Do you think Lothar will be there?" she asked. "Not that I'm afraid of him. I've faced him before." She paused. "Admittedly, I went right along with what he wanted me to do and fainted from the poison he gave me to drink, but I would be better prepared this time. He couldn't be any worse than Droch, surely."

Miach started to speak, then shook his head helplessly. "That's a bit like saying 'tis better to be slain by a blade in the heart than be staked out in the hot eastern sun and baked to death. Droch is direct and brutal. Lothar may drag things out a bit more out of politeness, but I daresay the end result is the same." He put his arm around her shoulders and led her back up the path. "In truth, I think it would be best if we planned to get into the glade and out as quickly as possible and leave Lothar out of it."

"And if he comes?"

He sighed deeply. "I think all we can do is prepare as best we can. The most important thing is what we already have, and that is your courage. The rest is all plotting and scheming and spells. It is the stomach to use them that will win the day."

She nodded because she knew he had it aright. Hadn't she thought the same thing in Ceangail? Perhaps they could take the evening, have a decent meal, then turn their minds to less serious matters.

"You're thinking about dancing."

She smiled without looking at him. "I've become soft, haven't I?"

"Nay, you haven't. You've just seen why I enjoy it so."

"Have you always been a dancer, Miach?"

"Nay, Morgan," he said quietly. "Just with you."

She nodded and continued on with him, saying nothing. There was no more to say. Their path was set out before them, and there was neither turning back nor altering what lay ahead.

She was past wishing there might be.

Sixteen

Miach walked through twisting passageways with Morgan, following the dwarf who'd been sent to escort them to the smithy. He was carrying the shards of the Sword of Angesand in a drawstring bag whilst Morgan carried the hilt. He'd had a surprisingly good night's sleep, but he suspected he was the only one. Morgan had been out in the lists when he'd woken and gone to look for her. She'd been fighting Paien and Glines at the same time and looking as if she hadn't slept at all. Her expression had given nothing away, but he knew her well enough to realize that she was extremely ill at ease. Matters weren't improving any as they continued on their way.

"Who will be here?" she asked, finally.

"You and I and the master smith," he answered. "He is the grandson's grandson's grandson of the man who helped Mehar forge the sword in the first place. He is quite honored to be of service to us."

She nodded, then looked up at him. "Are we enough to give it the power it needs? Won't doing so put us both in bed for a se'nnight?"

"Aye," he conceded reluctantly. "If we were to do a proper job of it, it might."

She looked down and watched the floor for quite a bit longer before she spoke. "Would Mehar and Gilraehen be willing to help, do you think?"

"That is the reason they came. They just didn't want to intrude on something you might have wanted to do alone."

"Would anyone else be handy?"

He smiled in spite of himself. "You can only pour so much magic into steel, love, before it bursts of its own accord, but we might manage a bit of power from Harold and Catrìona as well. I daresay they would come gladly, if you wanted them to."

She looked up at him. "You know I don't like asking for aid."

"I know. But considering what lies along the road ahead, help isn't anything to be refused at this point. Why don't I send a messenger for them when we reach the fire?"

She nodded and said no more, but simply held his hand and walked with him down passageways that weren't meant for men of any height at all. Miach ignored the necessity to duck continually, and continued on.

Fortunately, the smithy was spacious and the ceilings stretched up into darkness his eye couldn't pierce. It was cold, in spite of the furnaces. That was no doubt pleasing to the lads there, but he was sure it wasn't to Morgan. Her hand was already cold as death.

He drew aside a likely lad and sent him on with messages for the appropriate personages, then sat on a stool next to Morgan and discussed with the master, Ceardach, what would need to be done to weave spells into the folding of the blade. He listened, but in the back of his mind he wondered just how much of their own power Mehar and Gil had poured into the original blade and what it had cost them in trade. The current refashioning of the blade needed to imbue it with power as well, but he couldn't spare all his reserves or he would have nothing to offer Morgan at the well. He looked up and was, he had to admit, very glad to see Gilraehen, Mehar,

Harold, and Catrìona all coming into the smithy looking quite fresh and spry.

They would need to be.

It turned into a very long morning. It wasn't so much the actual forging of the blade that was difficult, though Master Ceardach was exceptionally particular about its crafting. It was the layering it with spells and pouring power into it that took time and effort. Miach didn't say anything, but he was very aware that the others were sparing him and Morgan the bulk of the work. Catrìona spent a goodly bit of time discussing with Morgan just how the blade should be balanced and how she preferred to feel it in her hand whilst Mehar visibly drained herself of power that went into the blade. Miach shot Harold a dry look when his grandfather several generations removed attempted the same thing with him.

"Your battle will come later, Miach," was all Harold would say.

Even with the lightened burden, Miach was more than happy when the work was done and he was able to go sit on a stool with his back up against a chilly stone wall and rest. Gilraehen sat down next to him.

"You know, Miach," he said slowly, "I don't think it would be a poor idea to keep that blade hidden."

"Do you mean send it back to Tor Neroche?" Miach asked in surprise.

Gilraehen shook his head. "Nay, lad, not that. As much as I would like to think you and Morgan will merely skip along a lovely path and find yourselves alone at the well with time on your hands to do a leisurely job of shutting the bloody thing, I . . . well, I—" He thrust his chin out and seemed to be looking for the right words.

"You imagine Lothar will be there."

"Don't you?"

"It wouldn't surprise me," Miach said with a sigh. "I know he's been there recently because he repaired a spell I had destroyed.

Worse still, there are signs that someone else is trying to open the well." He looked at his grandfather. "If we manage to gain the glade unmolested, I will be surprised. I'll be even more astonished if we have any peace to shut it."

"All the more reason to be prepared." Gilraehen looked at him seriously. "If I were you, I would go expecting the worst, with as many weapons as possible. Lothar's had a taste of Mehar's sword before and he fears it. It might be a handy thing for your lady to have hidden, don't you think?"

"What are you suggesting?" Miach asked, already knowing the answer. "A spell of concealment, perhaps wrought from Olc?"

"As repulsive a thought as that is, aye, that's what I'm suggesting."

"I could weave the spell so a single thread pulled would unravel it completely—and instantly," Miach said unwillingly.

"You're a clever lad, aren't you?"

Miach shot him a disgruntled look. "Why do I always feel as if I haven't quite graduated to long trousers when I'm around you?"

Gilraehen elbowed him companionably. "Because 'tis my duty as your grandfather just a step or two away from my dotage to keep you in your place. You *are* barely out of short pants from my point of view."

Miach smiled in spite of himself. Gilraehen of Neroche might have had a bit of silver glinting at his temples, but in all other aspects, he looked not a day over a score and ten. Dotage, indeed.

"I should live to see your length of days," Miach said quietly.

"Make sure that you do," Gilraehen said, suddenly serious. "For your lady and for the realm. I don't need to tell you to be careful, nor not to underestimate Lothar, but I'll tell you as much just the same. I'm quite certain he does little besides sit in his wreck of a hall and think on ways to vex his enemies. You in particular, these days. Be wary."

"I will," Miach promised. He glanced at Morgan, Mehar, and Catrìona, who were standing over the sword, apparently teaching it to sing, then turned to Gilraehen and his son Harold, who had sat down next to his father. "Thank you. I know what you both did this morning."

Harold shrugged. "Father and I have no pressing appointments for the next few days. We can sleep; you cannot."

"Not that that wife of yours will let you sleep," Gilraehen said with a snort. "You would think her years would have taken a toll on her somehow."

"Never," Harold said with a smile. "The woman will drive me into the ground someday. She is absolutely exhausting."

Miach didn't think Harold sounded particularly displeased by that. He leaned back against the wall and watched the three women gathered together, discussing spells and steel. He admired them all in turn.

Mehar was, he would readily admit, one of his favorite people. She was just as likely to sit down and tell a tale to a small child as she was to leap onto the back of some Angesand steed she'd talked the current lord of Angesand out of and ride like the wind. She was a weaver of cloth, spells, and love that had been felt in his family for generations.

Catrìona was, much as Harry had said, an effervescent spring that bubbled up continually into a fountain of merriment. Though she had certainly seen her share of sorrow, somehow when she entered a hall, the fire sparkled brighter and the music shimmered more sweetly, seemingly just to please her. She and Mehar were lovely, courageous, and full of magic that they had honed over centuries.

And then there was the third lass standing there. Miach looked at Morgan and felt something in his heart give way as it always did when he looked at her. She was terribly beautiful, true, but that wasn't what he saw now. He watched her moving in a world that was uncomfortable for her, yet she pressed on. He watched her take spells from Catrìona and Mehar and use them, though he knew she wasn't happy with how easily they came to her hands.

But she didn't flinch or shy away.

"Besotted, isn't he?" Harold remarked in a loud whisper.

"Very," his father agreed.

Miach looked at them both. "Can you fault me for it?"

They both shook their heads, smiling as if they understood perfectly.

"Your Morgan doesn't need you to," Gilraehen remarked, "but guard her well just the same. And tell her daily that you realize how fortunate you are she looked at you twice."

"I agree, Father," Harold said with a smile. "It works wonders."

Miach looked at them both wryly. "Any other words of advice?"

"Have you wooed her well?" Gilraehen asked.

"Ah—"

"Go have a nap," Harold suggested. "We'll have a list of appropriate ideas waiting for you when you wake. Really, Miach, you would think you could manage this on your own."

Miach favored his progenitors with a choice curse or two and had laughter as his reward. A nap, however, sounded like the best idea he'd heard all morning. Morgan needed it far worse than he did and he was completely spent. He pushed himself to his feet and went to stand next to his lady.

"Have I told you today how fortunate I am you looked at me twice?" he asked politely.

Predictably, she looked at him as if he'd lost his mind.

He shot his grandfathers a pointed look, then made Mehar and Catrìona bows before he took Morgan's hand. "I think there might be a free spot in front of a hearth somewhere. Let's go make use of it whilst we're able to."

Morgan nodded wearily, thanked Mehar and Catrìona for their aid, then walked with him from the smithy. She was silent until they'd reached the ground level of the palace, then she looked up at him.

"They spared us, didn't they?"

"They did," he agreed, "though they tried to be subtle."

"It was very kind."

"They're under no illusions about what you face, Morgan. I daresay you would have done the same in their place. For all you know, you will someday for someone else."

She shivered. "I can't bring myself to think about that." She paused for several minutes before she spoke again. "When do you want to leave? Tonight?"

"I think it best, don't you?"

She nodded, then put her shoulders back. "I'll look at the spells again whilst you work. I might see something new."

"Of course," he said, because he knew he wouldn't convince her to do anything else. He had the feeling, and it wasn't a pleasant one, that no matter how long or hard they looked at what they already had, they wouldn't find the last part of the spell until they reached the well itself.

He only hoped they would have the time to look for it there before all hell broke loose.

They left at twilight. He would have preferred to have gone with Morgan alone, but he'd never thought he would manage that. Sìle had flatly refused to be left behind and Miach didn't bother to ask Sosar or Keir what their wishes were. The only thing that surprised him was how adamant Morgan's companions were about insisting they would come as well.

"A sword is as sharp as a spell in the right hands," Fletcher had said wisely.

Miach suspected Morgan had already begun to introduce Fletcher to a few of Weger's simpler strictures, or perhaps it was one that she'd muttered so often under her breath that her mates had simply learned it perforce.

He didn't waste breath arguing with any of them. He wasn't sure they wouldn't need all the aid they could gather. He bid farewell to various and sundry progenitors, thanked King Uachdaran profusely for his hospitality and the loan of his smithy, then turned to the business of convincing the horses they wanted to fly again.

Hearn's horses were, surprisingly, chomping at the bit to once again wear dragonshape. Even the elvish horses were looking fairly enthusiastic. Miach turned them all into powerful dragons, glittering and fierce-looking. He looked over his shoulder to see how Morgan's companions were reacting. They were maintaining expressions of absolute stoicism. Well, save Fletcher who gaped, then turned and lost his supper in the weeds.

"Told you he'd be trouble," Paien muttered under his breath. He looked at Miach. "I said as much to Morgan outside Istaur last fall, but she insisted that we bring him along. Not to worry, though. I'll go slap some spine into him. I'll make him ride with me after I've done so. He'd likely fall off, otherwise."

Miach left him to it, made sure Glines and Camid were comfortable with reins and no stirrups, then left Sosar, Sìle, and Keir to sort out who was riding with whom on the elvish horses-turned-dragons. Once the company was mounted, he cast a spell over all their essences, then turned to Morgan.

"You don't mind flying?"

"I prefer it," she said grimly. "I need something to do."

He nodded, then began his own spell of shapechanging, watching Morgan as she did the same. Within the space of a pair of heartbeats, they were rising in the air and turning toward the west.

Two days later, Miach paced around the outer edge of their camp, wishing they had dared make a fire. Sìle had covered the place with his glamour and Miach had covered that with a Lughamian spell of aversion, but that hadn't guaranteed them anything besides a bit of peace. It hadn't provided any warmth, nor light past what the moon was willing to give. It was just as well; he couldn't look at Rùnach's notes any longer. He had all the spells memorized anyway. He suspected Morgan did as well.

"Miach."

Miach looked at Sosar leaning against a bare, misshapen tree. "Aye?"

"Go rest if you can, lad. I'll keep watch."

Miach shook his head. "I'm fine."

"You might be," he said quietly, with a nod toward the camp behind him, "but there are others who aren't."

Miach turned to look at Morgan. He'd thought she was asleep, but he realized now that her eyes were open. He bowed his head and rubbed the back of his neck for a moment or two, then nodded his thanks to Morgan's uncle, and walked over to squat down next to her.

"I thought you were sleeping."

She shook her head, but said nothing.

He found another blanket to put over her, then lay down beside her and put his arm over her waist. He propped his head up on his hand and looked at her gravely. "I didn't know you were awake, Morgan. I would have come sooner otherwise."

"I can usually at least scold myself into sleeping," she said wearily, "but not tonight. It isn't as if I fear dreaming any longer. Not now." She shrugged helplessly. "I'm not sure what ails me."

Miach smoothed the hair back from her face. "Dragon wildness," he said gently. " 'Tis a bit like too much rich food at supper. It leads to restless nights."

She attempted a smile, but didn't manage it very well. "Tell me a tale, Miach," she whispered. "Something pleasant. Something to take my mind off . . . well, off what's before us."

He tucked strands of hair behind her ear, one by one, before he trusted himself to meet her gaze and not reveal the depths of his distress for her. He took a deep breath, then smiled at her. "Of course, my love," he said, leaning forward to kiss her cold lips briefly. "I think I can bring to mind something that will suit you quite well. There are swords wielded, mages humiliated, battles won in glorious fashion." He paused. "There will no doubt be copious amounts of romance in it."

"I'm too unsettled to make the comment that last bit deserves."

He smiled. "Shall I try to keep those parts to a minimum for you?"

"Nay," she managed. "I think I've acquired a taste for your brand of it. Clandestine forays into places no sensible soldier would go, visits to elven palaces, pleasant mornings in dwarvish smithies. I'm not quite sure what you'll do in the future to outdo any of that."

"Flowers?"

She managed a half laugh. "I can just imagine what you grow in your garden, my lord."

"You'll find out by and by," he promised. "Now, come you here and put your head on my shoulder before I begin." He waited until she was settled, then took a deep breath. "There was once a lad, the youngest son of the eldest son of an obscure house in the mountains, who despaired of ever finding someone to love. If you were to ask my opinion, though, I daresay his heart was wiser than his head and knew that there was a gel he was destined to love the moment he first saw her—"

"Miach?"

"Aye?"

"You're not off to a promising start with this thing."

He kissed her hair, then felt for her hand and laced his fingers with hers. "Have patience. I think the lass will draw her sword soon and use it on her would-be suitor. You'll enjoy that bit."

She sighed and squeezed his hand. "I daresay."

"Now," he continued, "as it happened, this shieldmaiden had spent her youth on business of her own, learning to loathe all sorts of things that likely deserved it, and honing her skill with a blade far beyond what most men could endure."

"Save the lad, I assume."

"Well, he didn't neglect his studies with the sword, but he was nowhere near her equal. I've heard tell that after he and the gel met, he did his best not to let her thrash him completely whenever they met over blades, but I daresay it was a very dodgy thing, indeed.

But we're getting ahead of ourselves. It happened, as these things do, that the lad met the lass and he did indeed fall in love with her the moment he laid eyes on her, and he loved her more with every day that passed. There was a task laid before them, a very unpleasant one, but the accomplishing of that task is a tale better left for daylight. What we'll concern ourselves with now is what happened after their work was finished."

He waited for her to say something, but she didn't so he went on, describing in great detail all the court functions they would avoid and the lovely hours they would pass in the lists at Tor Neroche where he could personally guarantee she would not be training in the bitter cold that seemed to be a fundamental part of Gobhann. He turned then to things he was sure would please her, such as a view of the sea from the battlements at Tor Neroche, the fine stables that would house their Angesand steeds, and the private garden where they could go dig in the dirt and forget for a time about things of the realm.

He felt her hand resting on his chest twitch a time or two, then still. He continued to describe all the sorts of things they would plant in that garden until he felt her begin to breathe evenly. He stopped speaking, then carefully pulled his cloak over them both. He settled his pack under his head a bit more comfortably, then looked up into the sky and watched the stars wheel overhead.

He hoped for the ending he'd given her. He hoped for years with her after his work as archmage was finished, years of watching the turn of the seasons, of watching her with her family and his, of watching their children and grandchildren and grandchildren's grandchildren grow and take their turns on the world's stage. It wasn't a certain thing, as his parents could have attested. But he hoped for it.

Aye, he hoped for it just the same.

Seventeen

Morgan walked through the forest of Ceangail at dawn.

It was worse than she'd feared, and she had allowed herself to imagine quite a bit of awfulness. Spells covered the entire forest like a canopy, shielding it from the sun with layers of confusion and distraction. It was far too much like Droch's garden for her taste. She looked up and shivered. The spell overhead seemed to be mostly intact, but she could see where it had been rent and left dripping down through the trees, as if a great wind had tried to blow it away and only succeeded in shredding it against branches. She had no desire to examine any of it more closely to see how it was wrought. All she wanted to do was find the glade, then be out as quickly as possible.

She continued on, ignoring the magic that pressed down on her. It was more difficult to ignore the sensation of having been there before. It was the same thing she'd experienced when walking into her father's solar at Dìobhail, only this was a hundredfold worse.

She had to stop, finally. She looked at the ground, which seemed to be remarkably free of anything untoward, until she thought she could go on. She took a deep breath, then began walking again.

She had to do that more times than she wanted to count.

She paused at one point, because she couldn't catch her breath. Miach was behind her, somewhere, which should have comforted her. Her brother was with her grandfather and her uncle, perhaps even closer to her than Miach. Even her mercenary companions had swallowed their gorge and agreed to wear spells of un-noticing so they would be a help and not a hindrance. She wasn't alone, yet she felt as if she were the only poor fool for miles.

Sìle hadn't wanted her to be that fool. Even though the plan had been agreed on before they left Durial, he had balked that morning at the thought of her going ahead alone. She'd had no other choice. If something went awry, or any enemy attacked, she would be underestimated.

She had long last come to appreciate Miach's favorite ploy.

She had done other things to ensure success. She had used Miach's Duriallian spell of hiding to completely bury her magic, insisting that he listen to make certain she'd done it aright. She'd then taken the Sword of Angesand in her hand and prepared to hide its essence as well.

That had been more difficult than she'd expected it to be.

It had been impossible not to appreciate the perfection of the sword, not only because of the way it felt in her hand but also because of the sheer beauty of the blade itself. It was spectacular, crafted with skill that Weger's smiths would have given much to have called their own. Not even the magic she knew was folded into the blade lessened its magnificence.

On the contrary, it enhanced it.

It had been with sincere regret than she had laid over it spells of Olc that made her ill to look at and queasy to touch. She'd resheathed the sword just the same and promised it a good cleaning after the fact.

The wielders will come out of magic, out of obscurity, and out of darkness . . .

The words she'd read in the fall came back to her suddenly, though she no longer felt any fear when she thought of them. If anyone came from the last, it was her. She had no idea what the prophecy meant in relation to the well and Mehar had told her that she'd only seen the women who would wield the sword, not what their battles would be. Morgan suspected Mehar had known quite a bit more than she was telling, but she hadn't pressed her for what that more might have been. She had enough to think on without adding to it. She had, however, allowed herself to speculate how many times a year Mehar and Gilraehen had supper with Master Soilléir. Several, was her guess. Perhaps after she was finished with the task in front of her, she would give some thought to just exactly what they saw as they sat in his solar, lingering over their wine.

Unfortunately, she had no time for such pleasant ruminations at present. She put her shoulders back and continued on. Now that the moment was come in truth, she began to feel a remarkable calm, as if what she stood to do was no more taxing than convincing herself to leave the marginal comfort of her cell in Gobhann to go train out in a bitter winter wind—and to be sure she'd done that often enough.

She walked out into the glade before she realized where she was, then came to a stumbling halt.

She was prepared for all sorts of terrible things, but what she found in the glade was actually not as bad as she'd feared it might be. The worst part of it was realizing she had been there before.

She turned herself slowly about until she saw the place where she had gone with Ruithneadh to hide as her mother had begun to goad her father. She looked up and saw the evil that hung down from the spell above like so many repulsive, putrid vines. She suspected those spells had been intact when her father had visited the well, but whether they had been ripped when the well had spewed forth its vile contents or during some other battle she had no desire to know about, she couldn't have said.

She continued on until she stood just in front of the well. It was an unremarkable thing, not giving any outward sign of what lurked within. After a moment to get her bearings, she turned her attentions to the trees ringing the glade. She walked in a northeasterly direction until she could go no farther. A spell of illusion dripped down the bark of the tree in front of her like sap, but it moved easily enough when she brushed it aside.

And there, under her hand, was a word.

She was so surprised to find what she had been looking for where it was supposed to be, she could only stand there for a moment or two with her fingers digging into that mark and smile. It was the second major component of her father's spell of closing, which meant the first part should find itself to her left. She turned and looked directly across the glade for a tree that should have represented another corner of Gleac's battle plan, then jumped in spite of herself.

Trolls stood in the shadows of those trees, watching her.

She put her hand over her mother's amulet, but realized there was no need to do so. The creatures were not coming any closer. Still it was very unsettling to realize they were standing just under the trees—all the trees, including those directly around her.

She took a deep breath, left them unchallenged, and went to look for signs on the other three trees. She was amazed to find what she was looking for where it should have been found. It seemed too easy, but perhaps not. She never would have thought to look for a mark in such a place without having taken the steps that had led her to such a conclusion. Perhaps no one else would either. She never would have arrived at that conclusion if it hadn't been for six years spent in Gobhann, and she never would have gone to Gobhann if she hadn't spent the years of her girlhood in the care of Nicholas of Lismòr. She was starting to feel a bit like a tree in King Uachdaran's garden, with her life twisting and turning in patterns she wouldn't have imagined up on her own.

Patterns that had led her to where she stood at present.

She shivered, then turned and walked back to the well before she could think on that overmuch. She stopped in front of it and watched the evil bubble up and trickle down over the edge of the rock. It landed with an audible *plop* in a small well that had been dug there to receive it. Morgan drew Mehar's knife from her boot and sliced through the spell laid over the little hollow before it could create anything untoward. She put the knife back in her boot, then began to study the well, looking for the same sort of thing she'd seen carved into the trees.

She paused briefly, wondering if her father had come to the well beforehand and left his mark on the trees, or if he had done it just before he opened the well. Perhaps it didn't matter when her father had etched it there. All that mattered was that hopefully he had.

She looked first on the lid, that slab of stone that almost covered the opening entirely, then she made another circle, looking at the rock that made up the sides. She got down on her hands and knees and began to study the stone more closely.

She saw nothing.

She took a deep breath, then settled on a new strategy. She closed her eyes, which handily blocked out the sight of her trollish companions, and ran her fingers over every stone of the well.

She felt nothing, which left her more than a little agitated—and panicked. If she didn't find what they needed, they were lost. They would have to continue looking and that would mean more lives lost from Lothar's monsters. It would mean more time spent in places she had no desire to go and more encounters with mages she would have preferred not to meet.

She sat back on her heels, then heaved herself to her feet. The answer was in front of her; she was certain of it. All she had to do was find it. She pushed her hair back from her face with her scraped and filthy hand, then turned away from the well for a change of scenery.

Lothar was standing five paces behind her.

She almost screamed. She would have, if she hadn't managed to take all her fear and ruthlessly squelch it.

Fear crushed immediately has no chance to flower into panic.

She repeated that stricture a handful of times until she felt the clean edge of its truth straiten her soul like a particularly unforgiving pike. She clasped her hands behind her back and looked at Lothar calmly.

"Looking for something?"

"Actually, I think I might have found it," he said, with a satisfied smile. "Princess Mhorghain."

Morgan inclined her head the slightest bit in acknowledgment. "So I am. How did you know? Did Cruadal of Duibhreas tell you as much?"

"Never heard of him. And I didn't need to be told." He smiled again. "After I poisoned you in the fall, I began to think about how much you resembled someone else I once knew."

"Who?"

He shot her a look. "Your mother, of course. Naturally, I wanted to have a few more details about you from the king of Neroche, who currently languishes in my dungeon, but he was rather unwilling to give them, despite my tactics of persuasion."

Poor Adhémar. Morgan wasn't particularly fond of him, but she wouldn't have wished Lothar's tortures on anyone. She spared a hope that there would be something left of him by the time they reached Riamh, then turned back to what she faced.

"You might be persuasive," she said lightly, "but you're not a very good brewer of poisons."

Lothar drew himself up and glared at her. "I think you would find, my girl, that I'm quite adept at several terrible things that you daren't imagine."

Morgan shrugged dismissively. "Bore me with the details later. If you'll excuse me, I have business here—"

Before she could even begin to turn away from him, he attacked.

His spell of Taking slammed into her with the force of a score of fists, leaving her gasping in spite of herself. Fortunately, there was no power there for him to have. When he realized what she'd done earlier, he cursed, then tore at the spell of illusion that hid the well containing her power. Morgan searched frantically for something to counter it, but he was everywhere, attacking her from all sides. Her illusion was suddenly ripped aside as if it had been a flimsy spider-web.

Lothar then turned to the spell that hid her magic, seeking for a spot of weakness. Morgan realized, with an enormous sense of relief, that he would not succeed. She was very, very grateful Miach had appropriated a Duriallian spell or two at some point in the past.

She found her feet beneath her again and sighed silently. Then she very deliberately folded her arms over her chest. "Do you need any help?" she asked politely.

The change in Lothar's mien was swift and terrifying. Morgan wasn't unaccustomed to seeing that in the lads she had fought over the years, so she paid it little heed. Weger's strictures ran under the surface of her mind like a swiftly flowing river, loud and strengthening. She watched Lothar dispassionately as his fury exploded into spells of Olc that spun themselves around her and tried to encase her just as Droch had tried to encompass Miach. She waited until they had come within arm's reach, then slit through them with a simple spell of Olc that came to her tongue uncalled.

Lothar looked at her in surprise. "How did you know to do that?"

"Gair of Ceangail was my sire," she said contemptuously. "Did you think I was completely without any power?"

Lothar seemed to collect his fury and contain it. "I'm not sure exactly what I thought." He looked at her for a moment or two, then gestured behind her. "If you are as powerful as you claim, prove it. Open the well."

She snorted. "Why would I want to do that? So you can benefit?"

"You want to do it because I'll kill you if you don't."

Morgan lifted an eyebrow. "Do you think so?"

Lothar only smiled in answer.

She realized, as she lost her breath in a rush, that she'd had only a small taste of his power as he'd tried to take her magic. Miach had been right: Droch was a hammer; Lothar was a sinewy snake, wrapping his spells around her and waiting until she breathed out before he tightened them, leaving her less and less able to continue to draw in breath. She fell to her knees before she realized they had buckled beneath her. She began to see stars swirling around her, sparkling across the field of her vision, distracting her from the smile on Lothar's face.

She groped for her knife, but her fingers were numb and useless. She tried to put her hand on the Sword of Angesand, but her hand wasn't working and she couldn't find the sword's hilt. She tried to blurt out a spell of death, but Lothar's laughter carried her words away as if they'd been eiderdown whisked away on a brisk spring breeze.

She felt blackness begin to creep relentlessly toward her.

She gasped out spell after spell, but they were just words without any power behind them. Her steel was useless, her spells impotent, and she had no more breath for even trying to rip aside the spell that covered the Sword of Angesand. She tried to simply think the word she was to use, but it was just a word, nothing more.

She wondered how it was that Miach even dared stand against the man.

And then, quite suddenly, it was all gone. Her breath returned to her and the blackness receded. She looked up blearily from where she lay on the ground at Lothar's feet and saw why.

Miach was being dragged into the glade, bound in not only ropes but cords of magic that even she could see through the haze that had become her vision. The men holding him shoved him forward.

"I found him lurking in the shadows, Grandfather," one of the men said shortly. "Perhaps the woman isn't all alone after all."

Morgan didn't dare look at Miach. Obviously he'd seen her distress and allowed himself to be captured. She wasn't happy about needing a rescue, but she was also no fool. She was even more out of her depth with Lothar than she had been with Droch. If Miach hadn't distracted Lothar, she likely would have died right there in front of her father's well, without having done what she'd come to do.

She managed to get to her knees, but she could rise no farther. She groped for the spells of attack Miach had given her, but she found herself, for the first time in her life, afraid to use what she had to hand lest her plans go awry. Weger would have been disgusted.

Then again, she was facing Weger's grandfather, and Lothar was not without power.

She thought about Weger, about how Lothar had slain his father and brothers, likely because Lothar had known it would grieve him. If Lothar had any idea what Miach meant to her, he would do the same thing for the same reason.

But if he thought she loathed Miach, perhaps she could distract him with that loathing long enough to free Miach. Then, at least, Miach could engage Lothar and leave her at liberty to proceed with her plan.

Which she wasn't altogether sure hadn't been Miach's intention anyway.

She pushed herself to her feet, swayed, then steadied herself. She leaned over and tried to catch her breath.

"I can't seem to rid myself of him," she wheezed.

"Who? The wee one of Neroche?" Lothar asked in surprise.

"Aye," Morgan said, putting as much disgust as possible in her voice. "He follows me everywhere." And thank heavens that he did. She straightened with an effort. "I wish he would stop."

Lothar considered, then nodded to his lads. They shoved Miach so hard that he went sprawling—directly in front of the well. Morgan didn't dare look at him, but she could tell from where she stood that he was bound by more spells of Olc than she'd realized at first. She wasn't altogether certain that they weren't too many for him to rid himself of. And if she opened the well, the evil would wash directly over him and kill him.

She wasn't sure how this was any better, but it was done and there was no turning back. She rubbed her hands over her face suddenly, managing to snatch a look at Miach as he did so. He was watching her tranquilly, as if he willed her to know he trusted her.

She hoped that trust wasn't misplaced.

"I think I can aid you," Lothar said pleasantly. "In return for a favor from you, of course."

Morgan could only imagine what that would be. "I don't think I would like the favor you want," she said slowly. "I've seen what happens when that cap comes off and I have no desire to see it again. Unless, of course, the incentive inspires me. And I don't think removing the annoyance of the archmage of Neroche would be very inspiring."

"Then what would you say to being rid of him and having all his power in the bargain?" Lothar asked pleasantly.

She shook her head. "I don't want it."

He turned his dark, fathomless eyes on her. "And what is it you want, Gair's daughter?"

"No more magic," she said before she could stop herself.

"Easily done," he said smoothly. "I'll take the power from the well for myself, kill the archmage of Neroche so he doesn't trouble you further, then, if you like, I'll rid you of the nuisance of your power as well. Then I'll let you go, freely." He smiled, but that smile was a very cold one indeed. "That seems a reasonable trade, doesn't it?"

"I've heard worse," Morgan said with a shrug, though she doubted very much Lothar would allow her to leave the glade alive. She started to turn away, then looked back at him. "I have your word on all that?"

"Of course." He lifted an eyebrow in surprise. "Why would you think otherwise?"

Because every word that came out of his mouth was a lie, that's why. She nodded, as if she believed him, then turned away, calculating furiously. If she could, as the well was opening, manage to undo her magic and then free Miach's as well, the balance of power in the glade would shift. A pity everything useful was buried under layers of—

She froze. It took a moment before she could catch her breath. Everything was *under* layers of spells.

What if the end of her father's spell was burned into the *under*side of the cap?

Lothar made a brief sound of impatience. "Surely it can't be that difficult to use a simple spell of opening."

She ignored him. It was possible, wasn't it? If she had time to open the well, find the word, then slam it shut . . . she could do all that whilst Miach kept Lothar busy. Besides, her grandfather was also in those trees, as was Sosar, and their power wasn't insignificant. They could prevent Lothar from taking the well's power, surely.

She took a deep breath, then very slowly began the spell of opening she had used on the bottle of wine in her father's solar. She had only a fraction of her power free, but the spell began to take shape just the same.

Apparently, she wasn't working fast enough. Lothar was standing at her shoulder, his impatience a tangible thing. She pretended to hesitate, but that only sent him into a sudden frenzy of cursing.

"Stop it," she spat, glaring at him. "I can't concentrate."

He started to throw a spell at her—she saw it begin to form in the air—then he snapped his fingers and it was gone.

"Your sire would find your proficiency to be quite lacking," he said, looking down his nose at her, "but I have no choice but to make do with your pitiful self. Hurry, or it won't go well for you."

"I need room."

He sighed gustily, then turned and strode away. Morgan turned back to the well, shot Miach a look, then concentrated on repeating the words in the order she'd written them down.

"Make haste!" Lothar shouted from behind her.

In one single, smooth motion, she drew the Sword of Angesand

and spoke the word that stripped away its spell of concealment. It blazed forth with magelight as she slit the spells of Olc that kept Miach bound. She spoke the single word that released all her power before she even paused for breath, then pulled Miach to his feet as he did the same for himself. He squeezed her hand, then pushed past her and engaged Lothar. Morgan took a deep breath.

Then she spoke the last word of her father's spell.

The cover sprang open. Evil shot up out of the well, though not as fiercely as it had when her father had released it. She knew she should have moved, or called a warning, or woven some spell of protection over herself and those she loved, but all she could do was stand there, openmouthed, and watch the evil as it fell back down toward the earth.

It shied away from her. She realized, with a start, that the power that pushed the evil away was coming from not only the magelight of the Sword of Angesand, and not only from the amulet she wore resting against her heart, but from the sparkle of elven magic that sprang from the runes about her wrist and wove itself through that same magelight.

And then there was the song that her blade began to sing.

"Stop that!" Lothar shouted in fury.

Morgan didn't bother to look at him. She watched the evil as it tumbled over the edge of the rock to soak into the ground. The sight of it was at once both familiar and horrifying. All she could do was stand there and watch as it avoided splashing itself against her boots.

"Mhorghain!"

She looked up and saw Keir standing next to the well.

"Hurry," he said, turning quickly to thrust his sword through the heart of a troll. "Damnation, the spell of opening isn't holding."

Morgan saw that was true. The lid had begun to quiver in place, as if it couldn't decide what to do. She heard Lothar shouting behind her and realized that he was weaving his own bit of magic over the well, but she couldn't tell if he was trying to open or close it.

Keir leapt on top of the well with his back against the stone, holding it up by sheer strength alone. He stood with feet braced on either side of the yawning darkness.

"Find the last word," he commanded. "It must be here somewhere."

Morgan dropped to her knees and looked frantically under the cap of the well. It was too much in shadow to see without aid, so she made werelight and sent it skimming along every surface. She crawled to Keir's left to look behind him, but saw nothing. She scrambled to her feet and lurched to the right.

Engraved into the stone behind her brother was a single word.

She could hardly believe her eyes. She didn't dare rub them, though, lest it be a dream she had stumbled into and any stray movement might force her to wake. She looked at the word again, memorized it, then leapt to her feet.

"I found it," she said, feeling slightly giddy. "Keir, the word was exactly where . . . we . . ."

She found she couldn't finish her words.

There was a sword protruding from Keir's chest.

She blinked, then looked to Keir's left. Cruadal stood there, smiling disdainfully. Morgan leapt toward him only to have Keir shout hoarsely at her.

"Forget him and weave the spell, Mhorghain!"

Miach bumped into the back of her, almost sending her tumbling into the well itself. He cursed, then pulled her back away from the edge before he continued on with his own fight. Morgan looked at her brother. There was, and she could hardly believe it, an expression of peace on his face.

"Someone of Gair's blood must close the well," he said calmly.

"But," she said, blinking, "it cannot mean this. Grandfather and I can heal you. We've done it before."

Keir flinched as Cruadal wrenched the sword, then pulled it free. Morgan would have turned on him, but her grandfather was seeing to that well enough on his own, engaging Cruadal with spells and steel both. The magic became an annoyance to her, buzzing against her ears, drowning out what she thought Keir was saying to her.

She realized suddenly that it wasn't her grandfather's magic she was listening to.

It was Lothar's spell of Taking.

But it wasn't directed at her. She realized with a start that he was preparing to take the power of the well, just as he'd promised he would. And if he did, there would be no finishing him. Morgan wasn't sure where to turn first. Keir was struggling to counter Lothar's spell with Fadaire, Miach was fighting Lothar with very ugly spells of Olc, and the magic from her father's well had apparently now decided she was worth its notice, for it was lapping at her boots.

"Mhorghain, close the well," Keir gasped.

She wrenched her gaze up to meet his. "But you—"

"Weave the spell, then use the final word before you forget it."

Morgan realized she couldn't see her brother any longer and that made her angry. She dragged her sleeve across her eyes, then looked at him. "I have a very good memory," she said, because those were the first words that she could hold on to. "You don't have to do this!"

He looked at her, tears streaming down his face. "Mother would have been very proud of you. I'll sit with her soon, sister, far beyond the east where there is no more toil or sorrow."

"Oh, Keir, please," she begged. "Please, nay—"

"I'm dead already," he said with a faint smile. "I've been dying for years and not even grandfather's magic could mend it. This is how it was meant to end. I always wanted to undo what Father had done. Now, I'll have that chance." His breath rattled loudly in his chest. "Help me, Mhorghain. Help me do what I must."

Morgan found the words of closing on her tongue, but they were so bitter, she didn't think she could spit them out.

"Hurry."

She took a deep breath, held Keir's gaze with hers, then repeated the words she had no choice but to use. She paused, the last word shimmering in the air between them.

Keir looked at her one more time, then called to the evil. Whether it recognized his voice or his blood, she couldn't have said. All she knew was that it rushed back toward the well, almost unbalancing her in the process. It surrounded Keir, swirling up around him and surrounding him like a particularly generous cloak. He didn't protest; he merely released the stone lid and disappeared down into the darkness. Morgan whispered the last word and the cap of the well fell onto the rock with a crash and sealed itself with a faint click.

No more evil trickled from it. Morgan fell to her knees on ground that was simply innocent dirt, unpolluted by what had troubled it for a score of years. She heard fighting going on all around her, but she couldn't force herself to be a part of it. She had never felt such bone-wearying exhaustion, not even when she'd fashioned spells of death.

Perhaps it was her grief that had broken her.

She watched dully as her mercenary companions fought trolls, aided by elves she supposed Sìle must have called to himself. Perhaps they had been sent by Làidir. She wasn't sure and, worse, yet, she wasn't sure she cared. She had accomplished what she'd set out to, but she felt no satisfaction.

And then she caught sight of Cruadal.

He was fighting her grandfather furiously. He attempted to change his shape, but Sìle wrenched him out of his spell and sent him sprawling. He heaved himself back to his feet with a curse, then attacked Sìle with renewed fury, forcing Sìle back.

Morgan watched in horror as her grandfather stumbled over the corpse of one of Lothar's creatures lying behind him. He went down heavily. Sosar was there, though, and closer to the king than she could possibly have been. He reached down for his father's hand to pull him to his feet.

A shadow loomed behind Sosar suddenly, and a blade flashed in the sunlight as it descended.

Morgan threw herself to her feet, pulling Mehar's knife free from her boot as she did so. She flung the blade with all her strength at Cruadal.

She supposed 'twas nothing but dumb luck that it went into Cruadal and not into her uncle, who straightened suddenly. Sosar looked at her with very wide eyes, then turned and finished Cruadal with his sword.

That should have eased her, but it didn't. A white-hot fury clawed through her like a live thing, anger mixed with grief for a brother she'd had only a few days and lost thanks to Lothar and Gair and evil magic that came too easily to her tongue. She looked past her grandfather, who was getting to his feet, past her uncle, who was wiping his sword on the grass, over to where her mercenary companions and a collection of elves were fighting creatures made from her father's arrogance and Lothar's cunning.

She began to crush them with spells of death that fell on them like hammers.

"Mhorghain!" Sosar exclaimed.

She ignored him, relishing the power that rushed into her suddenly. She slew a score of monsters, then another half dozen, until there were only a handful left. She knew she should have felt spent, but she instead felt strengthened.

That was startling enough that it gave her pause. It couldn't be the evil from the well adding to her power. That was gone, drawn back into where it had come from. This power was coming from somewhere else. Somewhere human.

Lothar.

She looked to find him fighting Miach languidly, but watching her as he did so.

He spoke a word and the spell he'd cast over her left her abruptly. She fell to her knees, weary beyond belief. She stared at him stupidly, wishing she'd had the good sense to recognize his evil for what it was. She understood then the truth of Miach's words. Olc was a seductive magic and the learning of it cost a mage dearly. Using it, she suspected, exacted an even higher price.

As she listened to Lothar continue to speak, she realized that he was quickly reweaving his spell of Taking. It occurred to her that he intended to use it not on the well now, but on Miach. She threw herself to her feet and stumbled toward Miach. She flung herself in front of him and held up the Sword of Angesand and Mehar's knife both as a ward. She and Miach were instantly surrounded by light and song and the power of the runes that encircled both their wrists.

Lothar only yawned, then finished his spell.

Someone a fair distance away from her gasped, then cried out. Morgan whirled around in time to see Sosar fall to his knees, a look of absolute horror on his face.

Morgan turned back around in time to see Lothar stretch in satisfaction. He smiled pleasantly at Miach.

"You'd best hurry home, young one. I think you'll find that there's more to do there than you suspected—only now I am yet again infinitely more powerful than you are, making the fight even more difficult for you. But that has always been the case, hasn't it?"

Miach pushed past Morgan with a curse and a spell on his lips.

Lothar vanished.

Morgan pulled Miach back. "He's gone; let him go." She tugged on him again when he wouldn't look at her. "Miach, leave it. We must see to Sosar."

He cursed, then turned and looked over her head. He closed his eyes briefly. "I fear the worst, but we'll do what we can."

She resheathed her blades, then hurried with him across the glade. She dropped to her knees next to her uncle. She put her hand on his shoulder.

"Sosar?"

Sosar looked up at Miach. "It's gone," he said in astonishment. "My power is gone."

"All of it?"

Sosar laughed, but there was nothing but absolute desperation in the sound. "And just how do you expect me to judge that?"

Miach rubbed his hands over his face, then shook his head as if he sought to clear it. "We'll follow him."

"Let him go," Sìle said grimly. "I'll take Sosar home—"

"Nay," Miach said sharply, "we must follow. Only Lothar can restore what he's taken. Keir was adamant that was the case."

"And how," Sìle said heavily, "do you propose to force that bastard from Wychweald to give back what he's stolen?"

"When the right pressure is applied, Your Majesty, even the strongest man will fall to his knees and beg for mercy. Morgan, can you fly?"

"Of course," she said, even though she suspected she would be hard-pressed to merely propel herself across the glade.

"Your Majesty, bring Sosar after us," Miach said briskly. "We will follow Lothar and I will end this. But before I do, I *will* have back what he took from your son."

Sìle stood with his hands on Sosar's shoulders. "If you think so, Miach," he said, his expression very grave, "then we'll come. But what about this business here? Is it finished?"

"It will be in a moment."

Morgan watched Miach weave a handful of spells over the well. He was brutally efficient about it all, layering things over the stone that she wouldn't have wanted to try to undo. Even her grandfather pulled back, an expression of distaste on his face. Morgan walked over to stand next to Sìle, happy to have him to lean against as Miach continued his work. She understood Miach's fury and his grief. She only wished she'd had some of the former. All she had was grief and it chilled her to the bone.

Miach finished, then turned to Sìle. "Your Grace, please give the horses wings and follow us with Morgan's lads. I dare not take the time to do any of this for you."

Sìle nodded, then reached out and pulled Morgan briefly into his arms. "I'm sorry, Granddaughter."

She embraced him in return, then stepped back and looked up at him. "Sosar first," she said quietly. "We'll mourn later."

He nodded, then turned to gather up their company and send others to search for the horses. Morgan took the hand Miach offered her, but stumbled as he pulled her away.

"You'll ride," he said without hesitation.

She would have protested, but he didn't give her the chance. In his place suddenly stood a sleek, black dragon. She climbed between his wings and took the reins he'd provided her, very happy for something to hold on to as he leapt up into the air and clawed his way through the spells that covered the glade.

She was exceptionally glad for that first decent breath of clear air.

Morgan, I'm sorry about Keir.

Thank you.

You did well.

She clutched the reins, then leaned down and wrapped her arms around his neck. She was weary beyond any weariness caused by a long march or a terrible battle. Her heart was sick and she didn't think even a month of healing at Gobhann or an equal amount of time drinking Nicholas's brews would heal it.

Do what must be done first; grieve later.

She'd never dreamed a stricture would be all that held her together after a battle made up of terrible magic.

She supposed Weger wouldn't have been surprised.

Eighteen

Miach flew hard against a wind that continually beat in his face and tried to slow him down. He couldn't credit Lothar with that sort of power, but it wasn't out of the realm of possibility. He wanted to believe that Lothar wasn't omnipotent, though, so he chose to assume the wind had more natural origins.

He wished he could have dismissed the rest of the morning's tragedies as easily.

He'd only had a brief glance out of the corner of his eye at Keir holding up the well's cover, but it had been long enough to see Crudal's sword coming out of Keir's chest. There had been nothing he could do. It had taken all his strength and cunning merely to keep Lothar at bay. He'd heard the well close and realized only then that Keir hadn't escaped that closing.

He wished he'd had time to wrap his arms around Morgan and let her weep. She had accomplished something far beyond what anyone could have reasonably expected her to. Not only that, but she'd managed the feat in the face of all the chaos swirling around her and whilst knowing that Keir would perish as a result. Just the spells of opening and closing she'd wrought should have left her so drained she couldn't move. That they hadn't said much about her strength.

He'd wanted to be of more use to her, but it had been all he could do to fight off the spells that Lothar had been tossing about as casually as he might have handfuls of coins.

Aye, he would take her in his arms and hold her—but they would first see to Sosar. They would find Lothar, then he would spell the whoreson into undreamed-of agonies until he agreed to give up what he'd taken.

And then he would kill him.

He didn't see the other dragon coming his way until he almost collided with it. He was halfway to singeing it before he realized who it was. He wheeled away, then began circling downward, looking for a decent place to land and have a parley. He resumed his proper shape on the bank of a river, then turned to pick Morgan up from where she'd fallen to the ground.

"I'm well," she managed, accepting his hand up. "I just need to lean on you."

He put his arms around her and pulled her close. He supposed the gentlemanly thing to do would be to refrain from pointing out to her how badly she was trembling. He conjured up a pair of cloaks once he realized neither of them was wearing one any longer. He wasn't sure when he'd shed his and he didn't think he dared ask Morgan the same.

He wrapped them both up, then looked at the man hunched over five paces away, gasping for breath.

"Nemed, what are you doing here?" Miach asked in surprise.

Nemed straightened with a groan. "Cathar sent me to find you. Rigaud went to Durial to look for you, and Mansourah went to Ain-neamh for aid. I suppose I'm fortunate I chose the right direction." He took a deep breath. "We need you."

"I was on my way," Miach said. "I suppose you can thank Lothar for that. He told me we should prepare for a battle—"

"Prepare?" Nemed interrupted incredulously. "Miach, we're in the *midst* of one! Cathar's gathered together a formidable force, but we feared just the four of us trying to stand against Lothar and his minions wouldn't be enough." He shivered visibly. "His army is not all of this world."

Miach felt Morgan's arms tighten around him and realized belatedly that he was now leaning on her. He straightened with an effort, then gave thought to what his brother had said.

And then he realized what wasn't right.

"Four," he repeated slowly. "Nemed, don't you mean the five of you?"

Nemed blinked. "Don't you know?"

Miach hated those sorts of questions. "Know what? Who's at home?"

"Cathar, Rigaud, Mansourah, and me."

"Where's Turah? I sent him home almost a se'nnight ago."

"Aye, and he decided that he would sneak into Riamh and rescue Adhémar, the fool."

Miach flinched in spite of himself. He wasn't sure whom Nemed was calling a fool, Adhémar or Turah, but he supposed either—or both—deserved it. Adhémar could perhaps be forgiven for his foolishness; he hadn't intended to find himself inside Riamh. Turah had no excuse. He knew very well what a body looked like after having been in Lothar's dungeon.

"The bloody idiot," he managed. "What possessed him to do something that stupid?"

Nemed lifted an eyebrow briefly. "I would like to say 'tis because he had suddenly developed an overinflated sense of importance, but you know as well as I that arrogance is the least of his faults. He told Cathar that he'd learned of as-of-yet undiscovered depths of magic in himself and thought it might aid you if he went to fetch Adhémar and Adaira so you didn't need to." He smiled briefly. "To spare you a trip back where you wouldn't want to go and all that."

Miach closed his eyes briefly. "I told him he had more magic than he thought, but not *that* much." He looked into Morgan's upturned face. "He doesn't have enough to confront Lothar."

"Nay," she said quietly, "not that."

"If it makes you feel any better," Nemed said, "he planned to use his blade as much as possible, but I think things have gone badly for him. We've had no word and none of us has the talent of searching for his essence. Not that we'd be able to feel it anyway if he's inside Lothar's keep." Nemed paused for a moment or two, then looked at Miach seriously. "We're not cowards, Miach, but a trip inside Riamh is not something to be taken lightly."

"Nay, brother, it isn't. I'll go do the fetching. But what is this about Rigaud and Mansourah? How long ago did they leave?"

"Day before yesterday," Nemed said. "I thought you would probably be on your way home, so I elected to stay with Cathar as long as possible, then try to catch you closer to the border. We should hurry, though." He paused. "I think this might be a very ugly war."

"Hopefully Ehrne will lend us a few lads," Miach said, "though I don't know what Rigaud hopes to accomplish in Durial."

"He'll leave Uachdaran his cloak and likely return with a contingent of very sturdy fighters," Nemed said with a faint smile. "You know Rigaud. He has a gilded tongue."

"When it suits him," Miach agreed. He put his hand on Nemed's shoulder. "I'll go on and find Cathar's camp. Continue on for a bit and find our company, would you? The king of Tòrr Dòrainn and Morgan's lads are behind us, all flying."

Nemed nodded. "We'll follow hard on your heels."

Miach watched Nemed leap up into the air, then turn east. He waited until his brother was nothing more than a speck in the distance before he sighed and looked at Morgan. "Well?"

"I'm grieved about Turah," she said quietly. "There is no justice in being rewarded with harm when his only desire had been to save you pain."

"Nay, there isn't," Miach agreed, "and I hope he hasn't paid a terrible price for that willingness. Then again, for all we know he simply got lost. We might find him happily putting his feet up in some tavern."

She nodded, but she didn't look convinced. He wasn't either, but it was better than thinking about the alternative.

"Let's be on our way," she said. She looked at him critically. "Perhaps I should carry you this time."

He smiled. "I appreciate the offer, but I imagine I would fall asleep and fall off. At least flying will keep me awake. We should be there by dark, if we fly hard. I'll have a rest then."

She nodded, though he supposed she didn't believe him any more than he believed himself.

Nay, they wouldn't be resting anytime soon.

The sun was setting as he landed in the middle of the army's encampment. Perhaps he'd been more weary than he'd thought, for Nemed and Sìle's company descended only minutes later. Miach gathered them all up, then went to look for his brother's tent. Cathar's look of surprise when they walked in was complete.

"Nemed found you," he said, sounding vastly relieved.

"We were on our way," Miach said, shoving aside the almost overwhelming desire to sit down and fall asleep, "but aye, he found us."

"What made you come home now?" Cathar asked.

"Lothar told me to," Miach said with a yawn.

"He *what*?"

"I'll tell you the details later." He yawned again, because he couldn't help himself, then had help finding his seat by means of Morgan pushing him down into one. He looked for a chair for her, but she had already sat down at his feet, resting the Sword of Angesand over her knees. He sighed deeply, then looked at Cathar. "I need to see how my spells are faring, but I think I'd like your tidings first."

"You won't enjoy them, but you'll have them."

Cathar motioned for his page to serve ale all around, then began to relate the events of the past fortnight. Lothar had been busy, apparently, and not only at the well.

"I'm convinced he's been amassing an army for quite some time," Cathar continued, "though they are very poorly trained. If it weren't for their sheer numbers, I wouldn't have lost any sleep over them." He paused. "It is as if Lothar expected to have some sudden source of power to compensate for the failings of his lads."

Miach shivered in spite of himself. Obviously Lothar had decided that he was close to opening Gair's well, and once that was done there would be no reason not to use his newfound power and conquer Neroche whilst he was about it.

"We have five thousand lads," Cathar said, "but I'm not sure how we'll fare against what he has across the border. 'Tis impossible to have an accurate count, what with the spells of un-noticing that we can't see through. I don't think he has more than five or six thousand himself, but again, I'm not sure." He paused, then looked at Miach carefully. "It occurred to me that he might have found a way to harness what spews forth those creatures we've been battling."

"I think he intended to," Miach agreed.

Cathar's expression was very grim. "And will he succeed?"

Miach shook his head with a smile. "Nay, he won't. And you can thank Morgan for that."

Cathar closed his eyes and bowed his head for a moment or two, then let out a deep, shuddering breath. He lifted his head and looked at Morgan. "You brilliant gel. You did it, didn't you?"

"Aye," she said quietly, "but I had a great deal of help. Miach kept Lothar from killing me and my eldest brother made it possible for me to actually close the well." She paused. "He perished in the deed."

"Prince Keir is alive?" Cathar said in astonishment, then he winced. "I didn't listen carefully enough. I'm sorry, lass, to learn he fell."

She leaned back against Miach's knees. "I don't think he was sorry, for he knew what it would mean to those he left behind. It was a terrible sacrifice, though." She took a deep breath. " 'Tis done, and for that I am very, very grateful."

"It was well done, Morgan," Cathar said quietly. He looked at them all, then put his hands on his knees and pushed himself to his feet. "You all look impossibly weary. Let me see you fed, then pallets set up here. King Sìle," he said, making Sìle a low bow, "you will of course take the most comfortable couch—"

"Don't worry about me, lad," Sìle said, waving him off. "I've slept in much worse places recently and I'm hardened to the labor. Give the comfortable place to my granddaughter and we'll all soldier on with what's left."

Miach smiled to himself at Sìle's world-weary tone. Truly, the elven king had endured things his own father never would have tolerated.

He watched for a moment as Cathar began to rearrange things to see everyone settled, then he leaned forward to put his arms around Morgan. He rested his cheek against hers for a moment or two, then turned and kissed her softly. "Morgan?"

She looked back over her shoulder at him. "Aye?"

"I need to work on my spells. I hate to ask this of you, love, but would you stay awake and watch with me?"

She turned herself all the way around to face him. "Of course. Why wouldn't I?"

"Because I need more from you than simply sitting next to me and prodding me awake when I nod off. If you would, I'd like you to come along with me and set your own spells inside my spells of ward. You would know then when—if—they were breached."

Her mouth fell open. "By Lothar?"

"I am concerned he might try," he admitted. "I will cast spells of protection over the border, then put a very thin layer of Fadairian glamour over them just in case. Do you remember the spell of defense I taught you on our way to Durial? The one of Croxteth?"

She nodded.

"Come along behind me and set that just inside my spells. Instead of using yourself as the boundaries of the spell, use my spells as such." He paused. "Please let me know if you sense anything untoward."

"Very well," she said weakly.

He smiled, then leaned forward and kissed the end of her nose. "Morgan, you are the bravest soul I know."

She shook her head. "I think that would be Keir."

"He would appreciate that thought, but he would disagree with it. I'll tell you all the things he said about you when we've time later. He shared my opinion of your courage."

"I had him such a short time, but I'll miss him just the same."

"I know you will," Miach said softly. "He'll know it, too." He took a deep breath, then took her hand. "Follow me, love, and let's be about this. I think we both might want a bit of sleep before tomorrow. I don't think it will be a very pleasant day."

She nodded and closed her eyes.

He took one last look at her, then closed his own eyes and set to work.

He was up long before the sun. He'd done what he could to protect Cathar's army and the northern border, then turned his energies to shoring up the rest of the spells set over Neroche as a whole. He'd slept beside Morgan, only to wake suddenly and find Sosar sitting nearby, attempting spell after spell, as if merely repeating the words would somehow bring back what he'd lost. His look of devastation had been complete.

Miach had risen almost immediately afterward and left the tent to pace as the world turned toward dawn. He supposed he might now understand a bit of Morgan's feelings as she walked toward the glade near Ceangail. The time for preparation was past and the time for doing had come. He had spent years stretching himself and his power, greedily learning every spell he could lay his hands on, taking every opportunity to learn about Lothar's weaknesses, all for the moment he would soon face. He hadn't fared very well against Lothar in the fall, but he could not fail now.

The fate of the realm hung in the balance.

He realized with a start that Morgan was standing next to him. She wasn't wearing a cloak and he could see her blades tucked into various places on her person. He looked at her seriously.

"I don't suppose there's any point in asking you not to come with me," he said slowly. "Is there?"

She looked at him in disbelief.

He smiled and put his arm around her shoulders. "There are times, love, that I forget who you are."

She reached up and touched the mark over his brow, then she touched hers. "Miach, I don't want to say that I've seen it all, but I've seen many things I never would have dreamed of in my worst nightmares. In a manner of speaking, I have faced my worst fears and survived. This seems a simple thing by comparison. After all, these are just lads we'll fight, aren't they?"

"They were, once."

"Can they be slain with a sword?"

"Generally."

She shrugged. "I might be slow to use a spell of death again after yesterday, but I can use my blade repeatedly today and not suffer for it. It is, after all, what I've been trained for. I think I will be glad of it, actually." She shivered. "I never want to use Olc again in my lifetime."

"I hope you never have a need," he said quietly. "But you had cause yesterday."

"Have you ever been that angry?"

"To use those spells of death?" he asked. "Certainly, and the price was very high, which you discovered for yourself. I'm actually amazed that you're still on your feet."

"I'll sleep later."

He hoped she would have the chance. "You'll stay near me," he stated.

"How else will I guard your back?"

"How indeed," he murmured.

She smiled, leaned against him for a brief moment, then took him by the arm. "You need breakfast. You also need sleep, but 'tis too late for it now." She looked up at him. "After this is over, Miach, you're going to sleep for a solid se'nnight if I have to stand over you with a sword and see that you do."

"As you will, love," he agreed, almost to the point of taking her up on the offer, though he supposed it had been less of an offer and more of a threat. He took it for what it was and hoped they would have the chance for such a week.

He ate what he could stomach, listened to last-minute strategies discussed in the council that had convened in Cathar's tent. Various captains of divisions were there, along with his four brothers, an elven king, and a collection of mercenary lads who looked as dangerous as any rogue mage from the north. Well, three of them did. Fletcher looked rather green, but Miach found that rather reassuring. If Fletcher of Harding could be counted on to puke at the beginning of every battle, all was right with the world.

Cathar hadn't but gotten to his feet and buckled his sword about his hips when the alarm was sounded. Miach jumped to his feet and followed his elder brother outside in time to see a scout drop to his knees. He clutched his gut, blood still dripping across his hands and down to the ground.

"They began a charge without warning," the man gasped. "After demanding an even start, no less."

Miach exchanged a look with Cathar. They shouldn't have expected anything else.

"We're ready just the same," Cathar said grimly. He strode out of the tent and began shouting. "Captains, give no quarter today! There is room in this fight for mercy, but mercy will be ending what passes for existence for these poor creatures. To arms!"

Miach started to bend down toward the scout, but Sìle stopped him.

"I'll see to this one; you see to your business. I'll follow you with Sosar as I may." He put his hand on Miach's shoulder. "I wish you good fortune, lad."

"Thank you, Your Majesty," Miach said. He turned and looked at Morgan. He considered a final time asking her to stay behind, then discarded the idea. The truth was, she was likely safer next to him than she would have been elsewhere. At least if Lothar came upon her unawares, he wouldn't find her alone.

He took a deep breath. "Let's go."

She nodded and drew the Sword of Angesand. It burst into light and song, then settled itself into a more discreet glow. Its song faded to a hum that was both soothing and stirring. She took a deep breath, then an expression of calmness came over her features.

Miach looked at her in surprise. "You're drawing strength from it."

She nodded. "I think so. I thought about it this morning, when I realized I hadn't been as affected by yesterday's magic as I should have been." She reached for his hand and held it tightly. "We'll aid you as we can, the sword and I."

"I'll have you both gladly."

She hesitated, then smiled. "I don't think Lothar will have any trouble finding you now. Not with my sword as a beacon."

He laughed in spite of himself. "Nay, love, I don't think so either. Let's be about this and have it over with."

She nodded and ran with him to the battle's front where they simply joined in the fray.

He rallied men where hearts were faint and fought alongside farmers whose hearts were stout and hearty. He continually kept a sense of his spells, waiting to see where they were breached so he would know when Lothar deigned to grace them with his presence. And all the while, Morgan was within arm's reach, terrifying their enemies and bolstering the courage of their allies with her words and her marvelous sword that Miach was certain had never been wielded by a woman with more skill.

The battle raged on, unabated. He found himself tempted, more than once during that morning, to turn into a bitter wind and see if he couldn't slip inside Riamh and rescue the three souls held there. But every time he thought about it, he saw another group of men needing an extra sword, or a pair of lads on the verge of being overwhelmed. What point was there in wearing Weger's mark if he didn't use what he'd earned?

It was noon when he found himself standing deep in Lothar's domain, surrounded by his brothers, Morgan's kin, her companions, and elves from Ainneamh who had miraculously appeared when things had looked particularly discouraging. Cathar was leaning heavily on his sword, looking grimly at the carnage around them. But, as he'd said earlier, slaying Lothar's minions was truly the kindest thing they could do for them.

He supposed they had been men before, but they were that no longer. Whether they were bred to their horrible forms, or had spells wrought on them that changed them into misshapen demons, he couldn't have said. He watched Morgan wander for a bit, stooping every now and again to study what lay fallen at her feet. Perhaps it didn't matter how they had come to be. They were miserable and death could be no worse for them than a half life where they were slaves to the whims of a man who had no mercy.

The sound of wind made him lift his head suddenly.

It took him a moment or two to realize Morgan was fighting Lothar, who had appeared out of nowhere to engage her.

Only it wasn't with a sword.

Her sword was lying twenty feet from her and she stood there with her magic alone to aid her. She gasped out a spell of defense, the strongest she had, but Miach knew that it wouldn't matter. Lothar was weaving his spell of Taking and Morgan wouldn't be able to fight that, not now that Lothar had at least most of Sosar's power added to his own vast stores.

Miach leapt forward and put himself in front of her. "Hide your magic," he threw over his shoulder.

"And you think that will save her?" Lothar asked with a laugh.

"It did yesterday," Miach snapped.

"Luck," Lothar said distinctly. "And that was before I had the elven prince's power. I think you'll find me quite a bit less manageable than you might have before. Not that you were able to manage me then."

"The realm still stands."

"Only because *I* allowed it to," Lothar sneered, "or hadn't you considered that? And here is something else to consider, my young mage prince: once I have *your* power and that of your feisty lass there, I'll go back to Gair's well and this time I *will* have what it contains. After that, I imagine you won't have much of a realm to mourn the loss of." He looked at Morgan. "Are you in mourning today, my dear? Such a pity about your brother."

"Get out of my way," Morgan growled, pushing past Miach. "I'll kill him with my bare hands."

"Tsk-tsk," Lothar said, throwing a spell of binding at her. "So vulgar, my dear."

Miach caught the spell and destroyed it, then pulled Morgan back.

"Miach—"

He shot her a look of warning. She took a deep breath, then stepped behind him.

"I'm sure I can reach my sword," she muttered. "Leave at least a little something of him for me to use it on."

Miach thought he just might. He also appreciated the fact that Morgan at least thought he had enough power to best the mage in front of him.

They would all know whether or not that was the case very soon.

He threw away his sword and simply looked at Lothar. "The

bulk of your army is gone and we'll finish the rest at our leisure. I think 'tis past time you followed them into oblivion."

Lothar laughed. "Oh, that *is* amusing. Do you think so truly, Mochriadhemiach? Do you think that *you* can possibly stand against me?"

"I don't plan on standing against you," Miach said, refusing to be baited. "I plan to kill you."

Lothar smiled, then where he stood was naught but darkness.

To say it was unpleasant darkness didn't begin to describe it. Several voices around him cried out in horror, but Miach ignored them. He had, unfortunately, seen worse. Actually, he'd seen worse in Lothar's dungeon. He nudged Morgan backward.

Well, he pushed her, but she didn't seem all that unwilling to be out of the way.

He lost count, after a while, of the shapes he took and the spells he fashioned. He stopped counting times he destroyed spells Lothar threw at others. He certainly didn't keep a tally of the slurs Lothar cast his way, the slights, the petty little remarks—when Lothar had a mouth to voice them, of course—that were meant to sting in a particularly personal way.

He realized at one point, and mostly because Lothar told him as much, that Lothar was merely toying with him.

You haven't begun to see what I can do.

Miach resumed his own form, weary beyond belief and growing angrier by the minute. "Then show me, if you've the spine to do so."

Lothar smiled.

Then he became all the worst things Miach had seen in places where he wished he hadn't gone.

He was darkness that crawled with vile, venomous creatures, darkness that hid shapes of things Miach would have preferred not to see, doorways where creatures from unnamed places appeared suddenly and terrifyingly. Miach fought each in turn, countered where he could, simply ignored where he couldn't.

And then Lothar became Desdhemar of Neroche as she lay dying just outside the hall door, yet at the same time Lothar stood there in his own form, laughing down at her.

You couldn't save your mother then; you won't save the little wench standing behind you now.

Miach felt despair slam into him like a wave, a crushing wave that flattened him as none of Lothar's evil had done so far that day. He staggered backward and almost fell. He knew it was yet another gift from Lothar, but that didn't make it any easier to fight off. And why would any of the man's spells be cast aside so easily? He'd been perfecting his art for centuries, inventing new and terrible ways to make everyone around him as miserable as he was. Miach had seen that art firsthand and knew what those who died at Lothar's hand suffered before they were released.

Thought of Morgan suffering anything like it, suffering the same fate as his mother—and the thought of what his mother had suffered for his sake . . .

With a mighty heave, he threw off what Lothar had cast on him. He found his feet again, then straightened and looked his enemy in the eye. He gathered all his power, all the power that he had paid dearly to acquire, all the power he had a right to because of his mantle, all the power he desperately needed because of his love for Morgan; he gathered it all to himself and flung himself forward.

He wasn't sure if he'd moved as himself, or a single thought, or a shape he didn't want to identify. All he knew was he found himself standing with his hands around Lothar's throat, weaving spells of binding around Lothar to keep him in his proper form, and a fury rushing through him like a mighty wind.

"Before I kill you," Miach snarled, "give Sosar of Tòrr Dòrainn back his power."

"Never," Lothar gurgled.

Miach wove yet more spells of binding about him. Lothar struggled, but it was futile. He had overextended himself with that last bit of vile shapechanging and found himself caught between illusion and spite. Miach didn't care what the particulars were. Lothar was immobile and he had a score of other ways to further incapacitate him. He took his time wrapping around his great-uncle dozens of generations removed other things that were highly unpleasant.

He saw out of the corner of his eye that a collection of Lothar's sons and grandsons had gathered and were running toward him. They came to a very sudden halt, most of them having gone sprawling, thanks to his spells. He made certain they wouldn't be vexing him for at least another handful of hours, then turned back to Lothar himself.

"Reverse the spell you used on Prince Sosar," he demanded, stepping back and leaving Lothar standing there, immobile. "Reverse it and I'll let you live."

Lothar merely looked at him, his eyes hot with hate.

"Reverse it, damn you!" Miach shouted.

Lothar tried to spit on him.

Miach found the spell of Diminishing Keir had given him halfway out of his mouth before he realized what he was doing.

And once it was there, he saw no reason not to continue on with it.

He would drain the bastard once and for all of all that made him a mage, then leave him to wander the wastes east of Beinn òrain for the rest of his days. And after that was done, he would do the same to all Lothar's progeny. He would rid the whole bloody Nine Kingdoms of their blight. He had the means; there was no reason not to—

"Miach."

Miach ignored the voice, then smiled at Lothar coldly before he deliberately began the spell again. Lothar's eyes widened with what another might have called fear. If Lothar was terrified by the words, he could hear them at least another time or two. Perhaps the spell could be wrought very slowly so Lothar would have time to contemplate between each word just what he was about to lose. Miach didn't need the added power, but he would take it just the same—

"Miach."

He looked down and saw a hand on his arm. His first reaction was anger that he was being interrupted as he strove to lay out the best thing for all those around him, then he realized it was Morgan's hand. Her nails were chipped, her hand covered with blood and dirt. She squeezed his arm.

"Miach, not this way." She looked up at him, her green eyes very bloodshot. "Not this way, my love."

The anger he felt burning furiously inside him was so strong, he had a hard time pulling back from it. He felt someone else's hand on his other arm. He turned his scowl on that soul only to find Sosar standing there next to him.

"Don't turn into him to spare me," he said seriously. "Think about that spell you're weaving, Miach. It isn't Lothar's spell of Taking, it's Gair's spell of Diminishing. *Think*."

Miach looked back at Morgan. Her eyes were full of understanding.

"'Tis tempting, isn't it?" she murmured. "Keir said it would be. But think on the price you would pay, Miach."

He glanced back at Lothar. He stood there, bound completely, but there was no longer any fear in his eye. There was satisfaction there instead, as if he might actually have been happy to trade his power for Miach's destruction.

Miach looked back down at Morgan's hand on his arm. He saw the faint sparkle of elvish runes about her wrist, runes that promised things he would never be able to claim if he took even a single step farther down the path he'd started.

He looked up and stared at Lothar for another moment in silence.

Then he took a deep breath and very deliberately stepped backward.

"I will not become you," he said quietly.

"How noble of you," Lothar said scornfully. "Noble and weak. You'll leave the elven prince without what he treasures most because you haven't the nerve to destroy me."

Miach watched the spell of Diminishing blow away on the faint breeze that came in from the ocean to his left. That breeze was full of the smell of the sea, clean and crisp. He breathed it in a time or two, then looked at Sosar.

"I don't think I have to kill him to have your power back."

"It wouldn't matter if that were the only way," Sosar said with a faint smile. "I don't want it at the cost of your soul. We'll discuss it later, when we're slipping into our cups in front of a hot fire. Now, though, I think you have to decide what you're going to do with him."

Miach looked around him. Besides Morgan and Sosar, he was being watched by his brothers Cathar, Rigaud, Nemed, and Mansourah; Morgan's grandfather; her mercenary companions; and a complement of his own grandsires he hadn't realized were there. Yngerame of Wychweald stood to one side with Gilraehen, Harold, and Yngerame's son, Symon, the first king of Neroche. They were dressed in unremarkable soldier's gear, but their swords had obviously been well used. Miach turned to Yngerame, who happened to be, as fate would have it, Lothar's father.

Yngerame only shook his head. "'Tis your choice, Mochriadhemiach," he said. "I won't make it for you."

"Shut up, Father," Lothar snarled. "This is none of your affair. Or Symon's. This is between me and the *least* of your line. And he's a fool if he thinks his pitiful bindings will hold me."

Symon rested his hands on his sword. "I don't see you moving overmuch, brother. I seem to remember you in this same position several centuries ago, only it took me and Father both to do so. You'll notice that young Miach didn't need any help."

"He'll need help enough when I'm free and I come to kill *him*," Lothar spat. "I should have done so when he was weeping in my dungeon and saved myself this trouble."

"I never wept," Miach said quietly. He pushed aside the renewed desire to strip Lothar of everything he valued, then looked at his great-uncle. "Now, if you have anything to say, be about it before I put you where I won't have to listen to you any longer."

Lothar looked at him, then slowly smiled. "I do have one more thing to say." He took a deep breath, then made a strange, shrill call.

An answering call came from the keep in the distance.

Miach slapped a spell over Lothar's mouth, but that horrifying cry continued in spite of it, echoing in the keep. Miach looked for his sword, but before he could ask Morgan for it, Cathar chucked another at him. He caught it without thinking.

It blazed suddenly with bloodred magelight.

Miach gaped at the sword in his hand. It took him a moment or two, but then he realized what had just happened.

And judging by the gasps, so did several others.

Nineteen

Morgan wondered if she were seeing things.

It wasn't as if she hadn't seen enough in the past handful of months to make her rub her eyes more than once to make sure she wasn't dreaming. She'd seen knives tinged blue with magic. She'd seen swords shimmer with otherworldly light and sing songs apparently only she could hear. She'd watched duels with spells, gazed on the painful, glittering beauty of elves, and admired the twisting and turnings of the hidden palace of the dwarf king. She'd seen more Olc than she ever wanted to and watched the beauty that was Fadaire sparkle on the top of a torch in a particular tower chamber at Gobhann where magic was possible.

She'd also seen the sword Miach was holding blaze with light as it was doing now, only she'd been holding it at the time and protecting someone she hadn't known was the king of Neroche from finding himself impaled by a particularly gruesome monster.

Why was that sword now glowing for Miach?

She would have asked his brothers who had stopped gasping as if they'd been kicked in their guts and instead were gaping at him stupidly, but she was distracted by other things.

Miach had turned away from Lothar to face their company. The sword was still in his hand, still ablaze with that unearthly dark red light. He was wearing an expression of absolute astonishment. Morgan didn't take the time to ask him why. She was too busy watching a crown—and a rather robust one, at that—appear suddenly, shimmering in the air above him. It was a lovely thing as far as crowns went, magnificently cast and adorned with all manner of impressive gems. Considering how many crowns she'd tried to get out of wearing over the past month, she thought she might be a decent judge of their quality.

It wasn't a particularly solid crown, however. It seemed instead to be fashioned out of stuff that wasn't entirely of this world.

It was also settling itself on Miach's head.

A very impressive velvet robe, trimmed in ermine and embroidered with all manner of kingly insignia appeared as well, falling around Miach's shoulders like some sort of mantle.

She felt her mouth fall open.

Miach's brothers sank to their knees.

Miach fell to his hands and knees far less gracefully, as if he'd been crushed under some impossibly heavy weight and simply didn't have the strength to bear it.

Morgan looked around her again and saw that every soldier who had come to witness the spectacle there had also dropped to his knees. Her grandfather was staring at Miach as if he'd never seen him before. Miach's ancestors weren't kneeling, but they were watching him with very grave expressions. Only Sosar was smiling from where he'd gone to lean on his father, as if he didn't have the strength to stand through anything else on his own. He looked at her and winked.

"Interesting," he mouthed.

Morgan turned back to look at Miach wearing that bloody enormous crown and that regal robe and thought that perhaps she should bow as well, for that wasn't the crown of a prince.

It was the crown of a king.

She started to kneel, but found her hand taken suddenly. Miach had reached up and was clutching her fingers so tightly in his that it hurt. He shook his head sharply.

"Don't," he rasped.

She started to protest, but she made the mistake of blinking first.

The crown and the robe were gone. All other otherworldly manifestations were gone. It was just Miach, hunched over on the blood-soaked ground, gasping for breath and looking particularly green.

Damn it, when were those unsettling visions going to stop?

"Get up, you fools!" Sìle bellowed suddenly. "We're not finished here."

Morgan hauled Miach to his feet and spun him around so he was standing behind her with his back to hers. She killed three lads apparently bent on doing damage to the man behind her before she took another breath. She suddenly found herself in the middle of Nerochian soldiers she hadn't seen before, soldiers who seemed particularly concerned with keeping Miach safe.

She couldn't find any words to use to express her astonishment at what she'd just seen, much less anything handy to use as an intelligent question, so instead, she did what she she'd been trained to do: she fought and saved the thinking for when she had a cup of ale in her hand and a fire near her feet. There was a stricture for that, though she couldn't bring the exact wording of it to mind at present.

And so she fought with Miach's back to hers, fought alongside him, found herself pulled behind him a time or two when faced with a particularly burly opponent—though she would have been the first to point out that she did that for him just as often.

It might have been an hour, it could have been three, when the battle in the area around them was finished and their enemies slain. Lothar had been dragged over to one side and was currently under the tender care of a pair of Miach's progenitors. Morgan supposed they would be able to keep him in line now he was not only immobilized, but mute. She turned back to look at the keep in front of her, sitting on the edge of the shore. The ocean was lovely; the keep was not.

"Riamh?" she asked Miach, who was standing next to her.

He nodded wearily. "It was once, I understand, quite a lovely place. It is that no longer, I fear." He took a deep breath. "I need to go inside and find Turah. And Adhémar as well, I imagine."

She put her hand on his arm. "Miach, don't. Don't go in that dungeon. Let me go in your stead."

He jammed the Sword of Neroche into the ground, then took the Sword of Angesand from her and did the same with it. The magelight faded from both swords immediately. Morgan looked at them in surprise, then found herself pulled into Miach's arms. That was handy, actually, for the sight of those swords without their light left her somewhat bereft. She put her arms around him and didn't bother to fight her trembles. He would think they were from weariness anyway. And given that he was trembling in the same manner, perhaps it didn't matter what weakness he might credit her with.

"Don't go in there," she repeated, when she thought she could get the words out without her voice breaking. "Give me a minute to catch my breath, then I'll go."

"Morgan," Miach said quietly, "I wouldn't let you near that place if my life hung in the balance. It has nothing to do with courage or strength or what you are able to bear. It just has to do with me, wanting to protect you from horrors you would regret having seen."

She lifted her head and looked at him. "And who will protect you?"

"I'll fall apart in your arms in some deserted corner of the palace tonight," he said, with a very faint smile. He lifted his hand and smoothed it over her hair. "I've already been inside the keep, Morgan, and seen the worst it has to offer. After today, I don't think it will trouble me."

"Then take someone else with you," she insisted. "A handful of someones with very sharp swords."

"I will if it pleases you," he acquiesced, "though I don't think there's much to worry about. Lothar's kin behind us are happily trapped under my spell and I don't think Lothar himself will be doing anything else untoward today. I'll be safe enough."

She hesitated, then put her arms around his neck and held on to him very tightly for a moment or two. She wished with a desperation that surprised her that they were at Lismòr, lingering over wine in Nicholas's solar; or even at Gobhann, listening to the roar of the wind and attempting to choke down very bitter ale. She wished they were anywhere but where they were, standing on accursed soil and surrounded by events she wasn't sure she wanted to examine too closely.

She decided then that she didn't care for change.

Miach held her tightly for another moment or two, then pulled away. "Wait for me?"

She nodded. "I'll watch over the swords."

"Thank you," he said gravely. He reached out and touched her cheek, then turned and walked away toward the keep. By the time he reached the main door of the hall, he had been joined by Yngerame of Wychweald, Harold of Neroche, and his brothers Cathar, Mansourah, and Rigaud. She took up a post next to the swords and waited.

She soon found herself accompanied in that labor by her mercenary companions and Miach's brother, Nemed. He smiled at her and held out his hand.

"We haven't actually had a proper introduction yet," he said politely. "I'm Nemed."

"I'm Morgan," she said, taking his hand briefly. "Or Mhorghain, I suppose, if you'd rather. I am Miach's . . . um—"

"Betrothed," Nemed supplied. "Aye, I know. I'm happy he found you when he did."

She blinked. "Are you? Why?"

He started to speak, then looked briefly over his shoulder as someone called his name. "Forgive me," he said with a faint smile. "Duty calls."

Morgan watched him go, then turned to Paien. "What do you suppose he meant by that?"

"Timing is everything," Paien said wisely.

Morgan looked to Camid for his opinion, but he was only rubbing his long nose and looking with undisguised enthusiasm at the water to the north of the keep. Well, anything he might want to discuss would have to do with boats and since she had as little to do with boats as possible, conversing with him would be pointless. She turned to Glines. He was merely watching her with an expression she couldn't quite identify at first. It wasn't amusement, and it wasn't pity. She suspected it might have been an unhappy mixture of both.

"What?" she demanded.

He shook his head slowly. "Not a thing, Morgan. Not a thing."

She nudged her other companions out of the way and moved to stand next to him. She had to take several goodly breaths before she trusted herself to look up at him. "I'm not sure I know what happened there," she admitted. "I'm not sure I *want* to know what just happened there."

Glines looked at her gravely. "Adhémar is dead, Morgan."

"Do you think so?"

"I know so."

She closed her eyes briefly, then looked at him again. "I don't suppose you'd know much about Nerochian succession, would you?"

"I might."

"Noble blood will land you in trouble every time, Glines."

He laughed. "Morgan, you are hardly one to talk there, are you? But since I can see you want answers to questions you can't bring yourself to ask, let me tell you of it."

"Is this going to take very long?"

"Longer than you'd like, but you're too restless to sit, so just be quiet and listen." He clasped his hands behind his back and assumed the same sort of expression Miach did when he was about to relate some important bit of lore. "In the olden times, in the days of Gilraehen the Fey and his son, Harold the Bold—"

Harold the Bold and Exhausted, she corrected silently. She would have said as much to Glines, but then he would have wanted to know how she knew and then she would be giving him all the gossip Miach had given her and that would require ale and comfortable chairs. She had no time for that; she wanted answers to her questions. Perhaps she would give him details later, when she'd survived what she was sure were tidings she wasn't going to be happy about.

"The king of Neroche was, as I was saying before you dozed off there, in the olden days king and archmage both," Glines continued. "As time went on and the line became diluted, the offices of king and archmage were separated. There have been kings throughout the years who could have borne both burdens, of course, and archmages who could have done the same, but that hasn't happened for centuries. There was a prophecy—"

"Oh, nay, not one of those," she protested.

Glines smiled. "Uisdean the Wise said: '*The king will sit upon his throne with his sword sheathed and laid across his knees before the tide of darkness will be stemmed.*' Some have speculated that the prophecy meant the king would have to be powerful enough not to need the Sword of Neroche to win his battles. Others have thought that the king would need to give power *to* the Sword of Neroche, not take from it, for Neroche to prevail. In either case, the only way truly for the king to have that much power would be if he were king and archmage both. And only then would Lothar be bested."

"And what does that have to do with Adhémar possibly being dead?" she asked reluctantly.

Glines looked at her pointedly. "There is no possibility of Adhémar's being alive, Morgan."

"Why not?" she asked, finding that her mouth was very dry all of the sudden.

"Because when a king or an archmage dies, his mantle falls on his successor immediately. I suppose Miach could tell you quite a few tales about unsuspecting mages—and a farmer or two—fainting suddenly only to wake and find they were the next archmage of the realm." Glines smiled gently. "Adhémar's mantle fell on Miach, Morgan, but I daresay you saw that."

"I was delirious."

He put his hand on her shoulder briefly. "Cling to that if it makes you feel any better."

"It doesn't," she said, wishing desperately for a drink of something strong. She looked at Glines. "I can't believe it. Well, I can believe it because 'tis Miach and I always thought he would make a better king than Adhémar, but that was before . . . before—"

"Before you agreed to wed him?"

She took a deep breath. "I think I'm finished talking to you."

"But—"

She walked away from him before she was tempted to silence him by means of a dagger to his belly. She only managed a few paces before she had to stop.

Miach, king of Neroche?

She looked about her for the distraction of her grandfather or Sosar, but they were heading toward the hall door. She didn't want to go inside the hall and there was nowhere else to run. She settled for turning her back on Glines and taking up her vigil again near the swords driven into the ground. At least they were refraining from any further magical displays. She focused on them and their beauty until she saw things begin to happen near the keep.

Rigaud appeared in the doorway of the hall, carrying Adaira in his arms. Morgan didn't have to be any closer than she was to tell the queen was dead. Rigaud laid her gently on the ground, then closed her eyes. Morgan winced, then watched as Cathar and Mansourah carried Adhémar out and laid him next to his bride. There was no mistaking his condition either.

Morgan looked up and saw Miach and Turah standing at the doorway. Turah looked terrible, but at least he was alive. She hastened over to him, then drew his arm over her shoulders, taking some of his weight from Miach. She met Miach's eyes.

"Bad?"

He took a deep breath, then nodded. "Very."

Morgan looked at Turah. His eyes were open, but he wasn't seeing what was in front of him. "What can we do for him?"

"There isn't anything *to* be done," Miach said grimly. "There are no signs of bodily harm on him, which is fortunate. The rest can only be cured by time." He paused. "I suppose you could try your grandfather's spell of healing on him, if you wanted to."

"Not with you," she said with a snort, then she shut her mouth and winced. "Forgive me. Levity is misplaced."

He shook his head slowly. "I think, my love, that a bit of laughter may be all that salvages this day. Why don't we try that same spell again, only this time I'll begin and you'll be the one to repeat the last word with me. Then you can put me to bed when I faint."

She almost smiled. "If you like. But perhaps not here."

"Nay, not here. Let me sort things for a bit longer, then we'll return home and give it a go." He looked over his shoulder. "Glines, would you come take my place here with Turah?"

"Of course, Your Most Royal and Splendid Highness," Glines said deferentially.

Miach stepped aside far enough to let Glines ease under his brother's shoulder, then slapped Glines on the back of his head. Glines only laughed and shot him a knowing look. Morgan watched Miach walk over to talk to the men standing near the king and queen. He wasn't all that steady on his feet, which made her wonder just what he'd seen inside the keep.

Nothing good.

He did look over his shoulder, though, and smiled gravely at her before he turned back to his business.

"He's besotted," Glines murmured. "He'll drive his advisors mad when he spends all his time mooning over you instead of attending to matters of the realm."

"Shut up," Morgan said miserably. "This isn't fodder for jest, Glines." She cursed heartily, but it didn't ease her any. "The bloody king of Neroche—"

"And he was the bloody archmage of Neroche this morning. What's the difference?"

She glared at him. "If you can't see it, I won't explain it to you."

Glines only lifted his eyebrows briefly. "I see very well, thank you, but I think *you* might be looking at the wrong things." He nodded to his right. "There's a stone bench over there. Well, what's left of one. Let's see if we can walk Prince Turah over there, shall we? We'll discuss what those wrong things are whilst you're sitting down."

Morgan imagined she wouldn't be discussing anything with him anytime soon, but she was happy for something useful to do, so she nodded in agreement. It took a few tries, but they finally managed to get Turah walking in the right direction. They helped him sit, then sat on either side of him, keeping him upright.

Gone was the cheeky, teasing lad who laughed often and well. In his place was a man with no light in him at all. Morgan patted his back, but he gave no indication of having felt either her hand or the comfort she'd tried to offer with it. She looked over Turah's bowed head at Glines. He only shook his head grimly.

Perhaps Miach had it aright. There were just some things that were better not to see.

"How is the young prince?"

Morgan looked up to find that her grandfather was standing in front of her, wearing an expression of concern. She shrugged helplessly. "His body is here, but I think his spirit is very far away."

"I don't blame him," Sìle said darkly. "Death would be too kind a fate for that accursed mage. I hope it is dealt to him swiftly and without mercy." He squatted down and studied Turah for quite some time before he looked at her. "Would Miach mind, do you suppose, if I took away a little of the horror young Turah has seen?"

"Can you do that?" Morgan asked in surprise. "Would you do that?"

"I can and I would." He smiled briefly. "I like him. I wouldn't want him wedding one of my granddaughters, of course, but he could certainly come clean my stables for me."

Morgan smiled in spite of herself, then smiled again at the sight of Glines gaping at her grandfather. Sìle reached up and put his thumbs over Turah's closed eyes. She couldn't hear all the words he murmured, but Turah seemed to, for he shuddered a time or two. After Sìle removed his hands, Turah sucked in an enormous breath, then let it out slowly. He opened his eyes and looked around him as if he'd just woken up.

"Your Majesty," he managed. "Morgan. Glines."

"Your Highness," Glines said, inclining his head. "How are you?"

"I had a terrible dream," Turah began, then he looked to his left and his mouth fell open. "It wasn't a dream," he managed.

Sìle rose and put his hand briefly on Turah's head before he walked away. "It wasn't a dream, my boy, but it will fade in time. Do your best to allow it to."

Turah bowed his head and rested his face against his hands. Morgan put her arm around his shoulders and tried not to notice as they shook with his sobs. She wasn't adept at comforting others, but she did what Miach would have done for her. She rubbed Turah's back, patted him occasionally, and let him weep. When he sounded like he might be gaining control of himself, she looked around for something useful to give him. Finding nothing, she ripped off part of her sleeve and put it into his hands.

"Thank you," he croaked. "I don't usually weep."

"Neither do I," she offered. "Well, unless I've been poisoned by

Lothar. You could use that excuse as well I imagine, if you like." She smiled encouragingly. "You didn't fall apart too terribly, you know."

"Just don't tell Mansourah that I did at all. He'll never let me forget it." He blew his nose, wiped his face again, then stuck the cloth down his boot. He stared at the keep for quite a long time, then sighed. "Adhémar is dead, isn't he?"

Morgan nodded. "He is."

"Cathar must be a little walloped by it."

Glines looked briefly at Morgan over Turah's head. "By what, Your Highness?"

"By the mantle," Turah said. "What was Cathar doing when it fell on him? Did you see it?"

Glines cleared his throat delicately. "It didn't fall upon Prince Cathar."

Turah's mouth fell open. "It didn't?"

"Nay."

Turah considered for quite a bit longer, frowned, then shook his head. "I should have thought Cathar, but perhaps not." He looked at Glines. "Not Rigaud, surely. The realm will fall to shreds. I will be looking for somewhere else to live, for I'll *not* be subjected to how he'll expect everyone to dress."

"Nay, not Prince Rigaud, either," Glines said, smiling faintly.

Morgan found Turah gaping at her. "Nemed? Nay, not *Mansourah*?"

"It could have been you," Glines said mildly.

Turah shot him a dark look. "I'm still quite happily unburdened with a score of things I don't want." He looked at Morgan for a moment or two, then he began to smile. "Miach?"

She smiled, though she feared it had been a rather sick smile indeed. "Apparently so."

Turah bowed his head again, then he laughed. He shook his head another time or two, then laughed a bit more. It wasn't an unpleasant laugh, or one of disbelief. It was one of good humor, as if he'd just learned something that pleased him in a particularly lovely way.

"I am unsurprised," he said, shaking his head a final time. "It is as it should be." He smiled at her, a smile that was almost a decent echo of the good-humored ones he'd given her before. "And how did he react?"

"I don't think he had time to react."

"What about you?"

"What about me?" she hedged.

He put his arm around her shoulders and leaned close. "You'll make a glorious—"

"Stop," she warned. "Stop there and say not another word or you'll regret it."

He only smiled again, a better one that time. "Very well, dearest sister-to-be, we won't discuss the size of your betrothed's crown, the potential size of your own crown, or my stay in yon keep."

"I would appreciate that."

"What shall we discuss?"

"Why don't you just have a little rest?" she asked pointedly. "Talking is wearying."

He smiled to himself, then bent his head and studied the ground between his feet. Morgan looked around herself for a similar distraction, but there were none to be had. The swords reminded her of what she'd seen, Turah reminded her of where he'd been, and Miach reminded her of what he'd become. Even Lothar reminded her of a very unpleasant pair of days enduring more of his company than she'd ever feared she might.

At least she had escaped unscathed. She wondered if Turah had managed the same thing. She attempted a surreptitious glance at him, but found he was watching her out of the corner of his eye. She scowled at him.

"I was just thinking about you," she said. "Polite concern, nothing more."

"'Tis a promising start."

She tried to purse her lips, but there was something about Turah that inspired smiles instead. She managed one, then felt it fade all too quickly. "He didn't take your magic, did he?"

Turah muttered something under his breath, then a small clutch of flowers appeared in his hand, tied with a lovely green ribbon. He handed them to her. "Apparently not." He stiffened. "Did Lothar take your—"

She shook her head. "Not mine, nor Miach's. He attacked Sosar instead, at the well."

Turah closed his eyes briefly. "Poor Sosar. I can't imagine it." He looked at her suddenly. "You closed the well?"

She nodded. "I daresay it wasn't worse than your past se'nnight, but it was unpleasant enough."

He put his arm around her shoulders. "I'm sorry, love. It was well done, though." He looked at her seriously. "Not even Miach could have managed the feat, Morgan."

She shifted uncomfortably under the compliment. " 'Tis over," she said quickly, "and for that I am very grateful. I'm grateful this is over as well, though I'm not sure how the day will finish."

"Likely with my head on a pike outside Tor Neroche's gates," Turah said with a huff of a laugh. "Look at Miach glaring at me already. You'd think he'd have more to think about besides how to injure me when I'm already so crushed, but apparently not."

Morgan looked up to find Miach walking over to stand in front of them. He folded his arms over his chest and looked at his brother.

"Mauling my betrothed?" he asked mildly.

Morgan held up her flowers. "He made me these as well, if you're curious."

"But I didn't sing any lays to her beauty," Turah said, pushing himself to his feet, "which I'm sure would have been the tipping point in our relationship." He embraced his brother and slapped him several times on the back. "I understand congratulations are in order. Or are those condolences I should be offering?"

"What you should be offering is to keep your mouth shut," Miach said with a snort.

"Where's the sport in that?" Turah ruffled Miach's hair. "I'll have to do that a time or two more before you have the power to toss me in the dungeon, hadn't I?"

"Turah . . ."

Turah kissed him loudly on both cheeks, slapped the back of his head as Miach had done to Glines, then moved past him before Miach could retaliate. "I'll thank you later for the rescue. Did anyone over there bring anything to eat?"

Morgan smiled as she watched him go. He walked with the balance of a man who'd just spent the day cozying up to an ale keg, but at least he was moving. It could have been worse.

She looked at Miach and felt her smile falter. He was the same man, of course, but after the morning's events—

"Oh, nay," he said, reaching out and pulling her to her feet. "Don't look at me that way."

"What way?" she stalled.

"Morgan," he said with a sigh.

Morgan looked around for an avenue of escape. Glines was looking off into the distance, apparently doing his best to pretend he wasn't there. No aid from that quarter. She didn't want to bolt left, for that only led to a place she was certain she had no interest in visiting. She looked down at her hands in Miach's for a moment or two, then up at him.

"What?"

He opened his mouth to speak, but shut it at the sound of someone calling his name. He cursed lightly, then drew her into his arms. "Nothing has changed, Morgan. Well, *I* haven't changed," he amended. "And just so you remember, I went into Gobhann to fetch you once. I'm not opposed to going in after you a second time. I daresay I could pick the lock on the front gate, if necessary."

"Miach!" came the voice again from across the way.

He sighed, pulled back, then put his hands on her shoulders. His eyes were bloodshot and full of things she imagined he wished he hadn't seen. He started to speak, then shook his head. "Wait for me."

She nodded, mute.

He kissed her forehead, then released her and walked away. He wasn't much steadier on his feet than his brother had been.

Morgan watched him walk away, then sat back down because her knees weren't equal to the task of keeping her upright. She couldn't look at Glines, she couldn't look at Lothar's keep, she couldn't look at Miach. So she looked at the ground at her feet, just as Turah had, and tried not to think at all.

"I want you to remember," Glines said carefully, "that I knew you when you were a grubby little gel without decent table manners."

She shot him a glare. "I was never grubby."

He smiled. "I'll stay on and be your minister of protocol and deportment, if you like. I think you're going to need me. There are the formalities, Morgan, that visiting royalty require—"

"Shut up."

He laughed and reached over to tug on her braid. "Morgan, 'tis no wonder Miach loves you so. Tor Neroche will never be the same once you take the thr—"

She shot him a look that had him biting back whatever else he intended to say. It didn't, however, keep him from smiling. She would have been quite content to call on a fierce frown of displeasure, but all she could do was feel quite miserable. "I don't know why you're enjoying this so much."

"Because I am a connoisseur of fine irony. 'Tis a bit like fine wine, but has a better bite."

She imagined it did, which was why she preferred wine. And this was irony she could have done without. It was bad enough that she, a shieldmaiden of stern mien and unmagical tendencies, should find herself the granddaughter of an elven king. It was far worse that she, a mercenary who preferred to eat whilst standing and had a tendency to walk out on strategy sessions that lasted overlong, should find herself facing a lifetime of court niceties and endless ceremonies.

Glines did have a point. She likely would have been a part of those things if she'd merely been the wife of the archmage.

Though she suspected that the queen of Neroche would have a much harder time slipping out the back door to go tramp in the lists or poach a horse from the stables and ride off out the gates without a guard.

She gave Glines a final look of displeasure, because it made her feel better, then turned back to the contemplation of the ground between her feet.

It seemed the safest thing to do.

Twenty

Miach made his way back across the barren ground to Lothar's hall, trying to keep himself from stumbling. His head was spinning, which he happily and immediately credited to not having had enough sleep. It had nothing to do with what had just happened to him a pair of hours earlier, something he had never expected, never hoped for, and never once considered without having turned his mind immediately to something more pleasant.

It was slightly more difficult to deny the fact that he could now, without an effort, cast his mind over any part of Neroche and know with startling clarity what was happening. He could see, as if he stood in front of them, the walls of Aherin. Hearn was walking out of his front gates, casting a baleful glance at the sky as if he thought it might send forth rains to trouble the training of his spectacular beasts. He was wearing dark trousers and a brown tunic with a close-fitting coat over the whole lot, and his boots indicated that he had just come from the barn.

"Miach."

Miach blinked and he was once again standing in front of Riamh. His eldest brother the king and his bride the queen lay near the front door, unmoving. He wasn't sure what sort of spell had slain them, but he hoped they hadn't suffered from it. Well, any more than they'd already suffered from being held in a place where no light was possible and spells created horrors—

"Miach."

He focused on Cathar standing in front of him. "Sorry," he managed. "I'm distracted."

"I can't imagine why," Cathar said dryly. "I'm sorry to put you through any more today, but there's something inside you're going to want to see." He paused. "Perhaps it doesn't matter now that Morgan's shut the well, but I think you should see it anyway."

"In the dungeon?"

"Nay, not there."

"What a mercy," Miach said, dragging his hand through his hair. He managed a weary smile. "Lead on, then."

Cathar nodded, then turned back to the hall. Miach followed his brother back into Lothar's keep, glancing over the great hall as he did so. It was empty, for which he was very grateful. He wasn't sure what he would have done with servants if he'd found them there. Ending their misery might have been the kindest thing to do, but he'd seen enough of death for the day. He still had Lothar's kinsmen to deal with, and Lothar himself, of course, but putting innocent servants to the sword was one more thing than he could have stomached.

He followed Cathar up the stairs, along a passageway and then through an open doorway. He almost plowed into his brother's back before he realized Cathar had stopped. He steadied himself with a hand on the doorway, then looked over Cathar's shoulder.

"Is this Lothar's solar?" he asked.

"I suspect so, but I haven't had the pleasure of a visit before."

"Neither have I," Miach said with a grunt, "so I suppose we'll just guess."

Cathar stepped aside. "I'll show you what I found, but please don't take all day looking at everything else. I can't stand it here."

Miach nodded, then frowned. "We should hurry," he said suddenly. "There are still battles being fought along the border."

Cathar looked at him in surprise. "I should ask how you know that," he said faintly, "but I won't." He reached for a stack of papers sitting on a table. "The only reason I know about these is that we found another body in the keep. Not one of Lothar's kin, I don't think, and not one of his creatures. He was in a very small room with no door. For some reason King Yngerame seemed to know where it was and how to open it, but I didn't ask for details. There were a handful of papers in there. These match the hand that wrote the others. Symon thought you should see them."

Miach looked at the top sheaf and felt a chill run down his spine. *I am Acair, the last bastard born of Gair of Ceangail. My mother was the witchwoman of Fàs, who gave birth to me during my father's eighth century of life. I have agreed to give Lothar of Wychweald the spell of Diminishing in return for his aiding me in ridding myself of my brothers in the keep at Ceangail.*

Miach looked up at Cathar. "Did you read this?"

"Just the first page. That was enough." He shivered. "You don't think this Acair gave Lothar what he promised, do you?"

Miach considered, then shook his head. "I didn't hear Lothar use anything that came close to Gair's."

Cathar's mouth fell open. "How in the world do you know *that* one?"

"Keir gave it to me along with all the other spells he'd memorized from Gair's private book that he never let anyone see." He smiled wearily. "As we traveled together from Ceangail to Durial."

"Because you had to stay awake somehow."

"Aye, we did."

Cathar shuddered. "Brother, you know too many things. And what were you doing in Ceangail?"

"Finding Keir, among other things that I'll tell you later, when we have several cups of ale at our disposal. As for this Acair, I don't think we need worry about his giving Lothar any of Gair's spells. If Gair had even suspected Acair had known any of them, he would have killed him." He looked about the chamber with its stacks of books, ratty tapestries, and threadbare carpets, and wondered why it was Lothar hadn't attended to it better. It wasn't as if he didn't have gold enough to do so, or laborers at his disposal. Perhaps he spent too much time out in the world, wreaking havoc, to see to his own things.

"Miach?"

Miach pulled his attention back to his brother. "Should I search through this rot, do you think?"

"Surely not even Lothar would be stupid enough to leave everything of import in one place," Cathar said. "Besides, destroy this, and it will crop up again in a root cellar on some farm where he's terrorized the owners. I wouldn't bother."

Miach supposed they might come to regret that, but perhaps not. "I suppose there might be a handful of lads willing to keep watch over it until I can see to it."

"I doubt it, but you could try." He leaned back against a rickety table. "What are you going to do with Lothar, by the way?"

"I don't know yet," Miach said, sighing deeply. "It would be safer to simply slay him, but I daren't until I'm certain he isn't the only way for Sosar to have his power back. And as for anything else, slay Lothar and one of his sons will step forward to take his place—and we've no way of knowing which one that might be." He shrugged. "Do you have any suggestions?"

"Oh, nay," Cathar said, holding up his hands. "I wouldn't presume to offer an opinion. Black mages are your purview, not mine. Though if you truly do want an idea, why don't you stash Lothar in the dungeon at Tor Neroche and threaten the others with the same to keep them in line?"

"Do we have a dungeon?"

Cathar rolled his eyes and pushed himself away from the desk.

"You, Miach lad, have spent far too much time in that tower chamber of yours, learning things that make me nervous. Aye, we do have a dungeon, but on second thought, I don't imagine you want to put Lothar there. But you might want to find sooner rather than later a place to put him, if you plan to leave him alive." He started toward the door. "I wouldn't blame you if you didn't."

Miach would happily have put that decision off for another day or two, but he couldn't and he couldn't ask anyone else to make the decision for him. Not now.

He rolled up the papers and stuck them down his boot to join what Rùnach had given him, then followed his brother from the chamber. He paused after a handful of paces.

"Wait."

Cathar looked at him. "Second thoughts?"

"Aye." He turned back to Lothar's solar, considered for a moment, then wove one of Gair's spells of illusion over it. The Olc and the other nasty things the spell contained came far too easily to him, but given the day he'd had, he supposed he couldn't have expected anything else. He checked the spell for any flaws, then turned away and took a deep breath. He looked at his brother.

"What now?" he asked.

"I should be asking you that," Cathar said, pausing in the passageway to look at him.

Miach shot him a dark look. "Until our brother is buried, you are the eldest and therefore in charge. What next?"

Cathar put his hand briefly on Miach's shoulder. "Let's see to the end of the battle, then proceed from there. And did I tell you that you look terrible? Haven't you been sleeping well?"

Miach cursed his brother, who only laughed, embraced him briefly, then put his hand on the back of his neck and pulled him along the passageway. "Let's be out of this place. It gives me shivers."

Miach had a slightly more violent reaction than that, but he supposed by the haste in which his brother was dragging him from the keep, Cathar knew as much.

He stepped out the front door and walked down the steps, profoundly grateful for a breath of fresh air. He was even more grateful to stand to one side and allow Cathar to arrange for the bodies of the king and queen to be placed carefully in a wagon that someone had appropriated. Then his now-eldest brother turned to the assembled company.

"There are as yet small skirmishes that need to be attended to. We'll regroup in my tent after everything is finished."

Miach watched the company of his relatives and Morgan's troop off after Cathar. Well, most of them did. Morgan was still standing next to the two swords driven into the ground, looking very ill at ease. Glines was standing to one side of her, Gilraehen to the other, as if they protected her. Or perhaps they were trying to talk her out of bolting. He honestly wouldn't have been surprised by either.

He walked over to them, collecting another grandfather, the appropriate number of generations removed, along the way. He stopped a pace or two away and looked at Yngerame and Gilraehen.

"Thank you for your aid today, Your Majesties," he said seriously. "We needed it."

Yngerame shrugged. "I like trotting out my mediocre sword skill now and again." He looked Miach over for a moment or two. "I see you've improved yours."

"I owe it all to Weger's instruction and Morgan's patience with me in the lists," Miach said with a smile.

"She saved your sweet neck today more than once," Gilraehen informed him. "If I were you, I would finish up what needs to be done, then find a quiet place where you might thank her properly for it. Perhaps in verse. Accompanied by flowers or other such tokens of your affection."

Morgan looked at Gilraehen as if *he* were the one who'd lost his mind. Miach found that to be a vast improvement over having that look thrown his way, so he agreed readily with Gilraehen, then looked at Yngerame.

"I must do something about Lothar," he said quietly.

Yngerame nodded. "You must. You cannot leave him standing out there in the middle of the field and I don't think you want him cluttering up the palace. I wouldn't trust his children with him. He wouldn't survive the spring. And his sons and sundry are something you'll need to attend to as well." He looked at where Lothar stood, silent and bound by spells, then looked back at Miach. "When Symon and I bound him and left him in his hall, he didn't have as many descendants and they weren't all dark-hearted. We hoped that someone might redeem his line. Now, though, I fear there is no hope for any of them."

Miach rubbed his hands over his face, then looked at his grandfather. "I shouldn't be thinking twice about it. If ever there were a mage who deserved death, 'tis him. I owe him, if nothing else, for the deaths of my parents and my brother." He wondered if any of the consternation he felt showed on his face. "I can't bring myself to do it."

"I understand, believe me," Yngerame said. "I suppose you could search out a magic sink somewhere and lock him in it."

Miach blinked. He looked at Morgan to find her wearing an expression that he was sure matched his. He lifted one eyebrow. "Are you thinking what I'm thinking?" he asked slowly.

"Well, you did promise him something in return for his mark." She smiled faintly. "I'm not sure what he would think to find his grandfather deposited inside his gates with your thanks accompanying him."

"I think it might be worth the risk." Miach turned to Yngerame. "I wonder, Your Grace, if you would be amenable to a little trip south."

Yngerame was smiling. "To Gobhann?"

"It is a magic sink," Miach said. "And I'm sure Gobhann's lord would take particular care of his new guest."

Gilraehen smiled wickedly. "I think it's a wonderful idea. Lothar deserves it richly, but if I were him, I would fear for my life if I found myself in Scrymgeour Weger's hands."

"Then come with me, Gil," Yngerame said. "You can help me jot down the slew of curses Weger spews out when he sees what Miach has sent him."

"Gladly," Gilraehen said. He put his hand briefly on Morgan's back. "Mehar's at camp, Mhorghain, if you want to see her. She'll be interested in how you fared with the sword, I daresay. Grandfather, I'll be waiting for you near Scrymgeour's new inmate. Shall we collect Symon on our way south to keep us company?"

Yngerame nodded. "I'm certain he would relish the thought of watching his brother once again silent and bound. I'll be along in a moment." He waited until Gilraehen had walked away before he turned to Miach. "We'll be back tomorrow, I imagine. Later, if there's anything edible in Gobhann."

"Eat at Lismòr," Miach advised. "Nicholas sets a much finer table than Weger does. And why is Symon at the palace and not here?"

"He left to go guard your crown," Yngerame said with a smile. "He thought given how fond you are of wearing things on your head, you might appreciate that."

Miach didn't even have the energy to grunt. "Did he know about all this? Before it happened?"

"He knows everything, lad. He and Gil spend long winter evenings speculating about the fate of Neroche and its rulers. It isn't your time to join them on those evenings, though you will eventually." He started to walk away, then turned back and looked at Miach gravely. "Son, you did well today."

"Thank you, Grandfather," Miach said quietly.

"Your parents would be proud and your people will continue to be grateful." He stepped back. "Your work isn't completely finished though, children. Be careful whilst you're about it."

Miach watched him walk away, then turned and looked at Morgan and Glines.

"Well," he managed.

Glines smiled. "Aye, well, indeed. Let's go see if we can be of use, shall we?"

Miach nodded. He watched Morgan sheath the Sword of Angesand, then pull the Sword of Neroche out of the ground and hand it to him hilt-first.

"This is yours, I think," she said quietly.

He had to take a deep breath. "I don't think so."

"But I left your other sword behind," she said. "I think near where Lothar is."

Miach could see exactly where it lay, and Morgan had the location aright, but he wasn't going to go fetch it, and he certainly wasn't going to ask her to do it for him. The only problem facing him was that he had no sheath for the Sword of Neroche—it lay near his sword—and he wasn't sure he wanted to touch it again.

That would have been a bit like putting the last nail in his coffin.

But Morgan only continued to hold out the king's sword to him. He looked at her for several minutes in silence, then stretched forth his hand and took hold of it.

It blazed forth with a bloodred magelight that blinded him for a moment, then the light subsided into a glimmery sort of illumination that had struck fear into countless enemies over the centuries.

He sighed.

Morgan said nothing. She only nodded, then turned and walked away.

Miach looked at Glines, had a very low bow as his reward, then sighed and followed Morgan back toward the border.

Three hours later he was wandering restlessly about the camp. The battle was won with very few casualties, he'd found the sheath for the king's sword and put it up where it couldn't cause any more trouble, and he could easily sense that Lothar was on his way south in the tender care of a trio of former kings of Neroche who were amusing themselves by flying along the coast where the breezes made for a very bumpy ride indeed.

More important still, Gair's well had been shut, and he now had nothing but the future he'd looked forward to for several months stretching out in front of him, his to enjoy.

Only his future had completely changed.

He clasped his hands behind his back and suppressed the urge to run. Though the work was difficult, he enjoyed being the archmage of Neroche. True, he hadn't had a reason to think he would ever be anything else, but he had never been unhappy with his lot. He'd had privacy, he'd had freedom, and he'd had an excuse to duck out of unbearably tedious meetings with foreign dignitaries. He'd also had the license to distance himself from the insufferable ego that Adhémar had worn along with his crown and mock the king at will.

Now he would be in the thick of all that, the politics, the petty grievances between neighboring kingdoms, the painfully dull meetings with ambassadors he knew couldn't be trusted, and the even longer, even more painful attendance at the council of kings.

State dinners. Was there anything worse?

It occurred to him, accompanied by a sinking feeling that left him rather nauseated, that he was going to have to do a bit more growing up.

He looked for an avenue of escape. He was accustomed to outrunning his demons and his nightmares. He had never thought he would be outrunning a crown.

But since he had the feeling he might have company in that endeavor if he looked hard enough, he stopped wandering aimlessly and started looking for a particular gel. He strode through the camp, hurrying past souls before they could genuflect to him, and finally found the lass he was looking for.

She was standing near Cathar's tent, wrapped in a cloak yet still looking very chilled. Mehar was laughing at something Catrìona had said, but Morgan didn't join them. She merely stood next to them as if they were a cheery fire that she hoped to warm herself by. She didn't look as if it were working very well. Indeed, all she seemed to be succeeding at was looking thoroughly ill at ease.

He understood, completely.

He walked over to the little group, then came to a stop at Catrìona's elbow and made the three of them a low bow.

"Good afternoon, ladies," he said politely.

"Practicing your courtly manners, love?" Mehar asked with a smile.

"He's just naturally polite," Catrìona said, elbowing Miach companionably in the ribs. "I think he's trying to dazzle us with his lovely smile so we'll release his lady to him. Am I right, Miach?"

"You are," he agreed. "Might I borrow my betrothed for a bit? I'm in need of a bit of a run."

Mehar smiled in understanding. "Of course. I think whilst you're about your run, Catrìona and I will turn for the palace. Catch up as you can, children."

Miach nodded, made them a very low bow, then straightened and held out his hand to Morgan. "Let's go."

"Where?"

"Away."

She looked as haunted as he felt. She put her hand into his. "Gladly."

He walked away with her, but couldn't bring himself to speak. There was too much to say and most of it was about things he couldn't bear to think about yet.

It had been an overwhelming day, to say the least.

He waited until they were out in the open, out from under the poor trees Lothar had allowed to grow, then looked at her. "I suppose we should talk about today—"

"Later," she said. She took his hand and tugged on him. "Later, Miach, after you've outrun it for a bit."

He nodded gratefully. He ran until he needed to fly and she kept pace with him. He was reminded sharply of another afternoon, the first afternoon she'd changed her shape, when she was the one outrunning who she was. He'd never expected the tables to be turned so thoroughly.

Don't think. Just fly.

Her voice whispered across his mind. He took hold of her words and clutched them. They were, he had to admit, the most sensible bits of advice he'd been offered in the past pair of fortnights. He could just imagine all the pieces of advice he would be offered in the next few fortnights, advice about everything from what to say at supper so as not to offend all the way to how to match his silk tunics to his curly-toed court shoes. He supposed Rigaud would be offering that last one.

He pulled his wing back suddenly, wondering what he'd run into that had hurt so badly, only to find Morgan had singed him a bit.

Stop. It will be waiting for you when you get back.

He supposed she had that aright. She gave him a particularly dragonish look of challenge, then swept out toward the sea. He followed, gladly leaving behind things he would have to return to eventually.

But not yet.

It was very dark by the time they landed in the courtyard at Tor Neroche. Miach leaned over and gasped for breath, then fumbled for Morgan and threw his arm around her. He pulled her close and rested his head on her shoulder until he thought he could straighten with any success.

He heaved himself upright, then froze when he found himself suddenly surrounded by more than just torchlight. He was fairly certain Morgan had squeaked. He wasn't all that sure he hadn't as well.

All of Adhémar's ministers were there, along with the former king's steward, a handful of ambassadors from other countries, and Mistress of the Wardrobe, who was looking at him as if she were already sizing him up for what itchy, uncomfortable things she might force him to wear whether he liked it or not. He drew closer to Morgan.

"Let's run again," he murmured.

"I don't think you can."

Miach supposed he understood at that moment just how a tasty bit of vulture fodder felt. The king's advisors—who he supposed were now *his* advisors—descended upon him *en masse,* crowding around him, pressing in upon him on all sides. How they knew what had happened, he couldn't have said. Tidings traveled quickly, apparently.

He lost his grip on Morgan's hand at one point. He looked frantically for her but couldn't find her for the sea of robes, hats, and pieces of parchment being thrust in his face. He saw her finally through a break in the press. She was standing next to Glines, which he supposed he shouldn't have been happy about, but there was nothing he could do about it at present.

"Morgan!" he shouted over the din.

She waved, not looking particularly unhappy to be at liberty to flee, then she turned and walked away.

Miach singled out a face in the sea of faces in front of him. It was Sir Doigheil, the man whose entire existence was dedicated to seeing elves appeased at all costs.

Miach reached out and dragged Sir Doigheil close to him. "There is a very large contingent of elves arriving from Tòrr Dòrainn—"

"They're already here, Your Highness. Queen Brèagha arrived this morning with her daughters. I have, of course, seen them all situated in chambers befitting their exalted station."

Miach smiled in spite of himself. Whoever had selected the man for his particular job had chosen wisely. "Thank you for your diligence in that. If I might ask you also to please see to something especially comfortable for King Sìle's granddaughter, Princess Mhorghain—"

"Mhorghain?" Doigheil interrupted, looking stunned. "Mhorghain of Ceangail?" He gaped a bit more. "Is *that* who joined you on your accursed—er, I mean your *therapeutic* flying?"

"It was," Miach agreed. "She won't want anything fussy and she may want room for companions." He paused. "Please, *please* see that she's fed well."

Doigheil nodded, wide-eyed, turned, and then struggled to make his way through bodies that didn't want to move.

Miach took a deep breath, then looked at the remaining men clustered around him. They were all staring at him as if he alone held the answers to the universe and all its mysteries.

He was tempted to bolt.

He took a deep breath. Nay, he wouldn't run. He didn't run, not when it came to seeing to his responsibilities. If this was what Fate had decreed, then he would accept that decree and make the best of it. He'd spent all his adult life and a good part of his youth in the service of the realm and its people. King was, perhaps, no different from archmage, though it seemed bloody cheeky to think he might be wearing that crown, a crown he was certain would be three sizes too large and slip down over his eyes at an inopportune moment.

He wished, quite suddenly and quite desperately, that he'd even once asked his father how it had felt to have the mantle of the kingship fall upon him.

It had just never occurred to him that he would want to know.

He took a deep breath and looked at the men surrounding him. "Who's next?"

The response was deafening.

Miach suspected it was going to be a very, very long night.

Twenty-one

Morgan paced along the passageways of Tor Neroche because she couldn't sit still. She'd slept like the dead the night before—nay, it had been the night before that. After she'd abandoned Miach to that gaggle of busybodies, she'd walked down the passageway with Glines only for as long as it took someone to catch up to her and offer her a chamber large enough to accommodate half the population of Weger's tower. She had accepted, then invited everyone she knew to come join her there, just to keep the silence at bay.

She'd chatted for quite a while with her mercenary companions, then learned from one of Miach's brothers—Mansourah, she supposed, for he'd looked exactly like Turah only much more serious—that Sosar was resting comfortably, Turah was resting less comfortably, and Miach was trying to stay awake whilst listening to things that had needed to have been solved a month ago. Mansourah had then departed, looking vastly relieved that he wasn't the one doing the solving. Morgan had abandoned Miach to his fate, lain down, and slept until noon yesterday.

She'd spent the rest of the day before avoiding public meals and important people. She had passed a pleasant hour or two in the lists with a half dozen engaging lads who hadn't a clue who she was or what she was capable of. Leaving the Sword of Angesand under her bed had apparently been a wise thing to do.

She had visited Luath and Fleòd in the stables, then greeted the two horses of Hearn's she and Miach had ridden in the fall, Rèaltan and Reannag. The stables at Neroche were particularly luxurious, which she supposed would have pleased Hearn. She had the distinct feeling, however, that Luath and Fleòd were stirring up a fair bit of equine insurrection, for they seemed to think she was not only capable but willing to give them wings. When she'd politely informed them that she didn't know how, she'd had disbelieving snorts in response.

Hearn was going to have quite a bit to say to Miach about corrupting his horses with shapechanging.

She hadn't seen Miach, though she supposed neither had anyone else. He'd been closeted for the whole of the day with Adhémar's ministers. She knew this because she'd been sought out several times by official-looking young lads wearing crowns on their tunics who had come to tell her that even though Prince Mochriadhemiach was still in council, he had expressed concern about her care and wanted to make certain she knew he would seek her out at his earliest opportunity.

By supper, she'd been looking for another distraction and found it in the person of none other than Mehar of Angesand, who had been quite happy to jump off the roof of a tower with her and fly in dragonshape. Perhaps Mehar had once outrun her own demons, for she had certainly been willing to indulge Morgan in attempting to outrun her own. She hadn't offered much in the way of conversation outside of comments on the weather and the most likely spots for a good updraft. She said only one thing of import as she'd left Morgan at her door.

"I fell in love with Gil when I thought he was a stable boy," she had remarked casually. "The crown didn't change him. Or me, I daresay."

Morgan had tried to sleep on that, but it had proved a most uncomfortable pillow.

All of which left her where she now was, pacing through the hallways with a hood over her face to hide who she was and a cloak pulled close around her to ward off the chill.

She was having more success with the first.

She hadn't seen Miach yet that morning, but she hadn't been surprised by that. He likely hadn't managed either much sleep or any meals that hadn't been eaten whilst he was being badgered by ministers of this and that. Actually, so far that morning, she hadn't seen anyone at all.

Well, that wasn't precisely true.

She had seen and continued to see a steady stream of princesses and escorts that astounded her with not only their finery, but their beauty. She had no idea how tidings of a potential new lad on the throne had traveled so quickly or been responded to with equal swiftness, but there were, she had decided, many things that she just didn't understand.

"Watch your step!"

Morgan stepped aside as a particularly lovely woman almost ran over her.

The woman smoothed her hand over her bejeweled frock and straightened her crown, then looked down her nose. "When I am queen, you filthy urchin, servants such as you will pay better heed to where they're going!"

Morgan blinked. "Queen?"

"Aye," the woman said, drawing herself up. "I am come for that express purpose."

"And your name, Your Highness?" Morgan asked, because apparently she couldn't keep herself from taking a knife to her own breast and plunging it in to the hilt.

"Beatrice of Penrhyn. Of course."

"Of course." Morgan wasn't at all surprised at Princess Beatrice's manners, given that she'd encountered Beatrice's older sister in Tor Neroche several months earlier. And a pair of days ago, as well. "You must be grieved for your sister's demise," she said quietly.

"Briefly," Beatrice agreed, "but I like to move on to happier thoughts." She frowned at Morgan. "You are quite talkative for a serving wench. I suggest you learn your place before I don my crown. You won't like what happens to you otherwise."

Morgan imagined that might be quite true. She made Beatrice a small curtsey, then slipped past her and continued on. It was tempting to continue on right through the front doors and out the front gate, but of all the things she was, a coward she was not.

I fell in love with Gil when I thought he was a stable boy.

Mehar's words echoed in her head in a particularly stubborn way, as if she'd added a little spell to them to make them do so. Morgan sighed to herself. She'd fallen in love with Miach when she'd thought he was a farmer. Perhaps it wasn't his fault that he'd been chosen to be the king.

Though it was a little hard for her to swallow, Mehar's annoyingly incessant words aside.

She rebuked them sternly, then continued on to blessed silence inside her head. Or, rather, she would have if the damned ring she had on her hand hadn't begun a little song, a song that became a duet as the knife in her boot joined in.

At least the Sword of Angesand was safely and quietly lying under her bed where it couldn't offer either its opinion or its harmony.

She continued to walk through the passageways, avoiding piles of luggage and collections of princesses, until she found herself standing at the bottom of a circular staircase. She paused and listened for a moment, but couldn't hear anything that led her to believe there might be someone above. She began to climb the stairs.

In time, she found herself on a landing, facing a door that was ajar. She pushed on it gingerly and found that it swung in without protest. It was cold inside that tower chamber, but that might have had to do with all the windows set into the walls, floor-to-ceiling windows that made her feel as if she were almost flying.

There was a luxurious rug on the floor, slim tapestries lining the walls between the windows, and a substantial hearth set into another of those walls. Chairs were set in front of the fire with a finely woven blanket tossed over the arm of one, as if it had merely been left there carelessly after a happy conversation had ended. Morgan walked over and fingered the red material. It was marvelously soft and seemed to whisper comforting things as she touched it.

She wandered over to one of the windows, then sank down onto a handy window seat and looked out. The countryside was bathed in early morning sunlight. She could even see the ocean glistening in the distance from where she stood. It was a particularly lovely scene and soothed her as nothing had in days. She had no idea what the future would hold, if Miach would want her, if she could bear what he'd had suddenly thrust upon him—

The sudden crackle and pop of fire in the hearth startled her so badly, she leapt up and whirled around with a shriek. Miach stood in the doorway. He held his hands up slowly.

"Only me."

Morgan slipped her knives back up her sleeves, then turned away before she had to look at him. She'd forgotten in the haze that had been the past two days just how handsome he was.

And how much she loved him.

Nay, she couldn't say that. She'd thought of little else, actually, and when she hadn't been thinking about it, she'd been trying not to think about it.

She felt rather than heard him come to stand next to her. He was silent for several moments. It was all she could do not to turn, go into his arms, and burst into tears. But she wasn't a crier, her lengthy bouts of blubbering at Lismòr aside, and she wasn't about to indulge at present. She lifted her chin and continued to stare out the window.

"Do you like the view?" he asked at length.

" 'Tis spectacular," she said, but her voice cracked on the last word. She cleared her throat roughly, then tried again. "Aye, 'tis very lovely."

"It was my mother's private solar," he remarked. "I spent many a happy hour here with her, lying on the rug in front of the fire and imagining up what would hopefully be a brief stint as archmage of Neroche before I went off to farm in the hills near Chagailt."

She almost smiled, but she couldn't. She put her hand on a tapestry and tried not to dig her fingers into its weave.

"I don't think your stint will be brief," she said.

"Hmmm," was all he said.

Her eyes began to burn. She cursed, but that didn't help. She looked for strictures to recite, but Weger hadn't provided her with anything to use in the event that she might find herself betrothed to a man who had suddenly found himself king of Neroche. She was half tempted to blurt out a few spells of Olc in a last-ditch effort to harden her heart, but she didn't think she could go that far. Tears began to stream down her cheeks, but she would be damned if she was going to acknowledge them. She was a cold-blooded mercenary with scores of battles under her belt, ruthless, callous, in control of her emotions at all times—

"Morgan."

She made the mistake of looking at him. His eyes were very red. Perhaps in his own way he was just as miserably uncomfortable as she was. And that thought finished her off as nothing else could have.

She turned and went into his arms. She thought she might have wept a bit, but she wasn't particularly keen on determining that. She was fairly certain that Miach offered her some sort of cloth to use in wiping her eyes and blowing her nose, but then he took it away again and used it himself. She was positive he then spelled it into oblivion.

"Will you ever give me a gift that you don't take away and make disappear within minutes?" she asked.

He managed some species of laugh and hugged her so tightly, she gasped. "I told you at Lismòr that I am not adept at wooing."

"A handkerchief, Miach, that remains in the same chamber where you created it for more than a quarter hour. How hard can that be?"

He took her face in his hands, smiled at her, then kissed her softly. "Come sit with me before the fire and I'll work on one just to please you."

She found she couldn't move. He looked at her in surprise, then he put his arms back around her.

"What is it?"

She swallowed, hard. "I have been thinking of running."

He took a deep breath, then let it out slowly. "I know. I just don't know why."

She pulled out of his arms, then gestured at him with a jerky motion. "Well, look at you. King of Neroche, and all. You have a bloody crown!"

"I had a crown before."

"The new one will be bigger," she said pointedly. "And have you seen all those princesses downstairs? I think Adaira's younger sister is already planning your honeymoon. She informed me the servants, including me, would be better mannered after she was queen or else I would come to regret my cheek. And do you have any idea how many *other* women are downstairs, waiting for you to show your face so they can fall upon you like, well, like those damned faeries at Buidseachd did—only these gels have, I daresay, pedigrees to actually tempt you!"

Miach gaped at her in astonishment for a moment or two, then he gathered her back against him. He held her very tightly. She supposed, after she thought on it for a moment or two, that he held her so tightly so she wouldn't feel him laughing.

"Damn you, if I could just reach a blade," she said, her voice muffled against his chest.

He seemed particularly unintimidated by the threat. He merely continued to hold her close. He kissed her hair, then sighed, the deep sort of a sigh a body might indulge in when he was happy to be home after a long journey.

"Woman, you're daft," he said finally, sounding more amused than he should have. "Why would I look at any of those lassies downstairs? My heart is already given. Don't give them any thought. They're the same swarm that periodically descended for Adhémar. I imagine they kept their trunks packed for just such an exigency as this."

She was tempted to smile, but she managed to avoid it because the truth was just too brutal to ignore. "But, Miach, I don't look anything like any of them."

"Thank heavens," he said, sounding vastly relieved. He pulled back far enough to look at her. "Morgan, you look like an elven queen of old, grave and remote and so beautiful that any man who sees you will fall to his knees and feel himself fortunate to be allowed to merely stare at your loveliness. I'll likely spend most of my time in that position as well."

"Don't tease me," she warned.

"I'm not teasing you. Don't I already spend vast amounts of time simply staring at you in a besotted fashion?"

"Glines seems to think so," she agreed reluctantly.

He smiled. "He has it aright." He hesitated, then his smile faded. "Shall I tell you how I think we'll survive this? In truth?"

"Please," she said with feeling.

He took a deep breath. "I've given it quite a bit of thought, actually," he said. He smiled briefly. "It was the only thing to keep me awake during the past two days of interminable meetings."

"Was it, indeed?"

"It was, indeed. Now, here is my plan. When we must, you'll be Mhorghain and I'll be Mochriadhemiach. We'll wear our crowns and look important. Then we'll take our crowns off and be just Morgan and Miach. And nothing will change between us because I'll still best you in every game of cards we play—"

"Ha," she snorted.

"And you'll still come close to besting me on the field every time we cross blades."

She scowled at him.

He smiled. "See? I'll love you to distraction, you'll pour gushing praise upon my head all day long, and we'll be happy." He caught her left hand and held it up. "And I think you've forgotten something."

The circlet of runes glinted very faintly in the light from the window. She sighed, then looked up at him. "Perhaps my grandfather wasn't so far off with that crown of yours, was he?"

"I'd like to credit him with foresight, but I imagine 'twas just an attempt to irritate Adhémar," he said dryly. "And you're trying to distract me. I seem to remember that you promised yourself to me as we knelt before your grandfather. I definitely remember promising myself to you."

She settled herself a little more comfortably in his arms. "There is that, true."

"Then what has changed? Does it grieve you that we have the same length of life bound upon us? Are you unhappy that we are heirs of Tòrr Dòrainn's throne? Queen of Neroche, Morgan," he cajoled. "Think on what Weger will do when he hears."

"He'll likely fall off his parapet in surprise," she muttered. "Hearn will choke on his ale."

"Hearn will think it the most sensible thing that's happened in the realm for decades. I'm sure he'll give you all sorts of instructions on how to keep me in line and have the realm run in a way to benefit him the most."

"I didn't think Angesand was part of Neroche."

"The exact nature of our governmental relationship is a bit hazy and likely to remain so for the foreseeable future."

She looked at his chin for several moments, then met his very pale eyes. "What do you think about all this?" she asked hesitantly. "The business of the crown?"

"It has made your grandfather slightly less reluctant to allow me to wed you. He told me so himself this morning. The rest of it requires sitting down." He pulled away and took her hand. "That chair over there looks big enough for two, if we're friendly."

"You've said that before in another place."

"It was worth repeating here."

She smiled in spite of herself, then allowed him to lead her over to a very comfortable chair that was indeed large enough for them both. He pulled Mehar's knife out of her boot and laid it on the table next to him, then took off her boots and put his hand over her feet. Then he took a deep breath.

"I didn't expect this," he began slowly, "which I'm sure you know. I had hoped to make the best of what I was certain would be Adhémar's very long reign, then happily leave Tor Neroche behind. I planned to find a lovely spot to build you a sturdy house, with a training field in the back and a stable big enough for mares to keep Fleòd and Luath company and house their descendants. I had then intended that we should live out the rest of our very long lives in peace."

"And now?"

"We'll still do that last bit," he said, "but I think our lives may be rather more taxing before we reach that point."

She nodded, then sighed and rested her head on his shoulder. She felt him unbraid her hair, then drag his fingers through it slowly.

"Miach?" she said finally.

"Aye, love."

She chewed on her next words for a bit. "Are you frightened?"

"Terrified," he admitted with an uneasy laugh. "You?"

"The same."

He smoothed his hand over her hair. "But you'll stay?"

"I fear I won't make a very good queen." She paused, then looked at her hand resting on his chest. "Perhaps I should start by having a bath."

He laughed in a merry way that made her eyes burn in spite of herself.

"I love you," he said with feeling. "Morgan, I . . ." He took a deep breath. "I don't know how I could possibly manage this without you."

"You just want someone to sneak out the back door and fly with you."

"Aye," he agreed, smiling at her. "That and so much more." He leaned closer to her. "Stay."

She lifted her head and looked at him unflinchingly. "I don't truly think I could have brought myself to leave you."

He kissed her for her trouble. Well, that at least was something familiar in a swirling sea of things she didn't recognize and wasn't sure how to best. Then again, that wasn't anything different from her condition over the past six months, so perhaps she had nothing to complain about.

"Your mind is wandering," Miach murmured against her mouth. "Daydreaming about the joys of endless state dinners?"

She smiled and put her arms around his neck. "I was actually thinking about how you are truly the only thing constant and beloved in my life."

He caught his breath just a bit, then pulled her close and made quite substantial inroads into what she assumed was a reward for something approximating a term of affection.

It was quite a while later when a throat cleared itself quite uncomfortably from the doorway. Morgan lifted her head and peered blearily in that direction to find one of the king's pages standing there, shifting nervously. She looked at Miach.

"It's for you."

Miach sighed lightly, then shifted a bit so he could turn and look at the door. "Aye?"

"Prince Mochriadhemiach," the lad said, bowing several times, "they call for you."

Miach looked at Morgan. "And so it begins."

"Apparently so."

" 'Tis Adhémar's funeral today," he said quietly. "They would like to crown me tomorrow."

"So quickly?" she asked in surprise.

"I don't think anyone thought Adhémar would come back, so they've been preparing just in case. All is ready save the king's wardrobe. I fear the seamstresses are busily adjusting clothes they had intended to fit Cathar."

"Oh, Miach," she said with a wince. "How is your brother taking all this?"

"With vast quantities of relief and ale." Miach looked over his shoulder. "Run along, Peter, and tell them I'll follow in a minute or two."

"Aye, Your Highness." The lad smiled, bowed, and fled.

Miach turned back to her. "Where was I?"

"About to be late to a funeral," she said seriously.

"They'll wait."

Morgan shivered as Miach pulled her to him, buried his hand in her hair, and kissed her again.

Heaven help them, he was going to be more than a little late.

"When is this wedding?" he asked hoarsely.

"Probably not soon enough," she said honestly.

He laughed, buried his face in her hair, and held her tightly. "I agree. I'll talk to your grandfather about it later. " He pulled back and smiled at her. "I should go."

"I can't get up until you let *me* go."

He laughed uneasily. "I'm having a hard time with that."

She threw her arms around his neck again and hugged him tightly. "I love you."

"I love you, too." He held her for another minute or two, then reached for her boots and put them on her feet. He handed her Mehar's knife. "I think I may need to sit with my brothers today, out of respect—"

"I'll be fine," she said quickly.

"You might be, but I won't. After the funeral, I will convince Sìle to give you to me formally, in front of witnesses." He paused. "It might be a little unpleasant then for a moment or two. Actually, it might be rather unpleasant until then."

She shrugged. "If I can't face a gaggle of spoiled princesses, then I don't deserve the mark above my brow." She crawled off his lap and held down her hands for him. "You are going to be late if you don't go now."

He stood, put out the fire with a word, then took her hand and pulled her toward the door. "Want to fly after supper?"

"Please."

He hesitated, then turned and pulled her into his arms again. Morgan rested there happily until she heard someone from below calling both their names. She frowned. "Am I hearing things?"

"I think it's your grandfather. He'll come find us if we don't go now." He took her hand. "Let's be about this day of grief and have it over with. I think we may both wish for a bit of freedom tonight more than we realize now."

She nodded, then walked with him out of the solar and down the stairs. Sìle was indeed waiting for them in the passageway below. He looked at Miach with a scowl.

"Your ministers are prowling the passageways looking for you. I threw them off the scent, but I think they'll hunt you down eventually. I'll keep Mhorghain safe if you want to try to outrun them."

Miach made Sìle a very low bow. "Thank you, Your Majesty, for the head start." He leaned over and kissed Morgan on the cheek. "Meet me after supper on the battlements."

"She most certainly will not," Sìle growled. "I know what it is you want to do with her, and I'm telling you for the final time that elves do not shapechange!"

Morgan watched Miach laugh, then wink at her before he left at a trot. She smiled, then looked up at her grandfather and felt her smile falter.

"How do you fare, my liege?" she asked. "And how is Grandmother?"

He sighed as he drew her arm through his and started down the passageway with her. "I grieve for Keir and for Sosar and for all those who were touched by Lothar's evil, as does she. But we also credit you and your lad for having ended that evil, at least for your generation." He paused, then smiled briefly. "He's a good boy, Mhorghain. I won't complain too loudly at your wedding, though I am going to have a very stern discussion with him before the fact about what elven princesses do and do not do. He will *not* be leaping off the battlements at Seanagarra with you."

"Grandfather, you don't have battlements at Seanagarra."

"See?" he said pleasantly. "Already I feel better about this marriage. I'll feel even better about it after I offer young Miach a few more pieces of advice about the proper way to run a kingdom."

"I'm sure he would be grateful for them."

Her grandfather looked at her narrowly, as if he weren't sure if she jested or not, then he apparently decided she'd been in earnest. He harrumphed in pleasure and continued down the passageway with her. Morgan found it much easier to bear the grandeur of Tor Neroche when she was distracted by family.

But after her grandfather left, she would have Miach and he was much more likely to tramp about with mud on his boots than her grandfather was.

She took a very deep breath. This wasn't what she'd expected for herself, but that was nothing new. Miach hadn't expected it either.

Was it any more difficult to accept her heritage as a princess of Tòrr Dòrainn than it would be to think of herself as the queen of Neroche?

She hesitated, then shook her head. It was better not to think on it.

We'll take our crowns off and be just Morgan and Miach.

She held onto that thought with all her strength. It was, she was quite sure, all that would get her through the next few days.

Not to mention the rest of her life.

Twenty-two

Miach sat in front of his fire in his tower chamber, finished with his spells of defense for the moment. He leaned his head back carefully against his chair and remained still with his eyes closed, trying to catch his breath. It had been a very long day, though he supposed he couldn't have expected anything else. Funerals were actually quite rare in the house of Neroche, for which he was rather grateful, but they tended to drag on. It was fitting, though, that the day just passed had been full of last tributes to a king. Miach had been very relieved to have Cathar be the one receiving condolences from emissaries from other countries. It had been enough to endure the drove of prospective fathers-in-law who had wanted to pull him aside for a bit of a chat about the undeniable merits of their particular daughters.

He had tried to politely alert them to the fact that he was already betrothed, but he'd been told more than once that until Sìle of Tòrr Dòrainn had been seen to actually hand over his beloved granddaughter in front of a very large audience, Miach wasn't going to be believed. When he'd discussed with Sìle the possibility of that happening sooner rather than later, the elven king had vowed that he wouldn't be handing anything over until after Miach had a very large crown atop his head.

Miach had shown Sìle the runes about his wrist, but that had availed him nothing. Suggesting that he and Morgan might be better off eloping hadn't improved the discussion any.

He'd also wanted to fly with Morgan after supper, but he'd walked out of the great hall and into a collection of ministers who were convinced the future of the realm depended on speech precisely at that moment.

He had decided right then that things were going to run a bit differently when—and if—Cathar actually managed to get that crown on his head.

He would have insisted that such change begin then and there, but Peter had slipped up to his side and tugged on his sleeve. Miach had bent down to have Peter whisper in his ear that a certain mercenary gel thought he should send his ministers to bed and go there himself, then she would meet him on the roof before breakfast if he liked.

Miach had conjured up a lovely handkerchief, handed it Peter, and sent him back with an aye to the plan for the morning. He'd then done just as Morgan had suggested. He'd sent everyone to bed for a decent night's sleep, then retreated to his tower chamber to carry on with his usual tasks.

And now that those were seen to, he had other things to think on. The well was shut, Lothar was tucked safely in Gobhann, but there were still the questions of what to do with Lothar's kin and how best to rid the realm of Lothar's monsters that were still at liberty. Perhaps all he could do with Lothar's sons and their sons was to wall them into Riamh with spells they couldn't break through until he could bring himself to either slay them or wring promises from them that they would turn away from Lothar's path.

And given what he was sure would be the response to the latter, he supposed they wouldn't be going anywhere anytime soon.

The second problem was easier to solve. He had to rid the realm of Lothar's creatures as quickly as possible. He couldn't leave his people to face those horrors when there was aught he could do to prevent it.

He sighed, then opened his eyes. He jumped in spite of himself at the sight of his now eldest brother sitting in the chair across from him. Cathar reached down and picked up a mug of ale to hand to him.

"Thought you might need this."

Miach accepted it gratefully, drank, then wrapped his hands around the cup. "Been here long?"

"About an hour."

"You're always here about an hour."

Cathar smiled. "I lose track of time. I thought you might want a bit of company."

"Or a guard?"

Cathar shrugged. "That never hurts either."

Miach studied his brother. "Are you sorry about all this?"

"I'm thrilled," Cathar said without hesitation. "Rigaud is another tale entirely, but if you were to make him the minister of something important—like the silk trade with Sròl—he might forgive you for something you had no control over."

Miach looked down into his ale for a moment or two, then at his brother. "I didn't ask for this, you know."

"Bloody hell, Miach, didn't I just say as much?" Cathar said with a snort. "I know I spent more time worrying about my potential place in the succession than I did what horrors Adhémar was enduring in Riamh that whole damned time. I can't imagine you wouldn't have done the same in my place." He shook his head. "Nay, I was delighted to see that mantle fall on you. You'll make a fabulous king. I'll happily stand behind you and keep Rigaud from slipping a knife between your ribs."

Miach laughed uneasily. "I wish I was certain you were jesting."

"I imagine you do," Cathar agreed with a grin. "Not to fear; Rigaud will survive. The rest of the lads are, of course, behind you without question. They're also ready to troop to Melksham and see what King Nicholas can produce for them."

"And you?"

"I'm going to woo the widow Tonnag." He smiled. "She brews a particularly fine dark ale, don't you know."

"Well, you seem to."

Cathar cursed him, which made him feel much more as if things were as they always had been.

But somehow, they weren't. It was as if he'd suddenly become the steward of everyone and everything in the realm of Neroche. It was a bit like when he'd had his magic come back to him after he'd left Gobhann, only this was a much stronger sensation. He supposed if he'd tried, he could have sensed the essence of anything in the kingdom

He looked into the fire and searched for the trolls that had hunted him and Morgan before. He saw Hearn's men slaying half a dozen, Ehrne's kin doing the like with a different group of them on the borders of Ainneamh, his own guardsmen finishing off a handful more on the border of Riamh. He hesitated, then looked farther, to Ceangail and past that to Durial.

He was very surprised indeed to find how much he could see there as well.

He pulled his attention back to what he was searching for. There were no trolls that he could see farther east than Ceangail, which was a great relief somehow. He realized, with a start, that most of them seemed to be gathered at the well at Ceangail, as if they'd been called there. Which he supposed they had.

He sighed deeply and rubbed his hand over his face. The sooner they were seen to, the better for them all.

He pulled himself back to himself finally, then realized Cathar was still sitting there. He smiled briefly. "Sorry. You were saying?"

"Poor Morgan." Cathar sighed. "She'll be forever prodding you during supper to not neglect your wine."

"Trust me, I never wander off mentally when she's near."

"I can see why not," Cathar said. "She's a marvel. And if you're curious, she's downstairs, pacing through the passageways."

Miach pushed himself to his feet and handed his cup to his brother. "Why didn't you tell me sooner? I thought she'd gone to bed."

"She told me not to disturb you if you were working. She promised she wasn't bolting."

"A fact for which I'll be forever grateful," Miach threw over his shoulder as he strode to the door. He slowed to a stop before he opened it, then looked at his brother. "Do me a favor."

"Anything."

"I'm going hunting, well before dawn likely. I'll take Mansourah and Nemed with me, as well as whoever from Tòrr Dòrainn and Ainneamh will come along. I need to find the remaining trolls and finish them."

Cathar looked at him in surprise. "Why don't you send someone else?"

"Because I am still the archmage of the realm," Miach said quietly, "and my duty is to protect that realm."

Cathar stared at him for a moment or two in silence, then smiled a very small smile. "Mother would have been proud of you."

"Mother would have told me I was dawdling," he said dryly, "but I must go at least hold my lady for a bit before I go."

"Which she also would have understood," Cathar said. "But if you don't want me to go with you, what favor do you want from me?"

"Guard Morgan's back."

Cathar's mouth fell open. "Against the lassies downstairs?"

Miach shot him a look that had him holding up his hands in surrender.

"Very well, I'll be her personal guardsman. I'm sure she'll be vastly relieved to have me. And when those shrews turn on me, perhaps she'll keep *me* safe."

"I daresay she will." Miach opened his door. "Bank my fire for me, would you?"

"Demoted to servant already—"

Miach shut the door on his brother's laughter and loped down the stairs. He walked up and down stairs and along passageways until he came to the great hall. He stopped at the doorway and smiled at the sight that greeted him.

Morgan had pulled the king's chair up to the hearth and was stretching up to hang the Sword of Angesand on the wall. Miach watched her for a moment or two, then decided it was perhaps time to offer aid before she unraveled the tapestries with her curses. He walked across the floor and around the end of the table. He lit another handful of torches with a sweet spell of Fadaire, then looked up at her.

"Might I offer aid, fair maiden?"

She blew hair out of her eyes. "Either that, or fetch me a cushion. I only need another handsbreadth. I suppose I could stand on the arms of this chair—"

Miach reached up and took the sword from her. "Off, gel, and let me see to it for you." He changed places with her, put the sword back up on the wall, then jumped off the chair and pushed it back in. He looked at her.

"You're up late."

"I couldn't sleep," she admitted. "Well, that and I thought the sword should go back where it belonged."

"It belongs with you," he said quietly, "but you can keep it up there if you like." He reached for her hand. "The Sword of Neroche crosses it, you know, when the king is the right sort of lad to leave a sword on the wall."

"Which you might be?"

He shrugged. "I have a knife in my boot and a spell or two at my command. What else do I need? Well, save you. And perhaps a contingent of musicians to play for us."

"You've but one thing on your mind," she said with a smile.

" 'Tis a handy excuse to hold you in my arms," he admitted. "And it will keep us from discussing a half dozen things that require just us in my mother's solar, safe and warm under Mehar's weaving. Though I'll tell you that I think the Sword of Angesand chose well." He looked at her seriously. "No one could have done what you did, Morgan, and not just because you're your father's daughter. You have faced things that would have caused mighty mages to quake and you have bested them."

She shook her head. "I couldn't have done it without you. And if you want *my* opinion, I think the Sword of Neroche chose well, if it was the one to do the choosing."

He shrugged uncomfortably. "We'll see, I suppose."

She pursed her lips. "Miach, I have felt his power. I have a fair idea of what it took for you to do what you did on the field two days ago."

He took a deep breath, then smiled. "I wanted you safe and at liberty to dance with me, so let us be about that before we both find ourselves lost too much in memories of events perhaps better left forgotten for the moment. We'll have to imagine up the music, though. I can't conjure viols and flutes."

"And I can't sing," she said with a smile, "so I suppose we'll just make do."

He led her back around the table and across the hall. He stopped in surprise at the sight of a handful of musicians standing near the hall doors. One of the string players stepped forward and made him a bow.

"Prince Cathar thought you might be needing us, Your Highness."

Miach smiled. "Thank you, gentlemen. I daresay we would welcome your company."

The violinist elbowed one of his fellows. "Shut the door, lad, and let's give the prince archmage and his lady a bit of privacy."

Miach took Morgan's hand and led her into the midst of the hall. He made her a low bow, had an elegant curtsey in return, then he laughed and danced with her all the patterns he knew. He stumbled through a pair of them she'd learned from Brèagha, then finally pulled her back into his arms and simply held her close as the music continued to play.

"I love you," he whispered. "I wish I could begin to tell you how much."

He felt her hand running through his hair before her arms went around his neck. "You just did and I feel the same." She pulled back far enough to smile at him. "I don't want to let go of you."

"Very soon, you won't have to."

She started to smile, then she froze. She stared at him for a moment or two, then her eyes narrowed. "You're planning something you don't want me to know about."

He retrieved his jaw before it fell too far south. "What?" he asked, wondering if he might feign a bit of sudden deafness.

"Miach, what are you doing?"

He thought about hedging, but decided there was no point. He had planned to leave her a note, though that would have likely led to having it back on the end of her sword. He took a deep breath. "I must see to those creatures of Lothar's. They are rudderless, you might say, but still lethal in the right circumstances. I can't leave them to roam the realm unchecked."

"I'm coming with you."

He smiled, pained. "Morgan . . ."

"Miach, don't you dare leave me behind."

"I won't be gone longer than a pair of days and I won't go alone."

"But you won't take me," she said flatly.

He hesitated, then leaned forward and carefully rested his forehead against hers. "Morgan, my dearest love, I know who you are and what you can do. I also know that you have, over the last handful of months, faced things that no soldier, no matter how brave, should have had to face without the hope of a rest after the battle was won. You have earned your rest."

"And what of you?" she asked quietly.

"I'll rest when I return."

She put her head on his shoulder. "Is this how it will be? You leaving me behind at the first sign of a good battle?"

He smiled against her hair. "I don't think this will qualify as a good battle. I imagine I'll find these lads at the well and I would prefer to spare you another trip there. Allow me to ply a little of my very rusty chivalry on you, won't you?"

She sighed deeply. "If that's the case, then I suppose I should thank you for it. I could avoid that place quite happily, I think."

"With any luck, we'll both manage that in the future."

"I hope so," she said quietly. She lifted her head and looked at him. "Very well, I'll humor you. I'll terrorize your garrison, or attempt to keep my grandfather from terrorizing your ministers. I daresay the first will be the easier task."

"You could also keep Sosar company."

"I could." She looked at him thoughtfully. "Did Lothar take all his power?"

"Sosar won't discuss it with me. I don't know that he wouldn't with either enough time or enough sour wine from Penrhyn, but I haven't had the opportunity to ply him with the latter, and I haven't had the former to give him." He tucked a strand of hair behind her ear. "He might talk to you."

"He might."

"Did you hear everything I discussed with Keir?"

"Aye."

"And you memorized all your father's spells that he gave me, didn't you?"

"Unfortunately," she said with a shiver. "Does it matter?"

"Sosar said something about having talked to Keir about things he wouldn't elaborate on. Perhaps the particulars of Diminishing were amongst them. If nothing else, you'll take his mind off his situation until we can find a remedy for him."

She nodded, then reached up and put her hands on his face. "Be careful."

He smiled. "Morgan, nothing will come upon me unawares. Not now."

"No one is infallible," she said pointedly, "but you know that already." She sighed deeply. "You can't leave your people in danger."

"Our people," he corrected softly, "and nay, I cannot. Most of those monsters were drawn to the well anyway. It won't be hard to put them out of their misery."

"I don't like this, but I suppose there are times when you'll need to be off and doing without me. When will you go?"

"Sometime before dawn," he said. "I'd like to sleep for a couple of hours first, if possible. I suppose camping in front of your fire is out."

"As is a night in your hayloft, unless you want to find yourself skewered on the end of my grandfather's sword."

"I've already almost had that pleasure, so perhaps we should forbear for the moment. I'll at least walk you to your door."

She nodded, then slipped her hand into his. He walked with her across the hall, thanked the musicians for their fine playing, then continued down the passageways to where he knew Morgan's chamber lay.

He hadn't, not in his heart of hearts where he might have cherished dreams he would have told only his mother who wouldn't have laughed at him, imagined that he might be walking the halls of Tor Neroche with a woman he loved holding his hand. He certainly wouldn't have imagined it with what faced him being his own crowning.

He continued on with Morgan until they stood in front of her door. He reached for the latch only to have the door open before he could touch it. Sìle scowled at him.

"Wondered when you'd bring her back."

"Did you know I had her?" Miach asked in surprise.

"I peered into the great hall," Sìle said gruffly. "Couldn't bring myself to interrupt such fine dancing. At least you paid attention in your lessons and you won't shame her. I worry about you in other areas, but at least in this, you'll suffice."

"Grandfather," Morgan said weakly.

Miach only smiled and made Sìle a low bow. "That's very kind of you, Your Majesty."

"Here's kindness," Sìle said, opening the door fully. "We prepared a place for you by the fire. You can sleep safely tonight, at least."

"*Very* kind," Miach said with a smile.

Sìle grunted at him, then nodded toward the fire. Miach walked with Morgan over to the hearth to find two empty seats there side by side. Miach waited until Morgan had sat before he collapsed in the chair next to her. He smiled at Morgan's mercenary companions, who were already enjoying hefty tankards of ale.

"Your Highness," Paien said, raising his mug in salute.

Miach accepted a cup of ale from Camid and passed it to Morgan. He settled himself with his own, then relaxed for the first time in days.

He sipped for a bit, then set his mug aside and held out his hand. Morgan put hers into his, smiling at him. He brought her hand to his mouth, kissed it, then leaned his head back against the chair and closed his eyes. The conversation washed over him, leaving him feeling as if he merely sat about a campfire with well-known traveling companions. In time, he heard others join the group, Cathar, Turah, and even Sosar, but he didn't do anything past acknowledging them with a look and a smile. He was enormously grateful to be where he was, away from prying eyes, away from fathers who seemed to lie in wait for him around every corner, away from things he would have to slay on the morrow.

He was very grateful for the simple pleasure of the company of trusted companions.

He asked Cathar to wake him in a pair of hours, then closed his eyes and succumbed to sleep.

Four days later, he walked through the passageways of Tor Neroche, tired, hungry, and thoroughly sick of the work of death.

It had taken him far longer to finish his business than he'd expected, but he'd had no choice but to see it through to the end. It had been unpleasant and unrelenting, and he'd been very grateful Morgan hadn't been forced to be a part of it. She had enough of evil and darkness in her past; if he could spare her any more, he would do so without hesitation.

He ran bodily into his eldest brother before he realized that brother was standing in front of the chapel doors. Cathar turned around, then blew his hair out of his eyes.

"Finally."

"Finally, what?" Miach asked in surprise. "I hurried."

"You'd best continue to hurry. By my last count, there are eight kings and queens inside, waiting to watch you become the ninth. I've distracted them for four solid days with food, dancing, and the entire reserves of sour wine from Penrhyn, and that doesn't begin to address the number and kind of all the rest of the guests who've needed to be fed and distracted. I asked Morgan this morning when she thought you would be back and she said she was sure today. I think her exact words were, 'if he doesn't return today, I'm going to go find him and kill him.'" He smiled. "You must have sensed that."

"I daresay," Miach said with a weary smile. "Thank you for keeping watch over her."

"Not that she needed it, but you're welcome just the same." He smiled. "The woman is, well, you know what she is. She's already run through the garrison daily since you left; half the lads are in love with her, the other half terrified of her. That has occupied her mornings quite well. She's spent the evenings closeted with Sosar of Tòrr Dòrainn in the library, looking for heaven knows what."

"And the afternoons?"

"Arguing with Mistress Wardrobe." Cathar paused. "I thought it wise to demand all her blades before each of those encounters, lest something go awry. I didn't manage it today, though, so don't blame me if there's been bloodshed. I was too busy trying to entertain your guests to render your lady weaponless."

Miach nodded, then realized he wasn't altogether sure what he was nodding about. "Guests?"

"Inside the chapel, Miach," Cathar said, frowning at him. "Weren't you listening?"

"I was too busy thinking about food and a bath."

"Well, you'd best hurry with both. You're being crowned, oh, an hour ago, which means you're very late. But then again, so is your lady coming down the passageway toward us. There might not have been bloodshed, but I imagine there has been a fair amount of arguing."

Miach smiled, then glanced down the passageway. He had to find a handy wall to lean against just to keep himself upright. He looked at her for a moment or two, then turned to his brother. "What did you tell me about bloodshed?"

Cathar frowned, then shrugged. "I can't remember. Morgan has that effect, I think. As if she'd just walked out of a dream." He took a deep breath. "And before I start singing praises about *your* future wife, I think I'll take myself off to find the rest of the lads. We'll be waiting for you. Don't dawdle."

"I won't," Miach said absently. He continued to watch Morgan walking down the passageway toward him and felt a little winded at the sight. He didn't suppose he was equal to identifying what she was wearing. It reached to the floor, it was white, and the sleeves were long enough to cover the blades she no doubt had strapped to her forearms. She had on a crown, he suspected her hair was piled atop her head helping the crown stay there, and she must have been wearing some species of fancy shoe because those shoes tapped against the floor as she walked.

They almost drowned out her curses.

She finally stopped, hiked up her skirts, and took off her shoes with yet another curse. She continued on with a shoe in each hand, muttering under her breath what he was sure were dire warnings to a particular woman in charge of her clothing.

Until she saw him.

The look of relief on her face stole what of his breath she hadn't taken a moment ago.

He strode forward and caught her as she threw herself into his arms. He closed his eyes and held her tightly, unsure if she were trembling, or he was.

"You're home."

He managed an unsteady breath. "I told you I would be."

"You're late."

"So I keep hearing. It was worth it, though, to see you in your finery. Actually, it would have been worth it to see you in mercenary garb," he admitted. He put his hand very carefully against the back of her head and bent his head to kiss her. "I missed you."

She tightened her arms around his neck. "I don't want to talk about it. I didn't think you were in much danger, but I still want Master Soilléir's sight. That, or the gift of seeing your mantle has given you. I want to know how you're faring when you're not within reach of my sword."

"I think you might be entitled to both," he said.

She sank back onto her heels and looked up at him. "Is it finished?"

He nodded. "Finally."

She closed her eyes briefly. "It was difficult, wasn't it?"

"Did you see that much?" he asked.

She shook her head. "Nay, but I can see it in your eyes. Miach, I vow I'm serious about sleep. You can teach me to attend to your spells for a day or two so you can rest. Unfortunately, I don't think a nap is in your future today. The chapel is full of dignitaries. You're not going to be able to sneak in late and hide in the back. Unfortunately," she muttered, "neither am I."

"Nay," he said, reaching up to adjust her crown slightly, "you'll have to sit with the elves, I suppose. You'll fit in, I daresay."

"Save for the shoes."

He smiled. "You might have to put them back on."

"They are too high and they make a horrendous noise when I walk," she said shortly. "I prefer boots."

"Shall I lower the heels for you?" he asked politely.

She pursed her lips. "You can't. The gown has been hemmed at the precise length to drape over the shoes at their precise height so that I look graceful and slightly mysterious. Mistress Wardrobe told me so."

He realized his mouth was hanging open. "You can't be serious."

"I am," she said grimly. "You wouldn't believe what I've been through over the past four days. And nay, there is no stricture for it."

He would have laughed, but he stifled it at her warning look. He pulled her instead back into his arms.

"I vow we'll escape tonight," he promised. "One way or another."

"Please," she said with feeling. "My grandmothers have been here to keep me company, Mehar has flown with me, Catrìona has trained with me, but I wanted you. I don't wish another adventure on us quite yet, but at least we were together most of the time that way."

"I have a strategy," he said in a conspiratorial whisper. "Short meetings, short dinners, and long evenings of dancing."

"Can you do that?"

"Not yet, but ask me again in a handful of hours." He kissed her very softly, then took her shoes out of her hands. He knelt, put them back onto her feet, then spelled them into silence. He pushed himself back to his feet. "Better?"

"They feel like boots, if such a thing is possible," she said in surprise.

"What is the use of being betrothed to a mage, if he cannot make your court shoes comfortable now and again?"

She held him very tightly for a moment or two, then pushed out of his arms. "Let's be about this," she said briskly. "I have plans for you later in your mother's solar."

"I'll walk you to the chapel doors—"

She shook her head with a smile. "Sosar is waiting for me. And we'll be waiting for you."

He hesitated, but she made shooing motions with her hand. He took a deep breath.

"I'll be back."

"I know."

He smiled, made her a low bow, then walked down the passageway.

He looked back several times. Each time, he saw her standing just outside the chapel, watching him. He finally decided he should stop looking back, simply because he knew if he didn't hurry, he would be soon rivaling Adhémar for keeping guests waiting.

But he couldn't help one last look.

She was still standing there, watching.

He paused, then took a deep breath. The past was taken care of. All that was left was to walk, clear-eyed, into the future.

He turned, put his head down, and strode down the passageway.

Twenty-three

Morgan decided that there were perhaps worse things than facing a battle where she wasn't sure of the outcome. Listening to her grandfather disparage ambassadors from other kingdoms who had tried to have audiences with him whilst he'd wanted to be off to breakfast was one. Having her hair worked on by maids who seemed determined to pile it all on top of her head and make it stay there instead of letting it drip down her back as it so desperately wanted to do was another. Walking through the passageways of Tor Neroche and finding herself glared at by nobility she was sure she hadn't had a chance to offend was yet another to add to the list.

Wondering if Miach would get back to Tor Neroche in time to attend his own coronation had been the last but perhaps the most unsettling of all.

She hadn't worried about him, not truly. He'd managed twenty-eight years of life without her fretting over him, so she'd assumed he would survive another pair of days. She was, however, going to see what of value she had to bargain away to Master Soilléir for that spell of seeing. It would certainly be a mercy to Neroche's garrison lads who had paid a heavy price for the distress she hadn't wanted to admit.

"Mhorghain?"

She realized Sosar was standing in front of her, waiting for her with his hand outstretched. She took a deep breath. "Sorry. I was thinking."

"Out loud, if you want to know so you can avoid it in the future."

She allowed him to take her hand and draw it through his arm. He started inside the chapel, but she pulled back. It took her a moment before she could look up at him. "I'm not prepared for this."

"Mhorghain, love, no one ever is," he said quietly. "I think I can safely attest to that. Things come upon you that you don't expect and all you can do is soldier on as best you can." He smiled faintly. "I think you'll survive this well enough. You look beautiful, if that helps."

Morgan had to admit the gown was lovely. It was made from some sort of white fabric shot through with silver and adorned with minuscule crystals and pearls that didn't sing as she walked, but they certainly sparkled and shimmered in a particularly lovely way. Fixed to her hair so firmly it wouldn't have fallen off if she'd been bolting for the nearest exit was a crown of silver and diamonds. It wasn't heavy, but it wasn't discreet, either. If she'd been completely honest with herself, she would have said that it was a crown worthy of an elven princess.

She suspected her grandfather had had a hand in its design.

And that didn't begin to address her shoes that were as grand as her dress, only now they had been improved by a man who loved her.

A man who was about to be crowned king.

She took another deep breath, then peered into the chapel. It was, as she'd feared, filled to the brim with all sorts of visiting royalty she had avoided over the past handful of days. She supposed she might manage to scoot down the side of the aisle without being noticed overmuch if she hurried and if their seats were in the back.

"Where are we sitting?"

"In the front. Best seats in the place, or so I was told."

She shouldn't have been surprised. She put her shoulders back, her chin out, and grasped for her quickly disappearing shreds of dignity and courage. "I'd rather be in battle."

"I'd rather be down at the pub."

Morgan laughed a little in spite of herself. "Thank you."

He shrugged, but his eyes were twinkling. "You're welcome."

"I can do this now."

"Of course you can."

Morgan found that the first step was the hardest. The second was easier, but only slightly. The third was no good at all because it was then that she began to hear gasps and whispers—and those weren't because she'd fallen on her face. She decided to assume they were noises that mere mortals made whilst looking at the startling beauty of an elven prince. They couldn't have been because of her.

She concentrated on the collection of important courtly ministers who stood in the front of the chapel along with a priest. She continued to concentrate on those lads even after she heard her name travel through the crowd of guests.

In truth, she supposed what anyone else thought didn't matter. There was only one opinion she cared about and the man who would have offered it wasn't watching her.

But she was soon watching him. She hadn't been sitting with Sosar and her grandparents but a quarter hour before the company began to rise. She rose as well, then looked back down the aisle, wondering just what sort of getup Miach would have found himself forced into. She couldn't imagine feathers on his hat and long, curly-toed shoes, but given that she had been forced into uncomfortable shoes despite her protests, it was possible that Miach might have succumbed as well.

His brothers certainly had. They were dressed in things that were so fine and luxurious, she half wondered if they didn't fear sitting on chairs that hadn't been dusted prior to their arrival. Perhaps they were distracted by the curling toes on their shoes and didn't think about what untoward things might happen to the seats of their trousers. She exchanged a quick look with Sosar, who only raised one of his eyebrows and seemed to be fighting a smile.

She turned back to watch as Miach's brothers came up the aisle toward her, with Cathar in the lead, followed by Rigaud, Nemed, Mansourah, and Turah, who looked very much worse for the wear. She smiled at him and had a weary smile in return. It was past time to try the Fadairian spell of healing on him that he'd been refusing for almost a se'nnight. Perhaps they would, after Miach had taken off his crown so he didn't dent it when he fell.

After the lads had taken their places, Morgan turned back to look for Miach. She had to lean out a bit to look around a particularly portly man who seemed just as determined as she to catch a glimpse of Neroche's new king.

He was wearing boots. Morgan knew she shouldn't have been surprised, but she was relieved just the same. He had also forgone anything Rigaud would have been comfortable with. He was dressed, unremarkably, in black. He looked impossibly handsome and impossibly grave, walking with his hands behind his back and his head slightly bowed.

He did look up, though, when he passed her. He shot her a quick smile, then sobered again as he approached the dais. His brothers were standing all in a row next to the gilt-edged chair that sat there, quite empty.

Morgan tried to pay attention to the particulars of the ceremony, but it was difficult. It was all still so far from what she'd ever expected to have happen to him, she could hardly take it in. She listened to him kneel and swear an oath that he would protect and defend the people of Neroche. He was draped in a heavy velvet robe of red, trimmed in ermine. He was led to the throne, invited to sit, then Cathar stepped up behind the chair.

Morgan realized then that Miach was looking right at her. She held his gaze as Cathar set the crown of Neroche on his head, then she found she couldn't see him any longer. She dabbed very carefully at her eyes, then managed to see long enough to watch as Cathar then came and knelt before him to offer him his fealty. The rest of his brothers followed suit, with Turah the least steady on his feet.

And then the ceremony was over. Miach thanked the priest, then turned and embraced his brothers one by one.

"What now?" she murmured to Sosar.

"Lunch, hopefully."

She smiled up at him, then turned back in time to see Miach step off the dais. She was certain he would simply glance at her, then continue on his way. But he didn't.

He walked up the aisle, then very deliberately stopped and turned to her. He took her hand, kissed it, then made her a very low bow.

"Princess Mhorghain," he said, with a grave smile.

Morgan swallowed. "King Mochriadhemiach."

"Heaven help us both," he murmured, then he turned to her grandparents and made them bows as well. Then he straightened, smiled at her again, then excused himself.

Morgan watched him go, then caught a full view of the glares delivered her way by the princesses on the other side of the aisle.

"I'll guard your back," Sosar whispered.

"You might need to."

"I'm very good with a butter knife. Let's follow them into the great hall and I'll prove it."

She smiled in spite of herself, then accepted her uncle's arm. Sosar waited until his parents had left the row first, then pulled back.

"Seven other kings to go," he murmured. "We'll wait."

Morgan nodded, wishing that she'd accepted Glines's offer to give her a few lessons on protocol the day before. Too late now. She would simply have to rely on Sosar and hope that whatever mistake she made might be chalked up to elvish haughtiness.

Half a very long hour later, they were walking into the great hall. Tables had been set up and roaring fires burned in the main hearth behind the dais and the other two hearths on either side of the chamber. Morgan looked at the high table to find places there for all the kings and queens.

There was an empty chair next to Miach.

"A spot for you," Sosar murmured.

Morgan swallowed uncomfortably. "If I manage to get there without being buried under a pile of disappointed princesses."

"You could always call to your sword if things become a bit dodgy."

"I know," she said faintly. "I've done it before."

He smiled wryly, then led her over to a seat at one of the lower tables. "Let's go be discreet. I have the feeling this will take even more time than that business in the chapel. The only thing that will save us is the fact we'll have food in front of us."

Morgan sat with him, then watched as Miach hung the Sword of Neroche on the wall so it crossed the Sword of Angesand.

She felt her sword sigh, as if it were satisfied with the day's events.

Morgan was as well, for Miach's sake, though she was more than happy to now have something else to do with her hands besides wring them together. Eating was preferable to that, though the meal dragged on interminably. If it had been just eating, she might have had more patience for it, but it seemed that the whole of the afternoon was going to be taken up in formalities.

She could have sworn she saw Miach squirm more than once.

After the meal came the renewing of goodwill between kingdoms. Morgan tried to look interested, for she supposed she might be called on to make mention of those alliances at some point, but all she could do was lean her chin on her fist and try to stay awake.

She watched as Miach came to stand in front of the dais to receive gifts from each of the other kings. There were what she could only assume were usual gifts of jewels and bolts of silk, foodstuffs and blades. She imagined Miach's mother would have been very proud of his lovely manners in acknowledging all the things he was given. She was impressed by not only that but her own ability to suppress her yawns.

Sìle walked around the table last of all. Miach made him a low bow, which her grandfather accepted with his usual show of graciousness.

"Typical," Sosar murmured with a bit of a laugh.

Sìle folded his arms over his chest and looked at Miach. "I have given quite a lot of thought to what I shall give you, King Mochriadhemiach," he began slowly. "I have considered saplings from my garden, or perhaps a spell or two from my books—which you already have more of than you should," he added, not entirely under his breath. "Or perhaps I should just give you gold and gems from my coffers."

Miach inclined his head. "Whilst those would be kingly gifts, indeed, Your Grace, I wonder if there might be something else that would suit."

"I should think the trees would be enough." He threw Miach a sideways glance, then blew out his breath loudly. "Very well. Name what you want."

Gasps echoed in the chamber. Morgan supposed the souls around her had reason. It was doubtful that any king was so free with his things, much less a king of elves.

Miach clasped his hands behind his back and smiled. "I'll have your granddaughter, Mhorghain."

Sìle pursed his lips. "Will you indeed?"

"I will," Miach said, inclining his head. "Indeed."

Morgan watched her grandfather stare at Miach for several excruciatingly long minutes in silence, as if he willed him to break, or cower, or simply throw up his hands and concede the battle. Miach did none of those things. He simply returned Sìle's look steadily, as if he sought to, once and for all, prove where his heart lay.

Sìle sighed heavily, then walked away with a variety of things muttered under his breath that Morgan was just certain couldn't be either complimentary or polite. But he walked away just the same and made his way around the table to stop behind her chair. He pulled her chair out for her, then held out his hand.

"Come, Granddaughter," he said very gravely. "Your lord awaits."

Morgan was appalled to find her hand was trembling as she put it into her grandfather's.

There was absolute silence in the hall.

"Not too late to bolt," Sìle said loudly as they walked along the edge of the hall, then out into the center.

"Isn't it?"

He squeezed her hand. "I would tell you that it isn't," he said very quietly, "but I think if you left that poor lad standing there in front of the table, you would break his heart." He paused. "You could wed him for pity's sake, I suppose."

Morgan managed a smile. "I'd rather wed him for love."

"That's what I feared," he said, but he smiled as he said it. He led her over to stand in front of the high table, then he sighed once more before he put her hand in Miach's.

"I can't fathom why, but she loves you," Sìle said. "Here she is, lad. Yours. Again."

"Thank you, Your Grace," Miach said gravely.

Sìle clapped a hand on his shoulder, winked at him very quickly—likely so no one would think he'd gone soft—then walked away. Morgan looked at Miach and tried to ignore the fact that everyone in the hall was watching them. His hand around hers was warm, though, so she took courage from that. He bent and kissed her hand, then straightened and took both her hands to pull her close.

"You can't be serious," she whispered quickly.

"About what?"

"You aren't going to kiss me here. In front of everyone."

He frowned. "Why not?"

"I don't think you're supposed to."

"New traditions are always welcome."

"But—"

She wasn't sure what was louder as he pulled her against him and kissed her thoroughly, the blood thundering in her ears, the howls from disappointed parents, or the very undignified cheering of his brothers and her mercenary companions. He kissed her far longer than he likely should have, but he didn't seem inclined to stop and she wasn't about to insist.

She did feel a little flushed when he took her hand and led her around the table. She sat very gratefully in the chair he pulled out for her.

"Your proper place, Your Highness," he said with a smile as he sat next to her.

She leaned close to him. "Is it time to go flying yet?"

"Dancing first."

She smiled. "Enforcing the royal edicts already?"

"Aye," he agreed cheerfully. "There's little point in spending all this energy trying to balance this enormous crown on my head if I can't have the reward of a collection of musicians to do my bidding now and again, is there?"

She had to agree there wasn't. She watched him as he poured wine for her, then handed it to her. She drank, then set her cup aside and simply watched him as he received congratulations from those who approached the high table. There was a feeling that tugged at her, a feeling she couldn't identify. It wasn't unpleasant. On the contrary, it was quite lovely. Unfortunately, every time she reached for it, it eluded her grasp.

Miach reached for her hand under the table and laced his fingers with hers. She put aside her thoughts and turned to smile at him. There would be time enough for thinking later.

It was well after sunset before the newly made king of Neroche exercised his prerogative to leave the festivities early. Morgan went with him, accompanied by several very stern words from her grandfather about what were and were not appropriate activities to engage in whilst he wasn't sitting five paces away from them.

"We're eloping tomorrow," Miach said, rather less quietly than he might have otherwise.

Morgan had pulled him away before her grandfather could respond. She happily ran with him through passageways and up and down stairs until they reached the stairs that led up to his mother's private solar. He led her inside, shut the door, then locked it with a spell of Wexham that she was sure not even her grandfather could have broken through.

"At last," he said with a heartfelt sigh.

Morgan smiled as he reached out and pulled her into his arms. "It has been a very long day. For you, especially."

"It was worth every minute of it to have you here." He kissed her softly, paused, then kissed her again. "You were lovely and graceful and gracious today, Princess Mhorghain. But, if you don't mind, I would like an hour or two with your other incarnation."

"As His Majesty wishes," she said, feeling a little breathless.

"I wish it." He reached up and very carefully took her crown off. Or tried to, rather. He frowned thoughtfully during the first few attempts, scowled through a few more, then finally cursed as he made her turn around.

"How'd they get this bloody thing to stick to your head?" he demanded.

She shrugged helplessly. "I have no idea, but it took a good hour to do so. And don't ask me to help you. I don't have any idea how to get it off."

"Mistress Wardrobe and I are going to come to a right understanding," he vowed as he plucked pins from the back of her hair and tossed them on the table near one of the chairs.

"You sound as autocratic as my grandfather."

"When it comes to matters of removing your crown so you don't poke me in the eye with it when I hold you in that chair over there, aye, I intend to sound that way."

She laughed uneasily and looked over her shoulder. "You need a bit of dragon wildness to bring you back to yourself."

He put his hand on the top of her head and turned her back around. "You'll suffice me tonight. And you know I'm only saying the like to have you put me in my place. Hold still, Morgan, lest I pull your hair."

She held still as he tinkered a bit more, then smiled at his exclamation of triumph. He turned her around, then very carefully lifted her crown off her head and set it aside. Then he took his own off and laid it down next to hers.

"And now here we are, just you and I," he said with a smile.

"So we are," she agreed.

"Come sit with me?"

"Happily."

A handful of minutes later, he was holding her feet with one hand and dragging the other through her hair, a fire burned cheerily in the hearth, and she was reasonably comfortable in a dress that was probably worth more gold than she would have made in a year's worth of lucrative sieges. She reached out and put her hand against his cheek.

"Surviving?" she asked.

He smiled. "This is worth every moment of prior discomfort, despite the fact that I'm quite certain Sìle is sitting halfway down the stairs to make certain I return you, unmolested, to your bedchamber before too many watches pass. How long did he say it would take to compile the guest list for our wedding?"

"Again, too long, though I'm sure the time will rush by, what with all your administrative duties to keep you occupied."

He tugged gently on her hair. "That is cruel, Morgan."

She laughed a bit. "I'll hurry him along, if I can. I would like to have all the festivities over so we could sneak off to Aherin and just be ourselves for a few days, enjoying that sweet water you fashioned in the fall for Hearn's horses."

"I would, too," he agreed. He wrapped his arms around her.

"And speaking of passing the time pleasantly, I have a surprise for you tomorrow."

"What is it?"

"A visit from someone you love."

"Nicholas?"

"Aye."

"In truth?" she asked, surprised. "How did you know?"

He hesitated, then smiled faintly. "I saw him packing his things. Actually, he made sure I saw him packing his things." He shivered. "I'm not accustomed to this seeing yet. I'm not sure how Master Soilléir manages it so easily."

"Centuries of practice, no doubt," she said. She smiled. "I will be happy to see Nicholas, though I wonder why he didn't come to your crowning."

He continued to trail his fingers through her hair. "His turn on the world's stage is over, as he would say. I think he prefers a bit of anonymity, though it wouldn't surprise me to have him terrify half the garrison by arriving on wing, as it were. He does make, as you know, a very impressive dragon."

"Aye, he does," she said with a smile. She put her head on his shoulder and closed her eyes, letting the feel of his hand on her hair soothe her. She could, without much effort, imagine they were in any number of unremarkable places, continuing to be unremarkable people.

Though she supposed Miach, at least, had never been that.

She shrugged aside the thought, then turned her mind to trying to decide what the feeling was that had been trying to envelop her since the moment her grandfather had put her hand in Miach's. It wasn't hope, though she felt a substantial amount of that too. She opened her eyes and looked down at Miach's other hand that was covering hers atop her knee. The runes there that encircled his wrist and hers sparkled faintly in the firelight. Those runes had given her hope in many dark places over the past few days, but it wasn't hope that she felt either.

She shifted on Miach's lap so she could keep her head on his shoulder but look at the chamber they were in. The firelight flickered on the tapestries lining the walls, against the long windows, against the chair across from where they sat. No doubt Miach's mother had sat there often, enjoying the same sort of evening she currently enjoyed with that mother's son.

Morgan blinked in surprise. There had been only one blanket draped over the chair the day before; now there was another one laid over the chair's back. It was woven in blues and greens, shot through with gold and silver. She realized with a start that the border was full of runes of the house of Tòrr Dòrainn and Neroche both.

"Miach, where did that other blanket come from?"

"Hmmm?" he said, sounding as if he was also pulling himself away from some pleasant bit of reflection. "Oh, that. 'Tis a gift for us from Mehar. She wove the red one for me after my mother died to give me comfort. The other, she wove for us."

"Really? Why?"

There was a smile in his voice. "To give us peace."

Peace.

Morgan stared at the weaving for several moments in silence, watching the runes swirl and dance in front of her eyes until they finally settled into a pattern that was similar to the runes about her wrist, but not identical. Something more had been added, something that spoke of deep roots and rushing winds, bubbling brooks and fresh-tilled earth. And through it all was a profoundly beautiful magic that wove itself in and out of her and Miach, binding them both to Neroche and its people.

A magic that whispered *peace.*

Morgan crawled to her feet to go fetch it, then brought it back and settled back into her place. She pulled it over them both, then looked at him.

"I was wondering after supper what it was I was feeling," she said slowly. "After all the business was finished and there seemed to be nothing before us but perhaps troubles that wouldn't come close to tearing us in two to face. It's only now that I see what lies under everything Mehar wove that I understand what that feeling is."

"And what is that, my love?" he asked softly.

She smiled. "Peace."

He wrapped his arms around her and drew her close. "May we have long stretches of it, even if it is only something to be shared between us." He kissed her softly, then rested his cheek against her hair. "May we have it in abundance."

She closed her eyes and nodded. She had never considered the word or what it could mean, not during those long days in Gobhann where she had never thought to have someone to love, not during the past few months when dreams of darkness had continually assailed her, not even after she'd closed her father's well and felt nothing but grief and pain as a result. She'd had a taste of it that evening in Ceangail, when she'd seen her mother sitting in front of the fire, looking at her with love, but it had been fleeting.

She should have known she would find it in all its fullness with the man holding her close to his heart.

She supposed this was what their lives would be like. They would see to whatever business his crown required, then he would likely stuff his crown in a drawer with his seven rings of wizardly mastery, and they would carry on as just they two, farmer and besotted village wench.

She shifted a bit and Mehar's weaving whispered in reply.

Peace.

It had been worth the wait.

Epilogue

Miach leaned against the wooden fence that separated the lists from the more equine-populated parts of Aherin and watched as Morgan fought with Hearn of Angesand's second-fiercest guardsman. The first was waiting his turn, bouncing on his heels and stretching his arms over his head, as if he prepared for an excessively taxing bit of sport. In that, at least, the man had it aright. Morgan was so far superior to anyone she fought, it was a wonder any of them dared face her.

They were a bit more ginger with her than they had been in the past, which he knew vexed her, but he couldn't blame the lads. It was one thing to fight a stranger; it was another thing entirely to fight the queen of Neroche.

Of course, they'd used no such restraint when he'd been in the lists the day before, but perhaps Hearn's lads weren't as dazzled by his face as they were by Morgan's.

He watched his lady wife destroy the man before her, then call for another victim. Since he knew how that would finish, he allowed his mind to wander a bit. Of course, those wanderings involved Morgan, but that didn't surprise him. He was perfectly happy to engage in that sort of pleasant reflection.

They had wed over four months ago in Sìle's private garden, with only their family in attendance. Sìle's concession to the rest of the guests had been a more public sort of ceremony later that day in the great hall, a ceremony involving rings and promises of care and consideration. The feasting afterward had been spectacular and drawn out over several days. Weddings in Tòrr Dòrainn were few and far between and generally involved only a few select visitors.

For them, however, Sìle had thrown open his gates and allowed in a full score of souls. That he saw no irony at all in the thinness of his guest list had made Miach smile more than once.

Master Ceannard had come bearing gifts not for the bride and groom, but for Sìle himself, which Morgan's grandfather had accepted also without a shred of irony. Nicholas had come, of course, as had all Morgan's mercenary companions. Royalty had arrived from Durial, Ainneamh, and Camanaë. Master Soilléir had come as well, not only with a promise of spells delivered personally to Neroche when Morgan wished to have them but with Morgan's brother in tow.

Miach hadn't minded spending most of the first week of his marriage working with Morgan and Sìle to restore Rùnach's hands and face. Perhaps he would always bear the scars of what had befallen him, but they wouldn't be so severe. Rùnach had promised to divide his time between Seanagarra and Tor Neroche, which had pleased Brèagha and Morgan both.

After a suitable amount of time spent with one pair of grandparents, he and Morgan had traveled to Lake Cladach to spend another se'nnight with Eulasaid and Sgath before finally coming to beg a night or two in Hearn's hayloft. They had then returned to Tor Neroche and to the business of settling the realm.

He couldn't say it had been an easy transition for either of them. He still loathed even short meetings with self-important ministers and Morgan still fidgeted during state dinners. He supposed they would both learn patience eventually, but in the meantime he was finding ways to politely hurry people along and Morgan, well, Morgan could still be heard to recite Weger's strictures under her breath when things went on overlong. It cheered him to know that under all those exquisite court clothes he'd seen fashioned for her was still the woman he loved. He had endeavored to humor them both by providing dancing as often as possible after supper, and by happily flying with her after the dancing.

He watched with a smile as Morgan now did what she did best, which was leave every man in her vicinity on his knees in front of her. Hearn's finest guardsman was indeed very good, but he would not in this lifetime or the next come close to besting her.

"She's passin' good, ain't she?"

Miach looked to his left and found himself joined by two small boys. They were hanging over the top of the horse fence and watching Morgan with the same amount of awe he was wont to use himself.

"Aye," he agreed, "she is."

The elder of the two looked up at him. "We're on our way to be pages at the palace," he said, puffing his small chest out. "Me and my brother. We heard tell Queen Mhorghain was here in Aherin and Lord Hearn was good enough to let us come have a look at her." He frowned at Miach. "Don't suppose you'd know her, would you, sir, being but a soldier yourself?"

Miach caught sight of their father, standing on the other side of them, looking as if he would rather lay himself beneath Morgan's very sharp sword and perish than be where he was. He started to open his mouth—no doubt to chastise his sons—but Miach shook his head with a small smile. He turned to face the boys.

"I'd say you're from Istaur."

The younger boy looked at him with wide eyes. "How'd you know that?"

"I travel a good deal," Miach conceded. "What are your names?"

"I'm Gerald," said the older. "And that's Thomas."

Miach shook their hands politely, then found himself being ignored in favor of watching the woman out in the lists. He joined them without hesitation. Morgan laughed as she wielded her blade and the sound was so beautiful, Miach thought he just might have to sit down soon.

"Does the queen need a page?" Thomas ventured.

"Shall we go ask?" Miach asked.

Gerald looked, for the first time, his age, which couldn't have been more than nine. "But, sir, do you dare? She bears Weger's mark, you know."

"Does she?" Miach asked mildly. "Where did you hear that?"

"Word gets round," he whispered reverently.

Miach imagined that it did.

"The king bears the same mark," Thomas said, his eyes wide. "'Tis rumored he went inside Gobhann and earned it to prove himself worthy of her."

"Even so, I'd rather be *her* page," Gerald said, sounding as if he wished it very much. "She's so fierce."

Miach smiled at their father's groan, then nodded toward the field. "Let's go see what she thinks, lads. Stay behind me, though, lest the venture prove perilous."

Gerald hesitated. "But, sir, you don't even have a sword to defend yourself if she grows angry."

"Aye, but he has a knife down his boot," Thomas said. "Look you there, Ger."

"That's something, at least," Gerald offered.

Miach agreed with them that it was at least something, then he climbed over the fence with the lads and waited whilst Morgan put the finishing touches on Hearn's captain. He suddenly found a small hand slipping into his. He looked down and found Thomas looking up at him with an expression of such nervousness, Miach wondered if he might throw up. Perhaps this one could be given to Fletcher of Harding until they both mastered the urge to vomit in fear.

He walked with the lads and stopped a goodly distance away from where Hearn's captain was crying peace. He waited until Morgan had put up her sword before he approached.

"Your Majesty," he said, with a bow, "I have a pair of lads here who would like to make your acquaintance. If it pleases you."

Morgan walked over to them, then squatted down and looked at the lads. "Good morrow to you, good sirs," she said with a smile. "How may I serve you?"

"Serve us?" Gerald squeaked.

Thomas drew closer to Miach.

"I don't think they want you to serve them, my queen," Miach said. "I believe they want to serve you."

Morgan looked up at him in surprise. "How?"

"By being your pages."

"Does the queen have pages?"

"She does, if she likes the look of them."

Morgan frowned for a moment or two, then held out her hand and waited for Thomas to take it. She pulled him over to stand next to her.

"I daresay being the queen's page is not a task for the faint-hearted," she began thoughtfully. "I would need a pair of lads who aren't afraid of hard work. Or horses. Or coming out in the lists on occasion to give me a bit of sport."

"Oh," Gerald breathed worshipfully.

Thomas looked at her for a minute with trembling lips, then he threw his arms around her neck. Miach caught Morgan before she was borne backward, then steadied her. She thanked him politely, then looked at the lads.

"Well? You two look up to it."

"Oh, aye," Thomas said, pulling back and looking at her as if she'd just offered him one of Hearn's finest horses.

"Aye for me too," Gerald managed. He paused, then looked up at Morgan with a frown. "Why don't you have the Sword of Angesand there, Your Majesty?"

"Because I don't train with that sword," she said easily. She showed them her blade. "This is one an old friend made for me. 'Tis my everyday blade."

"Aren't you afraid you might need to be protected?" Thomas asked. "Did you bring a guard?"

Morgan smiled. "Just that lad there behind you."

"But he doesn't even have a sword," Gerald said in disbelief.

"He doesn't need one," Morgan said. She turned Thomas away from her and patted his back. "Go tell your father that I'll have you, then present yourselves at the palace when it suits your sire. I'm sure I'll want to talk to him about your care."

The boys nodded, but dragged their feet as they started away, as if they didn't particularly want to leave her.

Miach understood.

Morgan looked at him. "And just who are *you* supposed to be? The stable boy?"

"Aye. Come along, wench, and we'll have ourselves a pleasant afternoon in the hayloft."

The boys ran toward their father.

"He called her wench!" Gerald exclaimed. "Father, she'll have him hanged for that, for sure!"

Miach raised an eyebrow and looked at his wife. "Will you?"

"You're safe for today," she said. "And likely tomorrow as well. Take me somewhere I can sit and I'll think about the day after." She dragged her sleeve across her forehead. "I think I need a drink of your elixir, Miach."

He put his arm around her shoulders and drew her close. "As you will, love." He walked with her and was surprised by how hard she was leaning on him. He looked at her and realized suddenly that she didn't look at all well. "Morgan, you're green."

She shook her head gingerly. "I think I just overdid this morning. A rest will put me to rights. But let's send my new charges on their way before all manner of tales go round the pub about the queen and the stable boy."

"Please, nay," he said with a half laugh. He walked with her over to where the lads were jumping about their father like two enthusiastic pups. He leaned against the fence as Morgan discussed a few details with their father, then smiled at the look on the boys' faces when she told them that the stable boy was actually the king of Neroche and that the reason he didn't have his crown on was because it was likely under his bed.

"Another three conquests made," Miach said with a smile as he watched a very grateful father gather up his gaping sons and walk off with them.

She smiled, then went into his arms. "I think there's only one conquest I care about. Are you won?"

"Completely." He kissed her softly. "Come have a drink from Hearn's other well, Morgan. You'll feel more yourself once you do."

She nodded and took the hand he offered. He walked with her across the field and through the gate, then continued on with her in the shade of the hall to spare her any more sun.

He realized suddenly that she was very unsteady on her feet.

"Morgan, what ails you?" he asked in surprise.

Her only answer was to suddenly turn and lose her breakfast onto a handy compost heap. Miach waited until she straightened before he put his arm around her shoulders.

"Morgan, what is it?"

She shook her head carefully. "Nothing. I just need to sit."

He led her over to sit on the edge of Hearn's second well, then handed her a dipper of water. She rinsed her mouth, spat the water out, then accepted another to drink.

"Spectacular," she managed weakly. "It seems a shame to waste it."

He reached out and brushed a stray strand or two of hair back from her face. "What did you eat for breakfast?"

She waved her hand in front of her nose. "I don't want to think about it, given that I just experienced it again. It was likely the same thing you had."

He considered. He put his hand to her forehead, but there was no undue heat there. He frowned. "How do you feel?"

"As though I have contracted some sort of wasting illness," she said grimly. "Nothing tastes as it should—when I can bring myself to eat anything." She put her hand over her belly protectively. "We've had four good months, Miach. Perhaps that is all we were destined to enjoy."

He laughed in spite of himself and almost went swimming as a result. She scowled at him, but he ignored it and put his arm back around her shoulders, wondering how he might broach the subject he'd been thinking on for the last pair of fortnights. Wasting illness, indeed.

"Morgan," he began gingerly, "do you think you might be expecting?"

"Expecting what?" she asked, waving her hand in front of her face again. "Bloody hell, Miach, can you smell that? What sort of vile beast are they roasting inside for supper?"

"I can't smell anything," he admitted. He rubbed his hand over her back soothingly for a moment or two until he was certain she wouldn't reach for her blade if he pursued the subject at hand. "Morgan?"

"What?"

He took a deep breath. "I wonder if you might be, well, with child."

The next thing he knew, he was resurfacing from a good tumble into icy well water. He came up spluttering.

"Did you push me?" he asked incredulously.

She was standing up with her hands on her hips, looking down at him as if he'd suddenly sprouted horns. "You're damned right I pushed you," she said in astonishment. "What do you mean *with child*?"

"Well," he said reasonably, "it has been known to happen." Then he felt his mouth fall open. "Morgan, what in the *hell* were you doing in the lists?"

She folded her arms and frowned back at him. "Taking a bit of exercise. And only a bit, unfortunately. The lads were too intimidated to do aught but pretend to strike at me. I assume I can still count on you for a decent bit of sport."

He started to say *absolutely not,* but he had another look at her expression and decided that perhaps he should just keep his mouth shut. He heaved himself up out of the water, then clambered over the edge and sat down on the rock. He looked up at her.

"I don't imagine you'd want to sit inside and stitch for the next few months, would you?"

She sank down onto the edge of the well next to him. "Stitch what?" she asked blankly.

That, he supposed, was answer enough.

"Never mind," he said, trying to wring out his tunic and finding it a hopeless task. "Do you think we could go inside and sit by the fire so I could dry out?"

She nodded uneasily. "I'll pinch my nose closed." She looked at him, apparently rather panicked. "It could just be bad ale."

"It could," he agreed.

She rose, swayed, then steadied herself. She held down her hand for him. "I'll think on it."

He allowed her to pull him to his feet, but said nothing. He had the feeling the time for thinking was long past.

A pair of hours later, he sat at one of the long tables in front of the fire, dry, and nursing a cup of wine. Morgan was looking at the food in front of her suspiciously, as if it intended to merely reside for a bit inside her, then liberate itself at a most inconvenient time.

Miach buried his smiles in his cup.

He finally gave up on his wine and simply rested his chin on his fists and watched his wife as she ignored her supper in favor of discussing swordplay with Hearn. That, at least, seemed to bring some color to her cheeks. She was, in her own way, as opinionated about swords as Hearn was about his horses. In truth, she could have been discussing with the man what variety of turnip to plant in their garden and Miach would have found it fascinating. She was, as he had remarked quite often to anyone standing nearby, a remarkable woman.

"Besotted," Hearn said with a sigh.

Miach realized that both Hearn and Morgan were watching him. "What?"

"You're besotted," Hearn repeated. He turned to Morgan. " 'Tis a wonder he gets any work done."

"He manages," Morgan said with a smile, "even though he slips out of more council meetings than you'd suspect. But back to the matter of horses, my lord. I wish you would let us pay you for Fleòd and Luath, at least. Or let us return them to you."

Hearn snorted. "I won't have money for them, missy, and I certainly won't have them back. The last time you brought them home, they spent all their time corrupting my other beasts. All I hear now is *wings, wings, wings* until I'm ready to silence the entirety of my stables." He shot Miach a dark look from under his bushy eyebrows. "Don't you turn any more of my horses into dragons, lad, or I won't let you back inside my gates."

"At least I turned them into something fleet," Miach said with a smile. "They could be begging you to turn them back into slugs."

Hearn pursed his lips, then turned to Morgan. "Don't know how you live with him. You also flatter him overmuch. Too many more *my lieges* and he'll be impossible."

"I don't curtsey to him very often," she said, "but I do have particularly sweet kisses for any kind words thrown his way, including all those kingly titles, so I persist."

Hearn rolled his eyes. "I don't know if I want to know anymore, lest it upset my supper. Miach, how is the sweetening of my well coming along?"

"Nicely," Miach said, "but it might need a final bit of work. I'll see to it."

"When?"

"Tomorrow."

Hearn looked at them both, laughed, then shook his head and turned back to his ale.

Miach took that as dismissal enough. He thanked Hearn for the supper he at least had enjoyed, then pulled Morgan with him across the great hall and out the front door.

He slowed once they were walking across the courtyard, took a deep breath of fresh air, then looked at his lady.

"How do you fare?"

She shot him a look, then continued on with him for a moment or two in silence before she stopped and looked at him again. "Do you think it's possible?"

He looked about him to make certain he was comfortably far from anything he might be pushed into before he dared answer. "I think so."

She hesitated, then turned and put her arms around his waist. Miach gathered her close and rested his cheek against her hair. He closed his eyes, content to simply hold her and enjoy the very fine weather—and the fact that he was still dry.

"I don't know what to do," she said in a very small voice. "About . . . well, this."

He tightened his arms around her briefly. "We'll celebrate first, then we'll manage with the reality, just as we've done with everything else."

She was silent for another minute or two. "If it's a lad, we'll have to name him Hearn."

Miach smiled. "I imagine so."

"It would mean your brother might stop sneaking into our bedchamber to fondle your crown."

"Rigaud?" he asked with an uneasy laugh. "Does he?"

"I caught him at it the other day. He was completely unrepentant." She sighed, then looked up at him. "Thank you, Miach, for still being you beneath that crown."

"Who else would I be?"

She shrugged helplessly. "Power corrupts, sometimes. Instead, you take your duty very seriously and yourself with vast quantities of modesty." She smiled. "It suits you as well as your crown does."

He thought it might not be inappropriate to thank her properly for her kind words. He was just beginning to think he'd begun to make a decent job of it, when she pulled out of his arms, laughing. She leaned up and kissed him, then turned and walked away.

"Perhaps we'd best make certain of all this, Miach. Continuation of the line and all that." She shot him a look over her shoulder. "Don't dawdle, my liege."

He watched her go and smiled to himself. Almost a year ago, he'd been in Tor Neroche, feeling a chill settle over his heart as he watched the realm be assaulted by an evil he couldn't name and wondering, when he'd had the stomach to, if his life might ever include anything but darkness, weariness, and the endless grind of seeing to his spells.

And then Morgan of Melksham had walked into his life and turned it upside down.

He had loved her from the start, but he'd sorely underestimated how much that love would continue to grow. He loved her strength, her courage, her uncompromising sense of honor and loyalty. He loved that she looked at him blankly when he attempted the occasional courtly flattery, that she blushed when he brought her flowers, that she grew quiet and a bit misty-eyed when he found her a particularly beautiful blade in the treasury. He loved the dragon wildness that lingered in her eyes after they flew, the way she was still wont to turn him around and stand against his back when she was startled, the way she had mastered Sìle's look that warned overzealous ministers that they were nigh on to wasting the king's time and exhausting his patience.

And he admired to the depths of his soul how she had passed through the fires of her past and all that went with it, yet not allowed it to embitter her. She was Morgan, wielder of blades and reciter of Weger's strictures; and Mhorghain, heir to vast power and elven magic. And she was the keeper of his heart, which was his favorite incarnation.

And now, heaven help him, the mother of his future child.

She turned and looked at him. "Miach?"

"What?"

"Thinking about your turnip crop?"

"Actually, nay," he managed. "I wasn't."

She smiled, a very small, private smile he'd been favored with only when he'd done something that had particularly pleased her. Then she turned and walked away toward that hayloft that kings had despaired of ever sleeping in.

He smiled to himself and ran to catch up with her.